Saturday Writers

Elements in Writing

Anthology #9

Photograph for President's Contest
      courtesy of Ryan Jacobsmeyer, © 2015
      Used by permission

ISBN-13: 978-1522815273
ISBN-10: 1522815279

Cover design by Jennifer A. Hasheider and Cyn Watson
Cover illustration by Cyn Watson

First Edition: December 2015
10 9 8 7 6 5 4 3 2 1

Saturday Writers

Elements in Writing

Anthology #9

Edited by
Bradley D. Watson

For everyone with a hand in the creation of this book: From brainstorming theme ideas to advertising our contests, managing entries, procuring judges, proofreading, editing, and designing — so many of our members had a huge part. We thank you.

* * *

Our thoughts are with our fearless 2015 President, Tom Klein, as he battles evil.

Requiescant in pace:

Lilah M. Contine 1924 – 2015, Saturday Writers Member 2005 - 2015

Saturday Writers 2015

Introduction & Acknowledgments

Founded in 2002, Saturday Writers has spent the last 13 years attempting to live up to their motto: "Writers encouraging writers." Each year they search for new and better ways to assist their members in reaching their writing goals.

In addition to the monthly meetings with their guest speakers and excellent snacks, the group also hosts open-mic events, regularly scheduled contests, meet 'n' greets, critique groups (both off-line and on-line), and weekly write-in opportunities. The winners of our monthly contests are published in our yearly anthology.

This book is the result of our monthly contests for 2015 based on the challenge "Adding Elements to Your Writing" and featuring a different "element" each month. Submissions were accepted from our members, as well as other writers across the nation. The judges were often overwhelmed with the quality of the writing.

The stories, poems, essays, memoirs and flash fiction contained herein are the best-of-the-best: the winning entries from each contest. We are proud of each and every author represented in this work.

A special "thank you" to the group of volunteers who helped put this collection together: Rose Callahan, Susan Gore Zahra, Linda Schellenger, Tom Klein, Jennifer Hasheider, and Cyn Watson—who all volunteered their time and efforts to assist with the creation of this book. A special thanks to Rose, Linda, and Susan for their assistance with proofreading the final manuscripts, and Cyn Watson for our wonderful cover. This anthology would not have been possible without all of these people.

Thanks,
Bradley D. Watson
Editor

Table of Contents

PRESIDENT'S CONTESTS

PRESIDENT'S CONTEST: Poetry

PRESIDENT'S CHALLENGE: Flash

PRESIDENT'S CHALLENGE: Prose

CONTRIBUTORS

COOL DOWN

- Cold -

Meltdown

Sherry Cerrano

Footprints and drops of blood in the snow led into the forest, away from where the expensive car was parked. The mountain road to the ski lodge had been harrowing, but the drive paled next to the unexpected turn of events.

Upset in ways never before experienced, the young man tracked Carol into the forest. His legs became weary from trudging through the eighteen inches of snow. Yesterday, the snowstorm finished with a misty rain. Midnight, dry air accompanied with frigid temperatures descended on the forest, forming a slick, icy topping.

Dressed for the ski trip with Carol, Matt punched his foot down to crack and plunge his boot into the virgin crust. At first, each step, a labor of rise and stomp, rise and stomp, required his full attention, until his mind wandered off. In a dream state, his ambulation became mechanical.

Working hard to keep up with Carol, he was driven to make all this right again. He had to. Everything in his life had been working out. Becoming a junior partner in his law firm fulfilled goals Matt set for himself in high school: graduating law school, landing a job, and succeeding in his profession. His new car, his new girl, fell nicely into place.

Matt daydreamed of Carol in a wedding dress walking down the aisle, remembered her in her bikini on the beach where they met, and believed he felt her touching him. Tucked safely in his suitcase was his hope for a bright future, an engagement ring for the gorgeous woman who had ridden next to him in his new BMW. He imagined the two of them sitting next to a fire, the snow falling outside, and he would propose.

This morning before they left the city, Carol sat so gracefully in her nightgown at the breakfast table, smiling at him as she sipped her coffee and chattering about their getaway. Last night was the first time she agreed to stay over. It had been a perfect evening. Until the unexpected outburst in the car, Matt had been so sure of her feelings, of her values. After four months of being a couple, he thought he knew her.

This weekend would have finalized the next milestone in his life: an engagement to Carol. Now what? One phone call and his foundation trembled. Matt wasn't used to losing control over his life. Laboring on through the unfamiliar expanse, even his grasp of reality was in question.

The bloody wadded-up paper towel dropped to the ground, a crimson blotch on the pristine satin at his feet. Before his eyes, crystals hung suspended in the air. Pushing through the icy gemstones made his face wet. With each thrust forward, the frosty curtain parted and a glimpse of her stayed ahead of him, unattainable. Her willowy form beckoned him, not with jeans and a tight sweater, but with flowing, wispy filaments blown away from her body by the wind.

He stretched his right arm out to almost touch the image, but his rise and stomp were too slow. Matt's blood streaked face had to be what was frightening her, making her run away. Trudging on, he spotted her again and lunged for her but fell. His face hit the ice hard, cutting his cheek, which burned and felt raw.

Shocked out of his trance, he turned on his side to pull his feet out of the ruts made when he fell and tried to get to his knees. His hands pushed him up to all fours. He crawled forward, momentarily suspended on top of the layers of frozen precipitation, until his snow-laden gloves slipped out from under him.

Splayed out on the cold, solid surface, the girl looked down on him. This time she was real, wearing a white down jacket and gray snow pants. Her platinum locks blew away from her face. Her eyes held the same distress he saw earlier in the car. He cried out, "Carol, stop. Talk to me. What's wrong?"

Matt's urgency to rise, to touch her before she fled, caused him not to notice the steep slope below him. As he rolled onto his side, he caught sight of the drop off. But, it was too late to stop the momentum of his turning over.

Without traction, his body rolled out of control down the ridge, brambles tearing at his clothing, his nose, his left eye, spreading blood. His tumble ended abruptly when his left side whacked into a tree. Pain shot through his chest. He tried to take a deep breath, but gasped and could only manage short, shallow gulps of air.

Panic set in. His head spinning from the pain he felt with each breath, Matt realized he had no idea the direction from which he came. In a couple of hours, night and the low temperatures would be upon him. Alarmed that he would not be able to find the road in the dark, he patted his pocket for his cell phone. It dawned on him, it was on the charger in the car.

Matt decided he needed to get up. As he shifted his body, the pain cut him in two. He squeezed his eyes shut to gather the strength to try again. Lying still next to the tree, questions without the comfort of answers blanketed his mind. Would Carol help him? Could she help herself? Did she know he was hurt? Why had she been so inconsolable?

His body began to shake uncontrollably from the panic, aided by the cold. When he looked around, the wispy vision returned through the slits of his eyes, which he opened wide to see her better. The snow blowing off a fir tree, swirling downward into an opening, created the illusion.

Sleep—a temptation to forget the pain and snow piled on his body—was calling to Matt. He pulled his stocking cap over his burning face and resolved to get up in a few minutes. To distract himself from the pain, he replayed the scene in the car. He needed to figure out why Carol had reacted so strangely.

Only a few miles from the ski lodge, Carol took a call that lasted less than a minute. Keeping his eyes on the slippery road did not allow him to see her reactions as she listened on the phone. His only understanding of what transpired came at the end of the call when she said, "You can't do that? I'll return immediately." She slammed her phone down on the dash and let out a scream like an injured animal. The outburst nearly caused him to lose control of the car as the electrical shock of her shriek went through him.

"What's wrong?" Matt asked, his voice cracking.

"Turn around. I have to go back," she demanded.

"Tell me what's wrong," he said, not daring to look anywhere but straight ahead. The road was becoming steeper with curve after curve.

Carol yelled at him, "It's none of your business." Matt could not reply, stunned by her caustic tone and refusal to share the problem with him. Throughout their time together, she had never acted toward him with anything but sweetness, never a cross word, always even tempered. None of this made sense.

Shouting, she insisted, "Let me out, or I'll jump out." She began tugging wildly at her door handle. As soon as he found a decent shoulder, he slowed the car, trying not to use the brake. Her thrashing around calmed as they pulled over.

He looked at her. Carol's eyes were like a cornered feral animal, frantic desperation in her voice.

"Turn around. Take me back."

He grabbed her arms above the elbows, to calm her, to get her to talk to him. "There is no reason to be so upset. I can help. What is it?"

"You don't know what you're talking about. Turn around, or I swear, I'll get out."

"It's freezing cold. There is nothing here but forest. Talk to me," he said, squeezing her arms with the hope his touch would allow her to trust him.

She wrestled with him until he let go, not knowing how to help her. Grabbing her phone, she turned to open her door and said frantically, "I'll find my own way home."

When she moved to get out, he grabbed her left hand to stop her. Carol struck him with her phone, causing a cut on the thin skin covering his eye socket. A stream of blood flowed down his cheek. He unfastened his seatbelt and clumsily grabbed sheets from a roll of paper towels to press against the cut and stop the blood flowing from his brow. Matt followed her, taking long strides, hoping to stop her before she went too far into the woods.

Remembering how she lashed out at him stung him more than his painful ribs and the cold pressing on his body. Matt felt like a fool, building a fantasy life around this young woman who had either lied to him or was nuts.

Motivated to push through the pain, he gathered his courage and rose using his elbow, twisting away from the tree's trunk until he was swallowed by the dark realm of unconsciousness.

WARMTH . . . something tickling his nose . . . a truck's motor running . . . intermittent flashes of red and blue lights. Through fuzzy lenses, he thought he was entangled and thrashed to get free.

A red-haired, freckled woman hovered above him. Her hands gently held his shoulders as she said, "Lie still. You're in an ambulance. There's a good chance you have some ribs broken, but we won't know until we get some x-rays. Do you know your name?"

"M . . . a . . . tt," escaped slowly from his lips, as his dried-out tongue peeled away from the roof of his mouth.

"Do you know where you are?"

"Moun . . . tains. Carol? Where's Carol?"

"She's outside, waiting to talk to you. She's the one who called 911. I think she's in a hurry to leave."

The paramedic opened the door, stepped to the head of the gurney, and said to Carol as she stepped in, "Only a minute, we need to get him to the hospital."

Carol kneeled down and said, "Matt, one of the troopers is going to take me back. My son's father took him from my parents' home."

Matt's face twisted in confusion. "Son?"

"He's three and lives with my parents. His father is crazy. He doesn't have custody. I can't wait any longer. I have to go. I have to find my son," she said, visibly shaking.

His voice raspy, he implored, "Why?"

Carol's finger touched his lips like a feather to quiet him. Their eyes met, hers fierce with fear, his wounded. She stood and turned away. Facing the doors, she hung her head and said, "Matt, I am sorry. You had your whole life mapped out. Mine . . . is chaos, always has been. I didn't know how to tell you. I didn't want it to end." She pushed the doors open and stepped down. He watched his dream girl disappear into a state trooper's SUV.

The medic closed the doors and prepared for the trip to the hospital. Bumpy jolts, a wide turn, and a smooth take off with sirens blaring helped Matt feel his life had resumed, no longer stuck in the freezing woods. His injuries were not on his mind, the pain meds were taking care of that. He was thinking about the cost of believing in someone and how distrust casts a long shadow that comes with the brightness of day and darkens in the night. He stared at the back windows on the doors where he watched Carol walk away and realized it was no longer day.

Mrs. McGinty and Her Sensible Shoes
Rose Callahan

People around me stood in black coats, holding black umbrellas, thinking black thoughts, and it made me realize that today of all days I fit into the norm. I held back a laugh that was a sick mix of joy and anguish. Instead, I allowed a tiny smile to slip across my lips and wondered if my dad would have found the same humor in it as I did. Probably not.

"You're holding up well." A reassuring voice was whispered in my direction from an elderly woman who was too stubborn to allow age to cripple her. "You'll be fine, huh?" When I began to reply, she pressed her finger to her lips and "shushed" me.

Mrs. McGinty, with her square-toed shoes sensibly heeled with rubber soles, stood by me, but closer—within an arm's reach—to the casket. I noticed her scoot nearer to the priest, and those shoes of hers bumped into his, causing a brief break in the service.

"Go on, Father," she said, "I was just trying to keep a bit of the wind off of you."

She reached out to pat his arm with plump hands that I knew smelled of onion and beef broth mingled with the scent of Mr. Clean. The priest cleared his throat, and she continued, "Go on then. You're doing a lovely job."

As she wiped the moisture from her eyes and the drip off her nose, I took note that the powder, meant to hide the purple lines that broke across her face, tinted her simple, white handkerchief with a clay-like stain. Her face then contorted into a frown that brought the dimple of her chin into the soft lines of her jowls. She shook her head and said, "Mr. Watlow would have adored this service, simply adored it."

Which, I knew that he wouldn't have.

It was to his advantage that he did not, in fact, have to listen to this service; it was going well beyond his 30-minute limit on anything religious. A devoutly faithful man, he felt that prayer should be done privately. Never one to draw attention to himself, when asked why he hadn't been to Mass, he would respond in a reflective voice, "Matthew, Chapter 6." Mrs. McGinty was always saying a prayer for him. So when she insisted on helping me with the funeral, I couldn't refuse. Since I was now officially alone in this world, I felt it wouldn't do anyone a great harm to let her make the arrangements. It was the least I could do.

I considered it odd that in this dreariness, glints of light reflected off the cold drizzle collecting on the chain that held my wallet firmly to my slacks. It was made of steel strong enough to bear the weight of an industrial container or dumpster.

"Biker Chains and Wallets. Made for the Road. $9.99" read the sign above the wire bin where I'd bought it. At the time, I'd told myself that at $9.99, it wasn't real leather. I'd never ridden a motorcycle, and my car was a tomato-red 1991 Yugo. Still, it was sturdy and the wallet held two snaps on wide loops substantial enough to secure it tightly. I liked having something "Biker." I thought about checking the contents again: a five dollar bill, a slip of paper from a fortune cookie, and a photo of my family as it had been years ago. Knowing the photo was there flooded me with warmth, until a damp wind found its way into my jacket, coaxing hairs to stand on prickly skin. My shoulders tensed to shake the chill away, and I swore that the shiver was more intense on the scar hidden by the blue-tinted curls of my hair. Though it was too cold to wear synthetic leather, the fabric's crackle seemed to define me.

The air was whitewashed a gray that reminded me of a Benjamin Moore paint swatch I'd once seen called Old Soul. It softened the landscape's hard edges into obscured lines between mourners and headstones. The words spoken were no more than a hum to me. The priest knew little of my dad, but spoke of him in mournful tones and would raise his voice in practiced pitches that moved the crowd to shift uncomfortably amid the rain-soaked ground. Even though I stood in a winter rain, the pocketed patches of brown, dormant grass reminded me of my yard in summer, neglected since the last time I remember having seen my mother. I struggled to remember her funeral, yet could only recall images of my dad. He didn't seem to be as neglected when I was a small child, but the absence of his wife chipped away at him until nothing was left for me.

Memories of my father flickered through my mind like the scratched and faded images produced by a kinetograph. I'd see him with his back to the door mulling over scattered papers, and me standing in the doorway with my eyes locked onto him and my lips taut as I forced a wish for him to face me. The closest I'd get to my wish fulfilled would be for him to pause and straighten himself in his chair. I too would straighten as I waited for a smile or "good morning," but he'd slump back over his work as I'd move my gaze to the floorboards on which I stood.

I've seen this scene countless times and it always ends the same. And today, as the cerebral celluloid reached the end of its reel, the image broke into a field of whiteness that shocked me back to the interment.

Now, in a box glossed with the sheen of muddy ice, this man I'd come to call Ted faced the lining of his coffin.

When I was in grade school, Ted did make a few efforts to be available when I'd arrive home from school. Eventually, even that became a burden. One afternoon, I found myself at the door of our empty and locked house. I'd knocked, and when it didn't open, I stood and waited until the twilight crept onto the stoop. I'd rocked from foot to foot, and when it became dusk, the elastic of my socks loosened enough for the top bands to slip beneath my heels. Shivering and tired, I'd bent to adjust them, and I bumped my head hard against the metal handle of the door. Something warm trickled down my forehead. I can't recall crying or what I did next, except to lie down on a worn-out mat screen-printed with the faded words, "Welcome Home."

When I'd awakened, my eyes opened to see a pair of black square-toed shoes with rubber wedge soles. Mrs. McGinty had given me a gentle shake and pressed a cloth to my head.

"Now then. What kind of bed does that welcome mat make?" Before I could respond, she said, "It doesn't. Come along. I'll make you some dinner."

She'd helped me to stand and wrapped a red blanket around my shoulders that reminded me of Scottish Terriers and shortbread cookie tins. I pulled away from her.

"Oh. That's how it is, is it? The school got you fearing your neighbors, do they?" She pulled at the teacher's note safety-pinned to my jacket. "Well, I have something they don't."

She leaned in closer, reapplied the cloth to my head as I tried to pull back further and met my gaze with her freckled green eyes. I held my breath and stared at her slow moving lips as she enunciated, "Rutabaga."

I couldn't believe what I heard. My insides jolted as if I'd miscalculated a step from the curb to the street.

"Oh for Jimminy Christmas, boy. Rutabaga." She stood tall with her hands resting on the folds of her waist. "Don't you even know the secret word you and your mother came up with?"

I did. I stood there, wrapped in that blanket, eyes glazed and jaw slacked. The word that was meant to give me comfort and safety in times of distress, now betrayed me. When I realized that she knew my secret word, I gulped my tears deep into the back of my throat and spit out, "Yeah. I know it, but you shouldn't!" I can't imagine what lead me to wrap my arms around her, but I did as my breath stuck on bursting sobs.

"Well then, you know I'm not going to slice you up into little bits and serve you in a stew. Secret password and all." She held me firmly enough for me to know that I was safe.

"Come on, then." She led me through a gate into her yard and said, "And when you come in, wipe your feet and leave that attitude of yours at the door. It'll do you no good in my house." The wink she sent my way was comical and inviting.

Once inside, she gave me a plain mug of hot lemon water. I hadn't realized how chilly the autumn nights were, until I held that mug with both hands. I devoured the stew, but was careful to avoid the chunks of meat. I sat at her table feeling full and watched her move around the kitchen, humming as she worked. And as if a gent or beau asked her to dance, she took up a handful of her floral duster, curtsied, and then tapped her heels and toes in an improvised jig to a band in her head. The soles of her shoes would catch the floor and make a thudding screech like that of a swing's seat rubbing against chains that anchored it to its frame.

Rain hitting puddles replaced the sound of her shoes tapping in my mind. When the service completed, I stayed back and watched as silent figures moved to cars or gathered into groups to talk of whatever is discussed after a funeral.

I'll miss Ted, in the way I might miss someone I wished was a friend. Was I better, or worse, for knowing him? Had I missed out on something important? Had my mother been around, would my family have been happy? I looked beyond the silhouettes of people into the diminishing light above, and let the rain wash over me. A whole world of wish and worry won't make a difference now.

I knew that after the service, those who still felt an obligation to give me a few more moments of sympathy would meet me at Mrs. McGinty's. She'd been adamant that no one should pay respects to my dad in our unkempt house. She'll welcome them into her home and serve them finger foods and tiny desserts she'd picked up from the discount store. She'll speak of Ted with sincerity and mention that he was a "truly faithful man," that "everyone should strive to be like him," and that "God has forgiven him for not being a father who was always around."

"After all," I'll hear her say, "We should put God before all else. Mr. Watlow did as he thought was His will. A true servant of God."

Mrs. McGinty will raise onto her toes just enough not to be noticeable and with her voice a little above the muffled conversation around her, she'll add, "To help wherever I can."

I looked forward to the time when everyone will leave to go on with their lives, and the two of us will sit for a time with a cup of hot lemon water and talk before I return to my unkempt house across the street.

Most of the mourners had left the cemetery when I sat in my car to run the engine. I rubbed the red Tartan cloth braided around my wrist and relaxed as a sense of balance cloaked me against the bitterness of the day. I caught myself smiling, not a smirk, but a smile. I looked out the window to see Mrs. McGinty nod, rise slightly on the toes of her shoes and wink at me.

Mary Lynn's First Day in Prison
Jennifer McCullough

"Inmate, get up," the jailer boomed as he drug his handcuffs across the iron bars of Mary Lynn's cell, rousing her from a light sleep.

Her mouth was pasty dry. The film on her tongue tasted like rotten eggs. She sucked in her cheeks and rubbed them against her teeth in order to work up enough spit to wash out the putrid taste so she wouldn't vomit.

Knowing the jailer was not a patient man, Mary Lynn slid out of her bunk and walked briskly past the moldy toilet. As she reached through the ice cold black metal wall separating her reality from her past, a shiver went all the way down to her feet.

"You like rice, inmate?" the jailer said as he cuffed her.

Trying to avoid the jailer's cocky gaze, Mary Lynn stared down at her dry, cracked fingers and at dozens of tiny blood-crusted scabs where her skin had split in the dry winter air of the Pulaski County, Arkansas jail.

"I guess so," Mary Lynn mustered from between chattering teeth.

"Well that's a good thing, cause you're headed to the Cummins Prison Farm today, sweetheart," he said as his laugh echoed off the cinder block walls and crashed down on Mary Lynn's terrified ears.

"You gonna get all the rice you can eat down there if you work hard, inmate."

Her pale blue eyes filled with tears as she finally looked up at the jailer.

"Now by hard, I mean you're gonna have to keep those trustees down there happy, and by happy, I mean real happy, if ya know what I mean," he said, grabbing himself. "You can't go fightin' them boys like you fight me," he said as he pressed his lips close to Mary Lynn's ear.

"Now spread your legs," he yelled as he nearly kicked one leg out from underneath her.

Mary Lynn's knees buckled and she cried out.

"Your problem, inmate," he said as he shackled her ankles, "is that you think you got somethin' special right here, darlin'," he said, thrusting his hand between her legs.

"As I see it, you ain't nothin' but a dumb, white-trash, convicted felon."

The jailer's booming voice reverberated inside her head drowning out her own desperate thoughts for the moment.

"You best be glad I ain't got time for you today or else I'd teach you how to keep those trustees on your good side," he said as he grabbed Mary Lynn's breast from behind and squeezed it into her chest, forcing the breath out of her.

"Your limousine done pulled up out front, inmate. Sixty miles to Hell. All aboard!"

The jailer pushed Mary Lynn down the dimly lit hallway. Her shackles clanked against the frozen concrete floor like out-of-step clog dancers. As she approached the front door, blazing sunlight crippled her vision. Her delicate eyes had grown accustomed to the darkness during her six months of incarceration.

"My baby," Mary Lynn cried as her eyes darted back and forth through squinted eyelids. She tried to scan the jail lobby hoping to see her husband with their infant son, Nathaniel.

It was the first daylight she'd seen since taking a plea bargain.

"I want to see my baby," she screamed at the jailer as he pushed her out the door of the building and into the blisteringly cold April wind. Mary Lynn stumbled up the steps of a rust-speckled school bus that smelled of worse fear than the jail cell she'd just left.

Her lips quivered. The salty taste of snot and tears was all too familiar.

"Ah, sit down and shut up, honey," said a middle-aged woman from the back of the bus. The rasp in her throat betrayed a heavy cigarette habit.

"Don't nobody got time to listen to your whiney ass all the way to Cummins," a large negro woman bellowed as she laid her head back in her seat and closed her eyes.

Several wide-eyed does, themselves too scared to speak, peered back at Mary Lynn.

"Come here, sweetie, you can sit by me," Mary Lynn heard a woman say from somewhere in the middle of the bus.

Mary Lynn wiped her nose on the scratchy wool sleeve of her government issued long john and squeezed her eyelids together several times so she could see.

A wiry blonde woman waved her hand.

"Come on, I don't bite," the woman said as she patted the seat next to her. "Don't go pissin' him off before we get out of the parking lot," she said, nodding toward the 350-pound man who had stepped on the bus behind Mary Lynn. He was dressed in a tattered prisoner uniform himself, except he carried a 2-foot wooden blackjack and a pistol.

"That's right, Wanda," he said. "Now get this stupid bitch to sit down or all y'all's going to get the strap when we get to the Big House."

Mary Lynn's leg suddenly felt warm. As she sat down, she quickly smeared a puddle of her own urine around the floor of the bus so Wanda wouldn't see it.

"What's your name, honey?" Wanda inquired.

"It's Mary Lynn after Marilyn Monroe," she blurted.

Laughter erupted from the back of the bus.

"Don't listen to them. That's a beautiful name, sugar. You do look a little like Marilyn Monroe come to think of it."

"Thank you," Mary Lynn whispered.

"Whatcha in for, honey?" Wanda said as she slung her arm around Mary Lynn's shoulders.

"Uh, uh…" Mary Lynn fumbled as she felt her heartbeat rise from her chest into her throat all the way up to the tiny blood vessels in her ears.

"Murder," she said, finally.

"Murder?" Wanda quipped. "What'd you do, honey… kill a spider?"

Everyone on the bus roared with laughter. Even the nervous does, as well as Tex, the driver.

Mary Lynn hunkered down in her seat with her chin tucked firmly into her pounding chest. She covered her ears with her hands and began to quietly mouth the words to the Lord's Prayer.

"Oh, honey," Wanda said as she half-heartedly tried to stifle a snicker. "You got about an hour-and-a-half to toughen up that skin of yours, or else you're going to be in a heap of trouble."

"Now tell me — and I promise not to laugh this time — who in God's Earth did you murder?"

"I don't know," Mary Lynn said. "And I don't feel like talking to you anymore."

"Well, well. Looks like we got us a tough little bimbo on our hands, Tex."

"You don't say, Wanda. How 'bout all y'all ugly ass tramps shut the hell up and give me some peace and quiet," he warned.

Wanda shot an icy glance over at Mary Lynn but held her tongue the rest of the way.

The rolling hills of Little Rock were soon replaced by the flat Delta of Pine Bluff and half a dozen little towns southeast. The high springtime sun beat down on the east side of the bus and warmed Mary Lynn's face.

Occasionally, she caught a glimpse of her reflection in the window. She didn't look much like a 19-year-old fresh-faced mother and wife of a Captain in the U.S. Army anymore. Instead, she looked shell-shocked and gaunt, like the terminally ill cancer patients she used to tend to at the V.A. Hospital in Little Rock.

One day their lives were fine, and the next, they found themselves being ushered off to a strange and unimaginable hell, a place between life and death, but far worse than death, sort of like where Mary Lynn was now.

She had hoped for the electric chair. But second-degree murder, they told her, didn't come with that.

Instead, she'd get to pick cotton the rest of her life and think about what she'd done, if only she could remember what that was.

The heat from the sun warmed her weary muscles, and after a while, Mary Lynn dozed off to sleep, her head bobbing against the window of the bus like a sleepy child headed to school.

"Look at that beautiful boy," Mary Lynn's mother squealed as she entered Mary Lynn's hospital room. Mary Lynn tried to match her mother's smile with one of her own, but it wouldn't come.

"I just want to pinch those sweet little cheeks and kiss him all over," her mother said as she stroked Mary Lynn's matted hair. "He looks like you, sweetie."

"Really?" Mary Lynn said as she looked down at her tiny Nathaniel without so much as a flicker of pride.

"I don't think he looks like me at all."

"Oh, Marilyn? Marilyn Monroe?" Wanda's voice intruded into Mary Lynn's hospital room.

Just then, Wanda yanked a handful of Mary Lynn's hair, which jolted her awake and out of her seat.

"You think you're hot stuff, Miss Mary Lynn Monroe. Well let me be the first to welcome you to your new home," Wanda said as she kicked Mary Lynn down the steps of the bus and onto the dry parched grounds of Cummins Prison.

As the other women filed off the bus, they too took turns kicking Mary Lynn. They stomped on her head and hurled their feet toward any part of her they could manage to strike. No one wanted to be outdone, not even the first-timers.

Eventually, they were all ushered off toward a ramshackle barracks by two male prisoner trustees on horseback carrying shotguns.

Tex stayed behind. He drug Mary Lynn's limp body into a ditch between two outhouses and had his way with her.

She tried to scream, but her mouth was full of blood and teeth, and her throat was choked with vomit. Her lungs wouldn't fill with enough spare air to make any sound anyway. She felt a searing pain between her legs as Tex ground her into a wet, cold tomb of black mud.

When he finally staggered off toward some flickering lights, a near lifeless Mary Lynn mustered enough consciousness to realize darkness had fallen on the prison farm.

She reached out to stroke Nathaniel's angelic face in the freezing night air.

"Don't cry, sweet boy. Please don't cry," she said to the pitch black sky.

Mary Lynn could see nothing and everything at that moment.

She began to cry not from the physical pain but from a pain in her heart that no amount of time could heal.

"God, please forgive me," she whispered over and over.

In the distance, the sound of roaring applause echoed off the barren cotton fields.

Then music began to play as a part of Mary Lynn died, her heartbeat replaced by the reverb of a drum.

She recognized the famous voice.

It was Johnny Cash singing, "*I fell in to a burning ring of fire...*" on Mary Lynn's first day in prison, April 10, 1969.

The Rock on the Bay
Nicki Jacobsmeyer

Drowning, hypothermia or a life sentence, Frank's choices were limited and lacking promise. Cement walls and steel bars had been home for the past 23 years. His moral compass had been defined by criminals. Frank's charges of narcotics and robbery along with multiple escape attempts landed him on The Rock two years ago in 1960. That's when he was brought in by Allen West and the plans began. Frank Morris was convinced he was recruited for his intellect.

Frank was straddling the triangular raft that Allen designed, but he wasn't on it. Only the Anglin brothers, John and Clarence, were at his sides rowing like their life depended on it. Frank kept checking over his shoulder, half expecting to see the prison lit up from having found their papier mâché heads staged on their pillows. Only the winds pushing them from the west could be heard. Frank glanced back again and sighed. They were far enough away from the island that he could make out its battleship shape.

Clarence began to chuckle.

"What's so funny?" barked Frank.

"The raft," said Clarence.

"What about the raft?"

"It's triangular."

"No kiddin'," John contributed.

"It was supposed to be rectangle. That was the plan," said Frank.

"That was Allen's plan."

"It was THE plan."

"Hey Frankie, why you blaming Clarence and I? It wasn't our fault he didn't finish making the last inner tube."

"It doesn't matter J-Dub; he was too scared to come. And he thought he was in charge, calling all the shots."

"What do you know? You weren't there. He couldn't get out of his cell. The hole wasn't big enough," said Frank as he pulled his legs in tighter to keep from getting saturated.

It was high tide and the current was coming in with a vengeance. Their standard-issue navy pea coats would keep them warm from the 47-degree night air. However, the same water temperature was a different story. All three men looked at each other to ensure they each had kept their balance.

"Allen said you two helped patch his hole when it got too big to cover up," Frank said as he continued to paddle north towards Angel Island.

"Don't you say we didn't patch it good 'nough. We did Clarence, didn't we?"

"We sure did J-Dub, we sure did," Clarence said with a smirk.

Realization of the truth flashed in Frank's eyes as a wave overcame their raft. As all three men tried to keep their heads above water, Frank took full advantage. He reached for the spoon chisel he planted in his coat pocket. The wool of the coat was sucking in water like a sponge. Frank peeled off his coat before it dragged him towards the floor of the San Francisco Bay. Clarence did the same as he saw his brother struggling not to panic.

"John, take off your coat!" Clarence yelled.

John fumbled with his coat as he took in a gulp of water with the next wave.

Clarence started to swim toward his brother when Frank plunged the chisel into his side. Clarence clutched onto his side and let go of the raft as his scream pierced the night's air.

Frank didn't hesitate to put distance between them. He grabbed the raft and let the current take Clarence. John was regaining his composure when he heard his brother scream.

"Clarence, Clarence, you ok?" John asked as his eyes grazed the water's surface.

"There, he's over there," Frank replied, pointing towards the left. John searched in that direction until he spotted his brother.

"We got to get 'em! Hurry!" John said as he climbed back on the raft and began paddling.

Frank held the paddle, refusing to submit to John's request.

"The currents too strong, John."

Frank could tell Clarence was starting to tire from the blood loss. He was well over 300 feet away and struggling to keep afloat.

"But he's all I got, Frank," John said as he started to paddle with urgency. Frank looked towards Clarence to make sure they weren't able to reach him, when he disappeared under the surface.

"What the hell?" said Frank. He caught John's attention about the same time Clarence bobbed back up surrounded by crimson water.

"Nooooo!" yelled John. Frank grabbed John as he lunged towards his brother. Clarence's wails were muffled as he was pulled down again.

"Stop paddling. Don't move."

"What? I'm not stoppin'. We can't just leave him."

"He's gone. And unless you want to be a goner too, we can't move. We don't want to get their attention."

"Whose attention?"

"The sharks."

John cursed under his breath.

Frank and John sat silent. John stared towards the Golden Gate Bridge with empty eyes. Frank could hear his heart thunder in his chest as he shivered. Now that they had stopped for a minute, he could feel the frigid air seeping into his bones. The illuminating moon was already making its way across the night sky. After some time, Frank started paddling towards Angel Island. If they didn't get to land soon, they would be dead or at least wishing they were.

"We have to get to land," said Frank "It's only getting colder and we have to get dry." John didn't move a muscle. "He would want you to make it, John. Clarence would want you to make it."

John's eyes came to life at the mention of his brother. He nodded as he began to paddle. Frank was relieved. He needed John's strength. He couldn't get to Angel Island on his own. John's brawn and now renewed determination would give Frank time to get his bearings which seemed to be drifting away.

The raft was deflating from the whole ordeal and Frank realized they had been neglectful. He started blowing into the plastic tubing that inflated their makeshift raft. Frank started on Clarence's tube as John worked on his own. John's tube wasn't getting any bigger.

"What's the problem?" asked Frank.

"I don't know? It won't blow up," said John.

"Are you doing it right?" Frank said as he snatched the tubing from John. He blew into the tube but to no avail. John rolled his eyes. Frank began inspecting the raft.

"Shit."

"What?" asked John.

"The seal's broken on your tube."

"How did that happen?"

"Hell if I know."

"Now what?"

"Well, we can't sit on it anymore. It won't hold both our weight." Frank chucked the paddle to the side, slid off his tube, and lodged it under his chest as he began kicking.

"We're almost there," John said as he pointed to their destination. Frank could hear the questioning tone in his statement.

"Yea, we're almost there," replied Frank.

The one-and-three-quarter mile swim from Alcatraz to Angel Island was farther than it looked. The men were halfway there if they were lucky. Luck never seemed to be on a convict's side. They continued to kick in silence. Frank noticed he stopped shivering and was not reassured. His teeth had stopped chattering. He paused to hear his heart pound in his chest from adrenaline. He waited. Only a faint thump echoed.

"J-Dub?"

"Yea?"

"I'm sorry."

John looked at him with a questioning expression. Without a second warning Frank struck John's temple with his fist. Before John could react, Frank hit him again. He didn't waste any time when John's body went limp. He took his hand and submerged John's face under the dark water. John began to struggle but it was too late, his fate was sealed. When the struggle went out of him, Frank let go. Now there was room on the raft to get out of the frigid water. He drug his arm across the raft and took a deep breath to fend off the nausea.

Frank decided to lie on the raft and rest before his last push to Angel Island. He gazed at the twinkling stars and the falling moon. If he could just close his eyes for a while, he would get his second wind.

~

Frank's eyes fluttered open as he rolled his head to the side. The Golden Gate Bridge hovered in the distance.

"Allen," he whispered, "we're almost there. We did it."

The Bay's current continued to pull Frank toward the Pacific Ocean as the darkness flooded his senses.

~

"Is your name Allen West?" said FBI Agent Grant.

"Yes," replied Allen.

"Were you born on March 25, 1929?"

"Yes."

"Are you Alcatraz Inmate #1335?"

"Yes."

"Did you plan the escape with Frank Morris, John Anglin and Clarence Anglin?" asked the agent. He glanced at his colleague before eyeing the polygraph machine.

"Yes," said Allen. The needle didn't waiver.

"Was the hole behind your ventilator grill too small for you to escape?"

"Yes."

"Did you complete the final stitches and seals on the life jackets and raft used to escape Alcatraz?" asked the agent.

"Yes."

The polygraph needle rose and fell like the tide in the Bay.

Cold Trail
William A. Spradley

She felt closed in. The grayness of the fog made her uneasy. Imagining eyes watching her every move heightened her sensitivity to the bleakness of the low hills around the house. The house didn't seem to give the security she needed. Her nerves kept her fidgeting in her seat.

"Where's Wayne? Why isn't he home? He just isn't worried about how afraid I am. Oh what would I do if something happened to him? Oh please, God, bring him home." She stoked the fire and sat down with the 12 gauge on her lap.

Wind noises masked any noise from outside. The gray turned to black. Time seemed to have stopped. She had dozed in the chair when noises outside the door awakened her.

"Who's there? Who is it? Wayne, is that you." When no reply came, she stood up. Shotgun at the ready. When no answer came, she panicked. The door slowly opened and she saw a shadow. She pulled the trigger and the blast sent her back on the chair.

"My God, Flo, you shot me," Wayne screamed.

She stood up and shouted, "Oh, my darling Wayne, what have I done? Oh God, help me, I've killed my husband."

He lay on the ground in front of the door, blood flowing from his right shoulder. She rushed to his side and lifted his head. "Oh, dear Jesus, I have to get you help." She shook with fear.

"Help me over to the bed. It's too late tonight to get help. We have to get the blood stopped now. We can go into town tomorrow morning."

Tears streamed down her cheeks as she pulled him toward the bed. Together they got him into bed. She put a kettle on the fire for hot water to clean his wounds. Tearing up some undergarments to put in the water, she used them to cleanse the injury to his shoulder and arm. Adrenalin pumping through her body brought her to focus on treating the gunshot.

She spent the night by his side, cleaning him, putting cold cloths on his forehead, and using horse liniment to stem the pain. He slept in short intervals. She prayed for morning to come, but it remained dark. Fear gripped her heart and made the hours stand still.

The wind continued to whip around the sod house, increasing her terror. At one time when the wind slowed down, she thought she heard the howling of wolves. Frost on the windows sparkled in the moonlight as the clouds parted just before dawn.

When it turned light enough to see outside, she hitched the horses to the wagon and made a pallet on the wagon bed. She warmed soup in a coffee pot and wrapped it as best she could to keep it warm for a while. Gathering the Indian blanket and the sheets, plus all of the covers and quilts, she dragged him to the wagon using the last blanket. Struggling to get him into the wagon took all the strength in her frail body. She climbed up on the buckboard seat after covering him with the blankets and quilts, and then started toward Ogallala.

An hour from the house, the clouds returned and it began to snow. The wind turned the light snow into a driving blizzard. Everything turned white, and the blowing snow cut visibility to five yards in front of the horses. She pushed the horses faster and tried to find the trail. Only the base of the hills guided her. She thought she heard the sound of the wolves again. She kept the shotgun close on the bench.

She plodded on, unable to see the trail. Using only her instincts, the snow and poor visibility cast doubt on her ability to stay on the trail. The snow intensified, compounding her frustration. She was unable to concentrate on driving, and the wagon wandered.

The wind was now at her back, and she wondered if it had changed direction. Confused, she stopped the horses and tried to get her bearings. It was impossible. The driving snow hid everything.

She heard the sound of movement behind the wagon. When she turned toward the sound, she saw a pack of wolves, some black, some grey. They attacked the horses, nipping at their flanks and lower legs. She grabbed the 12 gauge and fired a shot at the closest one. She didn't want to hit the horse, so she fired at the hind legs of the lead wolf. The wolf let out a howl and fell away from the trail. Flo managed to wound three of the hungry beasts, and the two others decided it was not an easy kill and changed direction toward the hill behind her.

She continued on, exhausted with fear and shaking with cold. An hour later, the snow stopped. Able to see further now, she pushed harder. Half an hour down the trail, she came upon wagon tracks in the snow. They looked fresh.

"Someone's out here," she said. "They can help me. Wayne, someone's near. We can get help." The response came as a low moan.

Further on, the wagon tracks veered to the right. Then it came to her. "Oh, no. That can't be. Have I went in a circle? I can see the trail goes off to the left. The sun is on my right." Fear gripped her heart and pain shot through her chest.

"Oh God in heaven, Wayne. I'm lost. I hope I'm following the right trail."

The horses were moving slower. They needed water and feed. When she arrived at Willow Creek, she stopped and took care of the horses. Checking Wayne, his breathing was shallow and slow. She bundled him up with the Indian blanket and brushed the snow from his face. He was able to drink a little soup, but coughed up blood when she tried to give him water. He was unable to talk and nodded off to sleep. The sun drifted low on the horizon.

"Rest easy, Wayne. We're close. Just a couple of hours left. I'll get you there, darling. Hang on." The sun dropped below the horizon and stars shone bright. The clouds disappeared and the full moon lit the trail.

She came around the side of a hill and it was standing there. A white buffalo calf in the middle of the trail turned toward her, and it said, "I am Tatanka, the white buffalo. Follow me." It started down the trail. Moonlight made it glow.

She didn't understand it, but it calmed her and gave her strength. It was a sign. A sign that everything would be all right.

The horses seemed to take the white buffalo's lead and hurried on. They were reluctant to cross the Platte at the ford; the water was cold, and ice patches floated on the shallow river. She whipped them on. Knowing it wasn't far to help now, she talked to Wayne. "Wayne, darling, we are almost there. Help is not far away. The white buffalo is going to save us."

Finally, off in the distance, she saw the lights of Ogallala. "Thank heaven, we are going to be all right, Wayne. I can see the town."

Her hands were stiff with cold and frozen around the reins. It didn't matter to her, the goal was in sight.

They reached the outskirts of town and she shouted, "Help! Someone help. My husband needs help."

No one was coming out to help her.

Yelling as hard as possible now, "Please, please, help me."

Further down the street, three men came to the wagon, and one said, "What's the problem, ma'am?"

"It's my husband. He's in the back. He got shot and he needs a doctor."

Two of the men climbed in the wagon to check on Wayne. The other ran to get the doctor while the first two tried to help her down from the wagon. The two men looked at one another and shook their heads.

The doctor arrived and examined Wayne. The body was frozen and had no sign of life. He placed a hand on Flo's shoulder. "I'm sorry, ma'am. I'm afraid he's gone."

"No, no, that can't be. The white buffalo took care of us and showed the way. I took care of him. I talked to him all the way here and he talked to me. He just told me how much he loved me and how much he appreciated the care I gave him. He can't be gone. He's all I have."

"White buffalo? Ma'am, there hasn't been a buffalo in this area for years," said one of them.

The doctor told the men to get the undertaker and said to Flo, "Ma'am, I'm going to need some information."

Flo continued to tell the doctor that Wayne could not be dead; she had taken care of him.

He took her arm and led her to his house.

"No, we can't leave Wayne in the wagon. It's cold, he'll freeze to death."

"John and Henry will take care of him," the doctor said as he took her arm and headed down the street to his house and office.

"Tell them to fix him some soup and put more blankets on him."

When Doctor Evans got her to the office, he called to his wife to bring some hot tea for Flo.

When Flo had warmed a bit, Doctor Evans asked what happened.

"What happened? Nothing happened. Wayne just got cold."

"Ma'am, something else happened. Wayne has been shot. Do you remember?"

"There were wolves, and coyotes, and snakes. And Indians and a tornado. And the white buffalo led me here. Many things happened, but it will get better in a year or two."

"Ma'am how did your husband get shot?"

"Shot? Wayne was shot? It was so dark, and there was wind and snow and cold."

"Yes, ma'am, Wayne was shot."

She sat silent for a minute. Then she said to no one in particular. "We didn't see the darkness. It was there all the time, but we just didn't see it."

The Secret Fortune
Sherry McMurphy

Ice pellets pounded her windshield. Heavily moisture-laden clouds filled the sky. Thunder rumbled in the distance as Hattie traveled the curvy mountainous road. Daylight was disappearing rapidly as she pushed the boundaries of safety in order to reach home before the forest was fully engulfed in darkness. Oh, why hadn't she paid more attention to the weatherman that morning and stayed home? Because the newly opened resale shop in town had enticed her like a lighthouse beacon to a ship's captain. Thinking about the beautiful antique box she had just purchased made it all worthwhile.

Snow fell heavily, as she slowed her Jeep in anticipation of the dangerous and narrow curve ahead. Hattie switched the defroster to high and hung to the right edge of the lane as she entered the curve. Suddenly, a large black SUV came out of nowhere and rammed the back of her Jeep. She screamed and held tight to the steering wheel, checking the rearview mirror. In seconds, a second ram caused her to lose control. The Jeep spun around, hit the guard rail and rolled over and over down the mountainside. She could hear her screams as her vehicle crashed into a large tree and came to rest on its side. Her last thought before losing consciousness was why did the SUV purposefully run her off the road?

Nick watched the Jeep careen down the mountain in horror. He'd been following the black SUV closely and narrowly avoided smacking into its bumper. Probably would have if the SUV had not sped off in an urgency to leave the scene. He threw his truck in park, grabbed a flashlight and jumped out. Stepping over the guardrail, he scurried down the slick embankment. The Jeep's wheels were spinning, the front windshield and side door window were smashed. The car was still running, headlights beaming out into the woods.

Climbing up onto the car, he forced the driver's door open and looked inside. A dark headed woman lay suspended by her seatbelt as if lying in a sling over the console and into the passenger seat. Shaking her carefully, Nick called out, "Ma'am. Ma'am, you okay?" He received no response. Reaching around her, he turned the vehicle off.

Crawling out of the driver's door, he moved to open the back door and then lowered himself into the Jeep. Reaching through the bucket seats, he wrapped his arm under the woman's shoulders and supported her head while he released the seatbelt. Slowly, he lowered her down to the seat and stabilized her neck. Brushing her hair out of her face, he noticed a large contusion across her forehead and placed his handkerchief on it to stop the bleeding. He didn't notice any other injuries. He needed to get help.

Climbing back up the mountainside was strenuous and exhausting. He'd manage two steps forward and then lose more ground than he'd gained. Snow and sleet fell heavily around him as he fought to keep going. Ice pellets stung his face. His hands bled as branches and rocks tore at his flesh. He grabbed anything to help him climb up the terrain. Eventually, too bone-weary to continue, he gave up and made the decision to return to the wreck. With the harsh elements and falling temperatures, finding help tonight would be impossible. What he wouldn't give for his cell phone docked on the charger in his truck.

Rummaging around in the Jeep, he looked for her cell phone with no luck. It didn't take him long to realize the woman had to be a local and smartly packed a survival kit. He found two thick blankets in the back and two wooden crates. One housed a first aid kit that included warming packets and bandages. The second contained bottles of water, snacks, matches, a flashlight and warm clothing.

Nick arranged one blanket over the woman and the second over himself. She was still not responding to any stimulus but her breathing was slow and regular. All he could do at this point was to rest and hold out for help. With his truck sitting at the top of the mountain, surely someone would find them soon.

Nick awoke with a start. Someone was outside the jeep. Slowly and secretively, he maneuvered around in the seat in order to peek out a frosted window. He knew the visitors were not here to rescue but to do harm. A pounding sound came from the hood of the jeep and then again on the broken windshield. Nick turned toward the window and noticed the woman was awake. Her two dark eyes were trained on him. Placing his finger over his lips to quiet her, he shook his head and placed a hand on her arm to prevent her from rising up.

Bang! Bang! Two shots rang out into the frigid dark night. Nick flung himself over the top of the woman while simultaneously placing a hand over her mouth to muffle her scream.

"Shhh . . . keep down," he whispered. Scanning the windows on all sides of the Jeep, he could see shadows but nothing distinct. Reaching behind his back, he slid the Glock out of the back of his jeans and racked a round into the chamber. The woman jerked beneath him and attempted to scream again. Nick pushed his hand tighter over her mouth.

"Shhh . . . I'm not going to hurt you. You have to be quiet," he said, looking down into her terrified face. Suddenly, the back window shattered. Nick reacted instantly by firing off multiple rounds through the opening. Two men dressed all in black, wearing ski masks ran from the Jeep into the woods. Nick jumped out the broken window and dropped into the deep snow but it was too late to give chase. Armed and at the ready, he searched around the vehicle but only found deep footprints. His flashlight picked up some dark spots in the snow. Upon closer inspection, he realized it was blood. He must have hit one of them.

Returning to the Jeep, he hung one of the blankets along the back window in an attempt to block out the cold air. When he turned toward the front of the car, the woman sat staring at him in complete shock. Moving toward her, she flinched and grabbed the blanket to her chest as if it might shield her.

"You don't have to be afraid. I won't hurt you. What's your name?" he asked.

"Hattie. Why were those people shooting at us? Who are they? Who are you?" she questioned fearfully.

"I could ask you the same questions. Any reason someone would force you off the road? Try to kill you?"

"Kill me?"

"Well, from what I saw it was pretty clear, that black SUV intended to run you off the road," he stated.

"Who are you and why do you have that gun?" she demanded.

"Nick Finley, U.S. Marshall," he replied.

"U.S. Marshall? How did you end up in my car?"

"I was following the SUV that ran you off the top of the mountain. How's your head? You hurt anywhere?"

"Everywhere . . . I hurt everywhere. But no, not seriously injured."

"I tried climbing back up the mountain to where my truck is to get some help, but that didn't happen. Looks like were stuck here, at least for tonight."

"You think those men will be back?" she asked.

"I don't know, but I'm not letting my guard down."

Snuggling down under the blanket, Hattie tried to find some warmth. Consumed with fear, she kept her eyes focused on Nick who sat on full alert, waiting. The silence was deafening, until fatigue won out and her eyes closed.

"Hey, wake up," said Nick. "You can't go to sleep."

"I'm so tired."

"Ya, me too, but you're not croaking on my watch."

"They teach you all that charm in the academy?" she questioned sarcastically.

His eyebrows raised as if to say, "Watch it."

"What the hell were you doing out here on these roads anyway?"

"I could ask you the same question," she said with a sassy bite. "If you need to know, I went to a new resale shop in town. Oh, my box," Hattie cried out when she remembered her beautiful purchase. "Do you see a shopping bag anywhere?" she asked, frantically searching.

"This it?" he asked, holding up a pink shopping bag.

"Dang it, it's probably broken," moaned Hattie, reaching out to take it. Quickly, she pulled the damaged container out. Inside rested the antique box with the front broken into several pieces. Removing one of the pieces, both were surprised to find an exposed key and business card.

"Look. There's a secret compartment," said Hattie, pulling out the key.

"Where did you get this box?" demanded Nick, lifting the business card. Twenty-three was written across the back in large red numbers. "This is why you were run off the road."

"What? What do you mean? How do you know that?" screeched Hattie.

With urgency in his voice he asked, "Hattie, did you get this at the resale shop today? I need to know."

Without warning, the front windshield exploded. Glass flew around Nick and Hattie. She screamed and ducked, he drew his Glock. "Stay down," he ordered, cowering to keep his head out of view. A second bullet ricocheted off the steering column; a third shattered a side window. Nick returned fire before jumping out the back of the Jeep and taking immediate cover behind the rear wheel axle. Breathing heavily, he scanned the area. Nothing. Damn, they were sitting ducks.

"Hattie. You okay?" he asked in a muffled voice.

"Yes."

Out of nowhere a large black figure jumped Nick and wrestled him to the ground. He fought back, managing to get back on his feet, when the second attacker came at him. Nick wheeled around and kicked him directly in the face, dropping him immediately.

"Hattie, run. Run!" he screamed out, fighting with the attackers. He heard her scramble out of the back of the Jeep and saw the flash of her red sweater. "Run!" His arm was grabbed and twisted, forcing him to drop his gun. A strong shove had him falling backward into a snowdrift. Blow after blow was exchanged as he struggled to get up. Finally, Nick reached his gun. Rolling to the right he fired off two shots, hitting each target squarely between the eyes. Hattie screamed his name. Letting his head fall back he lay in the snow and tried to catch his breath.

Standing next to the highway patrol car, Hattie drew the heavy blanket tightly around her and took a sip of the hot coffee someone had shoved in her hand. In a daze, she watched everything swirl around her as if she were in a dream. Police stood everywhere. Red and blue lights flashed. An ambulance sat parked. A wrecker was pulling her Jeep back up the mountain. Nick stood across the road in deep conversation with what appeared to be other U.S. Marshalls. Did all of this really happen?

How could a simple antique box purchase almost cost her her life? Nick told her the key was to a locker at the bus station where thousands of dollars in drug money had been stashed. One of the dealers stored the key in his Grandmother's jewelry box, and when she passed away, all of her items were donated. They traced the box to the resale shop and witnessed Hattie purchase it before they could. Nick had been investigating the case for months.

When Nick finished up, he walked her way. Hattie went to him and hugged him tightly. "Thank you so much, Nick, for saving my life. I would have never made it without you," she expressed tearfully.

Nodding his head in acknowledgment, he wiped a tear away and said, "Why don't you let me buy you breakfast?"

Don't Forget the Peanut Butter

Douglas N. Osgood

Arctic air blasted at the window over the kitchen sink, rattling the glass in its frame. Blowing snow swirled furiously, unable to settle onto the blanket of white already deep from last night's blizzard. Light filtered through the haze of snow suspended in the air by the wind, sparkling off of the long icicles hanging from the eaves.

Looking out on the backyard, Joyce shivered involuntarily. Behind her she could hear the TV weatherman blather on about the overnight snowfall and chilling winds. This brought a derisive snort from her. *What did they know?* she thought. *Just yesterday morning this same bozo, so cocksure of himself, predicted that the storm would turn back to the north and miss them entirely. Sure it would,* no small hint of sarcasm in the thought.

School closings scrolling across the bottom of the screen caught her eye. Hardin R-I, Hardin R-IV, Herkimer School District, Incarnate Word Academy, Jackson County R-III . . . she had already seen Johnson City School District twenty times this morning, but waited to see it yet again. There it was, right after Jefferson College and JoAnne's School of Beauty.

She turned back to her work and dipped a wrinkled finger in the glass of water next to her. A single drop fell from her fingertip onto the griddle in front of her. It sizzled and skittered across the surface like a doodlebug over a pond. Satisfied the griddle was just the right temperature, she picked up the bowl of batter she had so carefully mixed just moments before. With practiced skill, she poured a small amount into two small circles on the hot surface. Almost instantly the aroma of melting chocolate filled the air. This was her mother's recipe for chocolate chip pancakes, and while they never seemed to turn out as well for her as they had for her mother, everyone still loved them.

"MeMaw, MeMaw," the girls yelled in unison as they entangled her legs in a death grip hug. Joyce had been so intent on the weather and school closings that she had not even heard her granddaughters come downstairs. Katie was eight years old and in second grade; Rose was five and had just started kindergarten that year.

"Good morning girls," Joyce said, mostly suppressing the laugh that came so easily to her. She bent down and wrapped her arms around both girls pulling them in tight to her.

Just as quickly, she stood and shooed them. "Go brush your teeth and wash your hands."

Rose stomped her foot and curled her lower lip out in a big pout. Brown curls of hair bobbed in unison with the pudgy finger she wagged at her grandmother. "Not fair, MeMaw," she whined. "You get chocolate chip pancakes for breakfast. We have to get ready for school."

Katie flipped long blonde tresses and rolled bright blue eyes. In her best I'm-the-big-sister-and-I-know-everything-and-you-know-nothing-you're-so-stupid voice, she said, "Silly, MeMaw only makes chocolate chip pancakes when school has been canceled."

Brown eyes suddenly wide, Rose turned to Joyce, her face begging for confirmation. Joyce simply nodded, a smile in her eyes. She noted that for all of her supposed confidence, Katie had also been watching her to be sure. Both girls began jumping up and down, mouths held open wide with silent screams of excitement.

Joyce stood and flipped the cakes bubbling on the griddle. "Now, run wash up and brush your teeth. I've got to finish breakfast and don't want to burn the chocolate chips." Tiny feet quickly pattered out of the kitchen and up the stairs.

Katie had been right, of course—snow days were for chocolate chip pancakes—a tradition Joyce's own mother had started all those years ago. A happy tear rolled down her cheek at the memory of her parents and her own childhood.

Joyce wasn't sure what woke her up. Outside, she could hear the wind howling; the glass, a thin layer of white frost clinging to the inside, rattled as the wind blew. Branches from the oak tree next to the house scratched against the siding right outside the bedroom she shared with her older sister, Grace. *Grace is such a princess,* she thought. *Just because she's nine and I'm only five, she gets to make me take the bed nearest the window during the winter. There's a cold draft from the window,* Joyce mimicked Grace in her mind.

Joyce's nose was cold. The bedroom was cool. Daddy turned down the heaters at night, and it always took time for the upstairs to warm after he turned them back up in the morning. Through the heating grate in the floor, she could hear the radio. Some man was talking about last night's snowstorm.

Something tickled her nose. Joyce sniffed. Was that chocolate she smelled? Next to her, Grace bolted out of her bed, racing downstairs as fast as her feet would carry her. Joyce was confused. Grace hated school, and it always took Mom several attempts to get her out of bed. Why was she up so fast today? Curiosity drove Joyce to brave the cool air. She jumped out of bed and raced after her sister, goose pimples rising on her skin as she ran.

Her mother stood by the stove, spatula in hand, carefully eyeing the pancakes on the large griddle. The distinct aroma of melted chocolate wafted through the kitchen. Joyce's mouth began to water and she grinned——Mommy never made chocolate chip pancakes. This was going to be a great morning. About then her eye caught the clock over the kitchen sink and realization struck just as quickly. A pout replaced the grin on her young face.

"Mommy," she whined. "Not fair. The kindergarten bus will be here soon. I'm not gonna get any pancakes."

Grace, who had been standing next to her mother, looked at Joyce and stuck out her tongue. "You better run get ready for kindergarten now, Joycie Poycie. You don't want to be late and miss your bus," she said, teasing. "I'll just have to eat your share."

Joyce dropped her head. Long brown curls hung down over her face, hiding the crocodile tears that were forming in the corners of her eyes. As she turned to leave, her shoulders heaved just once in silent frustration.

"Joyce, stay here." A deep voice from the corner behind the kitchen table. Then, in a high pitched squeak the same voice said, "Grace is just being a pot." Jimmy was their older brother. He was twelve, and sometimes his voice did that. It always made Joyce giggle, but not in a mean way. She could never be mean to Jimmy. He was her protector and often stepped in when Grace was being mean to her.

"There's no school today, dear," Mommy said. "You won't miss anything. Now go wash up, all of you. We'll have breakfast in just a few minutes."

"Don't forget the peanut butter, Mom," Jimmie shouted back over his shoulder as he left to wash up.

Static crackled over the announcer's voice as the radio alarm clock broke the night's silence. "It's the top of the hour, and we have a long list of school closings for you this morning," he said.

Joyce lay in bed, listening. Next to her, Ted, her husband of seven years, rolled out and strode to the window. He pulled aside the curtain and looked up and down the street.

"Looks like we got a foot, maybe a bit more," he said. "Plows haven't been out either, it seems. Bet there won't be school today."

"Hush, here come the J's."

The radio crackled, the announcer barely audible over the static. ". . . Hardin R-I closed, Hardin R-IV closed, Herkimer School District closed, Incarnate Word Academy closed, Jackson County R-III closed, Jefferson County—delayed opening, Johnson City School District closed, . . ."

"Well, I better go shovel out the driveway so I can get to work as soon as the plow comes through. Do you want to go back to bed? You won't have to go in, so you and Suzie can sleep in if you want."

Joyce thought about it a moment. One of the things she loved about teaching was that she could stay home with Suzie when there wasn't any school. She rubbed her expanding belly. And little Robert, too, once he came along.

"No, Dear. I think I'll get up. My mom always made chocolate chip pancakes on snow days. It was the only time she ever made them. I think I'll continue that tradition. Let Suzie sleep a little longer, but I'll have breakfast ready when you get back in from shoveling. Chocolate chip pancakes."

"That sounds great. Be sure to set the peanut butter out."

"Funny, my brother Jimmie always liked them that way, too."

Joyce shook her head, breaking the spell. Such good memories. She loved snow days. There was just something about the tradition of the chocolate chip pancakes on cold, blustery mornings. Little feet slapped against the floor as the girls ran back into the kitchen.

"Go sit down girls, breakfast is just about ready."

"Yeah," they shouted in unison.

"Hey, Mom. Are those pancakes just for little girls that don't have school? Or can a big girl that has to go in to work get some, too?" asked Suzie from the kitchen doorway.

Before Joyce could answer, Dave, Suzie's husband peaked over her shoulder and chimed in. "How about big boys that have to work?"

All three adults laughed, and Joyce pointed to the table, place settings for five already in place. "Please do join us."

"You even thought of the peanut butter for Dave. Mom, you're the best."

Cold: A Blessing in Disguise
Patricia Bubash

"Cold." Simply, hearing the word makes me shiver! I envision ice-crusted roofs, snow covered roads, frostbitten fingers, and frigid toes! For me, the word is linked to negative thoughts of discomfort: forced in-house stays, a stalled car, Boston! Have I made the point of my not-love affair with all things cold? My trial audience as I began to formulate this essay on the subject of cold was my husband. As we tumbled into our "cold" cranky car after church, buttoning up wool coats, pulling on gloves, and arranging the knit caps on our chilled heads, preparing for the drive home in the single digit temperatures, I turned to my husband. "What comes to your mind when you hear the word cold?" I asked. I anticipated a response that alluded to my "cold heart"—a term he uses on occasion to describe me! (Certainly, just in jest—our personal joke.) Or my question would get him rolling again, "Why are we here and not in Florida on the beach?"

This is an ongoing discussion every year when the cold of January sets in and our aging bones begin to complain against the decreasing temperatures. To my surprise, without hesitation, his reply, "Ice cream!" How unexpected was this? Very. Then, continuing, he went on to mention the pleasure of an icy cold beer on a really hot day, or a slice of summer sweet, cold watermelon, or the tangy welcome taste of cold lemonade on a steamy July day. Not to be left overlooked in his litany of good "cold" things, I began to chime in. I added gazpacho soup (the spicier the better!), and tangy cucumber soup, topped with a sprinkle of dill. Oh, not to be forgotten, the delight of cold southern sweet ice tea topped with a slice of lemon or lime, and don't forget, frozen grapes! A delicious cold treat.

We were on a roll—a roll of positive "colds." Who would have thought? We no longer felt the cold outside, only the warmth of the adjectives being tossed about inside our car.

One of my frequent quotes in situations involving conflict, disagreement, confrontation is, "It is all about the individual's perception." Jim just proved my theory with his positive assessment of cold. I was expecting negatives and getting positives. I do realize it was not the elements that he was listing, but rather food and drink! But, his choices were still in the category of "cold." The discussion between us continued with his usual analytical view of the topic in discussion: the cycle of the seasons of the year. (I was too busy with the menu.) It had not occurred to me that the seasonal change of fall into the cold of winter provides us with an escape from the fauna that causes us to sneeze, have itchy eyes and throats, sending us running to the nearest Walgreens for a cure for those miserable allergies! Remember when suffering, complaining about the discomfort of allergies, there is always the eternal optimist who pipes up with an easy solution to your misery. "Well, it is going to freeze soon, and then you will be just fine." And it is true, once the temperatures begin to drop to that medicinal 32 degrees, we usually are rid of those irritating, uncomfortable symptoms. Ahh, this is a cold that we gratefully welcome as it freezes out what has created such physical discomfort.

Populations of nasty varmints like mosquitoes and ticks, are also vanquished upon the return of the cold. Warmer temperatures bring out the insects that keep us scratching, itching, and uncomfortable in our own skin. But the coolness, cold of fall and winter allow us to enjoy walks in the woods, forests without the necessity of mosquito repellent and the all over body check for ticks at the end of the walk—oh, and I almost forgot one of my most feared minuscule creators of discomfort: chiggers! The misery of their body invasion lasts for days. As you scratch, take a cool bath in baking soda, anything to find relief, the cold temperatures that put these little demons to rest are suddenly very appealing.

Doesn't the resurgence, the first sight, of blooming tulips, creating a palette of pink, yellow, vivid red exhilarate our spirits in the spring? Moving from the cold of winter into the showy display of my favorite flower, tulips, lifts my spirits. Does anyone consider, as the tulip bulb pokes through the still, cold earth, that this process of hibernation is necessary for the bloom to rejuvenate, returning to its full splendor in the spring? The winter cold allows the blooms, trees, and all the greenery that brings pleasure to the eye to rest dormant, soaking up nutrients for the spring show to come after the thaw.

This cycle, which welcomes the season of cold, I find also applies to the rejuvenation of me. We have a cabin in the woods about fifty miles out of St. Louis. In the summer, it is crowded with families enjoying all the summer activities, outdoor events. Lakes abound for kayaking, swimming, canoeing, fishing, and, the latest, paddle boarding. As entertaining as the summer months are, my favorite time of year to be there is winter. The coldest weeks find me rearranging my schedule so we can spend quiet winter days in this remote cabin.

When we arrive, it is always cold. First order of the moment is to start a fire and quickly get a pot of coffee brewing. This is the one place that I do not mind the cold. I breathe in the frigid, crisp, clean air as I walk in the woods, loving the sound of crunching leaves, birds calling through the leafless trees. There is such a beauty in the bare branches lifting arms to the sky, a clean palate, uncluttered, with a wide- open view of the winter skies. I find a tranquility come over me in this environment that is not available in the clamorous, active summer months. Like my favored tulips, I am provided with this, my dormant time, when I can reflect, rejuvenate, knowing that this season will pass, and then we are in the throes of noisy, busy summer again. How can we really appreciate the warmth of spring, the heat of summer, without the experience of "cold?" Don't we know change is good!

I began this essay with a less than favorable leaning towards cold. Noting that when I hear that word, "cold," I tend to shiver, head for my fleece, feeling an imaginary chill. As a result of my previous comments, my few positives about cold, it would probably be a surprise to share that one of my very favorite television programs is "Living Below Zero." The show highlights the life styles and experiences of families that chose to live off the grid in remote areas of Alaska. I am fascinated by these personal stories of survival. The resourcefulness of the people, their ability to survive in the harsh, brutally cold and frozen tundra, is fascinating to me. I pull my flannel robe closer around me, hands wrapped around my hot chocolate, feeling the cold of Alaska as I watch these survivalists cut wood, hunt for food, store provisions for winter, and build houses. Their hardiness and love for the land is so far removed from my environment, I continuously question my husband as we stare at the television, "How can they stand the cold? It is SO cold there. Not just St. Louis cold, but really cold." As entranced as I am with their spirit, their respect for the bitterness of the elements, and the toughness required to exist there, I don't think I will be making a location move to Alaska. I will continue to watch faithfully each week, admiring their endurance and tenacity with my flannel robe and cup of steaming hot chocolate, easily prepared in the microwave.

Jim's list of "cold" things encouraged me to challenge his list with my own "stuff." I reluctantly share a childhood cold experience as it reflects on knowledge gained by age—my age! But it is a good experience, so I will get over my age sensitivity to share it. At the age of five, I was living with my parents in California Naval housing. These were very modest houses, not furnished with the latest modern appliances, thus an icebox was sufficient. (Yes, I am that old!) Twice a week, a frozen slab was brought in to produce the necessary refrigeration for our food. I wonder how many readers can relate to this appliance of the past? Twice a week, the "iceman cometh"—yes, there really was an iceman. The ice fit on a shelf inside the box—our answer to today's modern, ice making, crushed ice, or a glass of water, whatever you desire, marvels! But, the icebox had something to appreciate beyond today's appliance: a frozen slab that you could touch with a warm sweaty hand as respite from the hot California sun. (No, I never did attempt to put my tongue on its cold surface!) For a kid growing up without the experience of real winters, this brief moment touching the icy slab gave some indication of what I was missing: sledding down a snowy hill, ice skating (and the best part, savoring a hot chocolate after a few circles around the rink!), walks on crunchy snowy sidewalks, skiing, building a snowman, throwing snowballs at your friends or enemies, wrapping up in cozy wool sweaters, and quilted parkas. A winter wardrobe has always been more attractive to me than the summer clothing—the fabrics, materials, and styles suited me better than cottons and gauze. And then the boots!! Love boots.

Ironic that three different times in my life I have lived on islands. Places where temperatures never went below 70 or 80. I loved it. But as the months turned to the time of fall on the Mainland, when I knew folks would be pulling out the ski sweaters, furry mittens, and beginning to stack firewood for the fireplace, I was a little nostalgic—missing the "cold." Envisioning my friends laughing, socializing around the fire pit as the days of winter began. They would be scheduling dates for hockey games, headed to favorite restaurants, plays, all inside activities to stay out of the "cold." And, then my flash of insight: cold helps the economy! During those cold days of winter, socializing tends to be in the realm of indoor, which brings more customers to eateries, to indoor malls, to recreational facilities such as bowling alleys, pool, and any type of sport that provides physical exertion—inside! My summation for my observations is "cold is profitable!" And, for those of us who write, cold gives us a reason to stay inside creating, spinning out words on our computer screens for our latest writing projects.

With this final thought, embracing the positive side of "cold" in weather, in food, in drink, in winter activities, or creative writing, I finish wrapping my bright red hibiscus towel around my sun drenched shoulders as I head to the beach. Only so much "cold" can be tolerated.

#   #   #

A FLASH OF LIGHT

- Light -

Becky: Wife, Mother
Jennifer McCullough

Is she young? Thin? Does she even have a college degree, Becky wondered as she scrubbed the sleeve of his white dress shirt with one part bleach and nine parts sparkling water.

... looks like that gross shade of red his mom wears.

"What a tramp!" Becky said as her two-year-old twins scurried past the laundry room door.

The firstborn, Martin, doubled back. "Lady and the Tramp, Mama? We watch Lady and the Tramp now, pwease?"

"Ok, baby," Becky said to her dark-haired child as she quickly wiped the tears off her cheeks with the back side of a yellow-rubber-glove covered hand.

The blue glowing numbers on the VCR told her Roger would be home any minute.

He normally worked late on Tuesday nights, but had called earlier to say he was still tired from his out-of-town weekend sales meeting.

Sales meeting my ass. I bet you're tired, jerk.

Becky was almost always finished with the weekend's laundry by noon on Mondays. She prided herself on being on top of all things domestic, but lately she'd been letting things slide.

Not the least of which was her appearance.

Ugly cow, Becky thought as she caught her reflection in the hall mirror on the way to Roger's closet.

No wonder he's cheating on me.

Becky stuffed a wad of wrinkled undershirts in Roger's dresser then walked into the bathroom.

Her stretched-out jogging pants drooped like the skin of an English bulldog around her ankles as she sat on the toilet and cried. She'd lost some weight after the twins were born, but still wasn't back to her pre-pregnancy size.

She recalled all the other times she'd suspected Roger was cheating on her. His trip to Vegas for the fall conference. The time she went to visit her sister. The day she called his office, but his secretary said he was taking a vacation day. There were too many to count.

The distinct sound of four toddler feet leaving the wood floor of the living room pulled Becky back into the moment.

Don't come in here right now, boys. Not now. Jesus.

The boys' footsteps picked up speed in the hallway leading to the master bedroom but became quiet again once they reached the green sculptured carpet.

Two tiny voices called out in unison, "Mama, Mama?"

"Mama?" McKenzie said as he pushed open the door of the bathroom, his little face both surprised and frightened to see his mother so distraught. "You sad, Mama?"

"Mama cry? Mama cry?" Martin said, begging for an explanation. His forehead wrinkled with despair behind his tiny blue eyeglasses.

"I'm ok, boys," Becky reassured them. She attempted to smile, but instead cried harder.

Both children clung to her legs as she tried to stand, their sticky bare toes tangled in stretchy black fabric.

I can't just leave. I can't just leave my marriage.

"Let's call your Gimmy."

Immediately, their concern for Becky turned to distracted exuberance. They bolted for the door yelling, "Gimmy, Gimmy!"

But Becky wanted to run even more than they did. She'd been looking for a way out of her marriage since she found out she was pregnant with the twins.

She'd been on track to become the CEO of one of North America's largest industrial copper mines. The pregnancy itself wasn't what held her back. It was Roger. He'd always been supportive of her career until she got pregnant. At first, he didn't want her traveling to China. Then, he forbid her from entering the mine. He said the naturally occurring sulfur gas and petroleum fumes from the heavy machinery would harm the babies.

Despite her best arguments and a forged letter from her OB-GYN, Becky wasn't able to convince Roger she could do her job and be pregnant at the same time. When the twins were born eight weeks early, Roger was furious at her, even though she had taken a leave of absence when she was just six months pregnant to appease him.

Becky's resentment toward Roger grew more intense as the days she stayed home with the boys stretched into months. She wanted desperately to go back to work when they were four months old, but Roger refused to let her hire a nanny. Martin was visually impaired, so no daycare centers would accept him.

In the span of a few months, Becky went from being in the "Top 50 Who's Who of Female Business Executives in the U.S." to a tired, stressed-out, stay-at-home hostage.

Roger, on the other hand, seemed to thrive amidst family life. His career took off after the twins were born.

He was the top-producing sales rep for his tri-state region for eight consecutive quarters. His annual bonuses had been more than his previous two years' salaries combined.

"You don't have to work," he told Becky late one night as she sat reading Department of Natural Resources' revised statutes.

"But I want to, Roger. If I stay up on these regulations, maybe the Board will want me back."

"Well, your place is with the boys. My mom stayed home with me, and I think that's how it ought to be. I don't want our boys raised by people who aren't vested in their futures. End of discussion."

For a while, Becky tried to make the best of her situation. She joined a playgroup at the library, took cooking classes, and volunteered with the La Leche League. Although she managed to organize the house top to bottom, cut costs on things like paper products and laundry detergent by buying it directly from the manufacturers, and get the boys to swim lessons on time, her heart just wasn't in the domestic life.

When her psychiatrist asked her if she knew how many women would kill to be in her shoes, Becky countered with, "Yeah, well, I guess the fact that I want to be less of a woman makes me more like a man, then, huh? And how many women would kill to be in those shoes?"

Becky wasn't surprised when he didn't see the humor in her snarky remark.

The thing was—Becky desperately loved her boys. She took outstanding care of them and worked tirelessly to make sure they had good lives. She didn't know any other way to operate. Her dedication and work ethic applied across the board. Motherhood was no exception.

Her marriage, however, was a different story. She concealed her true feelings so well and so often, that she sometimes wondered if she should have become an actress instead of a business executive.

Becky was in the kitchen when she heard Roger drive up.

"Hi honey, I'm glad you're home early."

"I'm so beat. What's for supper?

Lamb chops drizzled in arsenic with a side of ricin.

'Where are the boys?"

Becky didn't answer.

"Becky, where are the boys?"

"Oh, your mom took them to the park."

"If it's ok then, I think I'll take a little nap before we eat."

A nap! Are you serious? You want a nap, asshole? I haven't had a nap in two years!

"Sure, hun."

I'll be right here slaving away while you sleep because you're so tired from having an affair, you bastard.

"Love you."

Go to hell.

Becky smiled back.

She knew other working women who had left their cheating husbands. Their divorces never turned out well. Judges don't like women who leave their men, especially ones who travel internationally 20 days a month and still want shared custody of their children.

Despite the fact that every muscle in her body ached to walk out the door, she stood in front of the kitchen sink washing her hands, her eyes glazed with tears, her head cocked to the side. She felt powerless to stop her life, her career, her youth, from trickling away.

Unemployed middle-aged divorced mother of two toddlers... Jesus.

Unemployed. Middle-aged. Mother. None of those identities seemed to match who Becky thought she was.

But it had been so long since she'd been anything else, she'd forgotten what it felt like to be young, happy, independent, and respected in the professional world.

Becky turned off the kitchen light and walked into the garage.

As she started the car, she told herself she could leave Roger anytime she wanted to.

She laid her head back, breathed in the exhaust that began to fill the closed garage, and smiled. For a minute, she felt in control of her life again.

I can do this one more day. I have to do this one more day... for my boys.

When she walked back inside, Roger was standing in front of the refrigerator with the door open.

He didn't look at her. He hadn't looked at her in a very long time.

"Since you're obviously not cooking..."

"Would you like me to turn on the light," Becky said.

"No, I can see."

"No, I don't think you can," she said as she flipped on the overhead light.

I don't think you can see even with the light on, Roger. But I can see you crystal clear.

The Great Race of Mercy
Nicki Jacobsmeyer

In 1925, the fatal diphtheria outbreak was running rampant, and the closest antitoxin serum was 674 miles away. Dr. Curtis Welch hadn't seen a case of "black death" in twenty years, but now it began taking lives from the Eskimo village of Nome, Alaska.

***

"Rosie, the doctor will see you now," Nurse Sara said as she guided them back to the exam room.

"It sure is busy," said Rosie's mother, Beth. The hacking coughs of children echoed through the hall.

"It's been like this for days. Since Dr. Welch is the only physician in town, the hospital hasn't slept."

Rosie's father, Michael, gave his wife a comforting pat. Nurse Sara got Rosie situated on the exam table then stated the doctor would be in soon.

Dr. Welch came in as Rosie worked through a coughing jag. The doctor placed his stethoscope on her chest.

"Sounds like you aren't feeling very well, Rosie."

Rosie shook her head.

Dr. Welch offered a sympathetic look as he asked her to open her mouth. Rosie cringed, trying to open her jaws. He shone a light into her mouth and grimaced.

Dr. Welch's cool hands palpated Rosie's glands on her neck. "Her glands are enlarged and swollen." He could tell Rosie was running a fever and placed a thermometer under her tongue to confirm. 103.5.

"Has Rosie been exposed to anyone who has been sick?"

"No, I don't think so."

"What grade are you in, Rosie?" Dr. Welch asked. Rosie held up three fingers. Bessie Stanley was in third grade, the doctor recalled. He had diagnosed her yesterday with diphtheria. She hadn't made it through the night.

"My, how time flies," Dr. Welch replied with a weak smile.

"Rosie, I'm going to have Nurse Sara get you a warm blanket. You rest while I talk to your parents, alright?" Rosie nodded.

Dr. Welch led her parents to his office where he stared at his sparse medicine cabinet. "Rosie has diphtheria," he stated without hesitation.

"No," gasped Beth.

"How can that be?" Michael said, confused.

"Diphtheria is extremely contagious. It is an airborne bacteria, one droplet is enough exposure. I'm sorry," replied Dr. Welch.

"Surely there is something you can do?" Michael said as he looked at his wife, stunned into silence.

"She needs the antitoxin serum."

"Then give her that."

"I wish I could, but there is no more serum in Nome."

January 26th

Dr. Beeson placed the last of 300,000 units of the antitoxin serum in a cylinder. He tugged at the insulated quilt to insure the tightest fit before he tied it in sturdy canvas. He handed the cylinder, with warming instructions, to Train Conductor Frank Knight.

Dr. Beeson mentally reassured himself this was the fastest way to get Nome the serum they needed. Even though Nome was located on the Bering Sea coast, it was icebound. The only aviation in Alaska was a biplane, and with their open cockpits, a pilot would never survive in the –60-degree temperature. The serum could only last six days outside in these weather conditions. As Steam Engine #66 pulled out of Anchorage, Alaska, Dr. Beeson bowed his head in silence.

***

In Juneau, Alaska's capital, Governor Scott Bone asked for the best 20 mushers and their dog-sled teams to participate in this relay for life to Nome. He instructed the relay to travel from the train station in Nenana to Nulato, the halfway point. There, a musher from Nome would meet them to retrieve the serum cylinder and turn around to deliver it safely back to Nome. Thankfully, the mushers drove segments of the trail on their daily mail routes.

January 27th

The train had reached the end of its 298-mile journey when it pulled into Nenana. The conductor had been told there would be a musher waiting for the serum. Sure enough, "Wild Bill" Shannon stood waiting with his nine malamutes ready to run. Frank cradled the cylinder as he got off the train and passed it to Wild Bill. He recited the warming instructions verbatim and shook the musher's hand.

"Good luck," Frank said, shielding his face from snow.
Wild Bill nodded and shouted to his team, "Let's go!"

***

Hundreds of miles away back in Nome, the dreary weather reflected the mood of the town. The only beacon of hope was the lit lantern outside the telegraph office. It would continue to shine bright until the antitoxin serum was delivered. The Health Commissioner was anxious that the serum wouldn't make it before his town perished. So, he requested the services of Leonhard Seppala and his team of 20 Siberian huskies to do half the route solo, a total of 319 miles. Seppala was instructed to retrieve the serum at Nulato. Seppala and Togo, his lead dog, had made the trip before in four days, but never in these weather conditions or matter of urgency. This would be the most challenging race of their lives.

Day 1
January 28th

Seppala was informed by telegraph that the relay had started and he was to leave Nome. He wore his warmest squirrel parka, sealskin pants and reindeer mukluks. He made eye contact with Togo's pale blue eyes as he mounted the sled.

"Mush!"

Togo obeyed without hesitation and took the team down Front Street towards Nulato. They had no idea that their destination was incorrect. The telegraph had failed to mention that the meeting point was changed to Shaktoolik, 150 miles before Nulato.

Day 2
January 29th

Seppala strained to see his wheel dogs in front of him as they drove through Safety. The whiteout was constricting Togo's view, so he led by scent, not sight. The bitter Bering Sea coast yielded ferocious winds and unrelenting snow.

The small village, White Mountain, was a welcome sight. The musher and his team were able to take refuge in the roadhouse. Seppala had to drop two of his dogs at the roadhouse. The hair around their groins had frozen and was restricting their stride, slowing them down. Time was not a luxury he possessed.

***

Rosie was bed ridden and her wheeze was getting worse. Dr. Welch could only catch a glimpse of the gray membrane forming over her throat, obstructing her breathing. Her parents' hopeful faces deflated at his melancholy expression and shake of the head.

Within just a few days, five patients were dead, 20 more diagnosed and over 30 suspected of having the illness. Dr. Welch looked out the hospital window to the telegraph office next door. The lantern remained lit, but time was running out.

Day 3
January 30th

The blustering −64 degree weather conditions were crippling Seppala's team. They were tormented by a lack of enthusiasm, and he had a hunch that some were afflicted with pneumonia. The wind chill was piercing his face like sharp daggers. He contemplated the longevity of the serum and hoped it was faring better.

A mile out of Koyuk, a crackling noise distracted him from his dogs' conditions. He looked up towards the sound and saw flames leaping across the sky. As a native of Alaska, one would think the Northern Lights would lose their allure. For Seppala, the dance of lights reminded him of his cherished childhood. As he pulled into Koyuk, the yellow-green band blazed a trail towards Nulato.

***

Henry Ivanoff and his team were less than a mile out of Shaktoolik, where he would pass the serum to Seppala. He was lost in his thoughts when his dogs became skittish and pulled off the trail.

"On by!" Ivanhoff yelled as he tried to bring order to the chaos.

He inspected the brush around them trying to identify if his dogs had smelled a moose. The 500-pound animal could trample and demolish his team with little effort. Ivanhoff wasn't going to wait around. As he got the last of the gang line straightened, he saw a flash of movement over his left shoulder.

***

Seppala was over halfway to Nulato and determination had him locked in the zone. He thought he heard a noise behind him, but figured it was the wind moaning. Perhaps sheer paranoia made him look back, but when he did he saw a shadow.

"Serum—turn back!" hollered Ivanhoff.

Seppala stopped his team with hesitation, leery of wasting time. Once he heard the musher's message, he shouted "Gee! Gee!" to his dogs to turn to the right and go back.

***

The past 72 hours had been brutal for Seppala and his team. He was still contemplating the ramifications if Ivanhoff hadn't been able to stop him to transfer the serum. The temperature had dropped to -100 degrees, so they had decided to insulate the cylinder more with rabbit skin when they made the exchange.

On the way to Golovin, Seppala had to make a critical decision. Cross Norton Bay with its 20 miles of treacherous frozen sea, or take the safe route and drive around, which would take more time. The serum would only last three more days at most. The town was counting on him, but so were his dedicated dogs.

He looked at Togo with raised eyebrows.

Togo howled to his team and they responded in kind.

With a flick of the wrist and a click of the tongue, they were off.

Day 4
January 31st

Togo and the team were rewarded with a few hours of sleep after their courageous trek across Norton Bay. Seppala napped in an igloo at Isaac Point while the serum warmed. They would be renewed by morning.

***

The blizzard woke the team with its icy blend and left a vanished trail in its wake. Seppala pushed them to Golovin knowing the end was in sight. Charlie Olson waited at the roadhouse as Togo brought the team in after running a total of 260 miles. Olson took Seppala's glossy eyes, cracked lips and shallow breathing as enough instructions.

Day 5
February 1st

Strong gusts had thrown Olson's team off the trail numerous times in the 25 miles to Bluff. His dogs' undercarriages had frozen along the way. Removing his gloves to blanket each dog allowed enough time for frostbite. Later, Olson winced in pain when Gunnar Kaasen went to shake his hand at the Bluff Roadhouse.

Day 6
February 2nd

Kassen and his team ran into Safety at 2:00 a.m. This was the last stop before Nome. The final relay musher, Ed Rohn, was fast asleep in the roadhouse having not expected Kaasen for a few more hours. Perhaps it was that Kaasen was a young 21-year-old, or that he called Nome home and there lay his loyalty. Most likely the idea of being the hero by delivering the serum himself was too attractive to pass up. Convincing himself he was doing the right thing, Kaasen grabbed the cylinder by the fire and strode out towards his sled.

***

At 5:30 a.m. Kaasen pulled down Front Street in Nome with only the lantern's light to guide him.

"Whoa!" he said as he pulled up to the hospital. Kaasen went to knock on the door, but it opened of its own accord.

Standing in the doorway was Dr. Welch. His face was a pasty white, his shoulders hung in defeat and his eyes were at half-mast.

"The serum, Dr. Welch," said Kaasen as he presented the cylinder.

Dr. Welch's eyes grew to the size of saucers and became glassy. His hands trembled as he took the precious serum from the musher.

"Thank you, my dear boy," he said with a lump in his throat.

***

The antitoxin serum was immediately administered to all patients. Dr. Welch was concerned Rosie's dose was too late, but she was resilient and turned the corner after a couple of days. Dr. Welch went to the telegraph office himself and extinguished the glowing light of the lantern. Over six days, 20 musher teams had traveled a total of 674 miles to save the town of Nome, Alaska. It was the great race of mercy.

A Flash of Insight
Carole Tipton

I've always enjoyed a good thunderstorm. A scientist once explained to me how the negative ions produced by storms affect the body's chemistry and produce a rush much like the feeling adrenaline provides. True or not, I'm sure that for most of my youth the feeling I enjoyed came from a twisted reaction to a bit of family history. A great-grandfather on my mother's side of the family was struck and killed by lightning in 1878, when my grandmother was an infant. Of course she was raised to believe that fear of thunderstorms was second only to fear of God, and she passed this fixation on to her descendants.

By the time her grandchildren were old enough to play outside at family gatherings, Grandma was a *very* old lady, and her father's death seemed like ancient history to us. We city kids couldn't imagine a farmer running for cover out in the fields in rural Illinois more than seventy years before. Grandma didn't even have a photograph of Great-grandpa Leo, so he remained a disembodied name in a grisly anecdote.

While we grandkids did recognize that there were dangers in storms, Grandma's fears made us into little daredevils. If we'd been called inside because of a burgeoning storm, we'd make our way out to the front porch a few at a time, and pretty soon we'd all be out on the sidewalk playing tag in the rain and shrieking at every thunderclap, until our parents realized what we were doing and called us in, this time to stay put—or else!

Especially vocal about this were the two maiden aunts who lived with Grandma and Grandpa. Oh, the lectures we'd get from them! Aunt Hilda was always the most appalled by our behavior and made her feelings clear! Of course we knew she loved us and meant well, but we thought we were bulletproof, as kids do.

Fast-forward twenty years, and I was a wife with three small children of my own. An evening in early spring and the owl-light of an approaching storm darkened the sky outside my kitchen window where I cleaned up after dinner. The deepening clouds made a black mirror of the bare glass in front of me. I watched the swaying branches of the river birch tree just outside and the rush of leaves rising in the grip of the whirlwind, and I remember feeling happy. A "good" storm was on its way, and though I'd long ago given up my childish antics where they were concerned, I still enjoyed watching them from a snug vantage point. My husband was working out-of-town that week, and my kids were engrossed in some game on the floor in the living room. Our cat was camped next to my feet on the throw rug in front of the sink, her paws tucked under; content, she waited to be fed. She knew the nightly routine. This coziness belied what was about to happen.

Never have I been able to put a definitive sequence to the events that followed, so sudden and apparently simultaneous were they that I could not have sworn to which came first. But there was an enormous blinding blue-white flash just outside my kitchen window. Had the birch tree then crumbled before me, it would have been no surprise! At the same instant, the back door in the kitchen, *locked before dinner*, flew open with such force that its doorknob left an impression in the wall behind it, and the glass bottom of the screen door shattered. In the same nanosecond, the cat leaped to her feet, arched her back, flattened her ears, and hissed like the Devil's familiar, *not* at the door, but at the space *behind* me. As stunning as these events were, my attention was focused on a voice coming from behind my right ear that urgently called, "Janey!" Just that one word, nothing more. So stern and clear was it that I had half turned in that direction with the word *what* forming on my lips before I saw in the black mirror of the window that no one was there! The voice was Aunt Hilda's. She was the only one of the relatives who called me Janey. She'd been dead for 10 years.

Shaking where I stood, I realized that the storm had moved on. As if the entirety of its energy had been spent in that instant, all that remained was calm and quiet.

Forty years later and I still get gooseflesh retelling what happened that night. Make no mistake—that reaction is in no way from fear. The voice I heard that night was that of warning, but also of protection. In that moment, I knew to the depth of my being that no harm was going to come to me. You might call the lightning strike a flash of insight. Aunt Hilda was gone, but her love remained.

An "almost" true story about my grand[mother]

Dem Dumpster Bums

Jennifer Hasheider

Carla Langdon never ate red M&M candies. I watched her plunk each shiny morsel into the trashcan after emptying the bag on top of her desk. Sometimes they made a *thunk* right to the bottom, and other times I heard them slide on sheets of paper before coming to a rest.

"I wonder what the cleaning people think when they empty your garbage and see all the red M&Ms," I said.

Carla looked over the edge of her desk into her trashcan. "Well, I can't bring myself to eat those. That color isn't natural."

"The candy shell on only the red ones isn't natural?" I asked this for clarity and to avoid the piles of work on my desk.

"Well, the brown and tan shells are closer to the color of chocolate. Red sets off an alarm for me." She shrugged. "Hey, did I tell you what I did the other night with Adam's red lamp?"

"The one you hate?" I knew she'd moved in with her boyfriend, Adam, recently and had gotten into some obsessive hate thing with a certain lamp he kept in the living room.

"Yes, with the weird cut outs in the bottom that show a frowning face on the wall when only the bottom part is on." I nodded, I knew more about it than her office partner should.

Carla rolled her eyes. "Well, I'd had enough of the damn thing, so I threw it out." I nodded, trying to push the story along. I had work to do. "In all of my complaining about that ugly thing, he never mentioned it had belonged to his great-grandmother."

"So, you threw out the ugly frowning lamp that belonged to Adam's great-grandma. Man, how did that go over?" Suddenly, I was rather enjoying this story.

"Yeah. I put it in the dumpster in the alley in the morning, then we argued about it all night. I finally went to dig it out of the trash, and get this—it was gone." She gripped the edge of her desk for emphasis.

"The trash had been picked up, or a dumpster diver had taken it?"

"Dumpster diver? You mean, like a bum?"

"Well, I don't know if they are all *bums*. Shoot, my grandfather goes around collecting treasures all the time. He fixes them up and donates stuff to his church or something." I grabbed a page from the file on my desk, preparing to work again.

"How do you know if the people are bums or are like your grandfather?" Carla asked.

I thought for a minute. "I'm not sure, actually. What's a bum anyway? I know in Hawaii they get people that go over to spend the winter in tent cities. They aren't really homeless, just taking advantage of being in Hawaii—*bummin' for the winter,"* I snickered.

"I don't believe that. I've been to Hawaii a few times and never seen any bums," Carla said.

"Well, people live in tents there. Next time you go, venture outside of your resort, you'll see them everywhere," I told her. "Heck, when I was kid there was a homeless guy in my grandparents' neighborhood who had saved a man from a burning building. We used to call him 'Cat Man' after that because he was a hero and lingered around in the alley like an old cat. He'd stand at the fence and watch us eat dinner in my grandmother's kitchen."

"That is totally creepy," Carla pointed out.

"Yeah, I guess it kind of is." I hadn't thought of it as creepy until that moment. "The person Cat Man saved turned out to be some rich dude. He rented Cat Man an apartment, but he lived there about two weeks and then abandoned it. He preferred to be homeless."

"Seriously? Why would anyone want to live that way?" Carla's face scrunched up like Barbie's when you squeezed it on top and under the chin.

"It's like when people who have been in prison for a long time get out, they go right back in by choice. Change is hard, and it's probably a lot easier inside prison than it is outside for them."

"Why do you know all of this?"

It was just in my head, like all the other useless information rolling around up there. "I guess I just pay attention."

Carla wagged a long, French-manicured finger at me. "I doubt it was an escaped prisoner trying to get back inside prison that stole the lamp from the dumpster."

"The prisoners aren't *escaped,* they've been released, because their sentence is up. And anyway, how can someone steal something that you threw away?"

I hoped Carla hadn't given her next sentence much thought when she said, "Well, I wanted it back, that's how I know it was stolen."

I scratched my head and laughed a little. "Maybe you can't tell when someone is homeless if they are *stealing* out of a dumpster."

Hearing "Carla in the Big City" stories were usually worth pausing for. They were good fodder for when I met the gang at Johnny's on Friday nights.

A few mornings later, I figured either Santa was trekking around the office, or Carla had on so much jewelry that she jingled when she walked.

"Good morning, Carla," I said, not looking behind me to confirm it was her.

"Hey, I saw that bum out at the dumpster this morning. I ran inside to get him a bagel but he was gone when I came back out. He's gotta be hungry, don't you think?"

"I guess?" I said, shrugging my shoulders.

"I think I'll make a sack lunch and leave it out there for him, like right on the edge of the dumpster where he'll see when he goes to open the lid."

I didn't reply, but I did shake my head: fodder.

Weeks later, when she dropped her heavy bag onto her chair and stood with her hands on her hips, I knew I was in for a story about a new adventure.

"I saw that bum this morning in the alley behind my house."

"Is he a bum or just looking for treasures in the dumpster?" I'd thought this adventure was over, but apparently she was still on the ride.

"He's a bum. No person in their right mind would go digging through dumpsters unless they had to, and that makes him a bum. Get a job." A tube of pink lipstick appeared from somewhere, and she applied a thick layer to round lips. "Well, I gave him money for lunch. He hadn't been taking the sack lunches, so I made him take cash." She smiled and cupped her chin in her hands.

"That's terrific," I said. I had a stack of files on my desk that was taller than me when I stood. I was ready to get started and get out early for the holidays.

"No, get this," Carla said. "He didn't want to take it, but I insisted. Some people are so proud," Then, over the clack of her heels on the way back to her desk, I heard her mumble, "Just take the money. Obviously you need it, ya bum . . ."

That afternoon it started to snow. "Hey, look, Carla, we're going to have a white Christmas after all." I pointed out the small window in our office. Thick, white puff-balls fell hard outside. It was the first snow of winter.

By Sunday, the roads had been cleared and I headed to my grandparents' house to celebrate the holidays. I was happy to get a parking space in front of the house rather than having to lug two bags full of presents up or down the street.

I stood next to the pristinely decorated fir tree, sparkling with white lights, silver and red ornaments, and red bows perfectly placed. I listened to tales of preschool drama, sports injuries and one story of a little guy who'd had a funny trip on nitrous gas during a visit to the dentist.

When I could take no more and figured I'd gotten the gist of what was going on in the lives of my eleven cousins, I headed to the kitchen to help carry the scrumptious meal to the dining room.

After the fine Christmas banquet, gift exchange, an intense game of "Rob Your Neighbor" and plenty of dessert sampling, my grandpa called all the cousins to the basement. We stood shoulder to shoulder near a heavy white door and listened to our instructions. "Only one for each of yous. Jes da one, now." He held up a finger to emphasize the words he spoke with a thick Polish accent.

We looked at one another. This was exciting stuff. What had Grandpa hidden behind the door? What could we have one of?

Grandpa opened the door and light immediately poured out onto the grey cement floor. The room was filled wall to wall with makeshift tables, and they were filled edge to edge with lamps, all with shades and all turned on. My cousins flooded inside.

"Take only one, now," Grandpa reminded us. I stood in the doorway watching the action. All the girls pointed and picked up lamps, inspecting them.

I watched my grandpa watching us, his proud smile as one granddaughter after another left his workshop with a new lamp.

A cousin held a lamp in her hand that her sister wanted. "You don't even have room for it," one said.

"I do. This red lamp will look fantastic in my dining room!" the other yelled.

My grandfather wasn't a big man, but when he stepped forward, the two women stopped their arguing. He took the lamp from their hands and set it back onto the table.

"Look, see here? It makes a smile face on da wall when it is lit only at da bottom." He demonstrated, clicking the lamp on then off for us.

I stepped forward. "So, Grandpa Rudnicki, tell me, has anyone ever forced you to take money for lunch on one of your treasure hunts in the alley?"

He stepped away from the lamp, laughing. He told us the story of the lady who moved in a few houses down, who had indeed forced him to take $10.00 to buy lunch one day. "She tinks I'm one of dem bums!"

I've Seen the Light
Jennifer Hasheider

I followed close behind Charlie, only letting his hand drop from mine when we stepped outside the dormitory's heavy front door. It had snowed since we'd gone up to his room and drank the night away. Now, the morning light was harsh and blasting off the banks of snow surrounding us. I held my hands in front of my face.

We took the shortcut to the diner. A quick cut through a backyard, a hop over a fence and across the railroad tracks, and we'd be in the parking lot. Two brand new adults, as hungry for greasy biscuits and gravy as we were for each other. I was ready to spend the rest of my entire existence with Charlie.

I loved that I could see breath puff from his lips in the winter air. I pulled mittens onto my freezing hands. Charlie had his shoved into his jeans pockets. "God no longer loves us, Libby," Charlie said, shivering. A cold breeze tossed fresh powder at us.

I laughed. Charlie had made a joke. It was never difficult for him to make me laugh. While I laughed, I ignored the rumble on the tracks below our feet. Charlie's hair stirred around his shoulders. I caught a trace of sweet smelling whiskey and cigarettes on the wind.

He tugged the collar of his denim jacket tighter on his neck. The skin around his dark beard was bright red. "It's friggin' cold out here, Lib."

I'm not sure why, but even this made me laugh. Maybe it was his perfect teeth behind the crooked, shivering smile. I was a dumb, young girl in love. I wanted to look at him and laugh with him more and kiss the cold off his lips. I reached for his hands, but my foot slipped off the metal rail and I stumbled. That's when the train crashed into Charlie. I was standing there with a grin on my face, and Charlie was gone forever.

I spent most days drunk or sleeping after that. Weeks ran together and eventually became months and suddenly years. Everything Charlie and I had planned disappeared. I couldn't save the world without him. I couldn't make my life without him and barely finished school. They mailed my degree to my mom's house. They probably felt sorry for me. Mom said I could live there as long as I wanted. The problem was, I didn't know what to want.

Two years later, on an unseasonably warm February afternoon, I happened to be sober. I headed to the art center in town where a local artists' meeting was being held.

The small room was full of cheerful people, and I didn't want to meet any of them. I took a seat in back, next to an older woman wearing a powder-blue sweater with flowers stitched onto the lapel. I thought she looked harmless.

A tall young woman with straight blond hair stepped to the podium and read her essay chronicling her journey through heart disease. This girl must have been close to my own age and certainly did not appear to be the recipient of six open-heart surgeries or someone I pictured when I heard the word pacemaker. She read about her children and writing them goodbye letters before each surgery. She had children, I was captivated.

The woman next to me leaned in and whispered, "Her piece is obviously over the word limit." She rolled her eyes and made a slicing gesture across her wrinkled neck.

I glared, appalled. Then, I heard the young girl at the podium say, "Of course I want to spread the word about this disease. I'm dying and I need a cure!"

I laughed. The proverbial lightbulb lit just above my head.

I sat there wondering what to do with my life, and Charlie had been robbed of his. The old woman next to me was going through hers, heartless. The young woman who knew to be passionate about hers was slowly having it taken away.

Now that I'd seen the light, now that I knew for certain that life doesn't care and does what suits it for reasons it doesn't have to explain, could I go on? I waited quietly in the back of the room next to the pucker-faced lady, and when the workshop ended, I walked out into the new day.

GROUNDED WRITINGS

Seven

Heather N. Hartmann

The crunch of rubber against gravel jolted Rachel McKinley awake. Her eyes rapidly blinked, fighting to make out any image. Blackness consumed her. The bile rose up fast and fierce; she was forced to swallow the bitterness of her own fear as she discovered tape secured her lips.

As Rachel went to rip the tape away, the realization that she was tied up sank in. Her hands were secured tight behind her back, ankles bound as well. Panic washed over her. She squirmed, bucked, and thrashed around. When her forehead smacked against metal, reality set in. She was locked inside the trunk of a moving car.

Squeezing her eyes closed, Rachel recalled her therapist's advice and counted to ten. The vise around her lungs loosened a fraction. She still couldn't see, but her mind was starting to think like the cop she was. They had to be miles outside the city to be on gravel roads. Shutting her eyes, she tried to recall her last memory. Cade. All she could remember was arguing with Cade. The details were foggy. Her head throbbed, the pain radiating from the back of her skull.

The car started to slow, and a cold line of sweat ran down Rachel's back.

When the trunk opened, Rachel was ready. She kicked up with her bound feet, pushing off the trunk floor with her back. She felt the solid contact of a jaw snapping.

"Bitch. Damn it."

Rachel squinted her eyes to adjust to the early morning sun streaming over her. Dark. She must have been in the trunk for hours. Last she remembered it had been dark. She kicked out again, but lost her leverage. She found herself half in and half out of the trunk. Bucking to try to gain some ground, she gasped when two hands reached in and plucked her out of the trunk.

Ready to head-butt whomever she came in contact with, she found herself skidding across dirt and gravel. The moisture on her lips had the tape peeling off.

"It's rare I get to work with such a fine toned specimen. Too often I am limited to the kiddy pool. Well, you know that. It's, after all, how you tracked me. It was a stupid foolish mistake on your part to think I'd fall for your trap. I might shop for the low lifes nobody will miss, but I am certainly not one of them."

She watched him pace, watched the anger in him build. Her last memory was walking into her apartment after an argument with Cade. The man pacing in front of her must have laid in wait to attack her. She tried to think of everything her team at the FBI had discovered about the serial killer they were hunting, who had instead found her.

The agents had discovered he hunted his victims in the park, where she had been playing a bum for three nights until Cade blew her cover when he came busting out of the surveillance van. She was new to the team, and everybody but Cade, her partner, thought she would make good bait. She knew in her gut Cade was already searching for her. She just had to survive.

"What's your name?" From her positon on the ground, she watched his lips peel back in a manic grin.

"You can just call me Lucky Seven."

The FBI—more like the media—dubbed him the Seven Killer. Every year he would reemerge in different cities and kill seven women. Never to be caught.

"All right, Seven it is." When Seven disappeared into a log cabin that sat about fifty yards from the car, Rachel wiggled her way to a tree. Her eyes rapidly took in her surroundings. Trees stood tall circling the perimeter. She listened for cars but only heard birds chirping. Because a cabin on a gravel road would be in the FBI database, Rachel clung to every ounce of hope she had. The cabin looked abandoned. Sitting up, she used the tree to help her stand. She looked for something sharp enough to cut the zip tie. Noticing a large rock, she hopped several feet, lost her balance and fell flat on her face.

The fear she thought she had under control rose up in the form of bile when Seven's shadow fell over her. When her eyes met his, she saw giddiness.

"I like my women alert, but you've proven to be a bit of a thinker. You've brought this on yourself. Remember that when you wake." Before she could blink, he injected her arm with a needle.

"What did you give me?" Panic had her sitting up in an instant, before the grogginess seeped in, and she swayed right into his arms.

When the porcelain shattered—cold coffee included—all over the wall, nobody was surprised.

"Damn it! We've been at this for hours and we're no closer." Cade paced in front of the murder board and avoided the recently added face: his partner's. He had let her down, failed at keeping her safe. He had fucking drove her to Seven, literally. Pinching the bridge of his nose, he thought about their fight. He knew it was a bad idea for her to be the bait.

Officially, she'd been missing five hours, but he knew in his gut it was eleven hours. Cade slammed his hand down on his desk. "Anything yet?" he asked no one in particular. He dropped her off shortly after 1 a.m., letting her storm off, believing he kept her safe. Five hours later, he arrived with coffee and her favorite donut to win her back to his way of thinking.

When she didn't answer, panic set in. He jimmied the lock and went in, weapon drawn. The only sign of struggle was the ottoman in the middle of the room. But he knew. The police wasted precious time canvassing the neighborhood, searching the house for clues and fibers that he knew wouldn't be there.

It was now noon, six official hours later, and they were no closer to finding her.

"Come on. We are smarter than this guy. Where would he take her?" He turned his eyes on his team.

"It has to be somewhere remote."

"But close enough for him to get back into town every two days to drop off one victim and kidnap another."

"Would he risk holding his victims close for convenience, or would he endure a longer drive?"

"I think he would go for the longer drive to be with them. It's part of his ritual. What do we know about the victims?" Cade asked.

"Cade, we've been over this for days."

"Well, start thinking the fuck outside the box, then." He turned on his heel and marched to their tech guy. "I want every remote area on the screen now."

"What radius?"

"Four hours from Rachel's place." Cade scrubbed a hand over his face when the search displayed on the large screen. "We don't have enough manpower or time to search every remote location. We need to narrow it down."

He turned eyes on his team and said, "Start talking. Anything that comes to mind, no matter how big, small, stupid, or insane you might think it is. Say it. Let's run over everything we've got. Something has to pop. Rachel's counting on us."

Rachel awoke with a start. Each hand was secured at the wrist with a metal cuff attached to a chain linked to the ceiling. Her feet were bound by chains to the floor. She stood forming an X. She bucked, thrashed, and found herself swaying. Her eyes darted around the room. Black curtains hung on the windows, letting in the filtered evening light. Whatever he had given her kept her out for hours. She knew instantly they were in his workroom. In front of her lay a metal surgical table and the young girl her team had been searching for. Her name was Bailey. Her legs were spread and bound. Her arms lay disjointed to her sides.

Rachel closed her eyes and focused on breathing. Forcing herself to look, she could see Bailey still breathing. She was cut in several areas, some wounds deeper than others. She assumed from the other victims Bailey had been raped, multiple times. She expected Bailey to also have internal injuries from a beating.

"Bailey." Her voice came out a harsh whisper. She imagined taking a sip of a cold glass of water as her throat ached. "Bailey." At her name the girl moved her head and looked at Rachel.

She was gone. She was still breathing, but her soul had checked out.

"I often like for my next victim to watch what her future holds—but you, Rachel, I wanted to surprise. Plus, Bailey was weak. She stopped fighting after the first broken bone. Such a frustration to me."

Rachel watched as he picked up a blade and walked to the table. "Wait, wait. She's had enough. I'm fresh."

"I know." And with that, he sliced her throat to the sounds of Rachel's screams.

He walked over and ran the side of the bloody blade down between Rachel's breasts. She bucked and fought to free herself.

"Feisty, I like it. You would be surprised how many stop fighting. It's always such a disappointment. Every once in a while, the flash of a blade will bring that fight back. But it dies quickly. But you, my darling, will never quit fighting. Will ya?" he said, leaning in to lick up her neck as she bucked and made a shot to head-butt him. He drew away chuckling. "Oh, darling, you will have to try harder than that."

Cade burst out of his seat. "I've got the bastard's location."

"What?" Every boot hit the floor.

"Your idea, Stevens—about how he would need gas—stuck. I started looking for gas stations with repeat customers every two days that paid in cash. A gas station in Middlestone has a repeat customer that lines up with our dead bodies showing up three hours later. I called the clerk. He knows of an abandoned cabin four miles into the woods, directly up the gravel road behind the station."

"The chopper will be ready in five," the senior agent stated.

Rachel knew he planned to move her from the chains to the table. All she had to do was not miss her chance. First, he moved Bailey out. Then he kept flashing his blade, telling her just how much he was going to enjoy her, but she didn't have time to be afraid. She had to plan. She had only one chance to escape. Once she was on that table she was dead.

Seven landed a few hits to her midsection before he unhooked the chains. Rachel waited until he laid her on the table and shot out with her feet, kicking him in the chest. He flew backwards. She was off the table and reaching for the knife before Seven regained his feet.

"Bitch. I knew you would be a fighter. That's okay. Like I said, I like them feisty. I even like a chase." He stepped back and motioned to the door. She knew they were surrounded by woods, and if she ran, she would be on his territory, waiting to be caught again.

She took a deep breath and charged full force at him, knife out. Seven blocked and they wound up on the ground wrestling for the weapon. As she lay under his weight, Rachel turned the knife up and froze at the gunshots. In an instant, his body weight slumped onto her, followed by warm blood. It was then that she heard Cade.

"Rachel. Rachel." He pulled Seven off before yanking her up into his arms. "Are you hurt?" Cade hugged her tightly as she clung to him.

"You came."

"Of course, I came."

Narrative Arc
Larry Duerbeck

My postal address is Labadie, Missouri, and little old Labadie, Missouri, makes Mayberry look as up-tempo alive as Manhattan. I drove down its drowsy Front Street and turned left into the Hawthorne Inn's parking lot. Big, special-interest vehicles and their plates (Colorado, South Carolina, Michigan) told me the restaurant still hosted some all-breed people, in from just up and over the two lane blacktops at Purina's dog show facility.

The mid-afternoon lull suited my desires just fine. Parking proved pleasant. I left my electronics, hopped out and walked in through scattered day-trippers lounging out on the deck. Inside, a few members of an intersex sports team, clad in first names and numbers, rallied 'round the bar. One family's serious celebration, complete with uncomfortable neckties and brooch pins on print bodices, held forth in apparently sedated good manners far to the left. Along the right, a couple of professional dog handlers, support staff, owners and exhibitors clustered at big circular tables for food, drink and talk. Always talk. I knew some faces, being in show dogs.

But my first order of business this day was dirt, not dogs. By dirt, I do not mean dishing the dirt gossip. I mean dirt.

There they were, the three of them. Much-washed milky-blue overalls, clean as fresh napkins; lightweight pressed plaid shirts; tans fading to reveal random and blotchy freckles. I was called before the door closed.

"Yo, Darryl! Right here, partner."

The three sat where they should. At a nearby four-top, across the entrance and just to the left. Of all the tables, theirs stated "Regulars" the plainest. On the fourth chair, a stack of straw hats sat up straight. The farmers were of that generation. No gimme caps. When they did wear caps, they donned fitted-to-an-eighth-of-an-inch ball caps. Baseball caps, bills forward. Cardinal baseball caps, filled with pride, and memories long, and love familial.

I lifted the stack. "Melissa." She stood right there. "Take care of these, please. And get yourself hatcheck tips. Three hats, four tips. Deal?"

"That's a good deal."

Off she went, off with them toward the office. I slid onto the chair. A brief change occurred, one worth telling. But first, some introductions on the fly. Or on my sitting, pretty much back to the door. Names, farmers' names. To my left, Schultenreith. Straight ahead, Klostermeyer. To the right, Baumhoeggen. Make it—.

Jack. Square cut, bald, with a gray-steel-filing fringe as wide as my hand, matching gray eyes. A chatty guy, if telegraphic. Writers edit adverbs, Jack deleted verbs. Catching.

Gus. Short for Augustus. Long, lean and lank. Imagine Jacob Marley after a week at a spa for the spirits. Chin up. Swept-back waves of spume gray hair that never saw a part, gas-jet blue eyes.

Fritz. One of those roundish Deutschers who stay nicely, politely inflated—buoyant right up to the end at eighty, ninety. Deliberately merry, a defense. I wore kid gloves for him, invisible and softly, softly. Combed, cornsilk hair was turning a late hoarfrost tone after decades of exposure to Vitalis. Hazel eyes.

Let's start here. "Everybody, one seat over!" Fritz laughed after his suggestion, exclamation, command.

"Whatever for?" That was Gus, bouncy as a flat tire.

We got to our feet amid a quickstep cascade of whitewater sentence fragments concluding with, "Help out the inn. Show off Darryl. Sport coat and tie. Facing the door. Better'n us old plowboys. One to the right!" Each picked up his beer and shuffled.

Melissa came back in time to witness our maneuver. "You-ou guys!" She yodeled her amused exasperation, then mothered us into our new configuration. Jack explained the while.

Here's a part: "Class, you know. Look. Cufflinks. Keep the property value up, Missy. Sorry for the bother. But newcomers. They'll see. Everyone welcome and the food good. A cut above. Like your service, sweetie."

"Bought and paid for."

Guess who? Gus, that's who. It sounded as laughably lugubrious as it reads. More so.

Fritz heh-heh-heh'd apologetically. "Give good tips, give good service. No complaints here, right? Either way."

Melissa smiled her approval on us. "The usual for you three?"

I piped up, "*My* treat, gentlemen. How's about an appetizer blitz?"

A definite go. Baked spinach-artichoke dip with extra tortilla chips, flash-fried spinach, potato skins, toasted ravioli, chicken wings, coconut shrimp. "And an autumn salad, split four ways," I finished up.

Melissa gave me the eye. "That'll be good for garnishes, Diamond Jim."

"Two, then?" A pursed lip nod. "And my usual." She zipped away for a Long Island iced tea.

Since Anheuser-Busch sold out, my table mates have gone their separate tastes. Heineken for Jack, Fritz favored Guinness, Gus stayed with Bud. "Why change now? What's the use?" A discussion of Cards' chances in the playoffs prospered until Melissa brought my drink.

Four glasses clinked. "To our very good health, gentlemen," I proposed. After obligatory swigs—.

"Well. Wondering. All of us." Jack set his Heineken down; he was ready to roll. "Here. Why? Happy to be here, of course. Free eats, too. But. . . ." Jack rolled along, all right. But he ran out of air eventually. Or punctuation. Full stops, maybe. My turn.

"I have come to clothe myself in silliness. Being a writer, silliness is attire I often adopt."

"Hee hee!" Guinness washed over Fritz's driftwood yips. "Silly, you say? I don't think so. Since we met you, why. Here's just one lil' ol' egg-zam-pill. We toast ever so much now. It's fun." He quit to allow for another incoming Irish tide.

The thread was picked up on my left, to knit together washed-up images. "An aid to gemütlichkeit. Off on the right foot. Good wishes. Used to think. A toast? Anything more than cheers? For a special event. Like the Leimkuhlers over there. Anniversary. A toast. Stuffy.

"And—"

"I toast Jehenna of a nice sunset now, with Riesling. Riesling was her favorite. I thank you, Darryl."

"You're all welcome. But Gus. That's special. Of course." I raised my glass. "To Jehenna."

Gus was the only widower. We toasted her and talked some more. We're like that. Subjects often delayed, but seldom forgotten. Never tell me I don't edit. Jack launched into a report on the latest book he had read. About the P-38 Lightning. At length, with joined detours. Melissa and a bus girl moved another table closer, so we could serve ourselves from it.

"We don't want to be too crowded. Got to have elbow room. Hahaa! I love it. Bring us another round, please. I'll pick up the bar, belles. Ha ha."

"Not for me," I told Melissa. "One of these is enough. Thanks, Fritz."

Melissa patted me on the shoulder. "Good call."

Soon, food arrived. Later, I spoke. "Gentlemen, you are of this good earth. Farmers. The Atlases upon whose shoulders the world rests. You are the ones I want to talk to, about dirt."

Edges off appetites, we considered second approaches. As wishes issued and dishes moved, I spoke again.

"My interest is . . . Theological."

So unexpected was this last word, the efficient, knowing and friendly distribution held up. Heads turned. Comments abounded. My favorite was, "Notes on eternal damnation, I suppose." Guess. Here's a clue. He finished his first Bud and set the empty glass on our other table.

"Not at all!" I protested. "Not after the finish line, but before the starting gate."

More ricochet responses brought another favorite. "Fundamentalism doesn't pay." My chortling stayed within, deep-hidden. No minister he, but if Fundamentalism did pay? Gus would have long since bid Martin Luther "Auf Wiedersehen!" to join a less critical clergy. However, cost analysis of return-on-investiture said no.

When I recalled, "In the beginning was the word," three heads grown variously gray nodded. "Now science is investigating smaller and smaller entities."

My introductory met with munch of potato skin, crunch of lettuces, snap of chip stuck and sunk in thickened dip and subsequent salvage "Ding dang dong, hee ho hum . . . Double dip. There."

"I am coming to believe that the very smallest of the small remains to be discovered. Discovered to be words. One unit of information words. Each from my Big Bang God's voice.

"God, being God, the universe was easy. Almost instantaneous. His words still echo."

Having their attention and voices, I addressed myself to the coconut shrimp.

"Well, heh heh huh. Well. What gives? What about dirt? Ho yesss. We know about that."

I polished off my Long Island iced tea. "Why just, why only echoes? Our drought last year—" And got the bus girl to go for some plain iced tea. While I heard agreement about where I was coming from.

"A bitch. Droughts come with the territory. But that one last year? A brute. Fields, fence to fence. Crops. Burnt crisp as those chips Fritz loves so much. Wine grapes? Fine. Deep roots. Worst year in about. What say you, Gus?"

"I'd say fifty years."

"You are coh-rect. Got her almost smack dab on the old schnozzola. Oh-ho yes. Ha-half a century. Right on. Last year we saw the whole year go up in summer smoke and dust." A bolt of Guinness was taken against bad times old and immediate, too easily remembered.

"What happened this year?" I asked.

"Ho ho hokay. Now you are talking!" Buoyant milky blue bottom rocked, all but bounced in happy abandon. "We had bumper crops galore. And all the grapes. Ooh la la!"

We laughed in easy and sweet, rural and communal cause.

"This year. Textbook case. A toast to it. Wonderful phrase. Bountiful harvests. A fine one. Out of books. Bountiful harvests all.

This year. Did my old farmer's heart so much good. And our Thanksgiving. Can hardly wait.

"Thanksgiving dinner. This year, a feast! A toast to Thanksgiving Dinner. Same as last year, of course. The way we do it. Every year the same. Last change in, oh, about—"

"Lad has more to say."

"Deed he do!" An affirmation trimmed in mirth. "You old stick-in-the-mud turkle. I like some new tasty, every year. Mm-mm-hmm!"

They all quieted down to regard their respective half-glasses, last choices, and me.

"Gentlemen, the writer's job is often to distill."

"Writer's moonshine. Ah." No need to guess, is there?

"Boil down, then. And please don't bring up sap. Think about this year, up till now. Doesn't it strike you that everything was all more? More than we should ever expect, even with our run of three ideal seasons. Like the word went forth? Make up the drought year. Corn, grapes, acorns on oaks. Everything. From the dirt up."

I gestured a certain personal and helpless sensibility.

"It's an ancient idea, I know. But still it haunts me. I may say Earth Herself spake a first, a miraculous word."

"Indeed. Indeed and indeed. Something there, all right. A small bang theory. Big enough for us, though. Miracles so vast. So all around us, what? Normal. Just things. Things just for the record books. Miracles or ledger entries?"

"Dandelions. Honeysuckle. Carpets of gold. And I never smelt so damned much honeysuckle so damned sweet."

"Ha-ha-hackberries and hawthornes. The dahamson plums. Tha-ha-hat jahamm-mmm." Plump hands palmed a burgomeister belly. "Concord grapes. Oh me and oh my. Those pies!"

"And," Gray steel eyes flashed up from last of autumn salad, "the Bible. Years like kine. Fat and lean. Lean and fat. This year. One of the fattest. Hands down. Fatter'n it should be. Logically. Way fatter. All from the ground up. Dead-set for the best. The biggest. The most.

"And—"

"First word. Dirt."

All attention pivoted and fixed itself.

"First word. Dirt."

Delicate as ash, dry as dust, his rising sigh rustled hairs along my neck. "Irony, Mr. Writer? Narrative arc?" Blue jets burned brighter, focused not too far beyond my graying beard. Not too far. Not anymore.

"First word. Dirt. Maybe. But."

A pause.

"Dirt always gets the last word."

The Last McGloin
Douglas N. Osgood

This is a night for thinking, and there is much on my mind. The light of the moon, just risen in the eastern sky behind me, reflects across the tranquil pond, as if painted there by an artist, one long stroke of his thick brush, heavy through the middle and more transparent towards the edges. Occasionally, its glassy surface is broken by a crappie drawn by the swarm of insects hovering over the moonlight's reflection. The resulting ripple breaking the line of light into a wave, turning the surface into a giant heart monitor, beating out the life rhythm of the pond. Invisible crickets and tree frogs chirp and croak to create a symphony of the night, the dramatic parts punctuated by the deep bass croaks of the bullfrog camped at the pond's western point. From somewhere, a car horn blares long, the piercing pitch rising as it approaches—an out-of-tune crescendo. And then, it's gone. Refusing to acknowledge the rude interruption, the crickets first, and then the tree frogs coming in on cue, fill the resulting quiet with their symphony, picking right back up where they left off.

Beyond the pond, dotted about the ubiquitous chaparral, are visible the distinctive horns of the cattle breed southeast Texas is known for. This is the Bar-M-Bar, my ranch, and all I have. It is who and what I am. Ranching this land is my life. Long horn cattle, large and powerful beasts as wild as the land. They, too, are a part of me and who I am.

Beau, named after the Duke's mount in True Grit, stands still under me, sensing my mood. From where I sit, only a very small portion of my ranch is visible. But this is the spot where I feel especially connected to it, as if here, on this hillock, an umbilical cord carries the soul of the land directly to me, nourishing my spirit.

Dad and I dug the pond over fifty years ago, when Uncle Dudly, lured by the easy money, sold out to developers, cutting our stock off from the watering hole McGloin herds had been using for over a century. This hill was built from all of the dirt we excavated to form the pond. I planted the pin oaks that shade it a few years later.

We burned out the chaparral that had overgrown the hill in the summer of '67, the day we got the telegram from the army. The next day we built the fence to keep the herd off it. Grass seed went down after we buried the silver box the army said contained my brother Robert's remains; it sure didn't feel heavy enough to have been all of him. Twenty years ago, I buried Dad here; five years later, it was Mom.

The big "C" took my Cecelia a few years back. We had built quite a life together here. She was and remains my heart and soul. Forty-three great years together, how quickly they went. My sons helped me bury her here, too. I always figured on taking my final rest right next to her. Now, I'm not so sure.

***

My heart specialist wanted me to come in for a follow-up visit; the test results were back. The long face when he walked in was all I needed to see to know it was bad. There weren't a lot of options—six to twelve months to live without open heart surgery. With the surgery the chances were fifty-fifty that I would recover and be mostly back to normal. The drive back from Houston took much longer than the drive in. I tried to think, but my mind had been a jumble of thoughts.

I was fixing lunch when the house phone rang.

"Now who could that be," I said to no one. "None of the kids knew I had a doctor's appointment this morning." The rug in front of the kitchen sink caught at my foot as I turned to get it, tripping me a bit. By the time I got to the phone, I was out of breath from hurrying.

"Yah, hello," I said into the mouthpiece, my drawl running the words together to more resemble a color than a greeting.

"Is Lee McGloin there?" it asked.

"I'm McGloin."

"Mr. McGloin, this is Matt Brossard, with Southeast Texas Development Corporation. Have I caught you at a bad time?"

Damned developers, I thought. I ought to tell him to suck eggs and die. Instead, the manners my sainted mother instilled in me came out. "No, this is fine. How can I help you today?"

"Well, Mr. McGloin," he started. Most folks I'd have stopped right there and told them to call me Lee, but this kid could go right on calling me Mr. McGloin. Damn developers. What do they do, pay all of the doctors to tip them off when someone might be needing to sell? Buzzards.

He droned on about the great planned neighborhood they were going to build: a small-town feel close to the city—a throwback to simpler times. Horse pucks, I say, but I didn't. Say it, that is.

"Mr. McGloin, there is a very tight window for us to make a deal on this. Our company is contacting several local ranchers with suitable properties."

"It's never even crossed my mind, selling that is. I'll have to give it some thought."

"Do you have a cell phone number I can follow up with you at, Mr. McGloin?"

"Son, anybody that needs to reach me can reach me at my home, or try again later. Kind of like how it used to be in a simpler time."

"Oh, ah, okay then. Let me give you my number so you can call me back once you've talked it over with your family. Just don't wait too long."

He gave me his number and I wrote it down. I didn't want to, but, well, I had just been to the specialist's office.

***

Arf, arf, arf. Tyrel's announcement that he has holed a jack rabbit brings me back to the present. Turning my mount, I see him, rear end high, tail going like a windshield wiper in a downpour, nose down in a hole among the scrub. "Hehehe," I chuckle under my breath. Until my eye catches something. The laugh stops abruptly as my face grows a glower. A longhorn standing next to the barbwire fence silhouettes against the glare of the bright street lights and neon store signs emanating from the newly completed Target plaza just beyond. It is a bitter reminder that my own brother, Thomas, made me the last McGloin to ranch this land.

For one hundred and eighty-nine years, McGloins have ranched here, ever since the first came down to southeast Texas with a land grant from the Mexican government. Through draught, disease, pestilence, and war, McGloins kept on ranching. Even the taxman couldn't take the land away, though not for lack of effort. But the big dollars of the developers made it look easy.

I shake my head, trying to dispel the resentment, and turn Beau back to the tranquil tableau before me—back to the umbilical cord—my spirit. What do I do? I wonder. Money is an issue, a big issue. I know I can't afford to hire someone to keep the ranch going while I recover. Recovery will be months, and my meager savings will not cover a hired hand for that long, *if* I could find one.

Bark, bark, bark. Ty's hunting song has grown more urgent. I sneak a quick look back, clouds of sand erupt behind him as he digs for his prey. I decide to leave him to it for a bit and turn back to my thoughts.

For many years, the clan rallied together when things like this came up—that's what families do, after all. But things are different now. Thomas and I have been estranged since he sold out a few years ago. My sons have no interest in ranching and no time even to help. Jorge is an orthopedic surgeon in Houston; Robert a lawyer in Austin. Both have families.

My only daughter, Juliana, has been hinting for years that she and her husband Dillon would like to take over the ranch when the time comes. They've always talked about being willing to help out anytime. Funny that when roundup time rolls around, when I could use extra help, Dillon is suddenly working "tons of overtime." Extra work that seems to end just in time for the post-roundup barbeque.

What if I cancel the surgery and just keep ranching until I keel over? That wouldn't be so bad, would it? To die doing the only thing I know on the land that I love. The boys would make sure I was buried next to Cecelia. Maybe I would be dust before a developer moved in—make me a permanent part of this land.

"What do you think, Cecelia?" I ask, finally speaking out loud. There is a whisper through the pin oaks, and a faint rustling of branches rubbing against one another. Is that just the wind? Is that her? She misses me. I sure do miss her. But I'm not ready to hang up my spurs.

Suddenly, a thought comes to me; from Cecelia, I wonder? What if I sell off most of the stock? I could send all but Tornado and Beau to the auction. Keep the prize bull and my best stock horse. The money from selling the herd would pay the neighbor's boy to see to things. He's old enough to handle that much, and he loves Beau. I tune in again to the crickets and frogs, allowing them to soothe my mind, while I think about how that would work.

A second, less welcome, thought interrupts the symphony. The doctor said there was only a fifty-fifty chance of recovering fully. What if I'm not able to return to my regularly scheduled life? I could die on the table, or never recover at all. What then? Or, what if the recovery takes longer than expected? Either way, I run out of money. Would I have to sign the ranch over to a nursing home? That wouldn't be fair to the kids.

I need to make a decision quickly. The surgery is already scheduled for next week. I can call the doctor to cancel it and let life just run its course. A call to the developer gets me the cash to live out my hopefully long life. Or the auction house to pick up my herd—a roll of the dice.

Gggggrrrrrrr. Ty must be close to catching that damned rabbit. Beau and I edge over to him. He's hidden by chaparral, but flying dirt marks his location like a beacon. "Ty, come," I say. "Leave it be, friend. It'll be there tomorrow." With a baleful look back, he reluctantly trots over to me and falls in behind Beau as I head slowly back to the pond.

The gentle sway of the saddle is hypnotic, and my thoughts turn back to my problem. Who do I call? That is what it boils down to. I guess I really just need to sleep on it.

I take one last longing look at the pond and surrounding ranch. With a nudge, Beau begins to amble back to the barn, Ty tight at his hooves. I can almost physically feel the loss of the umbilical cord as my connection is cut.

I sleep late for the first time since before Vietnam. Sunlight streams into the bedroom window and across my face until I can ignore it no more. A few minutes later, breakfast is over. My decision made, I pick up the phone and dial.

"Hello, this is Lee McGloin," I start.

I Hope You Dance
Jennifer McCullough

"Mom, I have some bad news," Anna said, pulling a tissue out of her white hoodie pocket.

Dozens of young yellow daffodils leaned in as an early morning breeze blew across the Butler Memorial Cemetery.

A male goldfinch caught Anna's eye as she bent over to sweep a pile of faded pine needles off the concrete base of her mom's headstone. Anna smiled recalling how pretty her mom had looked in the bright yellow jacket she was buried in six months ago.

Anna's allergies were getting the best of her, but she loved breathing in the smell of freshly-turned dirt and pollen. It felt good to be outdoors, and close to her mom.

She placed a flimsy plastic pot full of white pansies on steroids on the ground beside her mom's square slab of polished granite. The stone seemed so stuffy and formal for one so playful and down-to-Earth.

"You're going to be the only one here with a hanging pot, Mom. It's all Dollar General had, and the flower shop's closed on Saturdays."

Anna knew her mom always liked to stand out in a crowd, especially one as stoic as this.

E-V-A R-O-B-I-N-S-O-N. Unbelievable, Anna thought, to see her mom's name in such a state of perpetual existence, yet the woman it belonged to is gone like the best hour of the best day.

Anna's longing for what was had made her young life almost unbearable at times. Twenty-one years of memories came in sickly sweet servings and overwhelmed her with sadness whenever she overindulged.

"This is the first time I've been to see you that I didn't wish I was dead too, Mom. That's actually pretty good news, don't you think?"

Anna's eyes welled with tears. Her sparkly teal eyeliner began to flow down her pale cheeks.

Ever since her mom died, Anna had tried to convince herself that her mother was just an ordinary person wracked with faults, annoying habits and peculiarities, and therefore, deserving of but a reasonable amount of grief, like everyone else.

And she was.

But she was magnificent.

And deserved so much more.

She and Anna had been best friends, mother-daughter soul mates. They bonded the minute Anna was born in a crazy, underwater home-birth in a green plastic turtle pool in the living room of a 1968 double-axle Airstream travel trailer, illegally parked on the playground of the elementary school on a Saturday morning so nobody would bother them.

Eva Robinson was a nearly-famous driftwood artist, a college dropout, a three-time divorcee, a failure at all things financial, and utterly unable to say "no" to a stray, whether it be feline, flea bag or flea market. But she was wildly creative and funny, and her love for her only child knew no limit. In no way was she deserving of the kind of death ovarian cancer exacted upon her.

"I should have bought two of these, one for each side. I'm sorry, Mom."

Anna knew she didn't need to apologize. Money was tight. Her mom, of all people, would understand.

"'I'm just happy you're here, sweet girl,' is what you'd say, right, Mom?"

But Anna still felt the need to apologize. She apologized for something or other every time she came to visit, but it still wasn't enough. Anna took care of her mom every day for four years. Instead of hanging out with her friends, she watched her mom suffer in ways she didn't know people could suffer and still go on living. Because Eva Robinson was only 46 years old and full of psyllium husks, hemp seeds and organic homegrown vegetables, the cancer had a tough time breaking her down. But it did, eventually, and all Anna could do was hold her mom's hand, sing to her, and apologize for the pain.

Anna didn't sleep for weeks after her mom died. The guilt of wishing she could have done more to ease her mom's suffering consumed her.

Anna's back ached. She had just finished a 12-hour shift at the hospital and was on her way to her clinical study group. She sat down a few feet away from Eva Robinson and pressed her back against a tall pine tree. The damp ground soaked through her purple scrubs, but she was too tired to care. The sun at her back cast her shadow across her mom's grave. Anna felt strange being at eye level with Eva Robinson, but warmly comforted, nonetheless.

"Can you believe I got an A in Genetics, Mom?"

"After this semester, I'm done! Can you believe that? Your daughter: a nurse. Finally!" Anna chuckled as she wiped black mascara from under her eyes.

"We're going to have a graduation party in May. God, I wish you were here."

Anna pulled another tissue from her pocket and blew her nose. The bells from the Methodist Church over the hill began to chime. They reminded her of the song "Stay with Me" by Sam Smith. They were sad, but sweet in their gentle beckoning.

"I can't believe it's been six months already, Mom. Time is going by fast... too fast."

Anna swallowed hard.

"The Dean asked me to sing at graduation. He said he didn't know why I wanted to be a nurse with a voice like mine. Funny, huh?" Anna said as she smiled, the tears glistening on her lips.

She picked up a twig and drew a music note in the dirt then scattered it with the toe of her tennis shoe, which was crusted with little-kid vomit.

Anna watched a line of cars drive through the main gate of the cemetery. She hadn't noticed the hearse pull in first and park several rows away.

"Mom," Anna whispered as her hands began to shake, "I have the gene... the cancer gene."

Anna paused as if to give her mom time to process what she'd said.

"They say I only have 20 more years, maybe not that long."

A small group of people, heads bowed, arms around one another, began to assemble under a green canvas tent near the hearse. Anna could see the dark burgundy casket lined with pink satin, and for a minute, imagined herself lying inside it.

"I'm not sure I want to live, Mom, but I know I don't want to die," Anna's voice trembled.

"I think I need to sing," she said as she twisted two blades of grass together. "I know I've spent all this time and money on nursing school, and I promise I'm still going to finish, but after that, I think I need to go to Nashville to see if..."

Anna heard someone quickly approaching behind her. It was a young man she recognized from church.

"Anna?"

She wiped her eyes and turned her face into the sun.

"Hey, Anna...I'm so sorry to bother you." It was the minister's son.

"Logan, how's it going?" Anna said as she stood up.

"I saw you over here visiting your mom, and I really, really hate to bother you," he said, hardly concealing his impatient desperation. "But...," Logan nodded toward the memorial service in progress.

"That's Mrs. Atkins. Her husband really wanted us to have a couple of ladies from the choir here, but their bus broke down on the way back from choir competition this morning. Besides, you're the best singer in town anyways."

"I'm not really dressed for it," Anna said, wiping the mud off the seat of her pants.

Logan looked as if he might cry.

"What song?" Anna asked sympathetically.

"Uh," he fumbled in his suit-coat pocket until he found a crumpled piece of paper.

"Don't take life for granted...one door closes, another opens... and it looks like... Wow, Dad's handwriting is terrible. Uh...something like, don't sit down, instead you should dance."

"Yeah, I know it. *I Hope You'll Dance* by Lee Ann Womack. Not really a typical funeral song, is it?"

"I don't know, Anna. Just please come sing it. I have the music and a CD player over there ready to go. Mr. Atkins will be all kinds of pissed if I don't have anybody to sing this song. Dad will ground me and..."

"Hey, no problem," Anna said as she reached for the paper. "But are you sure I look ok? I'm not really dressed for the occasion. I'm going to stand out like a sore thumb. I mean, I have some kid's vomit on my shoes."

Logan gave her a quick once over. "You look fine! Nobody's going to notice your shoes once you start singing anyway. Come on," he said as he grabbed her hand.

As Anna rushed off with him, she glanced back at Eva Robinson and thought with a laugh, "What kind of strings did you have to pull up there to get all this done today? Don't worry, Mom, I'm going to dance! I am your daughter, after all."

Reflections
Audrey Clare

Weightless snowflakes waltz through the streetlights as she hurries back home. She's tired out from grocery shopping and thinks of something warm to drink. *A warm cup of coffee will taste good.* Then she remembers she is out of coffee. She crosses the street, avoiding the piled up snow that hugs the gutters.

Kat's Five and Dime sits on the corner of 12th Street and Walnut. Christmas lights illuminate around each of its windows, green, red and blue bulbs flicking off and on. Jingle Bells floods the air, repeating how grand it will be to take a ride in a one horse open sleigh.

With a quick move of her hand, she brushes flakes of snow off her shoulders and enters the store. She walks to the long lunch counter, along a sidewall, and sits down. She orders a cup of coffee.

Her mood is anything but jolly. She feels none of the Christmas spirit that she sees in the shoppers' reflections in the full-length mirror that takes up the back wall. She's been holding back the tears. "Not one letter from Bill, again, today." She quietly says to herself. As she brings the cup up to her lips, she watches in the mirror as an old man sits down next to her.

She sees the sadness in his face and recognizes his loneliness. It's the same with her, ever since her husband went off to fight the raging war in the Middle East. For a second, she lowers her sight.

When she looks back up, she sees his image in the mirror is fading, and bright streaks of colors and flashing-by scenes of a young man on a battlefield, takes its place. He holds up a slip of paper so she can read the written words.

In this field of death, this unearthly place, once here, a secret garden grew, where joy and passions played. Only here one rose is left, underneath the ice it's laid, all songs caressed to its awakening are forever–lost.

Jean's no longer aware of the few customers that hurry with their shopping before the store closes, or the music playing, "Silent Night, Holy Night," that fills up the room. She's completely mesmerized, and try as hard as she can, she cannot fully capture the meaning of what she is witnessing in the mirror.

And yet she feels a connection, a recognition as if she had seen, or someone had told her about this, and what she is seeing is now a part of her. She lifts the cup to her lips. Her coffee is still hot as if this very moment she's just been served. The old man, without her knowing, has left, and it seems to her he has taken the mirror images with him. Jean walks back out into the cold night. There's a deep sadness in her she can't explain away; she lets her tears fall.

The stars radiate against the dark sky. The wind skids the snow along, determined to cover over the busy city before dawn. A crowd has gathered. She hurries to see what is drawing their attention. It's the old man from the lunch counter, lying in the snow. He beckons her to come closer. She kneels down next to him. He whispers, "Don't cry, Jean, I am still with you."

The old man closes his eyes and lets the stars take him home.

Moments from My Wild Childhood
(In the Mountains of California During the 1930s)
Phyllis L. Borgardt

Introduction

I would like to share a few moments from my wild and very different childhood in the Sierra Nevada Mountain town of Auberry during the 1930s. My parents operated the Auberry Garage and Richfield Station. The sleepy little town of Auberry was full of interesting and very different characters. My sister and I learned to respect the differences in the mountaineers as we traversed from one adventure to another.

The Auberry Garage

The Auberry Garage had once been a blacksmith shop. In fact, the back half of the garage was part of the original building. As more people bought cars, there was less need for horses and carriages. However, in bad weather, horses could travel the unpaved roads.

Cars would get stuck in the mud. Most of the roads were packed dirt. Oiled roads would come later. The horse won out in bad weather over the stuck-in-the-mud cars.

My mother pumped gas. I watched as the red-orange and blue-green gas gurgled to the top of the glass gas pump only to see it sucked down as my mother filled an old Ford Truck. My father repaired and towed cars and trucks. He'd pull them up a canyon wall when someone missed a curve and drove off a cliff.

I spent many hours playing in the garage and running around the grease pit. I knew the rules and never got hurt. Strangers would remark, "How can you let your little girl run around the edge of the grease pit?"

My mother would reply, "Well, she knows better than to fall in."

Six Shooter Kate

When I was very young, my mother needed help with my care. I was a very active child, and Mother needed to help my father with pumping gas at the service station. The Richfield Gas Station and Garage was our mainstay for survival during the Great Depression of the 1930s.

Our little station was unique in the area and important for the town. Times were hard and pickings were slim for jobs. In the mountains, most everyone had a history, and some were more dubious than others. The past mistakes were forgotten if you did an honest day's work. Thus, the nursemaid that my mother selected for my care came from a dubious and questionable family background. The folks in the town said she was a hard worker and would give us a good day's work for little pay. No one had much money, so Mother selected the woman with the wild family background to be my new nursemaid.

My nursemaid had one brown eye and one blue eye. I thought it was nice that God decorated her so. It made her interesting, for the eyes did not line up, either. One wondered which eye was looking at you. I questioned, "Could she see through walls, with such eyes?" My nursemaid did her work, and my mother appreciated her help.

You need to understand, the mountains hold many a strange character. None of the characters were as strange as my nursemaid's mother, "Six Shooter Kate." "Six Shooter Kate" had been the bootlegger in the mountains for many years during the prohibition days. She drove a twelve-mule-team wagon full of booze up the mountainside to the Edison Electric Company base camp. The base camp held 500 hardworking single men, and there were few pleasures to be had. The company just looked the other way when the mule train and its cargo arrived. Kate paid the sheriff for his silence and shared her wares with the local folks. Kate was very successful, and no one wanted to see her in jail. She was just part of the local color.

Six Shooter Kate was someone that no one wanted to bother. Her reputation was not just dubious, it was "raunchy." She was a muscular-female type with a ready gun. No one wanted to tempt a large lady who could shoot the eye out of a squirrel half a mile away.

The Posse

One fine day, I lost my nursemaid. It was a warm spring day. The flowers were shooting up. Everywhere we looked we could see a profusion of shapes and colors. Sure enough, Six Shooter Kate came riding up in a bit of a hurry. She had an extra horse and pack mule in tow. I must say, our household was surprised. Mother paid Kate's daughter for the good care she had given me. Goodbyes were brief. Once in the saddle, Kate and daughter rode away in a hurry.

It took a while for the word to get around town that Kate was wanted in the valley below. She had been in some sort of altercation. Mind you, in those days there were no cell phones and very few party-line phones. However, word did travel fast in the small town. Even so, Kate and daughter were long gone by the time everyone heard that the sheriff was forming a posse.

Now, Six Shooter Kate had a good head start. The local sheriff knew it was not likely a posse would catch her. In fact, the sheriff didn't know what he would do if he did find her. She had paid him well for turning a blind eye to her bootlegging activities. He decided to have lunch before he swore in the deputies.

My father was one of the deputies. The sheriff and his deputies, like Kate, knew horses were better than cars on the rough mountain terrain. After everyone had lunch and his or her lunch had settled, the posse rode off in hot pursuit.

It was no surprise that Kate and her daughter were never found. She was an outlaw, but she was also a modern-day Robin Hood. No one in Auberry really wanted Six Shooter Kate behind bars. She was just part of the local color. Times were hard. Some mountain people protected her and shared her good fortune. They knew her history. They would say, "She don't bother us and we don't bother her. That's the way it is."

The Stampede

The cattle drive in the spring: the cowhands drove the cattle to higher ground and lush meadows. They would stand watch over the herd to prevent a wild animal from killing a new calf. The cattle remained in the high meadows until fall. Then, it was important to drive the cattle back down to the lower meadows before the snows arrived.

Two times a year, the cowhands would drive their cattle through our one street. We never knew when they would come. The vibration of the earth was the only advanced warning to move out of the way. There was no stopping the cattle and the yelling cowboys once they started down our one-street town. This was the cowboys' fifteen minutes of fame; all heads turned towards the sound of thundering hooves.

One day, I had a very frightening experience. I found myself all alone when the cattle coursed their way through the town. It just happened that my big sister was not with me. I was certain the cattle would find me as I hid between the screen door and door of the tank house, two doors from home. The cattle seemed to swarm like bees as they ran over the bridge and jumped into the small ditch next to it.

The stampede seemed to go on forever. Finally, my big sister found me clinging to the screen door. I was shaking when she scooped me up. My big sister took me to my parents. She reassured me that I had chosen a safe place to hide. Our parents expected us to make wise choices in dangerous situations. I'd done the right thing.

The Stampede: Up Close and Personal

Another time, I experienced the stampede up close with my big sister beside me. The cattle were even closer than before. They were way too close for comfort. That fall, the cowboys did what they usually did. They drove the cattle from the high meadow down to lower grazing meadows before the snows arrived. They were eager to return to their homes after spending most of spring and summer watching over the cattle in the high country. They were in a hurry. My big sister could see the cattle coming by way of the dust cloud they made. We could feel the ground shake and tremble. We were standing by the little bridge leading into Auberry. Suddenly, she grabbed my arm and pulled me under the bridge with her. It was none too soon. A thick cloud of dust surrounded us. We could hear the thundering hooves of cattle and horse as they stampeded over the bridge. The lead cattle were wild-eyed. All the cattle were on the run. A wooly cow's head in flight is a sight to behold. Its eyes bulge and nostrils flare. All of the cattle snort as they strain to keep up with the herd.

Today, a child welfare agency would say, "Where were your parents?" Well, we knew where they were, and they counted on us to come home when we were in trouble. We knew the mountains were dangerous. Our mother and father had taught us survival skills. This did not seem like an emergency. It did seem like a moment to remember. My big sister and I survived the stampede. Later, someone would say that experience builds character. I would reply, "Yes, if you live long enough to tell the story."

The Barn Dance

The barn dance celebrations were the highlight of our family's fun time. Life was hard in the mountains, and the people struggled to keep going. The barn dance was a chance to "blow off steam," "let your hair down," as the folks would say. It was a time when the Grange Hall was filled with "good old foot-stomping music." The ladies dressed in their best cotton dresses and the men wore clean shirts.

Over in the corner sat the older folks in a circle, swapping stories and passing "the jug" of "bootleg liquor." Here, the spirits were very high and getting higher by the minute. Much laughter swelled as the music of the fiddle played. The dancers flew around the dance floor to the "*do-si-do*" of the fiddle. The foot stomping shook the old Grange Hall.

This was Saturday night, and many could sleep it off on Sunday morning. Others, like my parents, would be expected to make their way to church and "stay awake for the service." Many a sore rib was had as my father nodded off in church and was jolted back to awareness by my mother's sharp elbow. Father displayed the "bobbing turkey neck" just before he nodded off. It made my big sis and me giggle. Such was the Sunday life in the little town of Auberry.

Our Close-Knit Family

Our close-knit family worked hard and played hard. The times demanded families to work together in order to survive the Great Depression. Simple pleasures, like the barn dance, were to be appreciated. Differences in the mountain people did not seem too great, for all were just "making the best of it."

COLD / LIGHT / EARTH : Poetry

Carole's Complaint
Sherry Long

My love's patient heat has for years now been ignored
By invading Nordic cold marching muddy through my house.
The feeble shelter of my heart I remade every day
And blessed it silently with aching prayers each night,
Only to see it fall to the battering of Indifference.

If you'd only see enough to come to a decision,
Either loving true or hatred bold, anything but pretense.
If you'd only make a division in your thoughts and ways,
To make kindly difference between the furniture and me.

The meager fuel's run out that kept my pale flame lit.
I'm not sure at all that there's even heat for one.
The fire has gone so low my soul is going numb.

You seem surprised I've found my voice and as I rise
To take my dusty unread life off of your moldy shelf
I am accused of selfish infidelity, poisoned spite.
Unjust wounds in one whose only prayers were tears.
But quietness is truly killed and anger rules alone,
An Empress shaking out of the sky every recklessness.

How could I have hoped so long or cared for you so much or
Given so very meekly what you could never take in kind?
Ears that never heard the other speak, oh this is such
A depth of deafness nothing cures and both of us gone blind.

My friends step back in their respect of my angry pain,
Whose love is sacrificial now that my cold storm blows in.
Each of us has our weather and our seasons to endure,
    First summer's heedless heat, then winter's lonely homelessness.

Smell of Old Barn Wood
Sherry Cerrano

The smell of old barn wood infused with dust from animals and dirt
    drifts past me.
Transports me to the white foam of a milk cow, and the flat, coarse
    hair of hide on her barrel belly.
While the faint perfume of an unidentifiable flower, sharp and sweet
    intermingled with dead grass floats by on a cool breeze,
Nudging away the sticky, heavy moisture-laden air.

The guttural trill of one bird, an intermittent cheeping,
A flyby twitter as the morning of late summer ages,
The deep-throated complaint of insects resume.
A swelling of buggy cha-cheering rises then dies away,
Begins again and dies away,
Begins again and dies away,
Wave after wave.

The smell of old barn wood infused with dust from animals and dirt
    drifts past me.
Transports me to the white foam of a milk cow, and the flat, coarse
    hair of hide on her barrel belly.
Kittens lap at milk with specks of dirt floating in a flat tin pan.
I'm eight and take advantage of kitties to pet their soft fur.

A whistle like "Hey, you" announces a bird.
For a time the aviary solos sound as the bugs work the background.
Trills, chirps, five-note songs take over.
A bird burp, burp, burps its life.
Comments resound of various sounds.
Before the bugs bow out, intermittent crescendos play.
All soften and take a backseat to the interstate roar.

Old barn wood infused with dust from animals and dirt.

Transports me to the white foam of a milk cow, and the flat, coarse
    hair of hide on her barrel belly.
The earth holds someone precious,
My grandmother gone close to fifty years now.

A single bird reports in like an old typewriter.
A mid-August yellow leaf drifts straight down on the dense air,
Against the green hue,
Alone, among the first to go with more to follow.
For a short time the birds are reverently still.
The insect buzzing becomes distant.
The busy traffic noise drones on.

Cows, cats, cacophony, cats, and thoughts of my cancer scare.

Dirt Farmer
Lester Schneider

The once-grand farm house now is scarred
Remnants of an era bygone
Decay and rust throughout the yard
On tools once horse drawn

The day begins at early dawn
With cock-a-doodle-do
Yesterday has come and gone
Time to begin anew

He makes their eggs and toast for breakfast
And buttons his bib overalls
He listens to the weather forecast
"It's time to eat," he calls

No movement from her since she fell
She stays confined to bed
A cord attached to a captain's bell
Hangs just above her head

He tends to all her morning needs
Then starts his work with dirt
He chops the cotton field's tall weeds
Constantly on alert

He toils for hours in scorching sun
To get the highest yields
The ring clangs loud before he's done
To call him from the fields

The moment in time has finally arrived
To end her earthly hell
No longer will she be deprived
Where angels hear her bell

With broken body and callused hands
He still has fields to tend
Hard work to meet his life's demands
And for sorrow to mend

His life-long labor with the ground
In the end is finally banned
To keep his body safe and sound
His offspring take command

He sits alone with a vacant stare
Rubbing fabric off the chair
No mortal comfort can quell his despair
He needs his dirt to care.

After The Wall
Jay Harden

In another hundred years, the people
  who knew the names on The Wall
  will be dead
  and The Wall will slowly become
  another meaningless monument in need of maintenance,
  marked for visitors by missing names and broken letters
  from aimless vandals seeking a purpose in their lives,
  not knowing, not realizing,
  they are silently erasing the examples they seek.

And the personal lessons learned from my war
  will fade and be lost,
  and surviving descendants of everyone will be left with
  the homogenized points of view in schoolbooks.

This is the deeper sadness I foresee
  beyond the grief and regret I feel at The Wall this day.

I suppose other wars will follow meanwhile
  to relearn the timeless lessons of this one
  for the latest generation.

Then someday, perhaps,
  the lessons little and long will finally be mastered,
  and wars to possess our common earth
  will no longer be needed at all.

If that comes true, then I will rest peacefully,
  knowing that what I did in the skies of Southeast Asia
  and what my combat brothers did in water and fire below
  meant something,
  and that will be enough.

That will have to be enough.

Gardening Without Guilt
R.R.J. Sebacher

Gardening I believe is a sacred endeavor

Truest intercourse with Mother Nature

Our hands sliding in and out of her moist earth

Planting seeds in the folds we've plowed

Smells both fertile and fragrant

Sweaty and dirty before we're through

At the end that pleasant pause

Like sex without religious hang-ups

The tenderness of transplanting sprouts

Then nurturing and protecting what we've sown

To see it flower and fulfill its promise

Are gardening shows pornography

Maybe we should never mention this

Or the enlightening pleasures of hunting and fishing

LIQUID THOUGHTS

Go with the Flow
Lori Younker

The sun emerges in brilliant red, a spectacular send-off for the men bound for the best fishing lake in the country. Bill's job is to secure the wooden rowboat on top of the van. He threads the rope through the metal hooks and uses a knot mastered in his youth on the lakes of Minnesota. Though the sky brightens by the minute, Bill can't shake the sense of doom that accompanies every trip to the countryside.

Yesterday, while he and Bataraa, the company driver, replaced the old tires, he reflected on how most trips ended. If he had his way, Bill would fill the back of the van with a variety of engine parts, a month's supply of beef jerky, a medical emergency kit, and in his pocket—cash for bribes. In mission training, his instructors emphasized the value of describing all possible outcomes when making plans. They called this the "work of worry."

"Who's ready?" Tom cheers from behind a camcorder, his wiry body buried in a navy sweatshirt with UCLA splashed across the front. Bill admires his friend's "anything-goes" attitude, wishing it would rub off on him. The camera points in Bill's direction, so he gives his friend a reluctant nod.

At the back of the van, Bill's son Pete uses his body weight to hold back a mass of fishing gear, the cooler, the tent, and the .22 rifle. Hanging from his arm is a plastic bag bulging with candy bars. "I've got the Snickers!" he yells and spins around quickly to slam the back door on their supplies.

A shout comes from the left. "Do we have enough toilet paper?" Tom's son James strides toward the van shielding his face from the camera. "Someone always gets the runs."

Ah, refreshing! Bill is glad he isn't the only one who wants to be ready for everything.

Inside the van, Tom's oldest son, Ryan, smooths the hair out of his eyes and kicks a flat of Pepsi under the backseat. "To control its consumption," he says.

The camera is aimed at Bill again. Tom asks, "So, where is this fine bunch of men headed for this time?"

Bill blows warm air into his hands. Though it's mid-June, the temperature dipped into the 40s overnight. He slides his hands into his pockets and plays along with Tom's spoof on the *Red Green Show*,,"Our destination is Ooghee Nore, a legendary lake in the grasslands of northwest Mongolia. And should I mention, the only lake for hundreds of miles? Where only the brave venture? Not to worry, we have a Russian tin can and an expert driver."

Bill remembers the winter hunting trip with their driver Bataraa. He used duct tape to repair a rotting radiator and squeezed more miles from one liter of gas than physically possible. Every man they met claimed to be hunting guides, all eager to check out his 30-ought six. On that trip, they started with five men but returned with thirteen. One of them was apprehensive every single minute.

"Ooghee Nore? Sounds exotic," Tom prompts.

"We've never traveled in that direction before, and there are no roads to get there, but if we're lucky, we'll arrive by sundown."

"Let's go, then," Tom shouts, and the six crowd into the van. They bounce out of the yard and descend the steep gravel road to the highway that follows the river.

Their first stop: the ruins of Karakorum, the original center of Genghis Khan's empire. Bill surveyed the stone fortress, trying to imagine the leader of the vast Mongol empire crossing the threshold of the main gate. With the north wind picking up considerably, their video recording becomes a humorous pantomime of Tom holding onto his baseball cap, motioning over his shoulder at the stone turtle and the architectural stupas that march in a perfect line on the grassy slope. Though no one can hear him, he begins his monologue with, "Six hundred years ago . . ."

With each mile, another layer of dust collects on the windshield. The van jostles along the path, sending its passengers forward and back, and from side to side. Bill's head slams against the window. He feels for a bump on his temple, and the rowboat squeaks and scrapes the roof above him, making him wish they had never taken it. Sure the boat is slipping, he insists they stop and tighten the ropes.

Getting out, Ryan remarks that it feels good to stretch their legs, and Bataraa sweeps the front window with a little broom.

Several hours into the day, the ruts disappear and a vote is taken to choose the way. The one they choose is an open stretch and comparatively smooth, leading them higher and further north. When a lone yurt comes into view, Bataraa says, "We'll stop and ask about the lake."

The housewife comes out of the yurt wearing the knee-length dress of the centuries called the "del." Her face is sunburned and leathery, and her smile reveals teeth as white as the hard cheese drying in a wooden crate on the roof of her home. "Ooghee Nore? I've never heard of it."

"We're still in Overhungai Province, aren't we?" The driver is seeking reassurance.

"Of course, but there's no lake within a day's drive on horseback." She sweeps her hand across the horizon.

With the risk of being rude, they refuse the customary milk tea and chatting. They point the van west. At nightfall, Bataraa pulls the van to a stop on a flat piece of pasture absent of rocks. He turns off the headlights to save the battery. In complete darkness, the younger men pull out the sleeping bags and stretch out under the stars while the older three curl up in the van, cramped, but out of the cold.

Morning dawns with skies of milky purple, and Bill creeps out of the van and shuts the door gently behind him. A strange stillness in the air amplifies the sound of animals murmuring. He looks around. It appears a herd of sheep snuggled up to the boys in the middle of night, and a yurt is less than fifty yards away!

Bill sees smoke rising from the stovepipe of the humble dwelling. No doubt, a family is preparing breakfast on the wood stove in the center of their home. Bill and the other men will be their guests for doughnut holes and tea.

Back on the road, the boys entertain each other with burping and long descriptions of where to purchase a decent backpack in the city. Bill must admit he enjoys their uninhibited conversation. Then, without warning, a village of wooden houses appears. The first building they approach is a shed with a serendipitous fuel pump where they meet an older gentleman who has stopped by for some cigarettes. He knows the way. "Go between those two hills to the west. Can you see them? Keep going and you'll find it."

The endless fields pass by, and Bill worries if all this lurching back and forth hasn't done some real damage. Perhaps his boat, designed and constructed by his friend Purnell, will never have a second try. Memories of its maiden voyage will have to be enough.

Christened *Pike Fever*, he and Purnell launched it into the frigid depths of the Tule River with plenty of congratulations from their wives. The boat floated—that's what mattered the most. The deep, black water swept the two men towards their destination. Along the way, city folk enjoying the warm weather held up bottles of vodka as they passed, and some stripped down to their waists to hale down a ride. Bill smiles at the memory and holds onto the strap above his head as the van takes a sharp turn.

Before noon, Ooghee Nore stretches out in front of them like a huge, glassy mirror that reflects the clouds and the blue sky above. This three-mile lake is teeming with northern pike, yellow perch, and Siberian taimen, the most coveted catch with its record-breaking size and a mouth of sharp teeth.

The moment the van stops, the boat flies down off the van and goes into the water with a splash and a shout. The teenagers play at fishing, build fires, and eat as many peanut butter sandwiches as they can make.

The second day brings what Bill calls "true success." The yellow spoon with its five red dots does its job as Pete appears to have a large fish on the line.

"Hold on! He'll give you a fight!" Bill yells.

Just as soon as Pete pulls the fish to shore, his catch takes off with lightning speed toward the deep. Pete struggles to keep his feet on the ground and is dragged into the water. He digs his heels into the sandy soil, and Bill holds him by the waist. Pete must hoist the fish to shore two more times before the fish exhausts himself and succumbs. The men huddle around as the creature writhes and twists under the strength of Pete's arms. Then, Bill runs for the measuring tape with a feeling of euphoria, and Tom grabs the closest camera.

Pete's northern pike measures well over a meter and weighs in at nineteen pounds. Bill looks up from gutting the prize fish to see two ranchers stop by on horseback to see how the foreigners are faring. If he has heard correctly, they are offering their daughters as brides for the young men. Dismounting, the two men say their daughters are prettier than the girls of the city. Everyone laughs.

There is fried fish for lunch with cold bread and Pepsi for everyone. One of the ranchers volunteers to demonstrate the art of marmot hunting. Even James crawls on his belly with the rifle dragging beside him. He twirls a white handkerchief over his head and moves closer and closer toward the prey.

To end the day, the sun-kissed men watch the visitors prepare barbecue the traditional way. After cleaning the marmot, they return the meat to steam in its own skin. Using a long stick, they turn the meat over the fire in quick little movements. The men listen to the fur sizzle and watch the carcass blow up to the size of a basketball. The dark meat bursts in their mouth with a unique flavor, but Tom can't resist. "Tastes like chicken, doesn't it?"

Smiles are as wide as the lake. Bill wipes his mouth with his sleeve, and the visitors say good night with candy bars tucked in their riding jackets. The horses kick up the dirt as they leave to the west. With the sound of the pounding of their hooves on the steppes, Bill wonders if Genghis Khan ate with his men on this very spot.

The third day looms dark, gray and threatening. Blustery winds make tying the boat to the van more than a challenge. The rendezvous with nature must come to an end, but it's not without an encore. A torrential rain persists. Strangely enough, though the van slides through the mire, Bill feels considerably lighter on his way home to civilization.

About fifty miles from home, Pete yells out, "Do you smell something?" Steam fills the interior of the van, and Bataraa confesses that the duct tape on the radiator hose is a year old. So he adds several more layers, and waits for the engine to cool down. The men's hot breath fogs the windows, but with a swish of their sleeves, they're off.

Just a quarter mile short of home, the van struggles to make it up the last hill. They will walk the rest of the way, leaving Bataraa to watch their things until they return with the car. It drizzles now, but Bill doesn't notice. In front of him, the two youngest boys carry the boat over their heads. They have no extra passengers, no injuries, no regrets.

f

Down to the River
Jennifer McCullough

The view from Dad's car didn't hold a candle to this. No, sir! This was Nat Geo, baby. This was Bass Pro meets *Smokey and the Bandit* meets *Escape from New York*.

Friends call me Pac-Man, and I'm not proud to say it, but on that day back in January of 2009, I was number eight on the FBI's Most-Wanted list. Number one in the state of Illinois, not counting Blagojevich. Of course, he wasn't on the run like I was when I hit the Martin Luther King Bridge just before dark, headed home to East St. Louis to see the folks. I was doing about 110–120 on I-44 through downtown St. Louis because, well, I was in a hurry to see the sun set over the Mississippi River. Reminded me of my childhood, you know?

Growing up, I used to watch the sun go down in that same spot every day in the wintertime, when Dad would drive us home at 5:14 p.m. on the dot. Dad was a St. Louis ad man, a real-life advertising guru just like Don Draper with his shiny grey suit, Lucky Strikes and Brylcreem hairdo, except Dad smoked Kools and had a Jheri curl back in the '80s.

I was a daydreaming Catholic-school punk kid who wore a uniform Monday through Friday and carried a pair of nunchuks on the weekends. I used to intimidate my little brother into giving me his allowance so I could play arcade games with my friends down at Doc's Bar & Family Diner.

I remember watching those sunsets and thinking I was getting to see God tuck the world in for the night. The panoramic red and orange sky was a sight, I tell you, where it met up with that churning river that twisted away into forever beyond the steel trusses of that bridge.

Back then, I was religious, I guess you could say. Now, I like to think of myself as spiritual. Life sort of has a way of doing that to you, ya know?

Dad's 1985 Buick LeSabre Limited Collector's Edition, with its whitewall tires and in-dash cassette player, loved sailing across that bridge, even if he didn't. He said the lanes were too narrow. I guess he never liked the fact that the only thing separating us from oncoming traffic was a thin yellow stripe of paint.

On warm summer days, Dad would let me roll my window down so I could smell the not-so-fresh air and see the water whirring by as he drove 45 miles an hour. Only the kids on the passenger side got to do this. If you were sitting behind Dad, it was too dangerous to stick your nose out the window, much less have your whole head exposed to oncoming traffic.

From November to March, seems like that dang bridge iced over morning and night. We'd spend 30 minutes inching across it, praying the cars behind us didn't go too fast and the cars in front of us went fast enough.

I don't think Dad ever did see a sunset, not like I did, anyway. He was always too busy driving the straight and narrow.

Of course, that never stopped him from taking a risk. Rain, snow, ice, you name it. Dad went to work and we went to school. He knew he had a sweet deal and wasn't about to screw it up. He would have moved us all west in a heartbeat, but Mom... she liked East St. Louis. Her mama was there, my grandmother, and you know how baby mamas and their mamas are.

Anyway, I thought my black 2008 Lexus RX 350 was going to love that bridge, too. Boy, was I wrong. Very wrong. Problem was, I paid cash for the damn thing. If I'd been making payments like a good boy, I doubt I would have been driving it like a bat out of hell over that bridge, trying to see the sun set, and I'm sure I never would have swerved in front of that semi. Mother bounced me like I was Frogger. I ping-ponged off one steel beam after another until I flew over the side, grill down, hanging like a 50-pound catfish on a 5-pound line.

I don't know what had me hooked, but something had me hovering about 20 to 30 feet above the water. I can only assume it was the sweet arm of the Blessed Virgin Mary.

Gravity, on the other hand, is a bitch.

When I came to, I too was grill down, face pressed into a huge white powdery airbag, which was pressed into the steering column, which was pressed into what used to be the dash, which was, I assume, smashed into the motor. I could barely see the hood, still hanging on like the canine of a 6-year-old boy: wiggly and good for nothin'. I was covered in blood, hot coffee and what smelled like windshield wiper fluid.

Brown, muddy water was everywhere. Up, down, right, left. No matter which direction I looked, it's all I saw. There was nothing beautiful about it. It was nature all right, but not the kind that inspires you. If you've ever seen one of those IMAX movies, it wasn't like that at all. It was OMNIMAX, only real man... and I was scared.

Every little gust of wind swung me that much closer to a watery death, and for the first time in my life, I prayed for a cop to find me.

Sort of.

In addition to a couple of outstanding warrants, not the least of which was a charge of first-degree murder, I was hauling about 250 pounds of marijuana for a close friend who was expecting me at 9 p.m. sharp outside Sindee's Night Club.

For you whippersnappers, that's back when pot was still illegal.

Even now, you got to have a license to haul that much weed... and know somebody.

The only person I knew, was a guy named Ted I'd met at Wash U who'd served time for hacking into the DEA's central database and getting his little sister out of a pinch.

Ted was a smart guy, a lot smarter than me. He had one degree in computer programming and was working on another to become an oncologist. That's a doctor who treats people with cancer. For some reason, he liked me and had offered to help me get on a plane to Honduras, which I had read was only slightly more dangerous than East St. Louis at noon on Sundays.

My plan was to deliver Ted's weed, stop in and see the folks, then hightail it out of dodge. I already had the fake ID, the plane ticket, and a wad of cash big enough to send every stripper I knew through four years of college.

Now, on that particular day, I thought God was working against me.

Sunsets are powerful things, man.

They've been luring men to far corners of the Earth since the beginning of time. And I thought this particular sunset was going to be the end of me. Turns out, it was.

Sort of.

I guess the cops ran "my" plates, because the first guy I saw swinging from a rope outside my busted driver's window addressed me as Senator.

He said, "Can you feel your right foot, Senator?"

"Yes, I can," I told him.

"Ok, how about your left," he says.

I said, "Yeah, but my toes are tingling."

Then he says, "Ok, Senator, we're going to have you out of here just as soon as we can."

Can you believe it actually crossed my mind to ask for a police escort to Lambert International if they got me out of that mess in one piece?

Then I figured that might be pushing it.

Instead, I stayed cool, played the part, and sat there all night listening to the Mississippi rumble through my bones. The cold air got to my feet first, then my hands, nose, ears and by the time I went to sleep, I guess I had resigned myself to letting it take my heart, too.

But I woke up the next day with a warm blanket wrapped around my head and shoulders. Somehow, they'd stuffed it through the broken window just in time for me to see the sun come up over East St. Louis.

In all my 29 years, I don't think I had ever witnessed a sunrise before. Drug-dealing college dropouts just don't seem to catch them.

But on this particular day, I was awake before 6 a.m. I was a "U.S. Senator," and best of all—I was alive.

Oh, and let me not forget… cradled in the arms of Mary, Mother of God, and about 50 first responders, some of whom would have undoubtedly recognized me if not for the broken glass that disfigured my pretty face.

See, I still have the scars after all this time.

"Senator, we have a plan to extricate you," a cool white guy with a buzz cut informed me. "But first we're going to have to cut the top off your vehicle and secure you to a litter."

I told those boys it sounded like a fine plan to me, and that they'd all get tax-payer funded Christmas bonuses if they got me out alive and in one piece.

As I sat there shrouded in a shiny silver blanket, so the flame from the blowtorch wouldn't send me to hell prematurely, I thought about Big D, the strip club owner I'd shot in the ass. The cops assumed it was a drug deal gone bad. It wasn't. I showed up early for work behind the bar one night and found him raping my girl, Tristy.

I don't think the cops ever would have promoted me to the most-wanted list if the mofo hadn't died, and I hadn't also stolen his car and his safe, but hey, brothers gotta do...

Funny thing is, all those guys working their asses off to save me in the freezing cold would have cut the line and turned around and gone home if they'd known my real name. Even funnier is the fact that some of them had sisters and girlfriends who worked for Big D.

And I'm the bad guy.

Thou shall not kill, though, right?

Right.

Which brings me to why I've called this place home for the past 31 years.

Technically, the law says I did not turn myself in that day, but I've always said that I did.

I guess somebody on that jury agreed with me, 'cause they gave me life instead of the chair.

Now, it would be easy to stand up here behind this prison pulpit and tell y'all how I lived a life of crime before I found God, but in my heart, I know that's not really how it happened.

See, I thought I'd always been right with God. I just picked the wrong day to go down to the river and pray.

An Essay: When Last I Saw the Sea
Robert E. Browne

"It is an interesting biological fact that all of us have, in our veins, the exact same percentage of salt in our blood that exists in the ocean, and, therefore, we have salt in our blood, in our sweat, in our tears. We are tied to the ocean. And when we go back to the sea, whether it is to sail or to watch it, we are going back from whence we came."

- President John F. Kennedy

Aye, when last I saw the sea, lo, many years ago now, I glanced about its broad expanse and went about my way; my shipboard duties to engage. I cannot remember the time or date, nor can I recall if the weather was fair or foul, but I can now recognize that it embraced me with its ancient lure, though I was not conscious of it.

I can sometimes recall the smell, not bad or good, but distinctive, somehow a smell of freedom and now missed, except for a vague recollection of it.

Aye, the many years I spent within its grasp, yet in mercy, the sea allowed my escape. There I watched the phosphorescent caps dance with the leaping fish from the crest of waves and fall to the valley between the swells to disappear again. Always new, yet always the same; unpredictable, yet always constant in its features.

Now, decades past, I wish that I had taken but one long-lasting moment to fix that image in my mind, so that now I could close my eyes and savor that aroma while picturing those waves, swells, birds and fish, to carry them with me forever.

When I listen intently, I can yet hear the boatswain's pipe sounding and the ship's bell ringing a stalwart crew to quarters to battle not just an enemy, but also the sea in its infinite diversity.

And in my last hours, I may arise to look at the ocean touching the sky, then understand that the beauty of the sea still lives within the heart of me: never more alive than when the sea, in temper stressed, may test a craft and worthy sailing men who disturbed her temperate rest.

I pray that in gilded, red and blue sunset I may see the face of God, master of all the oceans deep, and there await his nod.

The Chosen
Sue Fritz

Sparks bounded out of bed excitedly. This was the day she had been waiting for. It was finally here. She was finally old enough to be a part of The Choosing. It was an honor to be able to participate and an even bigger honor to be chosen. Many had gone before her. Her best friend Layla was chosen last time. Even though she missed Layla, she knew Layla was reaping the bounties of having been a Chosen one.

The commune was already bustling when Sparks joined the others. She found her friends huddled together in the shade. They were all talking excitedly about what was to come.

"I can't believe we're finally old enough to participate this time!" said Kierra. "Wouldn't it be great if all of us were chosen?"

"That would be awesome," said Jane. "But this is the first time our names will be in the chamber, so there's a chance none of us will make it."

"It's possible, though," said Sparks eagerly. "Look at Layla. Last time was her first time and she was chosen."

"I wonder what she's doing now?" said Kierra. "I wish we could see her again. I miss her."

"Don't you think it's strange we never see the Chosen ones?" said Babs. "I mean, after they've gone?"

"No," said Sparks, shaking her head. "Not strange at all. You know what the elders say. Being chosen is a great responsibility. We have a mission to complete, and even though that means we won't see our family and friends again, we are doing a great thing. Everyone in the commune will be proud of us. Our legacy will go on, and we will be an inspiration to those who will follow."

"But where do they go?" asked Babs. "And what is our mission anyway? Isn't it weird how no one really talks about it, except that it's a great thing to be chosen?"

"Our mission?" said Jane, staring at Babs in disbelief. "Our mission is to go to the airstrip with the others and move on forward."

"What's wrong, Babs? Don't you want to be chosen?" said Sparks.

"I don't know."

"What?" the other three said at the same time.

"But, it's such an honor," said Sparks.

"I know. But it scares me. I just wish I knew more about where the Chosen ones go," said Babs.

Kierra, Jane, and Sparks looked at each other. They were all thinking the same thing. Just then, an announcement came over the air-com system. Everyone was gathering in the square. Young and old huddled together, waiting for the drawings. The girls rushed over to find a good place near the front. The great chamber holding all the eligible names was placed on a table. As the director began his speech about the history of The Choosing, the chamber began to spin, mixing the names.

Sparks tried to focus on the director's speech, but her mind wandered. Why was Babs afraid? No one was ever afraid of The Choosing. How could she doubt the elders? Why didn't she want to be a part of this great event? She felt a jab in her side. Jane was poking her. The director was winding up his speech.

".....and so, my fellow members, let the drawings commence. Remember, you have a mission to complete. Your legacy will go on, and you will be an inspiration to those who will follow."

Applause erupted from the crowd. As the noise died down, the chamber slowed, and then stopped. The director opened the chamber and began drawing names from it. Name after name was called. Quietly, the Chosen ones gathered at the corral. The crowd remained silent, wanting to hear if their name was among the Chosen. Sparks leaned in closer to hear better. She was all aflutter when her name was picked, but she knew not to make a sound. Slowly she made her way towards the corral. Jane and Kierra were picked as well and joined Sparks and the other Chosen ones. Sparks was glad she would not be going alone. She couldn't believe it! Her first time to be able to participate and she was chosen. She was so proud of herself. This was going to be a great journey. How could Babs not want to do this? It was such an honor. When the drawings were finished, the silence in the square broke. Cheers roared from all. The Chosen ones were slapped on the back and congratulated.

Sparks, Jane, and Kierra jumped up and down and squealed.

"Can you believe we get to go together?" said Sparks.

"I know," said Jane. "It's a shame Babs didn't get picked."

"Yeah. Too bad for her," said Kierra, looking back at Babs. "But we get to go."

The three friends started giggling wildly as they followed the other Chosen ones to the airstrip. Everyone in the crowd was talking about what honor they were bringing to their families by being a part of the event this time. Soon, the airstrip was in sight. The group stopped and the director gave his last minute instructions.

"After you jump, you will feel some strange sensations. Don't worry. This is normal. You will get used to it after a few seconds," he said. "I need you to line up from oldest to youngest. Just follow the one in front of you and jump when you come to the edge of the runway."

Sparks found her place and moved along, getting closer and closer to the edge. She felt a flutter in her stomach. Must be nerves, she thought. She watched the several in front of her jump, and then it was her turn. A smile crossed her face. She spread her arms and leapt. Oh the sensations! It was amazing. The floating on air, the gliding gracefully. How could Babs not want to feel this? Sparks turned her head and saw Jane and Kierra. They had the same goofy grins on their faces as Sparks did. She closed her eyes so she could soak up the whole experience. Leaning back, she felt the wind as it caressed her body. When she eventually opened her eyes, she could see the Earth below. It was so beautiful. The older ones were getting closer to the ground. They were creating a beautiful white blanket as they landed. Sparks was mesmerized by its magnificence when her thoughts were interrupted by a scream. She turned to see a frightened look on Jane's face.

"What's the matter, Jane?" she yelled. But with the wind of falling, Jane didn't hear her. Sparks tried to cup her hands at her mouth to make the sound go farther, but one hand was missing. Well, not exactly missing. It was barely there. What's happening to me, thought Sparks. Just then she felt herself becoming faint. As she wafted through the air, her body became lighter and lighter. Soon she realized she was becoming transparent.

"Jane! Kierra!" she shouted, but it came out in barely a whisper.

Kierra was nowhere to be seen. Jane had shrunk to just a dot. Sparks began to cry. She thought about Babs, still at home. She was the lucky one this time. She wished she were back with Babs.

"Oh, Babs!" she cried. "You were right to be scared!"

As her tears landed on her body, Sparks became smaller and smaller. Why were some of the Chosen allowed to make that beautiful blanket on the ground while others, like me, are disappearing, she wondered. And that's when Sparks realized what the great mission was. It was to bring beauty to the earth during this cold, bleak time of year. It really was an honor to do this. And it was a sacrifice for those who didn't make it. Those who melted, like her. She closed her eyes and for the last few yards to the ground, Sparks was at peace. She felt herself melting and becoming just a speck, until plop. The last little milligrams that were Sparks landed on top of the beautiful blanket.

A few days later, the area experienced a warm front and the beautiful white blanket became mush. As the sun shone, a little speck rose from the liquid muck on the ground. Higher and higher it went, until it landed on a fluffy white cloud. Lying there in a soft white bed, the speck opened her eyes.

"Look," said a deep, gruff voice. "Her eyes are open."

"Isn't she beautiful?" said a sweet sounding voice.

"Let's call her Sparks," the first voice said.

"Yes, husband. I agree. Sparks is a wonderful name for a snowflake."

Cold, Hot, and So Sweet

Jay Harden

Being born a deep Georgia boy, I always assumed there was only one kind of cold refreshment worth drinking in this life—besides lemonade or an ice-flecked, nickel Co-Cola—and that was homemade iced tea.

Then, I got myself educated: first a warm-up diploma from high school, later a college degree just like the rest of the family had done—and expected.

And then I sauntered off into the real world from whence I mistakenly thought I had originated. I put on the blue military uniform of an Air Force officer (duly enlightened), left the sheltered South I had known, and made my way to the farthest coast of this country called California, where I discovered, to my shock and bodily delight, an unheard of drink called Orange Julius—this was in 1967, mind you—spun in a blender from crushed ice, orange squeezings, and a smooth, sweet milk-like powder. It was a fair alternative to Mama's iced tea, always fresh made and waiting for me back at the home place whenever I got leave.

Then they reassigned me to New England for flight duty, a place where no houses seemed permanent. Every one was built of cold, white siding, all flimsy looking (instead of red brick), seeming as insubstantial to me as the houses of the dimmer two of the Three Little Pigs. I could tolerate such accommodations for a time, but I was more offended when I ordered my first iced tea at the local Howard Johnson restaurant. I got only a cube or two of ice in the glass and felt cheated of fully chilled refreshment. When I complained, they corrected me like a new puppy, saying that locals felt cheated when the glass was mostly ice, instead of mostly the tea they paid for. I decided not to disagree with such rigid and ancient logic, though my own seemed more reasonable. After all, when a body is hot and thirsty, who would want to swig tepid tea? I got my thinking straight for this place of my new transplanting, suffered in silence (being a well-trained Southern gentleman), and never ordered iced tea in New England again, taking my solace in home-brew that my darling belle and bride served in our quarters on base at every meal, even breakfast.

For the rest of her life, and then the rest of my mother's life, I enjoyed iced tea made by two great masters of the art. Even now, my body and mind can actually recall the restoration they consistently gave to me. I still have and use their simple recipe, and it tastes almost the same, though missing their irreplaceable ingredient of encompassing care.

Many years later, I met another truly extraordinary feminine delight, similarly generous and loving. However, she was dissimilar to all the women I had ever known in a strange way, coming from a foreign land. Though she spoke what I was informed was The Queen's English, we had many amusing misunderstandings, based on pronunciation mostly, and vocabulary, too. Clearly, I was the one regularly uninformed.

I forgave her easily for consistently massacring many useful words: *aluminum*, *vitamin*, *schedule*, *controversy*, and my pet peeve, *aeroplane*. I also learned some new terms like *manky* and *infradig* that came in handy when I tried to impress others—provided they were sufficiently worldly and bright, and open to instruction. Eventually, I felt encouraged to teach her the language of the South, at least the sound of it, but I failed, in spectacular fashion, to teach her to drawl and slur certain crucial words like *Atlanna*, *Jawja*, and *bulldawg*. In spite of this, we still laugh and love each other.

But of all the missing education she taught me, my most important remediation was learning the genuine truth of tea. It seems that all my life I have been abusing this essential example of England and her superior culture. To my darling wife and her kind, iced tea was an abomination as low as ignorance of Shakespeare. My affection for her propelled me to a rapid re-education. First, I rejected "dust" tea: you know, those pale imitations packed into little white folded cloths with strings and tags. (I do, however, tolerate them for breakfast in a restaurant.) I learned of leaf tea, the good stuff with a flavor far superior to a soggy bag full of their leftover powdered particles. Then, I finally understood why King

George III and my ancestors took umbrage unto war over the shriveled, handpicked leaves of a finicky, subjugated tree.

Along the way, I developed my own independence regarding hot tea, as I had with the chilled kind. I insisted on lemon and sugar with both, but there are exceptions, of course. I absolutely will not condone her addition of clotted cream. The very idea revolts my digestion like chewing a stick of butter, and insults the lemon, too. And I prefer honey, when I can get it, over sugar, even if dressed in fancy cubes and delivered with silver tongs.

But otherwise, my lady and I are wonderfully compatible in every way: perhaps by the arbitration of shared true tea. I even rely on a good buddy who travels and furnishes me with highly desired first flush Darjeeling and Lapsang Souchong teas from Nepal of rare and excellent quality I jealously share with only a few deserving and appropriately grateful confidants.

My only failure with her (so far) is persuading my love to enjoy my ancestral affection for iced tea in a tall glass, cold as can be, under a sweltering summer sun down South. Her upper class education is, thus, incomplete, but I am patient anyway. In the meantime, she has taught me the joy of slow intimate conversation with mutual warmth and laughter over the soft clinking of china.

Being with her is a lovely habit. There we sit, eye-to-eye, heart-to-heart, and smile for smile, the English aristocrat and the colonial commoner, the Georgia boy and the elegant lady, balancing a shared life: the cold and hot of tea, sweet as our love, connecting us still.

Vacation's End
Bradley D. Watson

It was the last weekend before Mira's only vacation was over. One of those too short, never-ending-heat weekends, that you wish would go on and on because their conclusion brings with it a return to responsibilities.

But it was over. She stood on the white sands of Wista Beach, watching the families winding their huge beach-towels into a wad, closing their great turtle-shell umbrellas, and tucking all their belongings under their arms to make the slow trek to vehicles, waiting to whisk them back to lives that Mira couldn't even imagine.

For three weeks, Mira had played with the kids on the beach: learning to build sandcastles, eating her first—and only—hotdog, and laughing at jokes that she didn't understand. The children were so full of life, and the air was so clear and fresh. She took deep breaths, feeling it inflate her lungs, then expelling it with the enthusiasm of a child with a new toy. The sky was a brilliant cyan blue, and she realized she had been staring for hours into its beautiful emptiness, dotted every now and then with random jellyfish clouds. The sun felt strange on her skin, but she liked it. She wished her holiday could go on forever.

With a touch of sadness, Mira watched as the last of the tourists disappeared from the beach, like a great school of fish, turning and moving as one, vanishing over the rim of the hill. The rising tide of the ocean washed away the single remaining tower of her lonely sandcastle. The fading laughter of the children she'd made friends with so quickly was swallowed up by the gently lapping waves. The whisper of the soft breeze across the vacant expanse of sand was now the only remnant of her too-short vacation.

The rays of the evening sun lightly stroked her tanned legs, a feeling she would miss.

It's time, she heard her mother's voice in the distance.

"I'm coming," she said aloud, rising and crossing the deserted beach, her eyes closed, memorizing the feel of the sand beneath her feet. Unable to delay any longer, she placed a foot into the gently beckoning sea.

No one saw her wistful blue-gray eyes as they took one last look at the twilit sand.

No one saw her skin begin to shift and change.

And no one saw the little green-and-blue-jeweled fishtail give one last flick at the surface as it pushed her down, down, deep beneath the ocean waves, taking her back home again.

The Cabin
Pat Wahler

Not long after my eighth birthday, I nearly drowned. My dad's brother and sister-in-law, who also happened to be my favorite uncle and aunt, had invited our family to spend the day with them at their cabin by the lake. Aunt Sue and Uncle John built the small, sturdy cabin not long after they were married. It made a welcome gathering place for countless family parties and weekend retreats.

Life at the cabin seemed like the gossamer threads of a pleasant dream to me. In the afternoon, the lake reflected sun like a mirror. Though the adults hid behind hats and dark glasses, my cousins and I pinched our eyes into small slits which made us look as though we were perpetually frowning. We'd watch Aunt Sue ease into the water and grab a bright red towline. As soon as she waved, Uncle John gunned their oversized motorboat's engine to pull her up out of the water like a slender, pale mermaid gracefully balanced on a single ski. She'd smile as she leaned to the right and then back to the left, pushing up rooster tail sprays of water with each turn.

Nighttime brought a welcome cloak of invisibility from the watchful eyes of parents. My cousins and I chased after lightning bugs to the chirping serenade of cicadas. Occasionally, someone maneuvered a radio at just the right angle to catch a country music station, although the sound usually provided more crackle than melody. The adults nibbled chips with dip and laughed and gossiped in slow lazy drawls, until the moon rose high overhead in an inky, dark sky filled with a million pinpoints of light.

I counted the days until we could go back, despite the stinging red sunburns I nearly always achieved splashing in the shallow area of the lake. My mother's warnings about the dangers of too much sun were largely ignored.

Dad's warnings related to what he found important. He told me not to throw trash on the roadways and declared anyone who drove on snowy days deserved what they got. Dad worked as foreman of a road crew and spent hours outside, whether the streets sizzled or froze. After work, he'd join his friends at Jack's Corner Bar, playing horseshoes or washers and consuming, according to Mom, more drinks than ten pirates on shore leave. In the mornings, his eyes drooped, but he always smiled over the top of the newspaper when I came to breakfast.

"Morning, Kiddo."

He said nothing when Mom plunked a bowl of cold cereal in front of him, her lips pressed tightly together. I could always tell how she felt by what she put on the table. One night she spent a long time in the kitchen and set the table with her gilt-edged wedding china. Yet, it was only Mom and I who shared Dad's favorite meal of roast beef and mashed potatoes. She did little more than push the food around on her plate, so I wasn't surprised when the sound of loud voices woke me later that night. I covered my ears and concentrated on our trip to the cabin. No one could be unhappy there.

The morning we were to leave, Mom tried on three different outfits before she chose a pair of plaid shorts and a sleeveless pale yellow top. She stared in my closet with her hands on her hips. Her voice sounded less weary and more hopeful than I'd heard in a while.

"Here, Ginny, this will be perfect with your new jean shorts."

She pulled a crisp white blouse from my closet and hummed while I got dressed. Then she pulled my curls back into a tight ponytail and secured it with a blood-red ribbon tied into a jaunty bow.

"There, now. Don't you look nice?"

The mirror reflected Mom's smiling face. Her image made me smile, too, and I nodded my head in agreement.

Dad's voice growled from downstairs.

"Come on, let's go or we'll be late."

Dad never tolerated tardiness, whether on the job or at home, so we hurried to climb into his spacious Buick. Even though he told me we'd arrive in only two hours, I squirmed on the wide bench seat. Mom looked over at Dad and smiled, but he only rolled the window down and rested his sun-browned arm on the door. She turned to face the highway. Her shoulders no longer seemed as straight as when we got into the car. The ensuing silence prompted me to shout over the roar of wind and road.

"How much longer, Dad?"

"Almost there, Kiddo," he told me.

I twirled the end of my ponytail and waited.

As soon as the car stopped, I jumped out. The cabin looked faded but neat, surrounded by daisies, blue bachelor buttons, and tall purple coneflowers. Red and white striped towels were tossed carelessly over the porch railing. My favorite cousin, Tommy, Aunt Sue and Uncle John's only child, ran toward me with a whoop of excitement.

"Hey, Gin. C'mon. I want to show you the swing I put up."

We left the adults behind to unpack the car and followed the siren call of the lake.

Tommy was three years older than me and enjoyed displaying his superior accomplishments. He grinned and pointed to his latest creation in a shady grove of trees near the lake's edge. He'd secured an old tire to a tree limb with a roped tied in a convoluted ball of knots.

"We can swing right out over the water and jump in. How about that?"

My swimming skills hadn't yet gone much beyond a scrambling dog paddle, so I swiftly offered another idea.

"Or we could just swing out over the water and back."

Tommy looked at me and laughed. "My dad says in the Navy they keep throwing you into deep water until you finally figure out how to swim. Maybe we need to do that to you."

I glared at him. "I can swim fine. I just don't like to jump out of silly old tire swings." Tommy was not to be deterred. "Wasn't your daddy supposed to help you practice?"

"He hasn't had time, yet, that's all."

Tommy slanted a sidelong glance at me. "Maybe he's too busy with other things."

Something about the way he said the words made my eyes narrow.

"What are you talking about?"

"Mom says if your daddy stayed home more, your mama would be whole lot happier."

Unexpectedly, his remark made my eyes fill, and I turned my head so he wouldn't see. He gave my shoulder an awkward pat as though I were a cocker spaniel. I swallowed my tears and scuffed my shoe into the dirt. He offered an apology of sorts.

"Parents can be stupid."

I snuffled because I couldn't disagree with his opinion. Once my voice steadied, I responded.

"At least we're here now. The cabin always makes me feel better. I know it'll make them feel better, too."

"But what about afterwards, when you go home?"

"I don't know," I answered truthfully.

Tommy idly twisted the swing and let it go. We watched as it whirled around. I could tell he'd been thinking.

"Maybe there is something you can do."

I looked at him. "What do you mean?"

"What if you swung out over the lake and then fell right in?"

"Are you crazy? I'm not going to do something dumb like fall in the lake."

"No, listen, you could fall on purpose, in front of everybody. Your parents would have to save you, and then I'll bet they'd realize they ought to be a lot nicer to each other."

I considered his plan for a moment.

"I don't like the idea of jumping so far out in the lake. What if they can't save me in time?"

"Well, I guess then you'll be dead, and they'll be good and sorry," he responded philosophically.

This seemed like a poor bargain to me, but I promised to think about it. Then we heard the boat engine roar and ran to take our places on board the sleek white boat, resplendent with the words "Sue Ann" freshly painted on the bow.

I turned my face toward the sunshine and inhaled the mossy scent of river water, fish, and suntan oil. While we finally chugged back to shore, my skin sizzled with another sunburn. Dad and Uncle John debated baseball strategy while Mom answered Aunt

Sue's whispered questions in mumbled monosyllables. Tommy glanced at me with his eyebrows raised.

After dinner, the adults settled into their green woven lawn chairs near the water. I preferred to sit at the edge of the wooden boat dock dangling my legs in the river and half-listening to the murmur of conversation behind me. Tommy had run to grab a chocolate chip cookie for each of us, even though my stomach was already stretched tight with food. The cool water lulled me into a comfortable inertia as the late day sun shimmered and danced on the ripples my bare feet created. I reveled in the absence of angry voices or icy silence.

I heard Tommy's feet pound across the dock and my dad's rough voice yelled at him to slow down. He didn't, and the dock shivered as he grew closer with each step. I wondered how I could possibly eat another cookie just before something hit between my shoulder blades, pushing me into the water. I had no time to utter a sound before my legs slapped the surface and the sun disappeared. I sank like a stone.

My eyes were wide and wild as I turned my head looking for something to grab. All I could see was gray water surrounding me. My arms flailed and my legs kicked while I tried in desperation to rise from the water like I'd so often seen my aunt do. But I wasn't a mermaid and stayed in the depths of the river. I opened my mouth to scream and water poured inside. My lungs burned and my body began to grow curiously heavy. Then I didn't want to struggle anymore. It would be easier to let the river take me wherever she wanted me to go. My body relaxed into the water's cool embrace.

A heartbeat later, a pair of strong hands grabbed my arms and jerked me to the surface. I recall the warmth of the dock under my back as someone pushed against my chest until I sputtered and coughed. I heard my father curse, my mother cry, and my cousin's pleading words.

"I'm sorry. I only wanted to help. I'm sorry."

When enough water had been pressed from my lungs, someone pulled me upright, and I opened my eyes. My mother's smile wavered through her tears. Uncle John shouted, "She's okay," and my father's brown hands gripped my arms. I looked down and noticed the white stripe where he used to wear a wedding ring and turned my gaze back toward the river. A few yards away, I saw a bright red ribbon floating on a ripple of water. It bobbed up and down as though playing a game of hide-and-seek. Bedraggled but still buoyant, the ribbon drifted farther and farther away from shore. I watched it until my eyes blurred with salty tears and the red ribbon disappeared into the blue, orange and pink of the setting sun.

One Man's Hot Tub is Another Woman's Nightmare
Kathryn Cureton

My husband, Hick, and I often have differences of opinion. It's our dynamic. We have a prosecutor/defense attorney style of communication. One presents a case for something he desires, and the other tries to expose the holes in his logic. Even when it comes to exterior decorating.

Take the case of the free hot tub. Hick couldn't pass up such a chance. Never mind that we didn't have room in our house for a hot tub. No solarium, no enclosed patio, no redwood deck, no state-of-the-art spa. We certainly couldn't build an addition onto our home to accommodate a free hot tub. That would kind of negate the "free" part. So a major renovation was out of the question.

Hick never met a bargain he didn't like. And there's no better bargain than free. One of his colleagues had just sold a house, and offered to give away several items rather than pay to have them hauled off. He told Hick that he could take a 1991 hot tub that originally cost $3000. According to Hick, it had appreciated to a current worth of $4500. He borrowed a trailer, drove an hour to the city, and brought home his new 1991 hot tub.

The original plan was to install the hot tub behind the house, next to the swimming pool. It would be just outside the basement door, on concrete, with a view of the forest and frolicking woodland creatures. You could easily move from pool to hot tub. As a benefit, in cool weather, the hot tub was only three steps from the heated basement. The back section of our wraparound porch would shade it in the summer, and shield it from rain. It was the perfect solution for a gift hot tub. No renovations necessary.

Our 11-year-old son, Genius, was the first to tip me off regarding the change of plans. "Mom. He's going to put the hot tub *in the garage*."

I readied my case. "Who puts a hot tub in a garage? Where will the car and truck park? I'm sure the cats who live in the rafters, knocking down stored Christmas ornaments, will be pleased to have a roiling cauldron of water under their lair. They have been partial to drinking chlorinated pool water since last summer, but surely they are ready for a hot beverage. I'm certain those flighty felines will donate the hair off their backs for the privilege of living over a hot tub. Let's not forget that the garage reaches temperatures over 120 degrees Fahrenheit in the summer. Just what you need for hot-tub-sitting. Perhaps we can call it the Boiling the Flesh Off Your Bones Tub. And what about that view? To the left, two brown metal garage doors. To the right, three wooden shelves stacked with items we never plan to use again. Straight ahead, a bevy of fishing poles hanging on rusty nails hammered into the 2x4 studs. Above, a plywood patchwork laid down on the rafters, with cat tails twitching to and fro. Ooh, baby! Let's throw us a hot tub party!"

When confronted with my objections, Hick responded to a select few. Cat hair in the hot tub? He planned to build a wall around his free tub. A magical wall that could keep cat hairs from falling from the ceiling. The view? Hick suggested putting in some windows, using that $4500 he had saved by getting the hot tub for free. The temperature? Oh, we wouldn't be using the hot tub in the summer! Only in the winter. When we could don our swimsuits and walk around the porch and across the breezeway and down the steps to the garage, being careful not to skid a flip-flop on the ice, because a garage hot tub would be so much more logical for a soothing soak in the dead of winter than the big triangle bathtub with jets which was already in the master bathroom.

I let my points sink in for a few days. Gradually, Hick decided that he would really rather install the free hot tub behind the house, next to the pool. He set to work on his project.

Genius called me outside later in the week for a quick inspection. The hot tub looked new. It was shiny white inside, with wooden trim on the outside. Hick had already filled it with well water. I had a few questions for Hick.

"Why does it smell like chlorine?"

"I put some bleach in to clean it."

"It looks clean."

"I'm going to drain the water out. I didn't know it had to be level. It's about an inch off."

"This looks good. Better than I thought it would."

Genius agreed. "You can get in, Mom."

"Not now! It's freezing! And you just filled it up."

"I don't mean now. Later. In the summer. You said that you'd never get in it. But now that you think it looks nice, maybe you will."

"I'll think about it. Maybe." I had no reason to doubt that a hot tub had to be level. It was totally like Hick to install something without reading directions. But then I found out Hick's ulterior motive. I heard the free hot tub bubbling the next morning. So I consulted my little spy. "Why did Dad leave the hot tub on last night? I thought he was draining the water so he could level it."

"He's cleaning it, Mom."

"He put bleach in it last night. How clean does it have to be?"

"Well, after he filled it up...when he first turned on the jets...a big wad of black hair shot out of one of the jets. It was bigger than his hand. So then he poured in the bleach."

"Eww! I'm going to be sick! Who took it out?"

"You mean the wad of black hair?"

"Stop saying that! My stomach is churning! Yes! What else would I be talking about?"

"Nobody took out the big wad of black hair. It sucked back in. Dad said he'd let the filter take care of it."

"Eww! I'm going to vomit! My mouth is getting all watery. The filter didn't take care of it in those ten years the other people had it! I'm never getting in!"

"*Mom!* It's *just* hair!"

To this day, I have never dipped a dainty tootsie in the Free Hairwad Hot Tub. Hick and the boys soak in it. Hick even hot-tubs in the winter. He has made no mention of the wad of black hair. I figure that if it shot out of a jet again, and he disposed of it, Hick would brag like a successful big-game hunter on safari. Though he *would* stop short of taking a picture of himself standing with his foot on the hair wad, or nailing it above the fireplace.

Every time he parades through the house on the basement passage to his hot tub, I remind Hick that he *could* be mounting an expedition to Outer Garagia. Funny how he does not respond. I think I won this one. I rest my case.

BLOWN AWAY

Let the Breather Beware
Kathryn Cureton

Saturday morning, I awoke to find my husband, Hick, with his head buried under the quilt my grandma stitched for our marriage bed. That explained the reason my feet were hanging out. Though my feet were quiltless, I did have a plethora of yardage at the other end with which to make myself a burqa, a turban, a cowl-neck sweater, a comfy shawl, an executioner's hood, a poncho, a surgical drape suited for stitching a large facial gash, and a snood.

I pulled back the quilt and exposed the giant noggin of Hick. He sputtered and twitched and blinked like a mole dug up by hounds in the front yard. "What are you doing?" I think that's what he said. He sounded like Charlie Brown's teacher, what with that clear muzzle of his breather strapped across his nose and mouth. Some folks call it a CPAP machine. I call it a breather.

"You need to keep your head out so you can get oxygen." I left him there breathing, and went about my Saturday morning chores. When I came back to get towels from the bathroom, there was Hick, again buried under the quilt. I rescued him once more. Criminy! I was responsible for him, having saved his life already the first time. Hick mouthed me in his muffled way, and flopped over so as not to gaze upon his life-saver. I left for the laundry room to throw in the towels. You can expose Hick to oxygen, but you can't make him breathe.

I was joined by Hick a half-hour later while folding socks, underwear, and washcloths in the living room. He commenced a lecture on the finer points of breather operation. How it was a pressurized system. That oxygen was forced into his orifices through that mask, no matter what conditions were around his head. Hick copped a little attitude about my double-rescue.

"You should have left me alone. I cover my head with the quilt all the time. I'm fine. The oxygen comes from that little machine. It gets pumped through the hose and into my mask. Don't you have any concept of what a pressurized system is all about? You should.

You're a science teacher! It doesn't matter what's on the outside of my head, because the oxygen doesn't come from there. It comes from my machine."

"Well...how does your carbon dioxide get out of your mask? Can you take that pressurized system with you anywhere and still get your precious oxygen? Because you might as well be the first man to go deep-sea diving with a CPAP mask! Or maybe you could do a spacewalk from the International Space Station to tout the oxygen-pumping capabilities of that unbelievably efficient CPAP muzzle!"

Furthermore, to save my science-teachery reputation, I inquired as to whether Hick understood the concept of soup being a liquid, an entity that should not be piled to three times the height of the soup bowl, as Hick had done the previous week when he dipped up an entire arm roast into his bowl from the pot of vegetable beef soup.

To which Hick replied, "Depends on how solid the liquid is." I think, perhaps, his brain's lack of oxygen was starting to show.

I suppose I should relax and enjoy those times when Hick buries his head like an ostrich under the sand, turning her eggs in the nest. Once, he returned from a business trip to the east coast and brought us a little surprise, a sickness that started with fever and progressed to weakness, snuffling, whining, and coughing up chunks of vital lung tissue. I really hoped it wasn't Captain Trips, because I didn't feel like walking all the way to Denver, and I had not been dreaming of a little grammy-lady rocking on her front porch in Nebraska.

I did not want to be infected by the pandemic Hick was spreading across the country. During daylight hours, I vigorously avoided Typhoid Mary, Patient Zero, and The Original Swine Flu Boy all rolled into one, in the persona of Hick. I avoided bedtime like a sticky toddler all hopped up on birthday cake and Mountain Dew. When I forced myself to retire at 2:15 a.m., I could not fall asleep. Hick immediately rolled over and spewed his breather breath across my neck, over my right ear, and past my face. My face, with its attached nose and throat! Prime pathways for pathogens to follow while I snoozed the snooze of the unconscious. I tried to hold my breath, but I am not some freakish sort of David Blaine creature who can be buried in a coffin of water for days at a time without need of oxygen. Alas. I breathed. I became infected. I eventually recovered.

Some nights, I long for the simpler times. The times when Hick was dying every 30 seconds due to the cessation of his breathing. The days before the CPAP, when the only crimp in my right to the pursuit of sleep, restedness, and the pursuit of oxygen was Hick's leg thump. He would raise and slam a leg to the mattress like a referee pounding the canvas to count out the losing boxer in a heavyweight title match. This action flung me up and down like a jolly good fellow in a blanket toss. It was not conducive to sleep, yet it did not wreak havoc with my rest as much as Hick's antics once his breather was introduced to the marital bed.

With added oxygen through the night, Hick had excess energy to burn while sleeping. I suffered the stab of his raptor-talon toenail to my unsuspecting lower leg. That thing was like a crampon used by climbers on Everest to traverse a vertical ice face. I'm shocked that the sheets weren't shredded from the surgical sharpness of its edge. It could have sliced specimens of tissue thin enough for microscopic inspection in a forensics lab. My leg felt like maybe it did.

When resting his raptor-toenail, Hick used that excess oxygen for a workout involving his left elbow. No sooner had I plopped myself onto my side of the bed than I was stabbed in the back by the proximal end of Hick's ulna. It poked the space between my scapulae. (That's how I described the incident to Hick later, since he was so keen on throwing my profession back at me). Of course, I squirmed to get away, but it followed me, that pointy implement of torture.

I felt like a chunk of beef skewered by a kabob. A maraschino cherry pierced by a plastic sword. A cocktail weenie stabbed by a festive red-cellophane-frilled toothpick. Like a cube of day-old bread impaled by a fondue fork. Like a whale harpooned by a…well…a harpoon.

Hick refused to admit that his bony protuberance was in contact with my thinly-padded spinal column. He then moved the offending appendage, rammed it under my pillow stack, and denied that it was there.

"My arm is *not* under your pillows. Your pillows are on my arm." There was only one way to counter Hick's argumentative logic.

"Duh. I *know* my pillows are on your arm. So why did you put your arm *under* my pillows?"

Hick snorted and removed the intruding limb. The worst part, the salt ground into my inter-scapular wound, was that when Hick got up the next morning, he came back to bed and told me to wake him in an hour. He was going in to work late, because he was tired.

It's not like I want to deny Hick his life-giving oxygen. Sure, I might have contemplated putting a kink in his hose. But I'm pretty sure that is frowned upon by both law enforcement and the judicial system. Besides, I don't really need to resort to such extremes when a simple pillow over his face leaves less evidence. Especially when Hick insists on burying himself under the quilt of his own accord.

For now, I am not actively seeking to pull the plug on Hick's breather. I have resigned myself to nights of Hick's breath blasting the back of my head like winds sweeping down the plain in Oklahoma, while I envision his exhalations arching over my side of the bed like the red, white, and blue sprays of water from a fireboat over New York Harbor on the Fourth of July.

I have, however, decided to stop taking the quilt off Hick's head on Saturday mornings. Let the breather beware.

Leap Before You Look
Cathi LaMarche

"A zip line?" I asked. Unsettled, I stared at the brochure.

My husband flipped to the photos of people hanging from a cable over the Smoky Mountains' vast canopy. "Ever see such a view?" Michael asked.

"Look how far they are above the trees," our son Holden said.

Piper, our daughter, pointed to the brochure. "You can zip up to fifty miles per hour."

"You're really not helping your cause," I warned them.

Michael squeezed my shoulder. "It'll be exhilarating. You'll love it. Besides, you went whitewater rafting last year and survived. You even enjoyed it."

"Yeah, but the river wasn't . . ."

"Wasn't what?"

"Dangerous."

There. I said it. The "D" word.

"Wait," Michael said. "So the raging, level-four rapids with jagged rocks, hidden snags, and tumultuous waterfalls weren't dangerous?"

"Not really."

Holden sighed. "That's not what you said last year, Mom. Remember how you swore that we'd all be flung out of the raft into a watery grave?"

Piper tapped his arm. "Don't forget her reference to Davy Jones's Locker."

My argument against the zip line was flailing, much like I'd be if strung on a cable hundreds of feet off the ground. To strike some sensibility into my family, I blurted the unmentionable. "What if the cable breaks?"

Michael laughed. "Then we die."

Piper flashed the thumbs up. "Awesome."

"Instead of sitting here worrying, Mom," Holden suggested, "why don't you come with us? That way, we'll all die together."

Somehow that trumped being stranded alone in the cabin for the rest of the week, eventually forced to navigate down the mountainside to return home.

Once at the zip line company, we signed numerous liability waivers, which granted them immunity from our reckless abandon before we donned our harnesses, pulleys, carabiners, daisy chains, and helmets. When the professionals stepped away, I tugged at the children's straps to ensure they were tight.

Piper swatted my hands. "Would you stop, Mom? We're fine."

Holden said, "How do you know that you didn't just do something to my harness that would cause me to plummet to my death?"

I hadn't considered that possibility. "Do you think I should have them recheck it?"

He laughed. "Mom, I'm joking. Relax."

How could they all be so calm?

The company appointed two guides to assist us, and we headed over to the four-wheeler that would deliver us to the first of nine zip platforms.

"Once you reach the first platform, your feet won't touch the ground for two and a half hours," the driver said.

The kids cheered and sang "Dead Man's Party" as we snaked up the mountainside, while I clutched the handrail as the four-wheeler slid across the gravel road at every turn. The darting in and out of large ruts jostled my insides.

After the guides double-checked our safety harnesses, we circled up for instructions. Our guide Dave demonstrated how to ball up by leaning backwards and drawing his knees to his chest. "This will make you go faster on the zip line."

I raised my hand. "And why would I want to do that?"

Dave explained that people end up stranded on the line if they lose their momentum.

"And then what?" I asked.

"Then I have to go fishing."

"Fishing?"

He held up a bag attached to a long rope. "I throw this bag out to you and reel you in."

I nodded.

"That's assuming you catch it."

"And . . . if I don't?"

"Then I come out on the cable to retrieve you."

"Well, that would be embarrassing," I admitted.

Dave said, "That's why it's called the 'bag o' shame.'"

Holden laughed. "Let the teasing commence."

Mental note—balling up could be a good thing.

"Now, when you need to slow down, you'll need to starfish."
Dave leaned forward and splayed his arms and legs to resemble the
sea creature. "So, remember, I'll give you the signal to ball up or
starfish if needed."

I worried that I might accidentally ball up when I needed to
starfish. Dave explained that I'd either slam into a tree or knock
people off the platform like a human bowling ball.

My gaze scanned my family. "Do I get to choose which one?"

"Seriously?" Piper asked.

"Thanks, Mom," Holden said.

"Karma," I suggested crossing over the treetops toward our
first platform. I looked down from the swaying bridge and vowed
never to do that again.

Dave reminded us to watch for his signals on the receiving end
of the line. Then he leaped into the sky. The cable hummed as he
rocketed across the mountaintop. Cory, our second guide, waited
for the go-ahead from Dave to send us, one by one. Amazed, I
watched Holden, then Piper, drop over the ledge without hesitation.
Where did they get such courage? I wondered. Michael reminded
me by plunging off the platform, laughing while he twirled in circles.

Cory hooked my trolley to the cable, and my pulse quickened.

"Do people ever chicken out?" I asked, my chest tightening.

"Sure."

"What happens if you do?"

"You go sit in the barn for two and a half hours while
everyone in your party makes fun of you. But, you're not going to
do that."

I looked to the sea of green below and tried to jump—twice—
but my legs remained planted. Why couldn't I take the leap of faith

like the others? I looked at my family, who waved to welcome me to the other side. Slowly, courage overpowered fear. Closing my eyes, I stepped off the platform and fell into the open sky. The rush of the wind and the weightlessness as I sailed delighted my senses. Eventually, I opened my eyes to behold the forested, rolling hills. Soon, zip after zip, I sprung off the platform and into the majestic mountain air. Without hesitation. Without worry. Without fear.

When we reached zip line number eight, called Pirates' Plank, Dave instructed us to sprint down the runway before leaping, or we wouldn't gain enough speed to cross. "You might want to shout something as you jump. It's more fun that way." And off he zipped.

"I must go back to my home planet. My people need me," Holden shouted before zooming across the expanse.

"For Narnia!" came Piper's voice before she faded into the distance.

Michael chose "You've got to ask yourself one question: Do I feel lucky? Well, do ya, punk?" as his parting words.

As for me, "Cowabunga" seemed fitting.

The last two zips provided the opportunity to travel upside down and hands-free, and the end of the course brought a forty-foot rope drop, straight to the ground.

That day, we all learned to C.L.I.M.B. (challenge, learn, inspire, master, believe): the company's motto for overcoming fear and adversity. I admire risk-takers, those unsure if they will succeed or fail, live or die, but they forge ahead nonetheless. Instinctual and courageous, they refuse to fasten themselves to the ordinary and, as a result, experience extraordinary pleasures.

Nowadays, I follow Dave and Cory's lead, and I leap before I look. Then, with eyes wide open, I cherish the view as I soar across the vast horizon into the unknown.

Sleeping with One Wicked Woman
Jay Harden

She was one wicked woman: big, disturbing, fearsome, pregnant with pain, and black in the belly. She inhaled men and kept them alive, while she went about destroying—in an absolute way—other different men not to her liking. My wicked woman, the very embodiment of hell's unholy hatchet, loved me, not them. It did not matter that she had wrinkled skin, was called "ugly" to her face, and weighed a sinful amount, over 400—thousand pounds, that is. It mattered most that she was the mightiest of her kind, and that she was my mistress to control for a time. We developed a mutual respect, and, I, a strange love for her as we played with life and paid out death, night and day, seven miles high above the jungle green of Southeast Asia. I need to tell our story and honor my love for bringing me home safe again and again.

War is, among other things, boring and monotonous much too often—and both are seductions. It is glorious only to those writers and pretenders who have not experienced its extreme horror. You would think that boring war is a safe thing, but you would be very wrong. Boring sedates the active mind, especially the minds of the seasoned who take their skill and their aircraft for granted. Statistically, they were the ones more likely to "screw the pooch" and miss the target, putting our ground grunts at risk, or make an unforgiving error that endangers the entire crew. Knowing this, I felt a little smug as a young first lieutenant on my initial combat tour of duty. I was too scared—probably—to screw up. I prayed that if I did screw up, only I would die and no one else would "buy the farm." Such was the mindset of this twenty-four-year-old navigator hoping to beat the random monotony of repeated combat, return home to a pregnant wife, and enjoy my familiar and new human loves.

Every combat mission out of Guam lasted at least ten hours and as many as thirteen, depending on the whimsy of God's Breath: the jet stream. That high west wind could endow us with a ground speed exceeding 500 miles per hour. My mistress was fast enough for me and looked resplendent in the dawn sky, with her wingtips gracing the sky 22 feet above the horizontal and her eight contrails expanding bright, pure power against a graduated azure sky. My wicked woman was well above all inconsequential storms, the star of a serene landscape anchored to the pacific sea by an emerging melon of heated gold. That vision remains fresh in my mind's eye even today, still calling my incongruous affection.

Thorough training at five preparatory flight schools over the previous three years finally brought me over the battlefield below, fighting from inside the bowels of a bomber, the B-52D. We were linked as closely as a mother and child, mutually dependent on each other for survival, glued together by an intense edginess unknown to the rest of the world. I navigated; she responded—on target, on time, every time, sixty-three times in all. And from this inexplicable intimacy of profane purpose came a new kind of love from my hardening heart, a grimy, metallic gratitude for giving me oxygen and saving our boys below by killing the enemy, not me, after those bastards tried everything they could to bring about our mutual tumbledown from the dome of the world.

Along with the transcendent beauty of flight, I found a supreme contrast in war, too. The relentless demand for perfection to accomplish each mission and avoid being killed was simply wearing out my body and mind.

We were droning eastward at 40,000 feet on a single heading back to "The Rock," after another exhausting and thrilling combat run. There was little that I needed to do between the necessary celestial fixes every half hour, except to ignore my stress from compulsive wondering about what surprises might turn the mission into a nightmare. On this particular mission, I was leading a wave of six B-52s. I set the course and the rest followed, each 6,000 feet in trail behind the other, stacked up every 1,000 feet. All was well, so I unstrapped from my ejection seat and felt palpable relief from the heavy parachute I had shouldered for eight hours, so far. The pain increased every time I bent forward, as I must, to coordinate the dance of my minions: aeronautical chart, dividers, protractor, pencil, sextant computations, and trusty E-6B circular slide rule.

Craving different stimulation to stay alert, I left these tools of my trade undisturbed for a short time and climbed up to the forward cockpit. My oxygen mask was hanging on the side of my brain bucket, now a veteran with numerous scars and chips, smelling of dry oxygen and vague petroleum, my small, reassuring combat comforts. That weight imbalance strained my neck and ground into me yet another headache.

I am exhausted and yearn for sleep, but I cannot yield to such seductions because I am the navigator. Navigators never sleep; there is no checklist for it, and there is a checklist for everything. Never rely on your memory alone; always use the checklist. Rely on memory, rely on the comfort of experience, and you eventually screw up. Too many before me have done that, and I am determined to learn by their example. Fear of failing is my great and constant motivator.

The co-pilot in the right seat is asleep. Bob has just redistributed the fuel so we keep our center of gravity in the thin air outside that manages to support our 200-ton airplane anyway, an act of pure magic, when I have the luxury to think about it. He has the periodic but delicate job to coordinate twelve separate tanks as one balanced flow to eight ravenous engines. Done incorrectly, he will starve them; we will flame out and go down like a lost, lonesome rock. No one will see or hear our splash in the vast, dark deep. It has happened before to others. Bob is a captain, and I respect his high competence. I also envy his snooze.

The Aircraft Commander to the left has set the autopilot to fly my heading and barometric altitude, so he has nothing to do but monitor the radios with one ear awake as he, too, sleeps.

I know the electronic warfare officer is zonked out, hidden behind his wall of Top Secret transmitters and jammers. No one ever bothers him, and there is no missile threat homeward bound.

Likewise, our gunner has nothing to shoot. God only knows what happens back there 156 feet from the nose. We see him button up before takeoff, and see him next after full stop and chocks. He commands his own world and cannot be reached except in an emergency by the navigator crawling on a narrow catwalk through the unpressurized bomb bay, dragging his parachute and oxygen behind. "Guns" does not strap into an ejection seat like the officers. If he needs to punch out, he pulls down on a massive lever and the entire tail assembly of four 50-caliber guns falls off, leaving his feet hanging over the edge of eternity. The design is elegant and idiot-proof, not that "Guns" is an idiot; no gunners are. He simply rolls forward and out of the airplane, pulls his green apple for 10 minutes' worth of suckable oxygen, and, like the rest of us, expects a good chute from the Commander-In-Chief of the World. His unique seat is hinged so, at other times, he can stretch out to dampen the yaw and pitch of the tail. In other words, the only enlisted member of the crew is privileged with a recliner! Hell yes, he is asleep!

As my tired mind drifts back to the moment, I look upwards from the cockpit and see what few are blessed to behold, a vista more majestic than the Muir redwoods, more breathtaking than a clear day at the Grand Canyon. I am befuddled, struck senseless by this expanse of simple, incomprehensible beauty. At our altitude, the stars never flicker, never disappear, even in daylight. Each of them is a nano crystal of pure light, subtle size, and nuanced color. The eleven frames of the windscreen that keep me from reaching out, dissolve away in respect. The background night is the deepest and darkest and friendliest blue-black, somehow vibrant like the gentle, rumbling skin of a marvelous celestial drum. But the speechless part, the humbling part, is the endlessness of innumerable stars, their scattering so elegant, so random, it goes beyond any human masterpiece of art. My eyes cannot drink in all that glory, so my brain quits in stillness, my jaw falls open, and my heart tries to join that harmony. In this instant of my warring destruction, I feel protected by the innocence of heaven.

I can fathom the beauty of a woman, but not this, a beauty I cannot comprehend, a beauty forever engraved on my memory, a personal gift from my wicked woman. My heart and brain agree that this profound experience cannot be, must not be, the result of an indifferent universe. I am a latter-day Columbus suspended in time on the edge of all other worlds.

Too soon, the insistent demands of duty return me to the prosaic present of combat flying. I descend back to my position and strap in again with my mind in a clearer, softer place.

The bombardier to my left is asleep, too. His radarscope is blank like mine. There is no land to reflect a radar beam in any direction for hundreds of miles, only a transient, worthless blip every now and then from a ship at sea.

And then, against my own screaming iron will, I drift into and out of sleep, and succumb, in time, to that temptation more delicious than chocolate. No one but me knows that we are all asleep on duty, that we are all depending on my wicked woman for our sole survival, and I only realize this when I waken.

Consider the view below from God's eye above us. The entire crew on the lead B-52 is asleep. Eight unsupervised jet engines are blazing one throated chorus. We six are sealed inside an aluminum tube sweeping along in a bitter, cold, and icy wind not made for man, depending on a decade-old machine to feed us air and keep us warm. Five other BUFs follow us like mules down a trail, and I wonder: are they all asleep, too, as our wave leaves 48 expanding white streaks against the dark night? Is this snapshot ludicrous, a case of cosmic incredibility, or is it just comical, another of the unbelievable follies of war?

I can tell you this: if I had been caught sleeping, I could have been court-martialed for flagrant dereliction of duty, conduct unbecoming, and who knows what else: justifiably, too. I have no excuse for my actions, only this written confession past the statute of limitations. But my wicked woman saw my frailty as I slept with her, restrained her wrath, and forgave me. Because of our mutual affection, she took care of my crew and me when I failed to do it myself. The poets and I call that experience love. My lover was one wicked woman by design; it is true. She smelled, sounded, looked, and felt as no other lover I have ever known, and I owe my life to her.

In spite of one night of careless sleeping with my war mistress, she did not judge my youthful inadequacy. Mighty and ugly and deadly though she was, my wicked woman returned the loyalty to me that I gave her, and for that reason, I believe she let me live to tell the true story of our affair, kept intense and fresh by 45 years of memories and her silent, earned presence in a museum, forever kept from harm.

Internal Clocks
Larry Duerbeck

Our youngest Pembroke Welsh Corgi wanted out. Out of the crate, out of the family room, out of the house. Lillian wanted out, I wanted Lillian out. Sort of.

Her front feet thrummed the metal lattice of her crate door.

She wasn't shifting to get comfy. But maybe . . . Maybe she was . . . I turned over on the couch and snuggled into sleep-soaked hope.

Stage-two alarm.

Her high nasal demand reaffirmed what I snuggled away from, from what she already told me. On the living room's leather couch, I rolled over and sat up. I always thought of her whine as hypersonic and that it could be harnessed to good purpose, such as peeling off old paint. Her ego could drill into diamonds. She keened Ree-lease Mee-EEE!

3:15. She peeled me off the couch, to sleepwalk through doing just that. At the family room I turned on a light, the soft one above the three J. Bauer portraits of our early great German Shepherds. All five Pems bedded down here, in the family room.

Yep. Lillian, possessed of show-ring-high energy. Sometimes she needed a true "relief" run in the night; other times I believed she wanted to burn off some of that energy.

Lillian's crate stood across the room and down the line of four, farthest to my right. The tile floor sent up cold through my socks, the sleep of sleepwalking scampered away. So happy was Lillian to see me, she vibrated. The other four, all adult females, lay on their sides. Inert, or nearly so, they lifted eyelids in tacit thanks.

Opened the crate. Let Lillian out. Closed the crate. Lillian had already grown bigger than her mother, Lucy, lying becalmed in the next crate to my left. God made Lucy cute, compact and utterly laid-back at all times.

I followed Lillian's lead past the Corgis to the sliding glass doors that gave onto the big, fenced-in backyard, lined with long pens for the Shepherds. I slid the door open. *Wham*!

Torpedos los! A two-footed impact slammed into my right thigh. Lillian's thank-you and farewell. Sleep sank like the Lusitania. I'd salvage it soon. Now I leaned out. The night air smelt dark and dull, as from a matte-black palette.

I closed the door. The Shepherds in their outside pens were used to her untimely excursions—nary a bark.

Left the soft light on. Back to the couch. Set the internal clock for fifteen minutes.

The alarm worked. Into the family room and . . . The air told me. Bigger fish had been fried, old rotten fish in bad oil. That would have been better.

Some one of the Corgis had pooped in her crate. 3:35 and sleep retreated far away. I flipped on the big lights. The ribbons and trophies and plaques showed watery in the clinging, clear miasma. Even our newest, Lillian's Best In Match rosette atop her Vari Kennel, wavered in my sight.

A quick scan revealed all the Corgis down, Lillian's row still inert. Hmm . . . First things in proper order. I slid open the glass door. Lillian, happy after her amble, quickstepped to her crate. Circumstances rendered the night air light and bright, sparkly as champagne.

I closed the door and put up an impatient Lillian.

No bloodhounds needed to track down which crate, and it didn't take Sherlock Holmes to name the Corgi that didn't bark in the night. Here was the crate, across the room. One of two beautiful wooden crates, each big enough for any German Shepherd. The crate held Gigi. Her sister, Ginger, slept down the row, farthest from Lillian and in the wooden twin.

Ginger's crate faced Gigi's head-on, but Ginger didn't face Gigi.

Ginger was curled around and quiet, with a paw over her nose.

After telling her to stay, I opened Gigi's crate. Oh, dear. A brown lake, generally the shape and seemingly the size of Ohio, lay before me on her snuggly-wuggly, white woolly mat. Deep in the back lay Gigi, all eyes and those eyes unblinking.

"Come on out, Geej," I encouraged, over a silent prayer. Gigi tippypawed her way out, holding to my left and her right, answering my prayer. She kept herself studiously clean. Over to the door, slide, out. I left the door open, to call soft laudatory adjectives in her wake. Pristine being, incorrectly, but happily, the crown jewel.

"Pristine Gigi," I finished, sotto voce. A couple of Shepherds woofed, disgruntled. I shoved the door wide open, took a deep breath of sweet night air, called out "Quiet," took another breath and made for the mat.

I bent to the task. Two corners, two hands to slide the mat out.

Four corners, two hands. Careful! Gigi's steamy pool exuded permeating strength. At six feet, its effect was as bad as at two feet. But closer yet? I feared lesions on lung walls, the searing of sinus linings.

I shuffled to the sliding door, holding my breath and thinking of gyroscopes. Got it safely out and on the back yard grass. Idiot! I had walked out, still in my stocking feet. Quite the wee hours waker-upper, that dewy grass was.

The least of my worries.

Back inside, I rocked on an absorbent sort of welcome mat, charting my course. Gigi's whereabouts unknown, I closed the glass door and chuckled. She was one of the few Pems I've met with a sense of shame. Hence, the crate-bound silence. Her fine-as-furniture edifice featured an off-white Formica floor. Distant and quick inspection revealed telltale smears. These would be easy.

With a batch of small towels and two spray bottles, the cleanup took just a couple of minutes, including trips to the washing machine.

"There!" I announced. With a final flourish of dog towel over sheen of Febreze, I dried the crate floor. The towel went in the washer. I poured a shot of soap for the soak cycle and twisted the proper knob. *Chug—chug—chug.*

Let's see. I stood straight up, to check items off experience's itinerary. Then, I double-checked the immediate future. To the kitchen sink. Washed my hands. *Mens sana* and all that rot. *Chug—chug—chug.*

Back in the family room, I put the spray bottles back. *Chug—chug—chug.* Let in Gigi. Quickly in her crate, the short-legged embodiment of gratitude. *Chug—chug—chug. Pat—pat—pat.* Pushed the gate to; pressed the latches down, upper and lower.

I slid the glass door closed on ethereally woodsy night air, better far than Febreze. Shut the washer. Let everything soak. Turned all the lights off. Back to the couch. 3:50.

A short while later. A steady *chug—chug—chug* stole in low, to reassure my ears. "Good old wash machine," I thought fuzzily. "Good old wash machine." Even the words were vague. Good old wash. Words brightened, gained edges, serifs, a certain glow. Italics. And changed.

<u>Shut</u> <u>the</u> <u>washer</u>!

The repeating sounds grew more distinct, too. *Churk—churk—churk.*

Back on my feet. Hurry was contraindicated. *Chork—chork—chork.* Unless I wanted a string of dog vomit, to the door. Better a pool, or the great blessing of not being too late. I stepped into my kennel boots, standing at (ha ha) the foot of the couch, and approached.

"*Chork—chork—BLOARK! Kaff!*"

Too late. I held back. Let her finish up. "*Bluorff!*" Muffled this time.

There. I snapped on the big lights. Lillian, I saw, resented her rest's interruption. The others lay, curled in a way that told me they were being stoic.

Gigi, again. I opened the crate's door and thought of Maine hunting shoes. The pool to the left matched that brown rubber. The pool to the right came close to the leather's color.

Combined smell was humid, heavy and profoundly untoward. Deep in the crate, all eyes but blinking this time, lay Gigi. Not liking my choices, I encouraged, "Come on out, Gigi girl!"

I stood away. Gigi must have gathered herself and taken a canny Corgi's aim. For she sprang over and past every noxious drop, skidded on the tile, stood to flap her ears. Then, wiggle-wagging her butt, she made for the sliding door, just as jaunty as Pepe Le Pew. I was happy to be her doorman, aiding her clean getaway into the ambrosial night. I closed the door slowly. Now, the vomit. I knew, and of old, what to do. I juzz diddin' wanna!

But, I fetched a large towel, a bath towel for the Shepherds, and some more small ones. These would go, soon enough, on their big brother which I now spread out on the floor to abut against the front
of the crate.

First, though, I got up from my knees. I went in the kitchen and mixed a rum and diet Coke. A bit of a bracer for the task ahead.

4:15 and counting. I took a good sip, rolled it around in my mouth, swallowed, and left the rest as a reward. After the vomit.

Before the vomit, I walked out in the back yard, there to lead Gigi up into the special elevated pen. The long wooden enclosure had a semi-separate bed box in the back. Now the vomit. I smiled in the dark at Gigi, already abed. To the vomit.

Soupy, goopy gobbets and globs in mucoid loops and spools. Slimy, sliding strands with viscid, slithering filigrees of food and phlegm to meet, maneuver and mop up.

As from sulphur pits, disturbance rolled acid gas up in waves to caress my eyes. No wonder poor Gigi was blinking SOS's like a semaphore into the night.

The work proved dispiriting and disgusting. So much so I feared—that's the right word—I feared the effects would get the better of me. Outwitted and overwhelmed by dog spew.

But I prevailed! *Spritz, spritz* and last swipes of a fresh, small towel, the last towel on the pile. Bundle them all in the big one and to the washer. I drizzled in more detergent, set the machine for "Large Load," and started the "Ultra Clean" cycle.

Ultra clean. Damn right.

Washed my hands again. Got my reward, shut the lights down and headed for the couch. There, I turned the switch of an end-table light. Turned it on.

Then I picked up an old British mystery and enjoyed both bracer and book. Ran into fine old words I didn't know.
"Temerarious" and *"perscrutation"* and *"manciple."*

Both enjoyments barely begun, I put them aside. Set my internal alarm clock fifteen minutes earlier than usual, come the dawn. I snuggled into Technicolor dreams of Corgis skipping around and jumping over pools of stinking, steaming quicksand. Laughing, one and all, all of us.

5:45. I sleepwalked through pushing the button for coffee.

6:00. Kennel boots. Coffee. I poured Kahlua and rum into my Cardinal mug, stuck in a cinnamon stick, and filled it. Filled it a little short with the hot stuff. Because, what the hell. I went to the fridge for the aerosol can of whipped cream.

I was celebrating a joyous morn, and, loving cup in hand, I strolled to the elevated pen. Out with Gigi. She frolicked over the dewy grass, full of herself and more. Gigi had kept the long wooden pen immaculate.

No sign of it now, with her. Hell, Corgis have their own clocks, too. I raised my cup.

The first sip tasted great, a comfort warm and sweet and strong.

A fine metaphor, I thought, for Gigi. I looked a ways off at the fouled mat on the grass, at the last clue left. The first happy evidence of blessed messes yet to come.

I smiled and breathed in the spring morning air, cool and clean.

It smelt of nothing but fresh starts. Cup aloft, I offered a toast. "To morning sickness, Gigi!"

The English Teacher's Projectile
Gordon Smith

Fall was just getting started. They were preparing for the first football game of the year. The small school in the small town was not expected to win many conflicts this year. The last three years yielded records of 2–8, 3–7 and 5–6. But as always, they were ready to start over, to try to pull the proverbial rabbit out of the hat. Hope springs eternal in the coach's heart. As he and his staff looked around at his meager squad, however, he knew that it would take a major miracle for them to see daylight this year. The town needed wins. The Chamber of Commerce needed good publicity. It's amazing how the spirit of a town depends on its athletic teams. Everybody was ready to be happy and prosperous.

What they were not ready for was murder.

At the Thursday afternoon pep rally in the gym, the principal decided on a new approach. The band played every fight song they had in their repertoire. The cheerleaders jumped and pranced and were in their best form. Then, Mr. Wilson called upon the oldest faculty member to give a "rah rah" talk. After the tears subsided, he called for Mr. Brasington, a transplant from England who was the newest and youngest teacher, in the Chemistry-Physics department. Something old, something new. . . .

The students had always laughed about Mr. Brasington's accent and some of his expressions, but they really liked him. At least, most did. To say that he had no enemies remained to be seen. He forgot sometimes and fell back on such expressions as "brolly" for umbrella, or "biscuit" for cookie, "napkin" for diaper, or "projectile" for bullet. He even mispronounced "laboratory." He graded hard, and expected much.

After the first grading period this year, some senior students (notably football players) had received failing marks. One star football player was ineligible to play in the next game, making him extremely unhappy and his coach even more desperate than he had been. As someone put it, both looked angry enough to kill.

More than one irate parent had been to the school to complain about him, saying that he expected too much. Typical: "Why should my daughter need to know Celsius from Fahrenheit? All she wants is to graduate in May and get married."

Threats from two men who objected to his snide remarks about the American Revolution were actually reported to the school office.

At the rally, the principal called his name, and he did not stand. Everybody looked around. He did not seem to be present, but the principal knew that he had been there all day. So, he called on Miss Johnson, who said, "I hope we get a lot of runs!" causing the kids to snicker.

As soon as the bell closed the assembly and sent kids to their lockers and buses, the principal went straight to the science lab, thinking that perhaps Mr. Brasington had been delayed by having to counsel with a student or parent. Surely, he would not deliberately miss a school function without some good excuse.

Room lights were on. Walking through the lab, he found the teacher lying behind the large demo table. He detected no signs of life and called 9-1-1. Emergency personnel and police responded, and confirmed that he was dead.

He was lying face down. When an officer rolled him over, he saw a sizable hole in the teacher's forehead, almost directly between the eyes. What blood there was did not flow, but seemed to be almost dried or frozen in place.

Nothing in the room seemed to have been disturbed.

I was chosen to be the main detective. My name is Tom "Dog" Maness, so nicknamed for my tenacity in investigating. I sniff out clues and don't let go easily.

The body had been removed, so I did a thorough search of the room. There had been no apparent struggle. The materials-locker door was slightly ajar, but there were no gaps in the bottle lineup. I had reasoned that possibly a student had needed something to make drugs, and had been interrupted in stealing it. I saw nothing that was seriously out of order.

There was scrap paper on the floor (including a note from a lovesick boy), so it seemed obvious that the janitor had not been there.

Gradually, a picture formed in my brain. It could be that the killer was a parent who knew the day's schedule, waited near the front office as if ready to pick up a student after school, unnoticed in the rush for the gym. The perp could have figured that Mr. Brasington would be the last one out of his room, needing to straighten up a bit and lock the door before proceeding to the pep rally. I had no other immediate ideas.

Having done all that I could there, I headed for the coroner's office. He could give me only a preliminary report, which contained no really new info to add to the initial police findings. Mr. Brasington had apparently been shot at close range, probably as he stood behind the lab table. The wound was slightly larger than the coroner expected, so perhaps it was not caused by an American bullet.

This waved a red flag in my mind: Could this have been a "hit" by someone from the English guy's past, a grudge from the old days? Perhaps someone had been sent to America just for this mission.

But there was more. There was no GSR—gunshot residue that could be found around a wound from a shot fired at close range, as well as on the body itself. And there was a sour odor around the wound.

Still more puzzling was the small amount of blood in and around the wound. Why did it appear dried or frozen? He must have been shot sometime between the last class period and the close of the pep rally, a period of about thirty minutes. Blood does not normally clot completely that fast. The coroner had learned not to say "never."

There was nothing more that he could tell me at this point. So I went back to the school to look for more details.

It appeared that Mr. Brasington had been preparing for the next day's class, hoping to solve some problem, and setting up a demo. On the board behind him, his rambling scribbling was unorganized—such notations as "C+O," "sublimation: changing from solid to gas without becoming liquid," "Cardice," and a couple of formulas.

These notes seemed to have no particular order or usefulness, but I copied them anyway. On the lab table was his grade book, open to the last period. Thinking that perhaps some student on the roll had just learned about a failing grade for this period, perhaps making him ineligible for the game or some club membership, and had lost his cool and killed him, I looked over the roster. I made a note of a couple of failing grades. But as I looked back through the book, there were few other below-average marks in any of the classes. And, on a hunch, I scanned the book for anyone named "Cardice" or anything close to that. Nobody.

The only other item on the table was an empty plastic bottle, probably his drinking water container. So far, I was batting zero. But "Dog" never lets go.

I asked the principal to call a faculty meeting the next day in which I could throw out some questions. After the meeting, every teacher was to go to his or her class and ask if any student had been in the science lab after school the day before. They were to ask this in each class, all day. This was iffy, of course. Would a guilty student give himself or herself away? Would such a student even be in attendance on Friday? But perhaps some reflex, some reaction, even an absence, might be a clue.

A positive result was not long in coming. Mr. Johnson sent word that I should talk to Jim Allison. He readily volunteered that he had been in the lab on Thursday afternoon, just before the pep rally.

I obtained his address from the office and went to call on him and his mother.

He looked innocent enough (can't they all?) and not nervous. Or was he just so good at it that he could fool simple-minded adults? He could have been practicing his act all night, unable to sleep.

His reason for going to the lab was plausible. He was on the newspaper staff. He went to the lab to remind Mr. Brasington that he needed the school's video camera to get some shots at the pep rally, and at the game. "Mr. B" had checked it out from the media center for some unknown reason. Jim had told the teacher earlier that he needed it badly, so when he did not see Mr. Brasington, his heart sank. But as he walked toward the desk, he saw the camera on the lab table. It was running, so he figured that the teacher had been using it and had forgotten to turn it off when he left for the pep rally. He turned it off and took it to the gym. He was to keep it until Monday for some editing of the film.

I took the camera to my office on the chance that it might have picked up something important to my case. I rewound the tape and started it from the beginning. I got both sight and sound. And I found my killer.

Mr. Brasington had set the camera on the lab table, aimed at a central spot on its surface, and started filming.

The picture showed, and recorded the voice of, Mr. Brasington. As he talked, I was able to put the picture together. He was rehearsing his presentation, his experiment to be demonstrated before his classes the next day.

"Class, today we are going to experiment with 'Cardice.' This is the British word for what Americans call 'dry ice.'

"Cardice is frozen carbon dioxide, and it is easily prepared in the lab. In fact, I made a quantity of it today. I'll save the instructions on that phase, the making of it, for our next class. I have here some cardice pellets, a small empty, ordinary drinking water bottle, and a little water. We are demonstrating 'sublimation,' the changing of a solid to a gas without having it go through a liquid stage. I'll put some of the dry ice in the bottle with the water, and then cram a pellet of dry ice into the mouth of the bottle, creating a closed container that will trap the sublimated gas. The water accelerates the rate of sublimation, as well as greatly increasing the amount of pressure that the gas creates. Watch what happens then. Don't be surprised if you detect a sour, zesty odor from the gas."

As the camera watched, nothing seemed to be happening, other than a bubbling of the cardice in the water. Checking his watch, he seemed unsure as to how long the complete sublimation should take, since this apparently was the first time he had performed the experiment. It seemed to be taking a very long time.

Then came his big mistake: He leaned over the bottle, apparently to sniff the air, to be sure that no sour odor was coming from gas escaping around the pellet because he had not sealed it well enough. This would have lowered the pressure.

But he had. The experiment was a great success—or a great failure.

The tremendous pressure ejected the pellet with unbelievable force. The projectile hit him on the forehead. No pistol could have done a better—or worse—job.

The pellet of cardice disappeared, sublimated. All of the gas left the bottle, leaving just a sour odor, after quickly cooling the blood around the wound.

April 29, 1983
Sherry McMurphy

Finally, after a very long week, Friday arrived. To say that I was excited would be an understatement. I lived in Joplin, Missouri, and attended classes at Missouri Southern State College. I lived on campus in a dormitory with my friend, Erin Reilly, and we got along really well, but it was always nice to go home and see my family in Springfield.

By two-thirty, classes were over and I was flying eastbound down Interstate 44. Naturally, plans had already been made with my friends, and I was looking forward to meeting up with them later that night. The day was bright and sunny, and the forecast promised a rain-free evening. Perfect! No muggy weather to make my hair frizzy.

That night at ten minutes after seven, I was in my car zipping through our neighborhood on my way to a friend's house, when suddenly, rain began to fall on my windshield. Initially, I thought, "What the hell?" Then, when the tornado sirens began ominously wailing at an ear-piercing decibel, I thought, "Holy shit." Terrified of storms, I had to fight down the panic rising up inside. The fact that I just drove past my grandparents' house did not even register on my radar.

I had to get home!

Whirling the car around, I drove as fast as I could. The weather, now growing rather wicked, scared the hell out me. Heavy black clouds rolled and twisted across the darkening sky, while the wind howled and thrashed the tree branches in odd directions. I wanted my parents.

As I approached the driveway, my dad opened the garage door so I could pull in. I was told later that I was honking my horn all the way down the street, although I do not remember actually doing it. I ran into the house and was surprised to see my sister's two stepchildren, Carey, age six, and Chad, age four, in the living room.

"Where's Mom?" I asked my dad. It didn't matter that I was eighteen. I was scared and I needed her with me right then.

"Your mother went with Debbie (the neighbor) to Becky's ballet recital," he said.

What! No, Mom needs to be home.

"Put Carey and Chad's shoes on them. I opened the door of the crawl space under the house, should we need it."

"No! No way am I crawling under the house," I cried.

"Sherry, it's the safest place we can go."

"Dad, there's probably spiders and bugs … maybe snakes under the house. No, I'm not going."

My dad just gave me a look as if to say, "We'll see," and went out on the front porch to watch the storm with a neighbor. Most sane people would already be underground with the sirens blaring, but my father took the "watch and see" approach in regards to the storm. Considering the crawl space, I was completely fine with waiting.

Although afraid, I quickly opened several windows. (In those days, that's what you were supposed to do.) After putting Carey and Chad's shoes on, I sat them safely on the couch before timidly joining my dad on the porch. Surprisingly, the kids seemed excited rather than frightened, as if a big adventure was about to happen.

Abruptly, the rain stopped, the atmosphere became oppressive and still, encircling us in an eerie calmness. With panic rising, I turned to run into the house when lightning flashed across the sky, turning darkness into light and …

There it was!

The tornado, a white skinny-rope style, was definitely on the ground, eating up everything in its path. The twisting mass roared like a freight train and was just behind the homes across the street. My dad turned and said, "Let's go," but I was nowhere in sight.

The second I saw the tornado, I raced into the living room, grabbed Carey and Chad, and ran out the back door. I pushed them into the crawl space and was getting in myself before my dad even made it out of the house. Seconds later, he joined us and we clung to each other in fear.

Dad kept assuring us it was going to be fine, but I was absolutely petrified. Not having time to get our dog out of his kennel, I could hear Scout barking and the wind howling outside. I wanted to go back and get him, but Dad said absolutely not. (Terrified or not, I loved our dog.)

The floorboards over our head unmercifully creaked and groaned. Objects shook inside the house, crashed and broke, while the tree in the backyard bent unnaturally close to the ground. All we could do was hold on tight and pray.

After what seemed like an eternity, the roaring sound subsided and the wind finally died down. For the first time, I looked around and squirmed in disgust. Agghh!

"So what happened to 'No way am I getting under the house?'" laughed my dad.

"I didn't even think when I saw the tornado. I just ran."

Once Dad felt it was safe, we crawled out and witnessed the destruction left behind by the powerful twister. I ran to Scout and let him out of his kennel, so thankful he was safe.

Amazed to see our house still standing, we headed inside to take a look around. Posters on my bedroom wall had been ripped off, and household items had been slung around, but our home had defiantly weathered the storm. I was so proud of Carey and Chad, as they had absolutely been brave little soldiers.

The phone began ringing and I ran to answer it. Thank goodness it was Mom, and she, too, had come through safely, having ridden the storm out in the hallway at the ballet. Worried about her parents, Mom planned to go by their house prior to coming home, and we were going to check on Tom and Vicky.

I hung up the phone, and it instantly rang again. My sister Vicky was on the other end of the line asking if we were okay. On shift as a police officer, she relayed her ordeal. While sitting in her police cruiser in a major intersection, the tornado picked her car up several inches from the road, spun it around and dropped it back down. Other than crapping her pants, she was fine, but quickly asked to speak to Dad.

With the phone to his ear, I watched Dad listen intently, and then he turned white as a ghost. My brother Tom, working that night at Dillon's grocery store, could possibly be hurt after the building took a direct hit.

Dad, Carey, Chad and I began walking straight to the store in search of Tom. At the corner of our street, we turned right and froze, completely paralyzed by the sight that lay before our eyes. The neighborhood had been destroyed.

Our family home was built on Guinevere Street, the southern edge of the subdivision. Grandma and Grandpa lived on Morningside, the most northern street. Homes on both streets received minor damage, but the five interior streets were reduced to kindling.

Power lines lay stretched across the pavement, creating arcing sparks. Rooftops were in flames, broken gas lines leaked fumes, people were crying and shouting out in search of loved ones: while the walking wounded, looked around in a daze for help. Streetlights and trees lay everywhere, causing areas to be pitch black.

Utility companies, police, fire and EMS struggled to get into the subdivision, as homeowners rummaged through the debris searching for their pets and trapped or injured neighbors. Personal belongings blew in the wind, as owners tried to collect anything they could salvage. It was like stepping into a complete and utter chaotic war zone.

I looked over at my dad, and I saw tears in his eyes. I knew we were thinking the same thing. Did Tom survive the storm?

It was going to be dangerous maneuvering around, but we had a mission.

Alternating between a brisk walk and running, we followed Dad through the maze on our way to Dillon's. Several times, we were turned back by police, but my dad just found a different way to get around the debris and kept going. There was nothing that was going to stop him from getting to Tom.

The store was approximately a mile away, and we had just passed the halfway mark, when a car flew down the street towards us. It passed us then screeched to a stop. Tom jumped out of the passenger side.

My dad and I ran, grabbing him into a bear hug. As Vicky told us, the store took a direct hit, but we were relieved Tom was okay.

Tom's coworker was bringing him home because power lines had fallen across his car in the parking lot.

Tom walked back to the house with us where we found Mom waiting. We were all relieved to be home together. When I asked about Grandma and Grandpa, she laughed and said they were tough as nails. She had to wake them up when she went to their house. With the storm passed and the power out, they had decided to just go to bed.

Apparently, they heard the tornado sirens and Grandpa opened the front door. The wind blew him backward, and it took the two of them to get the door shut. Mom laughed and said, "The silly fools stood in front of the dining room window watching the storm blow their heavy metal lawn chairs over the fence." She could not believe Grandma and Grandpa had not taken the warning seriously and found shelter.

The wicked weather calmed that night, and thankfully no one ended up in Kansas. The effects of the storm would stay with us in different ways for many years to come. But on that night, all we could do was count our blessings and thank God that He had brought us all through it safely.

A SPARK OF INSPIRATION

A Runaway Burn
Doyle Suit

Dead sage grass stood hip deep in the meadow when Sam waded through the dew-covered stand of brown vegetation on Saturday morning. Each spring, they burned the worthless grass to make way for new growth in the fields. The family had planned the burn for today, but Sam's mother would visit a sick friend and his dad needed to deliver a pair of steers he'd sold.

Sam had recently turned sixteen and lack of confidence wasn't among his list of faults. He caught up with his dad before his red truck pulled away from the barn. "I can burn that meadow this morning. It's locked in with firebreaks and I won't need any help."

His dad frowned and shook his head. "Better wait. We'll do it next Saturday when you're home from school. Fire can get away from you when you least expect it, and you might need a lot of people to stop it."

"But I start baseball practice next Saturday."

The stern farmer pointed to the corner of the corral. "Can't be helped. You can load that manure pile on the wagon while I'm gone."

Sam made a face that expressed his frustration. If he wanted to make the team, he'd need to show up for practice.

When the truck disappeared down the gravel road, he kicked at the dirt. He didn't want to shovel manure, and he didn't want to miss his chance to make the baseball team next Saturday. The weather was cool, and a light breeze flowed down from the rough hills that surrounded their farm. Perfect day for a burn.

He trudged over to the corral to pick up a shovel and throw a few scoops of stinking manure onto the wagon. Minutes later, he decided. Tossing the shovel aside, he made a beeline for the kitchen to gather a pocketful of matches.

"I'll surprise them. If I get that field burned today, I'll be able to make baseball practice next Saturday." He glanced back over his shoulder. "I'll take care of the manure pile later."

Dew covered the tall brown grass, and a faint westerly breeze barely disturbed the cool morning air. The sun climbed the cloudless sky. He sucked in the smell of new grass springing up under cover of the dead sage. All around him, the land was wakening from a winter's sleep. A swampy area to the north and a cultivated field on the south would channel the fire toward a farm road that would serve as a firebreak. From the top of the hill, he examined the sage grass infested field, making sure he hadn't overlooked anything that might spoil his plan.

A partially completed pond intruded into the pasture across the road, and the contractor's bulldozer was parked on the raw earth of the new dam. Closer, a tank of diesel fuel rested on a trailer parked in the dry grass downwind from the firebreak.

Young second-growth pines dotted the rocky ground at the far end of the pasture. He broke off several branches and stacked them by the road to beat out spot fires that might jump the break. Bunched pine needles made an effective tool to smother flames. A barbed wire fence separated their land from a stand of mature trees on the neighbor's property to the east.

Satisfied he had everything under control for a successful burn, he tramped back upwind to start the fire. A handful of dead grass made a torch, and he set a series of small fires along the western edge of the field. The flames fizzled in the wet grass, and he waited a few minutes for the sun and wind to dry it. The light breeze freshened. His second attempt flamed briefly, but it also failed to ignite the damp sage.

Sam persevered and made a bigger torch, while the warm sunshine and rising wind combined to evaporate dew covering the dead grass. This time, the line of fires caught along the western edge of the field and spread downwind.

Both sides of the fire zone held the moving wall of flame in check when he ran along the barriers to make sure the flames didn't escape their intended path. Tongues of fire leaped higher as the burn gathered strength, and a brisk breeze drove it eastward. Heat from the fire dried the tall grass and the flames leaped higher.

Sam raced to the roadway and snatched a few of the branches he'd prepared, standing ready to beat out any spot fires that might cross the barrier. When the fast-moving burn reached the road, flames towered above him, and the smoke cloud enveloped him. He stood coughing, nose burning and eyes stinging, while heat from the inferno forced him to retreat.

Embers, driven by the freshening wind, flew across the road. Small fires sprang up, and he scurried to extinguish them. That worked momentarily, but the line of burning sage stretched a hundred yards, and new fires multiplied faster than he could beat them out. Heat from the approaching wall of fire scorched his skin and threatened to roast him.

The wind-driven flames jumped the narrow road without pausing and spread into the pasture, billowing to twice his height. His firebreak had failed. The violence of the inferno sent chills down his spine. Fear sapped at his strength as he swatted at the spot fires threatening to surround him.

A sudden vision of the trailer filled with diesel fuel resting in the dry sage jolted him into total panic. It stood directly in the path of the runaway burn. Images of the fuel tank engulfed in flames and exploding assaulted him. That rig must cost a fortune, and its loss would be his fault. No time to think about it. He'd have to fight fire with fire.

Retreating to the trailer, he set a semicircle of fire facing the oncoming inferno. He needed a firebreak quick. When the newly kindled fire started to spread, he smothered the newly ignited flames approaching the trailer. The backfire crept slowly upwind toward the impending monster, leaving a burned-over area in front of the diesel tank. Leaping tongues of fire singed hair from his hands and arms as he attempted to protect the trailer and contain the hungry monster.

Smoke-filled breaths came in gasps, and his pulse pounded. Wheezing and coughing from the acrid smoke, Sam flailed at the furious wall of flames. Sweat and tears obscured his vision, and he sensed the wind speed increasing. His puny backfire met the wind driven inferno barely twenty feet from where he struggled to extinguish burning embers that jumped the break. At some point during the battle, he lost the rest of the hair on his arms and parts of his eyebrows.

With scorched earth in its path, the wall of flames dwindled to clumps of smoking embers around the diesel tank. One disaster had been averted. Fire swept past the trailer and roared into the swamp along the north side of the field. Standing water reduced it to isolated flames that quickly died. The southern fork of the blaze encountered sparse vegetation on the rocky ground. Its fury diminished, but it continued to move toward the neighbor's forest. If the fire reached the thick underbrush under the trees, it could devastate the stand of timber. Fighting exhaustion, Sam raced to confront it.

Suddenly, his dad appeared at his side and snapped off a handful of pine branches. Working together, they stopped the fire's spread before it crossed the fence marking the neighbor's property. Another disaster averted. Relief that the runaway burn had been stopped allowed Sam to acknowledge his fatigue. He only wanted to find a place to lie down and rest. Instead, he stumbled through the charred field to examine the ring of scorched earth around the trailer.

His dad commented. "Good job with the backfire."

They walked the perimeter of the burned area and stamped out stubborn patches of hot stubble that could re-ignite the flames. His dad moved slowly, making sure the fire had been extinguished. Sam's knees shook, and he began to notice the pain from burns on his face and arms.

Finally, his dad tipped his hat back and examined the scorched skin beneath his smoke-blackened features. "Don't suppose I need to tell you that starting this job alone was not a good idea?"

Sam's burned face flushed brighter. "No, sir."

They made the short walk back to the house in silence. Sam's whole body ached and the persistent cough wracked his chest and throat. His legs trembled from exhaustion, and his shoulders slumped from embarrassment. He needed a cool bath and ointment for his burns. However, one positive thought penetrated his tired brain.

The backfire had saved him from the runaway burn, and he was definitely smarter than he'd been earlier that morning.

The Lake House Conspiracy

Douglas N. Osgood

Carol.
To not quote of the
famous movie ... the
fat man caught ... and the
and right ... goon. Enjoy.

Does she know? How could she? How does the government know anything? F'ing NSA's listening in on everyone's cell phone. Do they pass information to other agencies? Is that even legal? Did I talk about it on my cell?

John stole a glance at the woman that sat across the desk from him. Furtive. A caged animal looking for escape. Hunched over as she was, John saw the hag from Weird Tales; the contents of the folder she was so absorbed in, her crystal ball, revealed his deepest secrets to her.

How do I play this? Do I throw Vinnie under the bus? But what if she doesn't know?

The vein in his temple throbbed—he was sure she could see its staccato beat. John imagined her counting each pulsation. If she didn't know he hid something before, she would know now.

It felt like hot air blasted from the vent over his head. *Doesn't the government believe in air-conditioning?* A single bead of sweat crawled down his cheek like a fly. He brushed at it, but, like a fly, it came back in another spot. *Why do they keep these rooms so hot? Is that part of their plan? Is she trying to sweat it out of me? Why isn't she perspiring?*

Wait, did she say something?

"I'm sorry, ahh . . ." *What was her name?* John cast a quick look at the desk. Her business cards sat on the corner. *That's it.* ". . . Agent Hechler. What did you say?"

"I asked if this is all of your bank accounts, Mr. Mistretta?"

"Yah, yes. Yes, that's all of them."

"You're sure?"

"Yup, that's it."

"What about your wife? Any others? Safe deposit boxes? Anything?"

"N..no. Just what you got there."

"Hmmm. I see. Okay." She turned the folder to him. "I've highlighted a couple of very large deposits. Seem highly unusual."

The collar of his white oxford soaked through. His tie became a silken noose. John couldn't breathe. *Here it comes. Why did I let Vinnie talk me into this? I'm screwed. Will she go easy on me if I give him up? Oh, what do I do?*

"Can you please explain these? Where did that money come from?"

John took a deep breath, but it caught in his throat. He swallowed hard; it hurt. *What do I say?*

"Mr. Mistretta? Please explain these deposits."

"Yah, about those." He looked the statements over, groping for an explanation. *There, twelve thousand plus deposited in October. I can explain that—maybe she'll accept that for the other.*

"So, yah, expense reimbursement from work. I spent part of August and September visiting clients in Singapore and Hong Kong. Company reimbursed me for flights, meals, hotel, stuff. You know."

"I'm familiar with the concept, Mr. Mistretta. So, you expect me to believe that your company reimbursed you over two hundred thousand dollars for trips you took?"

John tried to laugh, but it came out more a nervous titter.

"No, no. It's just the twelve thousand."

"I see. And the other deposit? The one for two hundred twenty thousand. What is that, Mr. Mistretta?"

John's heart raced, his breathing shallow and rapid. His chest felt like it was in a vice. *Oh, God, am I having a heart attack? If I keel over right now, would this all go away? Damn you, Vinnie. Why did you have to bury a body there?*

"Mr. Mistretta? I'm waiting for an answer." Her voice was even and controlled. "There's an agent right outside that door that can take you to lock-up if you don't want to cooperate." Her index finger pointed at the door behind him, and her eyebrows arched high on her forehead.

John felt Agent Hechler's eyes boring holes into his skull, willing an answer to her inquisition, but she said nothing more. The silence dragged on; it grew oppressive. He looked around him, taking in the room for the first time. *Government puke-green walls. Cripes, can't the government spring for something nicer?* He reached to his collar and pushed his fingers inside, a vain attempt to loosen the tie.

His fingers came away clammy with sweat. *Or were they that way already? Can't they turn on the f'ing A/C?* The room spun.

"C..can I get some water, please?"

"After you tell me about the two hundred twenty thousand, Mr. Mistretta."

"I don't feel so well. Please, Agent Hechler, can I just get some water now?"

"Fine. But then you need to start talking to me."

John hung his head, then nodded once. Defeated.

Agent Hechler walked out her door, closing it behind her. A breath of conditioned air slipped through and kissed the back of John's neck. The kiss of death. Goose pimples raced down his spine.

How do I word this? How much do I say? I have to tell her about the body, about Vinnie. Stupid, stupid, stupid! This is what I get for listening to that asshole. But I wanted to believe him. It all sounded so perfect.

A bottle of water, condensation already thick on the plastic, was thrust in front of his face. He hadn't even heard her come back in. John took the bottle and broke the seal. He drained the bottle in one gulp. Torrents of refreshing relief flooded his parched throat.

"Mr. Mistretta? I'm waiting."

Time to come clean.

"Okay, Agent Hechler, the truth is this. I had this property I inherited fifteen years ago out on Reservoir Lake. My wife and I had been living there for the past couple of years."

"The address on Solitude Lane?"

"Yah, that's the one."

"Nice, what's a place like that worth?"

"When my old man died, we were offered three hundred grand. Almost took it then."

She jotted something on her pad, then nodded. "Go on with your story."

"So, last summer my buddy Vinnie approached . . ."

"Vinnie who?"

"Lodestro, Vinnie Lodestro." She scribbled something on her note pad, then rolled her wrist a couple times, signaling me to continue. "He approached me about selling the place to him. He said he liked how secluded it was—we were the only house on that lane, and we owned all the land around the cove. With all of the trees, it was real private back there." As John got deeper into his story he forgot about his nerves, got more comfortable and just lost himself in the narrative.

Agent Hechler finished writing and looked up. "I get it, very private. When did you move into the place?"

"Four years ago. We were living at our place in town, but the son was out of college and back with us there. So we left him in the house and moved out to the lake."

"Rent?"

"Ha! You're joking, right? I even covered all of the utilities. Too good to flip burgers and no jobs in his degree field." She rolled her wrist again. *Keep going.*

"So, Vinnie offered us half again more than it was worth."

"Lot'a money."

"And things weren't going well at work. Business was way down. We needed cash."

"So you sold the place to this Vinnie Lodestro?"

"Couldn't not. Moved back into our old house and kicked the kid out—we'd gotten used to our privacy, if you know what I mean." John raised his eyebrows a couple of times and laughed. But the laugh sounded forced. Nerves. He'd made a sexual comment to a federal agent. *Was that a crime? Stupid!*

Agent Hechler ignored the remark. She said nothing.

John continued, "That money, the two hundred twenty thousand, that was a down payment. Our deal. Two-twenty a year for three years. Always a cashier's check. One payment each year. See, here's all the paperwork."

Agent Hechler accepted the folder John passed her. She looked over each page. The room was silent as a tomb while she read. John started to sweat again.

She finally looked up. With one hand she removed her glasses and tossed them aside. The clatter when they hit the desk echoed in John's ears like a claxon. He rushed on with his story.

"So, Vinnie . . . he . . . he said I could just deposit the check and not worry about reporting it to anyone. Said it was all taken care of."

"Do you always listen to this Vinnie?" Agent Hechler twisted her mouth around the name as she said it, slurring the word.

"He knows about this stuff, but I wish I hadn't this time."

"But he was right, nothing to report there. Now, about . . ."

"We needed the money. Honest." He rushed, anxious to get his story out before he lost his nerve. "We didn't know what he was going to . . . I mean, how he was going to use it."

"And what did he do with it?"

Sweat beaded on John's forehead. A drop ran into his eye. It stung and he rubbed at it, glad for the momentary distraction. *Here it is. Here's where I sell him out. Oh, God!*

"He b..buried a body on it."

Agent Hechler's eyebrows almost struck her hairline, but she said nothing.

"He just showed up. It was the night before we closed the deal." John hurried on. *Get it all out now. Don't think, just tell.* "My wife and I were spending one last night there. You know, couple'a glasses of wine, romantic . . . well, you get the picture. Up drives Vinnie in his Audi. I don't think he saw us. The place was dark, our car in the garage. A big goon gets out, pulls a shovel from the back seat and starts digging. Vinnie did the same.

"We were scared, so we didn't do anything, just watched. Pretty soon they were done, so the goon pops the trunk. They pull something out wrapped in a tarp. It looked heavy—like a big man. They dumped it in the hole and I saw . . . I saw a hand flop out as they dropped the tarp. Filled the hole back in. Took off. We got dressed and left right after."

John sagged in his chair. Sweat dripped from his brow, from the end of his nose. *There, it's out.* He felt better. Telling the story had been cathartic. *Breathe deep. Just deal with the consequences as they come.*

"Quite a story, Mr. Mistretta. But, I think you have me confused with the FBI. They're across the hall. You're free to go. Stop in and tell that story to the G-men on your way out, if you want. Or don't. This is the IRS, and we only care about unreported income."

Man's Senselessness
Sue Fritz

Patuk woke with a start. Something was wrong. He wasn't sure what, but he could sense the shift. He stood and stretched. Walking to the front of his home, he peeked out. Seeing no imminent danger, he cautiously stepped outside. Glancing around, the Alaskan forest looked normal. The balsam poplars beside him stretched to the sun, just like always. Forest creatures were scurrying about scavenging for food, their normal morning routine. Still, something was different. It made him uneasy.

He didn't like starting his day with this feeling, but there were things to accomplish. First on his list was breakfast. Living out here in the wild wasn't easy. He would have to hunt today for food since his supply had run low. Giving the forest another look, Patuk started on his way. The family was counting on him. He shoved his unease down deep and turned his thoughts to prey. After walking only a few yards, he heard a twig crack behind him. Turning sharply, he saw Unimak close behind him.

"What are you doing, Unimak? You are too young to go hunting with me."

"Mother said I should come. She thinks I will be a great help."

"She does, does she?"

"Yes. She said to listen to you and do exactly what you say."

"Are you able to do that?"

"Yes, father."

"Well, then, make sure you do just that."

Patuk did not want his son with him, not on this day. Not with the unease he was feeling. But there was no arguing with his son's mother. He continued silently. His keen eyes darted back and forth, looking for an easy target. Unimak followed silently. He would make a great hunter someday, Patuk thought.

The pair continued on through the forest. They veered from the path, going deeper into the shrub. As they traveled, Patuk forced himself to focus on the hunt. A deer would be the best prize. The meat would feed the whole family and last for a while. A rabbit or fox would do, but then there would have to be another hunt sooner than he wanted.

"Father," Unimak whispered. " I smell something funny."

Patuk stopped short and turned to face his son. "Hush," he said. "You will scare away the prey."

"But…"

"Now, Unimak."

"Yes, father."

They traveled deeper and deeper into the bush. Patuk noticed that the once sunny sky was now hazy. Funny, he didn't think it was supposed to rain. They had better find something soon. The quicker they found their prey, the quicker they would be back home and Patuk could shake off this feeling of dread. The haze grew thicker as they went. It became harder to see. They were nearing the stream when Patuk first saw the outline of a figure…a deer standing near the water. He looked at Unimak. A silent communication passed between father and son. And then, there was an ear piercing sound as the attack began. Patuk aimed for the throat while Unimak went for a leg. The deer didn't stand a chance. It went down quickly, falling half-in and half-out of the stream. For a split second Patuk was happy. Mission accomplished, and on the first piece of meat they found. But his joy was short lived when the realization of his unease surfaced. Just yards away, he heard a soft crackle. The wind blew and the crackle turned to a roar. The amber color emanating from the trees meant only one thing.

"Unimak, run, there's a fire in the forest."

Unimak struggled to get a grasp on the deer's leg to bring it home with them. Because of his small size, the deer kept slipping from his grip.

"Leave it! We must get back home and warn the others."

"But the deer. We need the food."

"We need to run Unimak, as fast as we can. We must save the family first."

Patuk and Unimak ran through the forest. The haze, which Patuk now realized was smoke, made their journey difficult. It was hard to see which way they needed to go. Several times they had to turn and retrace their steps to get back on the path to home. After a while, Unimak began coughing from the smoke and the exertion from running at high speed.

"Father," he gasped. "I can't breathe. Go on without me. Save the others."

"No," said Patuk. He picked his son up and continued running. The fire seemed to chase them as they went. The once silent forest was now full of the rush of panicked animals and the rumble of the fire. The blaze was spreading quickly. Patuk wasn't sure he was going to make it home. Maybe they should have stayed by the stream. The water would have kept them safe from the fire, but the smoke would surely have gotten them. Besides, they had to make sure the others got out. His legs were aching from the extra weight of his son. He loped on, barely staying ahead of the fire. As they neared home, Patuk put Unimak down and let out a warning sound. He raced into his home. No one was there. Thank goodness. They must have smelled the smoke and left. Patuk and Unimak continued running away from the fire. They reached the Chena River and swam across. The land on the other side was safe. The air grew clearer. It was getting easier to breathe. The two headed to the family's designated meeting place. In all their years living in the forest, they never had to use it. Patuk was grateful they had made the plan previously. Slowing their pace, Unimak started to cry.

"I don't understand, Father. Where did the fire come from?"

"It is the stupid humans, Unimak. They build their campfires and carelessly put them out. They smoke their cigarettes and toss them aside. They do not care what happens to the thousands of acres of forest that get burned. They do not care what happens to the homes of all the animals."

"Why don't they care about us, Father?"

"Because they are the most selfish beings on Earth."

"I was so scared."

"You were brave, son. I am proud of you. You did not panic."

With that, the two wolves continued on to the family meeting place. They were thankful to be united with the others. They were thankful that they survived this fire. Hopefully it would be the last.

Not Exactly Somewhat

Larry Duerbeck

This work is dedicated to Mr. Randy Schuppan

Ivy-covered walls? Like Wrigley Field? No? Oh. . . . Like at Harvard and Yale. I see. Hmm. Well—

There may have been some ivy on some walls somewhere on campus, but none was visible to those in the multipurpose lecture hall. Not even through the windows. Especially through the windows, because there were certainly none of those inefficient amenities.

The room's cosmetics comprised a sere cornhusk hue highlighted by a timid caramel taken too soon off the heat, linoleum flooring with the polished sheen of cinderblock, and metalwork painted a French blue that was to cerulean beauty what French defense was to World War II—in name only. An insipid, carefully considered palette to provide a one-scheme-suits-all setting.

The rotational professor did his academic best, what with shined Bass Weejuns, tailored slacks, tweed sports jacket sporting leather buttons and elbow patches, button-down shirt and knit wool tie. All coordinated to echo his full beard and shock of hair. He made as clichéd and as individual an image as a fingerprint, though limned in brown and not police blotter black.

On the podium, his image of cliché attempted to preserve its referential potency. But . . . Professor John Dexter Degener, he of some and several degrees, stood before his audience as just another teacher. Possessing only a better handle than so many another whom Chance had happened to prop up before so many a student for so many a year. For so many, then, Professor Degener held less interest than would have an android, a robot, a computer, a hologram hovering in his stead. For so many, yes, but there was the exception.

The exception came to class complete with textbook, notebook and pen. The exception sat, class after class, smack dab at the center of the first row. The exception, after two weeks and six (Mon-Wed-Fri) classes, provided a tall, slim, ongoing sight to see, from spikeless golf shoes up to partless pompadour. Bright golf course colors proved the exception's rule.

Today the exception had perhaps outdone himself, and Oz, in greens. Plus, he brought with him a thick binder. Professor Degener started class by addressing the exceptional student. "Drew Hazlitt. Your first-day card of introduction piques my interest the most. You, alone in the class, flatly state that you are a writer."

Drew nodded.

The professor continued, introductory card like a forgotten cigarette in his eloquent left hand. "Should you be here? English Composition One-Oh-One? Why are you here?"

Drew smiled. He could have been lolling in an easy chair. "Sir, it is always well to keep close contact with the basics. For most writers, I believe, a facile hand with commas and hyphens—"

"Commas and hyphens!" The professor almost exclaimed his class awake. "Facile—No one has a facile hand . . . A firm and ready grasp on those!"

"Yes, sir. True. But they are among the *prima mobilia* of style on the page for readers to enjoy. And the pleasure brought to readers by the well-played apostrophe!"

"Indeed." Professor Degener stared at his exceptional student for a long, order-in-the-court sort of moment. "You are somewhat interesting. Why the binder?"

"Not exactly somewhat." Drew grinned. "I think. As to this . . . admittedly hefty accretion..." He flapped the thick slab, a massy volume softly bound. "I brought it with a mind towards asking you after class. I'd like to put you in my collection of teachers' lives. It stops with high school's blessed cessation. I mean graduation. May I talk with you as the semester wends its wearisome, I mean winsome, way? Conference hours, whatever you like."

The professor asked into the microphone, "May I see that?" He stepped around the lectern, off the podium.

Drew rose from his wraparound desk, moved to meet him and hand it over. "An honor, sir."

Professor Degener riffled the pages. He frowned. "May I borrow, read some of it?"

"Well, of course. For so long as you like. I hope you find something to enjoy. As I say, it's an honor." Drew headed back to his desk, comfortable as a club pro in deep blue, cool-breeze evening.

Copious sheets enfolding characters unknown, the collection of untold lives told was laid to temporary rest on the lectern. Professor Degener pursued another point of interest. "Drew. Do you play golf?"

"No, sir."

"Then, why?" The card flashed high in his hand before being returned to its spot in a leatherette folder. "Why the outfits?"

"I intend to make enough money writing to someday join a private country club. The doing of which requires coin of the realm. Considerable coin of the realm. Also, secondhand? Here's good, cheap advertising. I believe I am recognizable, even memorable. For good, for ill."

"I should say." The professor pivoted his attention. "Shall we move on to the predicate?"

Drew surprised the professor again, by answering what was a patently rhetorical, class-wide question.

"Pwedicate! Great."

Some teacherly instinct gave the professor pause. He heard something so exceptionally exceptional that advantage had to be taken.

"Mr. Hazlitt. Would you care to address the class on the predicate?"

Mr. Hazlitt showed great enthusiasm.

After a moment the two had traded places. Drew took over the dais—podium, lectern, microphone and all. In the vacated wraparound, Professor Degener observed with welling astonishment.

"If you choose to listen, you all may gain much by my vacuous boobery. For a long time, I found rough sledding with the predicate. Just as a word. Its meaning kept slithering through my hands, my wits.

"When I first met up with predicate, and oh! I was a wee sprat! I ee-mee-dee-ately confused it with other words, swirled it in with other sounds. Apricot, for one. Predicament. I was that kind of kid.

"Not until a couple years ago did I really determine to catch up with it. I went back to childhood and renamed it in a kid's squeaky voice.

"Pwedicate! Repeat after me, if you like. Pwedicate!"

The hall filled with self-conscious, high-pitched "Pwedicate!s" and good-natured laughter.

"Now what is the pwedicate!?; what is the etiquette for the pwedicate!? I'll borrow from Steve Martin. To find the pwedicate! you need merely say, 'Excu-use me!'

"Every proper sentence has a subject and verb. Find the subject and its adjectives—qualifiers, if I may—and say, 'Excu-use me.' Then? Send that part of the sentence along. Goodbye!"

Drew waved.

He leaned toward his listeners, confidential. "Everything left is the pwedicate!" He leaned back.

"Please, imagine you're at the local stock car racetrack. Somebody asks, 'Did that red car run?'

"You answer, 'That red car ran.'

"The pwedicate! in your answer is 'ran.' Now imagine you go on to say, 'That red car ran circles around everybody else's earlier this evening.' The pwedicate! is 'ran circles' and so forth. Everything that follows. There you have the pwedicate!"

More laughter and a few "Pwedicate!s" flitted through the air. Drew's eyes roved the tiers of students. He waited, spoke again.

"Now, I have a question or two. So, if I may call you back, sir. How does the pwedicate! figure in complex and compound sentences, with defining and non-defining clauses? And what is the pwedicate!s dwead, I mean dread, effect on the high-and-mighty hyphen?"

The two switched back to their original orientation. Professor Degener soon fixed his finest, grimmest gimlet gaze.

"Mr. Hazlitt. You would leave me the easy parts." A clearing of the professorial throat, amplified overture foretelling serious lessons of the most dismal description.

"The pwedicate!—"

His squeak saw the students lean forward, on his side more than ever, riding Drew's coattails.

The semester wended its way to a wintry close. Snow lay on tree limbs, some few flakes idled down. Large lancet windows in the walls of the teachers' commodious lounge displayed the monochrome, nearly still life to fine advantage.

Located in the campus's oldest building, all its distractive amenities were grandfathered in and fiercely guarded. Professor Degener cast an appreciative eye around the waist-high bookshelves: virtual wainscoting of at-random academic interests, the arched and timbered ceiling with its succession of hanging amber-glass lights, sconces high on cream plaster walls, lustrous tables and leather club chairs.

He aimed his steps for one of those, hard to the right of a quoined and buttressed fireplace. The whole subset area invited warm welcomes, invited collegial exchanges, invited the viewing of images in the flames: invited, inevitably, dozing.

Professor Degener was wide awake. He waited in the club chair, thick binder on his lap. Atop that lay a paper-clipped sheaf of typewritten pages. The title page uppermost, showing itself simple and starkly readable. A glance would take it in.

A Professor's Life
by
John Dexter Degener

After a last glance, he looked back at the entryway, open oak doors a frame.

"There he is!" the professor called. "The youngest aide on campus. Right on time." Drew Hazlitt walked in, a living flame. "What on earth do you call that color?"

"Fiery coral. I had to ask, too. Seventy-five percent off."

The professor didn't stand up. He tapped the top paper by way of companionable explanation. "Sit down, Drew."

"What do you think of it, sir?"

"I think you could ease up on the sirs, if you like."

"Uncomfortable."

"Fine." The professor leaned back. "First day of the Christmas vacation and here we are. I'm flying out, by and by. Down to business. God, is my life dull. In comparison."

Professor Degener leaned forward and slid the typewritten pages on the fire. He stayed forward to rub his hands in classic fashion.

"I have copies," Drew observed mildly. "You just had the original, sir. It's funny.

"Everyone, each person thought his or her life was dull. Things just happened and here we are. The P-51 ace who became an English teacher. The math major who taught music. The Russian lady émigré who was in fact a serial escapee. The scientist who left Monsanto, having felt the call to teach science.

"Just wait until you see the second draft. After Christmas. Answer me this, please. Which room do you like more? That lecture hall or . . ." Drew caressed the chair's luxurious arms. He edited some words. "Here?"

"I like this room more. Of course." Professor Degener turned his face from the heat for another look.

Drew's eyes followed in appraisal. He spoke. "The oriental rugs. Three deep, here and there. An *embarras de richesse*. I wish they'd use some as tapestries. Replace those portraits of bygone bigwigs. Tapestries'd look good under those medallions, those gems of stained-glass quatrefoil windows.

"And right here. This is one hell of a fireplace. A reminder that to be Gothic is to be giddy."

"But . . ." The professor chose not to add to the list. "I love the lecture hall. I'm a teacher. First, last and anywhere."

Drew smiled into the fire. "Now that's interesting. I'm a writer, which means I'm a student. Ever and always. Hey, sir. How do you think they get this excellent firewood for this excellent fireplace?"

The teacher stared at him. "I have no idea. Why?"

The writer got up and laid on another log. He picked up and waved the brass-handled poker as a fencer his épée. "Could be an interesting story.

"I like the hall. But I love this room. Do you have a ride to the airport? Save you taxi fare." Drew put the poker back and sat down.

The teacher stirred and stood. He handed the thick binder down. "Touché. I'll be back with my little bit of luggage in a bit.

"Drew, I'd buy your book. Merry Christmas."

The student looked ridiculous, right at home, relaxed with lives in his hands. "Larval though this may all be. Thank you. What do you think, sir," Drew eyed the poker, "about some mulled wine ere we depart?"

"I wouldn't put it past you."

"Indeed." Drew stretched and yawned. "Wine. And, for toasting, bread."

Wilderness Surveyor
Stan Wilson

Levi Easton entered the office of the Surveyor General at Vincennes with butterflies in his stomach. The handsome young man outwardly radiated the confidence of an experienced frontiersman. Inwardly, he was a shy youngster. His curly blond hair and sparkling green eyes gave him a younger appearance than his twenty-four years.

He grasped an old Louisville newspaper ad for a surveyor. His heart raced, fearful the job no longer existed. Nervously, he combed his fingers through his long golden locks. The surveying office's makeshift drafting tables were piled high with drawings. An Indiana territorial map hung on the wall. A gray-haired old man bent over a small desk covered with maps, didn't bother to look up from his work.

"What you need?" a grumpy voice asked.

"To inquire about the surveyor opening."

"Don't need a greenhorn. Last one got mauled by a bear. If you know anything about surveying, speak up, or move along."

"Apprenticed four years as a draftsman and surveyor's rodman in London. Came to America two years ago to work with master builders of water-driven mills. These are examples of the work." He offered a set of mill drawings to the old man.

"Don't sound like a Brit. You're timely. There's an opening for assistant to William Harris. These drawings look good. They're signed by a Levi Easton. That you?"

"Yes, sir."

"The job's on the Wabash River near its confluence with the Ohio. Harris is laying out a town called Harmonie. Pays two dollars a day. Interested?"

"Definitely."

"Expect Harris back next week. Tell Nate Ewing at the Trading Post, Josiah sent you. He'll put you up. Get yourself a good horse and a brace of pistols. There are disgruntled trappers and settlers in the area, along with numerous Indians. Don't believe they're dangerous, but best be prepared. Watch for the black bears."

"I can protect myself. The chestnut stallion and packhorses outside are mine." As Levi turned, his fringed buckskin jacket flipped open revealing a pair of flintlock pistols.

Josiah said, "Maybe you could. Ewing's place is three blocks south of the Territorial Capital."

The Ewing Trading Post was a beehive of activity. They sold everything from dry beans to a box of nails. Levi put his horses in their corral and asked to see Nate Ewing.

"Mr. Ewing, Josiah told me to see you. Thought you might put me up a few days. I'll be working with Harris surveying Harmonie."

Ewing answered, "Room and board fifteen cents a day, or you can help in the store in exchange until Harris's back in town."

"Appreciate being able to lend a hand. Hate being idle."

Ewing remarked, "Happy to hear Harris is doing the survey. He's a good man. George Rapp asked me and my partner to do it, but we don't have the time. Got a sketch Rapp sent, which you can have. It'll give you an idea what's involved."

Levi's soft, pliable deerskin Indian-style clothing set him apart from the average guy from the east coast.

"If I might ask, where did you get the outfit?"

Levi said, "At Boone's Mill on Blue River—the other side of the territory. When working in the brush I needed something that would holdup. A squaw made it for me."

"She did an excellent job. Haven't seen that quality of work since the French trappers were in this area."

***

Levi's picture-word stories of his exploits in London generated him a following at the Trading Post. The favorite ones were three-legged dog stories about one that walked on its front feet. Until someone reminded Levi he'd said the dog had lost its front right paw.

The town's people ventured, "Harris, with his crispy military demeanor, and Levi, with his laid-back approach, might kill each other once they are on the trail."

Harris arrived the following week and took a liking to Levi, the teller of tall tales.

"Levi, last summer, forty miles south of Vincennes, I placed a survey marker. It'll be the northern reference. Still need to run a line from Corydon. The area's primarily swamps with poisonous snakes and bugs strong enough to carry off your horse. Rapp wants the town's center point set no later than August first. Still want the job?"

"Very much."

"It's yours. Hopefully, it'll be a dry summer. We'll pick up Indian guides south of Sugar Loaf Mound. They're good workers and know the area well. One of the squaws keeps a clean camp, and she's a mighty fine cook. Double-check our supplies, especially sugar and salt. No stores where we're going. Leave the squaws and my dogs alone. Questions?"

"When do we start?"

"At daybreak. I've told Josiah to credit you thirty cents a day for your horses and ten cents for surveying equipment. He's forgetful on purpose. I pay the Indians."

The Indians were from the Miami tribe. They spoke a mixture of French and English. The survey party now numbered two whites, four braves, two squaws, a papoose, three dogs, and twelve horses.

"Levi, I've assigned Hawk to work with you. He speaks excellent French and has assisted me on several projects. The folks at Harmonie are German, for the most part."

"I'm not great at French or German, but can follow a conversation enough to know what's going on," Levi replied.

"Should be sufficient. Most of the time Rapp and his sons speak English. With luck, we'll make the northern marker by noon tomorrow. You can take half our crew on to the Corydon marker and start bringing the line this way. Hawk helped me set that reference. I'll work your direction once I get to Harmonie."

Crossing White River, the lead packhorse became stuck in quicksand. The Indians knew what to do and went to work immediately calming the animal. Several hours of daylight were lost, which delayed the turn toward Corydon.

***

When they approached Buzzard Roost, Levi noticed Hawk had removed his rifle from its boot, resting it across the saddle. Puzzled, he nodded toward the gun.

Hawk responded, "We picked up three outriders when working with the horse at the river. They turned east when we did. They're less than a quarter mile back of us on the left and closing. The whippoorwill you hear is Little Bear. He didn't go with Harris. He's following the riders. There's a large rock outcrop after the next bend. It's time to find out what those fellows want."

Hawk's daughter, Nina, and Yellow Feathers rode point a hundred yards ahead. They took up positions with the packhorses behind large boulders.

Levi unbuttoned his jacket to allow access to his pistols and pulled the tie off his rifle's boot. He'd never been in a battle. He felt tense and palms were sweaty. They rounded the bend as they heard the outriders gallop toward them.

Levi and Hawk scrambled for cover when they got to the massive rock outcrop. The three riders were led by one wearing a beaver skin robe.

"Hold it right there!" Levi yelled.

They responded with a hail of lead balls. They'd attached several flintlock pistols to rawhide slings around their necks, allowing them to quickly fill their hands with one pistol after another.

The scene became chaotic with screaming orders and firing wildly. One cornered Nina. He aimed at her the same time she squeezed the trigger of her smoothbore blanket gun. His bullet creased her arm as he fell dead in the saddle.

Yellow Feathers was shot in the leg, but his tomahawk found its mark, deep in the chest of the one wearing the beaver skins. The last outlaw was killed with shots from Levi and Hawk. A deep silence fell over the trail.

Levi and Nina received minor wounds when creased by bullets. Little Bear had a flesh wound.

Nina said, "Yellow Feathers has a ball embedded in his thigh, it'll require a doctor to remove." Three outlaws and a packhorse lay dead.

Levi went through the group's papers. He found a journal the leader carried. The three had sold furs in St. Louis and went on a drinking spree at the brothels. After exhausting their money, they crossed into Illinois, killed a settler's family and burned their cabin.

Two of the braves required medical attention. Nina gave them an herb mixture to reduce the pain.

Levi said, "We're only a day from Vincennes, Yellow Feathers and Little Bear should return immediately." Nina bandaged and coated their wounds with sulfur power. The two wounded braves mounted for the painful trip, taking with them the outlaws' horses to ensure they could ride straight through.

Levi wrote a report and included the journal for the U.S. Marshall. They buried the outlaws alongside the trail.

Five days later, Little Bear's brother, Shadow, caught up with them at Corydon.

He reported, "The doctor praised Nina, said all would fully recover. Little Bear went to catch Harris's crew at Harmonie. Yellow Feathers will remained at the Sugar Loaf camp until his leg has healed."

***

The first fifty miles, the survey progressed quickly. Then the weather turned sour and the streams flooded. Miles of dangerous swamps were filled with venomous snakes. They were only able to complete thirty miles the month of May—by late June, the rains stopped.

Hawk said, "We should be to the bend in the Ohio near Angel Mounds at a village called Evansville by mid-July. Expect we'll meet Harris there."

On the evening of July the tenth, Harris rode into their camp. He said, "Congratulations, you made good time. Yellow Feathers' back, but moving slow. Left him in Harmonie to locate the street markers."

Levi replied, "Couldn't have done it without Hawk and your crew."

***

"Levi, Rapp wants a series of small water mills to drive machinery for workshops around the town. Told him you're the man to design them and he'd need to pay you $500, plus ship a wagonload of their best apples to you at Ewing's Trading Post this fall. You'll owe me a bushel of those apples for cutting the deal."

"I appreciate it. Would like to keep Hawk and Little Bear to help contour the mill creek's grade and flume runs?"

"Okay, except you can't have Nina. Love her cooking. I've been dreaming of her evening campfire with the smell of fresh biscuits. I'll tell Josiah you'll be back by September."

***

Levi met Frederick Rapp, who gave him a tour of the town. Levi and his helpers were given a cabin while they did the project. Frederick, who'd been trained as a surveyor in his native Germany, quickly became Levi's friend. They spent many hours talking about ways to help power the growing town.

***

Levi said, "Frederick, while your concept of using water power for many small commercial projects is desirable, it's not practicable due to Harmonies' terrain without major movements of earth."

Rapp asked, "What are your recommendations for our consideration?"

"You'll need a canal running the length of the town. The best location is between Main and Brewery Street with the mill stream running north to south. I've surveyed and marked the location and grade."

"In addition, your major water-driven mill should be built south of town. A river cut-off several miles long needs to be dug from the Wabash River to run it. I've marked what would be the best path on the town map. I have a set of detailed drawings for building the mills."

Frederick said, "Levi, you've confirmed what we've suspected for some time. I have a bank draft for you. I am adding a second wagon of apples for the Indians. My father and I appreciate dealing with honest folks."

"Thanks, Frederick, that's more than fair."

He replied, "Tell Harris to bid on the new state capital layout at Indianapolis. I helped write Indiana's constitution. The territory will become the 19th state of the nation this winter."

<u>WATER / AIR / FIRE: Poetry</u>

Paradox the Other Side of the Mekong
R.R.J. Sebacher

Point man morning patrol

This grey day I am fog

Literally a cloud collapsed

Too condensed to rise above the ground

Damp and chaotic filled with the unseen

Danger both real and imagined

Stalking silently in this drizzle

In a world of magnificent sound

Listen—For the clatter of man

      Or tingling change in background

Slow and stealthy—Aware I belong

Reality a surrealistic landscape

No dewy eyed dreams to dissipate

Ecstatic tintinnabulation all morning long

Smell the strong spices oozing from their pores

Endorphin overload as we assume the mantle of gods

Flank and slaughter some poor squad

Not really different from our own

Remembrance
Cathleen Callahan

Water from some high place
falls, shatters over a round, wet boulder,
spills a shower of liquid light into a pool
stirred softly by the fine, shining spray,

inviting a sojourner to unwrap,
fling aside frocks and masks worn in the everyday,
shrug off inhibitions that whisper through ordinary time,
step into the bliss of this cool, cleansing cascade,
lift one's face to the wet rays that drench hair and body
with streaming, tumbling light,

fully exposed to the natural world,
fully removed from the cares and vetoes
of life outside oneself.

This is wholeness,
this is truth—
these naked moments into which one wades,
first with courage, and then with peace,
baptized with remembrance—

Ah, yes.
This is who I am.

Soul of Stone
R.R.J. Sebacher

You asked about the statue in the fountain
With snakes for hair and water rushing from her eyes
I acquired her on some godforsaken Cambodian mountain
I am too old for any more lies

You know I am at times subject to crushing depression
And have done things foul and awful
Fate decided on a moment for these to coincide
Sadly like the worst of things—these were lawful

There is no need to speak of these
Suffice to say my heart dove down a cleft
Soul rushing after for my body to end what's left
Worse the sun was warm with a flower scented breeze

My mind had reached the point of clarity beyond surreal
Then I saw her from her lovely naked rear
She said she would make me pay for the terrible things I did
I whispered that this was Just—into her ear

When she turned I saw the snakes upon her brow
We looked into each other's eyes as they began to fill
She turned to stone and I brought her home
Where I keep her still

I know that you will think me mad
Please excuse me—for an old man this is too much
When we are alone—we hold each other's hand
And listen to the water's hush

Reluctant Avian of Our Time
R.R.J. Sebacher

Imagine this paper pale blue

Of a just dawning sky

Ink pure white

Of three cranes

Stroking across that sky

There for a moment

Song not the scratch on slate

Black raven scavenging the guts

Of a world writhing

Upon the white heat

Of Earth's dying star

Poetic Art of the Fly Fisherman
R.R.J. Sebacher

First you give a reading

To both stream and local hatch

This will determine presentation and lure

What temptation your audience will find most pure

Casting in the air all about

Until you get a feel for the line

Placing it down point perfect

Possible prey lying still hidden in the depths

A dashing Rainbow or bloody Pike

Worthy of a winter's war story

What would incite this battle of wits

A lovely nymph pinned perennially

On a flap above his heart

A wooly ant or some other noisome insect

Rattling about his brain on a hat band

Entomology to ichthyology

Master and lover of these words

Famous for the sharpness of his hooks

He carries them imbedded in his soul

Karmic Fires
Cathleen Callahan

I am past the karmic fires

that raged

through verdant fields

of my life,

consumed my dreams

now burned to ash,

blackened to soot,

blown to dust sparkling in the sun.

August Dog Days
Debbie Hedges

Glassy lake, window of gold
Suits tied tight
Tubes bulging under cup-hooked arms
"Last one in is a rotten egg." I call
charging for the dock.
Tennis shoes stampede, raising plumes of dust
along the narrow path.
A slight breeze tickles my nose delivering the scent
of mud, sand and water.

At water's edge, a copperhead
slides lazily along the glassy surface.
Toes dig in, stop on a dime
"Da-a-ad!"
    "Shut up, you baby, or we can't swim,"
    my older brother warns.
"Poisonous?"
    "No doubt."
"Got a plan?"
    "Maybe. Launching rock bombs
    might scare him off."
"It's hot. I'm going for a soda."
    "Tell and I'll pound ya."

Skipping to the ice chest
digging out a Vess.
Popping the top off . . . *hisss*.
"Ooo . . .," I whisper. "A snake."
Mom jumps. "Where?"

River Poem
Marcia Gaye

Always arriving,
Forever leaving,
River of constants,
Never repeating.

Always arriving,
Forever changing,
Never repeating.
Constantly singing.

Catch the current's weight
Muddy tarnished silver
which whispers, which sings
which murmurs, which roars,
Its voice poured ashore.

Offer a grateful nod
For what it brings
For what it takes
For what it leaves
For what it carries on.

Saturday Writers 2015

NIGHT DREAMS

The Difference between Light and Dark
Sue Fritz

Marlene sat on the exam table at the doctor's office, gently fingering the bandages covering her eyes. She couldn't believe her lifetime of darkness was soon going to change forever. *What will it be like?* she wondered. Will it be as amazing as she always imagined? Will it be as beautiful? She thought about the freedom she would finally have. No more relying on the kindness of others. No more banging along the sidewalk with her stick. No more stumbling over unseen obstacles or bumping into moved furniture. Soon, she would be able to walk and look others in the eye, just like everyone else. She would finally understand the oohs and aahs a rainbow could bring out. She would finally see color. As she sat contemplating the joys to come, the doctor walked into the room. She knew it was him by the sound of his footfalls. She had heard it often these past few months of coming in for consultations and then for the surgery.

"Hello, Marlene," he said. "How are you doing?"

Marlene loved the sound of his voice. It was smooth and dreamy, and seemed to flow all around her.

"I'm doing great, Dr. Klinger," she said. "Just anxious to see if the surgery worked."

"Well, we will know soon," he said. Touching the bandages on Marlene's eyes he said, "Are you ready to get these off?"

"Yes, Dr. Klinger."

"Do you think you will regret your decision? After all, you are paying a great price for the change."

"I know, Dr. Klinger. But I know it's going to be worth it," she said. "I just can't believe I finally I have this opportunity."

"Well, the advances in science and medicine these days are astounding," he said as he laughed heartily.

Gosh, I love his laugh, Marlene thought. Any man with that kind of laugh must be handsome. She couldn't wait to get the bandages off and look him straight in the eye. Even more, she could not wait to get the bandages off to look herself in the eye.

The door opened again and Nurse Rayne entered the room. Marlene knew it was her because she always wore the same perfume.

"Hello, Nurse Rayne."

"Hello, Marlene. You must be excited this day has come."

"Oh, yes. I have waited all my life for this."

"Are you sure you won't miss anything by making this sacrifice?"

"No, Nurse Rayne. I put a lot of thought into my decision. I have had 50 years of living this way. It's time I get to have new experiences."

"Ok, Marlene, we are going to pull off the first layer of bandages," Dr. Klinger said. "I want you to keep your eyes closed until all the wrapping is off. Then, we will have you slowly open your eyes."

"Ok, Dr. Klinger."

The bandage tickled her face as it was gently unwrapped. It fell to the exam table. The next bandage came off and landed on the floor.

"Last one, Marlene. Ready?"

Marlene took a deep breath. "Ready."

As the last bandage came off, Dr. Klinger whispered in Marlene's ear, "Good luck."

He put the bandage on the table. Marlene's eyes were still closed. Dr. Klinger laid his fingers on her eyes so she would know it was time to open them. She scrunched her eyes and opened them slowly. At first things looked blurry, but after blinking a few times, it cleared up.

"I can see, I can see," she said as she bounced up and down on the table. She looked at Dr. Klinger, who was smiling. She saw his mouth moving, but she could not hear him. Marlene jumped off the table and hugged him tightly. She thought about Nurse Rayne's question. What would she miss? She would miss Dr. Klinger's voice. But that's ok, because it isn't like she would be seeing much of him anyway. She stepped back and took a really good look at him. He wasn't quite what she imagined. He was short and rather dull looking, not at all the man that should have that wonderful laugh of his.

He gestured for her to sit back on the exam table. She sat and he handed her a mirror. Marlene hesitated. *This is the first time I will see my face,* she thought. *What if I am ugly?* Everyone always seemed to like the way she looked, but what if she didn't like it? She glanced at Dr. Klinger. He smiled and guided the hand holding the mirror to her face. She gasped. She was beautiful. Tears ran her down her face as the enormity of the change came over her. What a miracle!

"Thank you, Dr. Klinger," she said. He nodded and smiled as Nurse Rayne guided Marlene out of the room. Marlene headed for the exit. As she passed through the waiting room, she noticed a young boy with his mother. His big brown eyes looked up at her. He had bandages on his ears. She smiled at him, but wondered why he would choose that change. The things those beautiful eyes have seen. Why would he give that up?

Taking a deep breath, Marlene pushed open the door and left the clinic. The bright sun stung as she stepped into the open. She had felt the warmth of the sun many times, but the light was harsh. She pressed her hand to her forehead, shielding her eyes. She stumbled and bumped into a man on the sidewalk. He looked at her and his mouth moved angrily, but Marlene could not hear him.

"I'm sorry," she said. He scowled and stalked off. She tried to open her eyes more but the searing sun would not let her. *Dr. Klinger did tell me it would take time for my eyes to adjust,* she thought. She continued to stumble down the sidewalk. On the corner was a man playing the saxophone. In the past Marlene would always stop and listen to him. His name was Charley. She loved talking to Charley. He played beautiful music and sang even better. She stumbled into him and grabbed his arm to steady herself.

"Marlene, are you ok?" he asked. But Marlene could not answer him. She did not know what he said. She squinted at him and started to cry.

"I can see you, Charley. My surgery worked. But the sun is so harsh, I'm having a hard time walking."

Charley hugged her and tried to comfort her. As she stood in his embrace, Marlene realized she would never hear Charley sing again. She would never hear his voice. All the wonderful sounds of the world were gone to her forever: birds singing, children laughing, streams rushing. She knew what the price was for the surgery, but she was so wrapped up in what she was getting that she didn't think through what she was losing. *What have I done?* she thought.

Flappers and Bootleggers
Douglas N. Osgood

Photos hold memories like a strong box. I found this one going through Ma's stuff. Five shirtless boys by the pond, tents pitched, fishing rods slung over our shoulders. Only Ben was missing—he missed that summer. I was transported back thirty years; pond stench burned my nose as if I were there again.

We spent every summer there. Grams and Gramps would let all the cousins camp by the pond. Six boys living in tents and sleeping bags for eight straight weeks. Mornings, we would help Grams and Gramps with chores, then rush back to the pond after lunch to swim, fish, be pirates, or whatever. They had so much land, we felt like we were alone on a deserted island: our very own kingdom. Once we tried roasting a pig like we were Lord of the Flies, but that didn't go so well. Grams had a table full of boys that night. Such happy times.

Until the summer of '74. I was thirteen and had just finished eighth grade. Ben found a job that summer and couldn't come down, so "cool" cousin Tommy was our leader. He was fifteen and kind of a hippie with long hair and a guitar. A rock radio station out of Buffalo barely came in on his transistor radio—tinny and static-laden. The Stones, the Who, Led Zeppelin, and Queen played as loud as we wanted all summer.

Every night Gramps brought down whatever Grams had fixed for us: brownies, a fresh berry pie, or cookies. He would stay for a while, and we sat around the campfire watching the stars and listening to stories from his younger days, or some ghost story he made up. Gramps had a ton of them, and we never minded when he occasionally repeated one. It was a ritual repeated every summer night and we loved it.

One night in '74, he told us about one of the regular customers at his garage. Gino "Fatty" Bianco was a famous bootlegger. No one else touched his car; Gramps was the only one that knew about the whiskey tank hidden under the back seat of Fatty's 1927 Model A, or the emergency drop flap.

Gramps regaled us with stories of flappers, speakeasies, and Fatty running Canadian whiskey over the Queenston-Lewiston Bridge. Gramps had *never* talked about *this* before. He knew a real, live gangster!

"What happened to that car, Gramps?" we begged.

He hesitated before answering. "Boys, I've never told anyone this. Fatty gave me that car just before the G-Men busted him. Owed me some money and knew the feds had him, I think. The car was worth a lot more than he owed me."

"Where's it now?"

"Wrecked it back in '34. What's left is in the cave behind the old barn."

Complete silence. A naked woman could not have gotten our attention at that point. Robbie asked, "What cave behind the barn?"

Gramps face grew real grim in the firelight. "Boys, forget I told you about it. Your Grams'd have a conniption if she knew I'd told you about it. That cave's dangerous. And haunted."

"*Haunted!* Gramps. We gotta see it."

"No. Forget it."

No amount of pleading would get him to say any more. The next night we pestered him so that he finally said, "Boys, if you won't leave it alone, I'll send you all home to your parents right now. Promise me this is the end of it or I'll do just that. I don't want you in that cave or anywhere near it." He made each of us promise to forget the whole thing. Which we did, with our fingers crossed.

It was the topic of conversation all night. We just had to see the cave and the car. Gramps' barn was in the middle of a flat, open field and the floor was concrete; we couldn't figure out where the cave could be. What was Gramps talking about?

Vince was the one that caught on. "Hey, Gramps said 'old barn.' Where's the old barn?" None of us knew.

That afternoon, we went exploring. Grams and Gramps had several hundred acres, including two hundred acres of forested hillside: all rocky crevices and moss covered boulders left over from glacial advance and retreat. In places, the snow wouldn't melt entirely until late June or early July. The rocks could be slippery because of the moss, and some of the drops would be thirty feet or more.

Every day, we searched for that cave, afraid Gramps would discover where we had been and send us home. It was a complete accident that we found it. If it hadn't been for Robbie, I don't think we ever would have. From above, a rock bridge covered it, and from ground level, honeysuckle formed a blanket over the rocky crevice; it looked like any other solid rock wall.

It was late afternoon and we were tired. Four days had turned up nothing. Robbie was only a month younger than Tommy, but big and awkward, so he got picked on a lot. He slouched into that wall of honeysuckle to relax against the rock behind. Instead, the vines gave way. He crashed to the ground in a tangle of honeysuckle, like he had been caught in one of those nets from a Tarzan movie. I think he expected us to laugh at him, but we were too busy staring at the barn behind him. Later we all wondered that we had never noticed it before. Saplings grew in the ruts, but anyone could see a road had been there.

Thick vegetation all around and the rock bridge above cast a heavy shadow on the fissure. The air was rich with the wet odor of decaying vegetation. Moss covered most of the barn like flaking green paint. The wood under the moss was grey and rotting.

A mad scramble through the vines ensued, as we dashed around the barn like a swarm of bees, but it was as if the barn grew right out of the rock face. The only way to any cave behind was through the inside—but the big double doors in front were padlocked shut.

The lock was rusty, like it had been there for forty years, which maybe it had been. Tommy found a heavy oak branch somewhere. "Come on," he yelled and stuck it in the gap between the doors. Five boys hung on that branch like monkeys, tugging and prying. "Come on, harder. Pull, pull, pull," shouted Tommy. *POP!* The padlock finally gave way. All five of us stumbled backwards at the abrupt release. We must have looked like something out of a Three Stooges movie.

Tommy tugged at the doors. *Ssssssccccccrrrrrreeeettttttch.*

I swallowed hard.

"G...Gramps said this place was h...haunted. M...maybe we ought to just go back to c...c...camp," said Jimmy.

"Y...yeah," I chimed in. "I'm with Jimmy."

"No, Gramps said the cave was haunted, not the barn. You'll be okay. I'll protect you. Besides, that's just rusty hinges."

Inside, the barn was dark and damp, and we couldn't see anything. Robbie had his Cub Scout flashlight with him. Its light was yellowish in the gloom, like the batteries were dying. We crept in, single file on tiptoes. Were we hiding from the ghosts? Even Vince, the adventurous one, seemed reluctant. My heart was beating through my chest, regardless of Tommy's assurances.

Inside, the smell of mouse urine and decaying flesh flooded over us in a tidal wave. It filled your mouth and nose like a gag. Jimmy threw up right there. I almost did, but forced it back down.

"Oh my God, look out!" shouted Tommy. In the faint light, I saw him duck down, arms swatting over his head.

A giant spider-like creature hung down from above, its body huge and round with eight legs protruding in front. It was suspended from the ceiling by a thick web line. My heart, already racing, leapt into my throat. It took me a second to realize the screaming I heard was my own. *Oh, no!* Tommy and Robbie were down, rolling on the floor. *Did it bite them?* "Tommy!" I shouted.

Vince, who was ahead of me, kicked Tommy. *Why would...? Was it on him?* Tommy grunted and then snorted. He and Robbie were only laughing. The "spider" was just the distorted shadow of a hanging rake.

"Assholes!" I meant it, though Ma would have washed my mouth out with soap if she'd heard.

The rake was the only thing in the barn. Along the back wall, another pair of double doors gaped open, a giant maw leading into the darkness beyond. Once he stopped laughing, Tommy waved his arm forward. "Come on, there's nothing to be afraid of." We all marched forward, feeling better. In spite of our anger, Tommy had shown us how silly our fears were.

The cave was much darker than the barn, and the smell changed—sweet, almost hypnotic. Robbie's flashlight seemed fainter, like the darkness was devouring its light. We could only see a few feet ahead. I snuck a look back, but couldn't see the barn. I shuddered. Suddenly I was cold.

Thump.

"Ouch." Robbie ran into something, and we all bumped into him. The smell and darkness of the cave was forgotten in our excitement.

"You found it."

"Cool, no doors, just like Gramps said—in case it went in a lake."

"Let's get in."

And we did. Tommy jumped into the driver's seat, his brother Jimmy got shotgun. Vince and Robbie sat on either side of me in the back. Awesome. We were pretending to be bootleggers chased by the coppers.

Everyone was laughing, so no one noticed it right away—the car's motor was purring. Suddenly, its headlights flicked on and the cave disappeared.

"What the . . ."

We were looking through a window. Inside, flapper girls danced the Charleston. A pianist banged out a bawdy jazz tune.

"Coppers," someone shouted. Instantly the music stopped and everything went dark. The headlights blinked out, but the engine roared to life. Suddenly, we were racing along a city street, only a crescent moon for light.

The car made a hard right turn without slowing. "Help," Jimmy screamed. Tires squealed all the way around the corner, and we careened ahead. My hands gripped at Vince's arm, my knuckles white.

I looked up front. Jimmy was gone! What happened?

"Dump the load," someone shouted, it wasn't any of us. We fishtailed: an erratic dance, while 90 gallons of Canadian whiskey flooded the road behind. We hurtled ahead. Another hard right, then a left, right, left, left, right, and we were racing down a country road. Fog swirled about us. Trees replaced buildings. We sped headlong down the twisting road.

A lake materialized right in front of us and we missed the turn. Airborne and heading right for the drink, we all screamed. Suddenly, a bright light, white and intense, blinded us. We were back in the cave. Gramps shone an electric torch in our eyes.

It took me a minute to release the death grip I had on Vince. My pants felt wet; I had peed myself. I staggered and almost fell as I climbed out—I grabbed the car for support.

"Nooooo! Jimmy!" Tommy pushed past me to the heap against the cave wall I hadn't seen before. It was Jimmy.

Gramps was already kneeling beside my cousin. Jimmy wasn't moving. He was rushed to the hospital while we were sent to pack our things; our summer was over early.

Jimmy was okay—just a concussion. Gramps dynamited the cave opening the next day. He made us watch, then he took us home.

We tried to talk about it once, at Gramp's funeral. I got sick. Jimmy couldn't remember anything after finding the barn. I wish I could forget.

Was it real? A hallucination? I don't think we'll ever know. I reached into my pocket for my lighter—some memories are better left buried.

Dark Matter of the Heart:
A Theoretical Love Story

Sarah Angleton

Whatever Clive might say, I am not a stalker. I can see how the evidence might be interpreted that way, but if he would just give me a chance to explain, try to see things from my perspective, I know he would understand.

Well, of course I don't know that he would understand. He is intelligent, a tenure-track professor in the philosophy department. But he gets confused. I can't blame him for it any more than he can blame me for my rationality.

As he approaches, I stir sugar into my cup of diner coffee. I don't need to do this. The coffee is hot enough to scald my lips, molecules dancing around one another like writhing horny twenty-somethings at a night club, occasionally escaping into the fresh air as swirling steam. The sugar will dissolve without my assistance. Still, I stir. It gives me something to do with my hands as I watch him cross the diner.

He wears a pair of faded Levis, loose and rumpled, probably gathered off the floor this morning to be worn for the fourth or fifth time since their last washing. With this he has paired a tucked T-shirt and ridiculous sport coat that I am surprised to see doesn't have elbow patches.

"Andrea," he states, as if I don't know my own name. It is not a greeting. It is not friendly.

"Clive," I smile and blow the steam rising from my coffee, puckering my full lips.

He sits and runs his fingers through his sandy hair. Seeing him, a sullen waitress comes to our table and asks him what he'd like. Clive orders a latte with almond milk, and the waitress rolls her eyes.

"This place has changed since I was last here," I say. It can't hurt to start the conversation on a light note. "Used to be you could only order decaf or regular."

"A lot has changed since you were last here, Andrea." Clive sighs and slumps against the back of the booth.

"I know, Clive. I'm sorry." I am not sorry.

There is silence between us when the waitress returns. She places a steaming cup of molecular orgy in front of Clive with an apathetic, "Here you go."

When she leaves, I place my elbow on the table and rest my chin on my hand, fixing him in a gaze that I hope conveys an invitation to speak.

Evidently it does, because he asks, "How was Switzerland?"

This is not where I expected to begin, but I am pleased. I recently returned from a fellowship at CERN, the largest particle physics lab in the world and home of the Large Hadron Collider. It was the opportunity of a career, of a lifetime. As a theoretical physicist, I could not pass up the offer, but it did require sacrifice. Though he claimed he was proud of me, Clive had made it clear that he was that sacrifice.

I understood then. And I understand now. The entire known universe is ruled by the law that with increased distance there is decreased attraction. It seems logical that it would be the same with people.

Except that my field of study is dark matter. I look to that which can't be observed except through the gravitational forces that hold the known universe together, despite the expectation that it would pull itself apart.

"Switzerland was good," I say, grateful for the ease of small talk, yet knowing there is much I will not say.

I will not tell him, for example, of foreign lovers, of brilliant researchers by day who were gloriously experimental by night. Nor will I bore him with the science about which he cares little. I will not explain that eighty percent of the matter in the universe neither reflects nor absorbs light and can be neither seen nor defined.

What I do say, while reaching for the hand he slides away, is, "I missed you."

"I missed you, too, Andrea." I can see he does not mean it. "But I have moved on."

"The yoga instructor." She is bubbly and sweet, uncomplicated and compliant. She is blonde and tan. I am none of these things.

"You have to stop following us," Clive's words are half muffled as he speaks into his cup of pretentious latte.

"I'm not following you." And I am not. I tell myself that it is an unexplained force that pulls us together, exerted by something I cannot see and cannot control.

It could be love, if love defies explanation, and I believe it might. I am an attractive woman, capable of finding a better man than this surfer-turned-philosopher in an ironic sport coat and unwashed blue jeans.

Yet I cannot deny that I have missed him, that I long for him, that I am unsure if I can continue to exist without him.

That is the eighty percent of what I think but cannot say.

"What we had was good, Andrea." Now he takes my hand, still extended on the table. "But it's in the past. I'm happy. I want you to be happy."

Clive releases my hand, warm with the memory of his skin against my skin. He stands and pulls out a worn leather wallet, dropping enough money on the table to cover both our drinks and a generous tip for the sullen waitress.

"That's it? That's all you want to say to me?" I am incredulous, though I do not show it.

"I think that's all there is to say." He leans over the table and kisses my cheek, and I breathe in the scent of his aftershave.

He turns to go, eighty percent of what should be said between us still unsaid, unmeasured, unanalyzed.

I watch him push past crowded tables. A bell tinkles as the door opens and closes behind him. He will climb into his Charger and take the highway toward campus, traveling fifteen miles out of his way to avoid the morning traffic. It is what he has done every weekday since I returned from Switzerland.

I follow him out and climb into my own car, a new Tesla S, a gift to myself after winning the CERN fellowship. He is still sitting in his car, his cell phone to his ear, when I pull out of the parking lot. He is probably talking to the yoga instructor, updating her about his morning meeting with me, assuring her I will no longer bother them.

I doubt he is telling her that there is still an unexplained matter of attraction between us, of immeasurable, indefinable love. But then I expect even a philosopher would have trouble imagining such a thing. The laws that govern the human heart, like those that govern the universe, must derive meaning from more than thought. Such laws require careful calculation and measured experimentation.

This is the thought that bounces around in my mind as I merge onto the freeway toward campus, toward my office where I will continue to draw on the data collected from the collision of high-energy particle beams in the largest particle accelerator the world has ever known.

My hope, the hope of theoretical physicists, is that in these high-speed particle collisions, we may detect the absence of small amounts of energy and momentum that would indicate the otherwise undetectable escape of dark matter particles.

And from these collisions, we would come one step closer to understanding this eighty percent of matter we cannot see, yet which, like love, draws together the observable universe in defiance of expectation. This is what I should have said to Clive, the words I searched for, but could not find.

My quick slide across two lanes garners angry honks from fellow freeway travelers, but I just make the exit onto the highway and turn back toward the diner, driving away from campus.

I see the black Charger within a few miles. This stretch of highway has little traffic and Clive has opened up his engine. Pushing the limits of the car's capabilities, he approaches rapidly. I stomp my accelerator, too, enjoying the rush of adrenaline that comes with irresponsible abandon.

120 miles per hour. 130. 140. An impressive feat of engineering, the electric Tesla delivers on its performance promises. It is a precision instrument designed to exceed limits and explore the unknown eighty percent.

I watch Clive disappear just for a moment below the rise between us and I guide the Tesla into his oncoming lane.

The Box

Jennifer A. Hasheider

A jagged line of fine powder dragged across the road. I tapped the brakes at my driveway, reaching in the wrong direction to open our garage. Old habits. In my van, the button had been next to the visor, but in the car it sat on the dash. A dirty orange basketball rolled on the passenger side floorboard and came to a rest against the seat. It'd been there since my husband picked it up out of the neighbor's yard in the fall. "Tell Michael I had to get his damn ball out of Bill's yard again this morning," Paul had said.

I pulled the car into the garage, careful not to get too close to the wall or the three bikes parked in a neat row on the other side. I turned off the engine, grabbed my purse from the passenger seat and opened the door. As soon as my shoe stepped onto the cold cement floor, the light came. I greeted it.

"Good evening, Little Light." I didn't try to touch it. The glowing puff of whiteness usually backed away from my hand, so I'd given up trying. It followed me to the door like I knew it would, hovering just out of reach. I walked inside and it didn't follow. It never did.

Next to the kitchen sink, I eyed the box on the countertop. They'd delivered it one day before the funeral, when I still questioned if anything was real. Inside were the contents of my ruined van. I suspected my sunglasses were there, Michael's Nintendo game, books, the atlas Paul tucked under the floor mat for me, just in case I ever lost my way. I'd debated a few times about whether they'd have actually bothered to pack fast food wrappers and empty cups.

I ran my finger along the edge of the box. The night I received it had been the first visit from the light. Somewhere in my brain, or maybe in my soul, I knew there had to be a connection, but I wasn't ready to make it. I patted the box then went to my bedroom. It wasn't full dark, but my day was done.

Sometime in the night I'd been talking in my sleep again, mumbling. The echo of it played in my head when I woke. I went to the kitchen and pulled a stool over to the box. I draped my arm onto the counter and lay my head there. I could see the fibers of the brown cardboard. It was wavy, not smooth like you assume of the material. Paper tape was stuck to the side. Over and over it repeated the *Tinylite* brand name.

"Why did you leave me, Paul?" My voice was quiet. I wanted the box to answer me, but it sat there simply being a box. I looked toward the garage. Was Paul the light? Was it Michael? I felt the slow familiar sting start in my nose, then my eyes burned and finally tears trickled down my cheeks. I allowed myself a few minutes of sadness and pain, something I'd only done a few times over the past months. Then I stood, ran my hands through my hair, wiped my face and filled my lungs. After a few seconds, looking out across the house, the darkness and silence confirming my loneliness, I opened the box.

At first I thought I'd dropped into a radiant lavender abyss. Then the smell of sticky sweet maple syrup dropped my brain back into place, and I realized I was in my bed surrounded by a sea of purple sheets. It was daylight and someone was in the kitchen.

"Hello, who's there?" I called.

"What, Mom?"

It was Michael. It was my son's voice. I pulled my legs from under the covers and hurried to the doorway, but then I was afraid to look around the corner.

"Michael?"

"Yeah?" His head popped around the fridge. "You slept late today." He disappeared from sight.

I wanted to run after him. My heart pounded but my feet felt like they had become part of the hardwood floor. I willed them forward. My son stood at the counter, a waffle on the plate in front of him. He didn't bother with utensils and took big bites of his breakfast while he flipped pages in a magazine.

"Don't forget, I have practice after school today."

I jumped. Was Michael real? My first instinct was to run into the bedroom and put my head under the covers. Could this be

Michael? The door from the garage opened and my husband, Paul, came into the house. My heart raced and my hands shook. Surely if I ran to my bed, I'd find I was still there.

"Hey, babe." He kissed my forehead on the way to the coffee pot. Flesh on my flesh.

I leaned against the refrigerator and watched my family. My husband's lips had calmed me.

Paul drank from a red coffee cup and looked over Michael's shoulder. They commented on an article.

This was a good dream. Not like the sounds of shrieking tires and bursting glass that sometimes sounded so real to my ears that it tickled the fine hairs deep inside. Michael's voice from the backseat, not aware the accident was happening, he'd have asked "What?" in response to Paul's panicked moan. Some nights, Michael's last "Wh—" echoed over and over in my head like a slow turning fan.

"You feel okay?" my husband asked.

I cleared my throat. "Yes, I'm good." I smiled. How far would I be allowed to go in this dream? "How are you two?"

"Good," Paul said, "I want to check out the seafood restaurant Bill talked about. You free for lunch later?"

I studied Paul. How far?

"You remembered I'm off work today, right?"

"I, yes. You are off work today. Yes." I'll play along since I'm here.

Michael rinsed his plate in the sink. "You're going to change the light in my bathroom today, right, Dad?"

I laughed and they both looked my way. The light fixture had gone out in Michael's bathroom, and he showered by the light that came in the opened bathroom door. Yes, this was all familiar to me. This was the morning before the accident.

Could I bring them back if I changed my dream? Maybe they'd be alive when I woke up if I did. I glanced at the counter and there was no box sitting near the edge, taped shut, waiting for me to open it.

"I don't think we're going to get to that stuff today, Michael," I said.

"Why not? It's dark in my bathroom," Michael whined.

"Michael, your mother must have other plans for me. We'll get that stuff after your practice tonight or maybe this weekend after your games." My Paul, he always had my back without question.

"What do you think if we all skipped our plans for today and hung out together instead?"

They looked at me like I had two heads. Sure, they're dead and standing in the kitchen, but I'm the weird one.

"You'll let me take off school today? I'm not even sick," Michael said.

"Yes, I'll call in for you. 'Something's come up.'" I made bunny ears with my fingers. "I'll grab a shower, then we'll have some fun. Okay?" I could tell they were unsure of my motives, but this was my dream so, my rules.

After humankind's fastest shower, which in fact I didn't recall taking, I walked into the living room with soaking wet hair and found my boys enthralled in a video game war with each other. I watched for a few minutes. Their matching long-fingered hands smoothly operated the buttons and knobs on the controllers. Paul's silver wedding band gleamed in the bright sunshine pouring in the window.

"Well, I know we've got all day," all my life if we're lucky, "but I don't want to spend it just sitting here. What do you guys want to do?" I asked and then added, "Besides play that game?"

Paul got up from the couch and walked quickly toward me. His feet moved faster than his body. He held his arms to me and I walked toward them. Holding me tight, he yelled my name, "Diane!" and again, "Diane!"

"Why are you yelling?" I tried to pull away so I could look at him, but he had a tight grip on my middle. Michael wasn't on the couch anymore.

I saw the tiny light flitter by my head. Paul pushed me away then pushed both fists into my chest. "I'm not getting a steady pulse. Do you guys have anything?"

"Paul?" I was sinking.

The light flittered in my eyesight again. Suddenly, my eyes seemed to burst into reality.

"Ma'am? Can you hear me? She's back. We've got her!"

"Paul?" I felt my voice in my chest. It boomed in my ears. There was ringing there, and shouts and sirens. I saw thousands of snowflakes swirling in the flashing lights all around. I turned my head and saw a crushed brown box with a "Tinylite Fixtures" logo on the ground next to me.

"Diane!" I heard Paul's voice. I looked for him. A paramedic's jacket reflected light into my eyes. I found Michael standing above me, crying. Kneeling in front of him was Paul, near my hip. He rubbed my hand. "That damn basketball saved you, baby." He had tears now. "Michael's damn ball." He pointed. I saw the deflated, dirty-orange basketball next to a mangled, broken piece of my van.

Silent Screams
Stephen Hayes

Army brats have no say where their parents are posted. I was miserable when my father, a career officer, was ordered to a base near Berlin. Once again I was torn from my friends, and this time I was dragged to a rickety house at the edge of a dark forest. As always, I held my tongue, all the while wishing for a way to punish my parents, make them pay for all the abuses I was forced to endure.

Unlike American houses, the main living space and most of the bedrooms were upstairs, but my room was down a narrow hallway on the ground floor. Shortly after we settled in, my teenage brother horsed around in the backyard, trying to drown spiders with a garden hose. He was pleased to be relocating once more. Unlike me, he had seemed almost desperate to make this move. After a while, he wandered away to scrape rust from his recently acquired jalopy, forgetting to turn off the faucet.

Later that night, after everyone had gone to bed, I jerked awake. The hairs on the back of my neck convinced me I wasn't alone. I tried to blame the feeling on the erratic hissing of the old radiator in my room, or maybe it was my brother who always claimed to be sleepwalking when he appeared beside my bed. I pulled the string dangling from an overhead light bulb and tried to comprehend the scene surrounding me.

Spiders, projecting nightmarish images and illuminating hordes of creepy-crawlies, clung to the walls and to the light bulb. The pink bedcover, with me for as long as I could remember, had become a sweltering blanket of musky spiders. I remembered the garden hose my brother had been fooling around with and realized he'd neglected to turn off the water, flooding the basement beneath my room.

Leggy arachnids, scrambling down the string towards my hand, leapt onto my arm. They found my hair, crawled over my unblinking eyes, inched beneath my nightgown, explored me with bites. My mouth gaped like a harpooned fish, but the marrow-freezing scream rising within me was stifled by a large prowling spider which had found a humid hide-a-way. My love for God and all things good metastasized into rage.

No one came to my rescue that night.

When my parents found me in the morning, I was unable to speak. By then, the spiders had crept away to mock me from their hiding places. You must believe I tried to get over this trauma, although it pleased me to know my parents were finally being punished for ripping me away from my friends every few years, and for failing to shield me from the constant evil they allowed to live with us.

The passing years have not changed things very much. My parents seldom come to sit by my bed, and though I see my brother every day in my mind, he has not paid a single visit. However, I'm no longer uprooted; a cocoon protects me from all but the spiders. When not being tormented by them, I'm alone with my thoughts, haunted by the blurry faces of girls on my brother's arm, girls like me, whose smiles died too quickly. I wonder what he said to keep them quiet. Are they also tormented by spiders? I think about all those moves as a child, how eager my brother was to shove his things into a battered suitcase and vanish to places where no one knew him.

Outside, I hear voices telling me the spiders are only in my mind, these incidents never happened. They're wrong. Even now, with eyes clenched, I still see them, feel the heat of the spiders' bodies enveloping me and seeking refuge in places even I never explored.

They're coming now—look at the size of that one, smiling with my brother's face, multiple arms and legs tucked beneath a white coat. As always, I scream, but no sound escapes my mouth.

Black on White Experience
Phyllis L. Borgardt

Last September I had hip replacement surgery. The operation was a great success, but I died—briefly. What was it like to die? I witnessed a scene of black images on a white screen, which drew me back to my life. Let me explain.

My son Philip, who is a physician, watched as my blood pressure dropped, the signal on the monitor flat-lined and my face turned dark grey. He could do nothing to reverse the phenomena. I had signed a do-not-resuscitate form preventing interference with my end-of-life. It was my choice to die when the time came. I chose life when I understood that I still had a task to complete.

The process of dying was simple and painless for me. It wasn't dramatic. No bright light appeared. No heavenly angels sang. First, I saw a white screen. Curious, I watched as some black spots appeared and then turned into patterns. The patterns metamorphosed into paw prints on a path. When I saw them, I thought immediately of Commander, my little Shih Tzu that I'd left at home. I wondered, *Who will take care of my old friend?* Later, I'd say to myself, *Funny how the mind works.*

When I awoke, sensing I had a mission to accomplish, I was in the intensive care unit. Something in my 80-year life was not yet complete. *What could be so important?* My husband and I had raised three children. All were independent and successful. That part of my life's work was done. *What had drawn me back to life?* Love for my animal friend had moved me to follow the black paw prints. The path was set before me.

While recovering in the hospital, I had lots of time to review my life. I'd experienced a pivotal moment for some reason. I noticed that regrets for things undone seemed less important. Yet I kept feeling there was something I needed to do. The question was, what?

I'd witnessed so many changes in my 80 years: radio to television, peace to war, depression to prosperity, and Sputnik to the moon. Anybody can read about those changes in history books. There was no book where my children and grandchildren could find my stories. They knew very little about my personal experiences.

My children were fortunate. They had it all: a good education, life without poverty, and a chance to choose their own lifestyles. They knew nothing about my passage from poverty to prosperity. I had not wanted to burden them with tales of hard times. For myself, I'd chosen to look forward and never look back. Gradually I realized I'd kept from them the story of ordinary people's struggles in the '30s. That was not right.

I had my answer. My story needed to be told. Funny how a simple thing can bother you so very much, I thought to myself. I decided to write my story, a memoir of my childhood. I'd create a permanent record in black and white. I'd leave a trail of happenings for all to follow—just like the black paw prints on the white screen that guided me back to this life.

At first, thinking about the past brought to mind old wounds and misgivings. I relived harsh moments from the Great Depression of the '30s as if they had just happened. I remembered Mother crying because there was only five dollars in the bank account. Father had just spent the rest on a trailer we didn't need. I could hear my big sister crying as she did when she went to bed hungry.

Soon, I began to set down the lessons learned in those almost-forgotten days.

Slowly, I discovered the positive side to the poverty I experienced as a child. The isolation of living in the mountains brought out my creativity. I learned how to turn a bad situation into a positive one by writing stories and drawing the world around me. At times, I used paints and brushes to record life as it was. At others, I created another world and another me. I became a princess in a castle. I used color to brighten up an otherwise drab existence.

I'd sheltered our three children from poverty. But I'd also sheltered them from learning many of the life skills that challenging situations nurture. They'd not had the advantages of growing up in the risky California Mountains. For them, I began to write about living with Piute Indians, of witnessing my mother at work in her soup kitchen, of escaping stampeding cattle, of avoiding rattlesnakes while hunting Easter eggs, and watching my interesting nanny ride off with her mother—the outlaw and bootlegger, Six-Shooter Kate. There are still experiences I can't tell my children. All families have their secrets.

While writing down stories for my children, I realized I was writing for other children, too. The first book my near-death experience led to is finished. But I still follow the path that guided me back to life and new understanding of its value. I continue to fulfill my mission: recording my stories in black ink on white paper.

Night Passages
Carol Mingo-Revill

One afternoon, as I was in the kitchen doing the dishes, I overheard my husband on the phone rescheduling his art show opening. "My dad is dying, and it may be any day now. Also, my wife is dealing with chemo side effects and needs me to be here." I felt so sad listening to him. How did our life become so painfully pitiful all of a sudden?

The last time I saw my father-in-law was shortly after my diagnosis of breast cancer. We were sitting with him in a locked ward of a facility for people with memory impairments. He had long since stopped calling any of us by our names, but there was still a glint in his eyes showing that he knew, on a deep level, who we were. I was thinking how weird it was to be there with him after thirty-six years of marriage and not be telling him that I was ill. In my mind I thought, "He is alive, and he will never know about the diagnosis or even if I should pass on from it all." He was trapped in his own world, alienated from his beloved family and everything he held near and dear to him.

As time passed, I became involved in a rigorous treatment plan and I was no longer able to visit hospitals and other facilities, in order to keep myself healthy as blood counts drop during chemotherapy. I kept up-to-date with his progress from my husband, but was far removed from any involvement with his care. It wasn't long before his dad declined and family members were spending more and more time with him to comfort him.

It was very hard not being able to visit my father-in-law and support my husband, Bill, the way he had supported me when my father passed. Cancer was now alienating me from my family, and I did not like the feeling of the disease having control over me. The passing of a parent is a time when a wife needs to be present for her husband and be by his side as he stands at the side of a dying parent. I considered it my duty. Sadly, I could not be anywhere. Not by Bill's side at the hospital, and little support at home, as I was dependent on him when the treatment side effects had me in their grips.

The situation had me engulfed in sadness and also made me feel like an outcast. When I was first diagnosed with cancer, I would wake up in the morning ready to start my day. Then, as I got my bearings and began to think about the day, I would remember. I. Had. Cancer. My stomach would tighten, and any zest I had upon awaking for the day was depleted. When I shared this experience with a friend who worked in the prison system, he told me that the inmates claim to have the same experience when they first go to jail. As the prisoners rise in the morning and begin to shake the sleep off, they then remember they are incarcerated. I never thought that I would be able to relate to someone in prison, but now that I was in a sort of prison myself, I completely understood. I realized that my father-in-law and I had something in common. The depth of his disease put him in a prison of mind and body which prohibited him from having the faculties to even talk about it. I felt imprisoned in a new world of medical terms that were a whole new language unto themselves, which I struggled to understand, and a scary treatment that was supposed to save me, but also put me in danger for other health issues. I wanted to run away and hide until the danger passed, and simultaneously wanted to break everything in sight to get rid of the anger for this disruption in my life. "Please, just let me wake up and have it all be a dream, and let me have my day-to-day life back," I would plead with God every night. At least I had the luxury of expressing all of those feelings to anyone who would listen. Unfortunately, my father-in-law was robbed of ever complaining or cursing his fate, in the fort of silence that surrounded him.

On one particular weekend, as my husband and family spent the day at the hospital, I decided to muster all the strength that I could manage and attempt to have a home-cooked meal on the table when my husband arrived home. It had been a while since I went to the grocery store and cooked dinner, as Bill had taken over these tasks for me, allowing me to work at my job on my good days and not have to worry about running the house. I dragged myself around the grocery store getting all the ingredients and was thrilled to be out of my house partaking in an everyday task. Back at home, I settled into the kitchen and enjoyed the fussing around, grateful to be motivated to do so! I knew it would be a big surprise for Bill, and I hoped it would, in a very small way, make up for all the time I could not be available to support him when he needed me.

When he came home with his brother, they were both delighted to indulge in a home-cooked dinner of a stuffed chicken, sweet potatoes, and green bean casserole. I was thrilled that I pulled off getting dinner on the table, a task I took for granted for many years. After dinner, the three of us sat down and relaxed.

It was the first time I had seen my brother-in-law since my father-in-law went into hospice. All I knew of what was going on was what my husband had shared with me. The week before, members of the church choir visited him at hospice to sing at his bedside. My husband took pictures and recorded the music so he could share it with me. We sat in the living room, my husband, brother-in-law and I, with the lights off and just shared memories of the family and their dad. We discussed how beautiful the songs the choir sang to him were and how it brought us to tears. We all agreed it was such a special gift for him at this turning point. It was family bonding time, and I was a part of it now. It made me feel good to feel connected to my husband and his brother during this intense time. We chatted into the night about death, dying, and the situation at hand.

After my brother-in-law left, we turned in for the night. I was lying in my bed with my eyes closed, feeling at peace because I had been part of the family process in a small way. Suddenly, I began to see images of dark green before my eyes. I had been working with an energy healer before my surgery, and she told me that when I meditate and see dark green that it means physical healing was taking place. I had this experience one time when I was first diagnosed with breast cancer. I had meditated so many times since then and concentrated on dark green, hoping it would manifest before my eyes for continued healing. It never did. Tonight, without even trying, there it was right in front of me—a big crystal-like ball of green. The color was even deeper and more beautiful than the first time I saw it. Without any effort, it had appeared, and I felt a comfort and hope that my energy work and chemo were making a positive impact on my health.

A smile broke out on my face as I sailed off to sleep . . . or something not quite like sleep. I felt myself fall deeper and deeper into a chasm. And as I felt myself dropping deeper and deeper, I had a sense of fear. I wondered, if I continued to fall this deep, would I ever be able to come back up to consciousness? I must have felt secure that I would, because I just kept going. Down. Down. Down. I did not know what was exactly happening to me.

And then I found myself sitting next to my father-in-law's bed, and I began to breathe along with him. I was very close to his face, and I was taking every breath along with him. Breathing in, breathing out, breathing in, and breathing out. Waiting to see if he would take his last breath. At one point, I was confused about who was dying . . . was it him . . . or me? As this was happening, I tossed and turned in my bed, and I tried at times to pull myself out of the situation, but there I stayed by his side for what seemed to be the entire night. Breathing. With. Him.

The next morning, the side effects hit me hard and I did not get out of bed. My husband came into my room to kiss me good-bye. He had a feeling he needed to get to the hospital early. When he arrived, it was only a few hours before his dad was at the threshold of life and death. He called me and the rest of the family. I no sooner hung up with my husband when my son called. He was in a panic. He didn't know where he, as the oldest son, was supposed to be. Should he be at the side of his dying grandfather with his dad, or come and take his dad's place taking care of me, fighting cancer and debilitated from chemo side effects? It broke my heart that this was a choice he was struggling to make. I encouraged him to go be with his dad and take my place next to him, as I would be fine in my bed just waiting for the side effects to pass.

I layed around almost the entire day in my bed, all alone, while my husband and son sat vigil with other family members at the hospital. I dragged myself up to play a quick game of Scrabble on the computer, but my head was too fuzzy to hold up, and I headed back to bed. Night fell. As I looked out of the door in my bedroom, I realized not one light in the house had been turned on all day. I pulled the blankets tighter to me feeling darkness envelop me. The energy in the house felt eerie, and I felt fear creeping up on me for the first time that day. I was drifting in and out of sleep. So foggy-brained from the chemo that when a text would come through from the hospital, I struggled to open my eyes. When I could finally force my eyes to see straight, I just stared at the cell phone until I could muster up the energy to pick it up. The texts were either from my husband or my son explaining to me what was happening. My husband would update me on his father's vitals or share that he had taken his last breath, but then text back that he was breathing again. Death was slow in coming. I would hold the phone up to read the messages, and then my arm would flop on the bed as I threw the phone down. It seemed that as the evening got darker, the texts came faster and more furiously as death crept closer and closer, though not yet arriving.

It was after midnight when my husband slipped into bed next to me. He had taken his exhausted ninety-year-old mom home and left his brother at the hospital. It was not long before the call came.

Now, my husband was grabbing for his phone in the dark.

If you write from the heart you'll always be (w?) right ~ *Diane How*

And Night Fell
Diane How

The rolling hills of the Ozark Mountains in Missouri were my stomping grounds as a child. I was free to roam within the sound of Grandma's voice. In the country, a car approaching on a gravel road could be heard from miles away. Sound traveled far, allowing me to do the same.

My grandparents' clubhouse was a converted chicken coop with a magnificent eastern view, perfect for watching the early morning sun rise as it cleared fog from the valley below. Mighty oaks, towering sycamores and fragrant cedars surrounded the rest of the property. It was nearly perfect, even without running water or indoor plumbing.

A typical day started with a hearty breakfast of pancakes smothered with Karo syrup and a couple pieces of smoked jowl. A pot of water warmed on the stove while we ate, so that by the time the table was cleared, dishes could be washed. Chores came first, but once they were done, the rest of the day was mine. The moment Grandma gave the nod, the screen door banged behind me as I hurried outside to explore.

I often wandered the woods admiring all nature had to offer. Among the many wildflowers were spiders and snakes, but as long as I didn't bother them, they didn't bother me. Each summer, my confidence grew and the distance I traveled expanded. On occasion, the freedom to roam propelled me to unexpected places.

It was late afternoon when I decided to take my little sister, Carol, on an adventure. The plan seemed simple to my twelve-year old self: Down the rugged driveway, made from slabs of flat rocks, up the seldom-traveled gravel road that bordered a creek, and over a few hills. If I timed it just right, we could watch a beautiful sunset. I had scouted out the location a few days earlier while riding in the back seat of my grandfather's '59 Ford.

It was my duty as an older sister to teach Carol some of the many things I had learned over the years. I pointed out Queen

Anne's lace growing among the many weeds along the roadside, identified fields of wheat and corn, and even decided to unveil the truth about some tiny yellow and white flowers my sister wanted to pick. "Grandma calls them pee-in-the-beds, but they really don't make you do that. I picked them once."

We stopped at an opening between some trees to watch water ripple down a creek bed. When Carol asked if we could go for a swim, I told her that Grandpa once warned me that a farmer would cut off my pigtails with a butcher knife if I got caught trespassing. I wasn't sure if he was serious, but I decided not to risk it.

The sound of flies buzzing nearby disrupted the lesson.

"What's that?" My sister's eyes widened as she pointed to the left.

I looked in the direction she pointed and instinctively pulled my sister away. Maggots and flies covered the hind leg of a cow. It was matted with dried blood and some hide was still attached. It couldn't have been there very long, I reasoned, or else there would be only bones. "We need to go."

Disturbing thoughts rattled around in my head as we continued down the road. *What killed it? Was someone lurking in the woods waiting to mutilate again?* Images of the farmer with the big knife flashed through my mind. Fear settled in my stomach and made me uneasy. Looking for a distraction, I began singing, "The ants go marching one by one, hoorah, hoorah," My sister skipped to the tune, and soon the horrific scene was behind us.

We topped the final hill just in time. The sky turned purple, then pink, as the golden globe descended beyond the cornfield. It was spectacular and well worth the long hike to see it. We stood in silence as the sun faded beyond the horizon. And night fell. And I do mean fell! Being left in total blackness had not been part of my plan. Even the moon had taken the night off, leaving the distant stars to flicker alone. My confidence dissolved as quickly as dusk.

My heart raced and my pulse pounded in my ears. Finding our way back without so much as a flashlight made my stomach knot again. I was going to be in big trouble when we got back. *If we get back.*

"I'm scared," my sister whimpered.

"Pretend you're blindfolded and we're playing Pin the Tail on the Donkey. We'll be ok." I followed the sound of her voice and moved closer, swooping my hand in search of hers. She squeezed tight once we connected.

One step at a time, we inched our way back, trying to stay in the middle of the road. As our eyes adjusted, our pace quickened and the steady rhythm of gravel crunching under our feet, mixed with the hum of locusts, was almost musical. *This isn't so bad.*

The positive thought dissolved quickly with the sound of splashing of water. The twisted thoughts about the dismembered animal resurfaced. Something in the distance caught my eye. I paused and reached for Carol's hand.

"Ow! You're squeezing too tight."

"Shhhh." The hair stood up on my neck when I saw a speck of light filter through the dense trees. *Oh my God. Someone's out there. What am I going to do?* No one ever traveled this remote area, especially at night. The light flickered closer. *It's him. He saw us looking at the cow. Now he's going to kill us.* In the darkness, I searched for a place to hide. My heart raced so fast I felt it would explode.

"Stay behind me. When you get the chance, run. Run as fast as you can," I whispered, now frozen in fear. I drew in a deep breath as the shadowy figure approached and shined the light on us. This was it. I'd protect Carol even if it meant he'd kill me.

Heavy boots stomped on the gravel as the silhouette moved within an arm's reach. I swallowed hard and grimaced in anticipation of the unknown.

"Where have you been? We've been looking everywhere for you. Your grandma is worried sick."

The glow from the flashlight revealed Grandpa's furrowed brow as he stood with one hand on his hip, shaking his head.

"Watching a sunset," I managed to utter. My sister ran from behind me and hugged Grandpa's leg. His frown melted into a smile as he wrapped a comforting arm around her.

"We'll talk about this in the morning."

"Yes, sir." I closed my eyes and released a long sigh. The cow could wait until morning. I had all I could handle for one day.

Healing
Tom Klein

Like a doctor re-breaking a leg so that it can heal straight the second time, Dale Lewis dreaded the pain today would bring. He knew he had to work through this in order to move forward, but it didn't make his walk any easier.

The grass beneath him was freshly mown, the fall air crisp and clean. It was early in the morning, a beautiful mid-September day, the air was calm and not a bird in the sky. The only sound was a few small engines buzzing as the maintenance crew cut the grass and trimmed around each headstone in the next section. Dale was headed toward the big, lone oak in the center of section 27A at St. Peter and Paul Cemetery. His goal lay just past the tree and one row to the right.

Today was his first walk along the path in nearly four years. He walked behind a row of headstones to his left, each engraved with some poor soul's dates and name. Even without reading today, he remembered every name. It had been an almost daily ritual for the first year after she left him. Eventually, at the urging of family and friends, it slowed to once a week for a few years until a new job took him 300 miles away.

Rose Mary Wilson stepped out from behind the big oak and Dale froze for a moment. He looked back over his shoulder, his car still running where he had parked. It would be so easy to turn around and leave, but he put his head down and continued forward.

"Dale," she called out and waved.

He looked up and returned the wave, then looked off to his right, watching the lawn mowers work in section 28 as he continued to walk.

"Dale, it's great to see you again. You look good."

She held out her arms and smiled.

"I was surprised when I got your note in the mail. It was silly, you asking me to meet you here today. Where else would I be? What has it been . . . three—no—four years?"

"Rose," he replied, walking into the comfort of her embrace. They held each other for a full minute, just letting the silence soak through them. When they broke, he could see the redness had returned to her eyes.

"I come here often," she said walking one row over. She wiped her eyes and continued, "Always like today, on her birthday, but never on the anniversary of the accident. Richard lies next to her now." She pointed to a fresh headstone to the right. "It's been six months for him. He's protecting her like a good father should."

She paused for a moment, catching a few broken breaths.

"I'll join them, eventually, on the other side of Richard. Our family will rest in peace."

"I was sorry to hear about Samantha's dad. I really like Richard. I respected him and the life the two of you built for Sammy, but I . . . I just couldn't make myself . . ."

"I know. I know. Sam's death has been unfair to you. You have so much ahead of you."

They both stared at her headstone in silence.

Samantha Wilson
Beloved daughter of Rose Mary and Richard
September 14, 1987 – April 4, 2007

"You know, if only I had . . ."

Rose grabbed his hand in both of hers and pulled his eyes off the grave. "Now you listen here, Dale Lewis. What happened to our Sammy was *not* your fault. It was that drunk driver. That bastard crossed the center line and took her from us. And he walked away without a scratch. This was not your fault and you've got to let it go!"

"But if I would've driven home from U of I, instead of insisting that she drive up to meet me for the weekend, we wouldn't be standing here. It was so selfish, and now she's gone. Gone forever."

"No. If you drove home that night, I might be standing with Sammy and your mother at your grave instead. It was an act of fate. You cannot change that."

He hugged her again and sobbed, "I am so, so sorry."

Rose broke the hug after another minute and held him at arm's length, her hands at his shoulders. "I'm glad you moved on, but when you dropped off the radar, Richard and I feared the worst. I was so glad to get your note in the mail."

She opened her purse and pulled out the envelope.

"Dale, I know you loved Sammy. You two would have been great together. I might have had grandchildren by now, but that is not the path our lives took. She wouldn't want you to have a broken heart forever."

"That's what my therapist said."

"Therapist?"

"Yeah. I finally realized I needed someone to talk to, so I found someone. When it came out, it poured out. Eventually he convinced me to move on, find a different city, start fresh."

"Good, good for you," she said, letting go of his shoulders.

Dale stepped over to the headstone, reached in his pocket and pulled out a strip from a photo booth. It was him, a college freshman, his high school sweetheart Samantha on his lap, giggling at one of his jokes. There were five photos, the last was her giving him a kiss. He squatted down, placed the pictures on the headstone and placed his hand over her name.

Then, as he used a finger to trace out the April date, he continued, "He, my therapist, said I had to make peace, move on. That's why I left four years ago. Took a job in Chicago. Tried to forget. I did for a while, but it didn't seem right. Deep down, in a small, dark part of my soul, it still seems wrong."

Dale stood and turned to face Rose Mary.

"Part of me still feels hollow. I loved Samantha, I guess I always will. But now, my new life, it feels like cheating. So I wanted to let her know, let you know, that I'm alright and hope you feel it's okay that I moved on."

Rose Mary started to cry and moved over to hug him.

"It is, Dale. Richard and I loved the both of you."

She broke the embrace and wiped her tears.

"But . . . but it just wasn't meant to be. I wish the world for you."

Rose Mary looked over Dale's shoulder toward the car idling by the road. She pointed and asked, "Who is that young man?"

A boy was jogging toward them while a woman leaned against the hood of the car.

"Dad," the boy yelled out. "Dad, is this the lady you wanted me to meet?"

"Yeah, come here."

As the boy got to his father, Dale swooped him up high and then held him on his hip.

"Rose Mary, I'd like to introduce you to my son, Samuel Lewis. Sammy, this is Rose Mary, the friend I told you about."

"Well, Sammy, it is a pleasure to meet you," she said as a tear rolled down her face. "And little man, is that your mother over there? Back by the car."

"Yes, ma'am. That's Mommy. She said I could come over here if I walked real careful not to step on the people. But Dad, where are all the people? It's just you and this lady."

"Well, Sammy, sometimes people move on, but they leave a part of themselves behind in a place like this. We can visit them, love them."

"And we hav'ta watch where we walk so we don't step on their heads. Right?"

"Yes. You were very careful. Now, run back and tell Mommy I'll be right over."

Dale set him down and Sammy trotted back across the grass to his waiting mother.

"He's a beautiful little boy. You must be proud."

"Yes. And over there is my wife, Theresa. She's the real saint for putting up with me and my drama. I'd like you to meet her, and she'd like to meet you, too."

"That sounds like a lovely idea."

She turned him so he faced her.

"Dale, put the past behind you. You have enough on your plate raising that young man to be a fine gentleman like his father. Now, let's go meet Sammy's mother."

Rose Mary took his arm and they started towards the car. A puff of breeze blew at their backs, and Dale turned to see the wind pick up the pictures he left, spiral them up and out of sight.

A Noisy Mystery
M.L. Stiehl

My friend, Lyle, and I were walking home from the picnic very late in the evening. We passed through the thick part of the woods while it was dark and scary. We were just kids but remembered from early childhood the stories of the boogie man, zombies, and bad men with guns. We didn't normally think too much about that stuff, but darkness changes things. Though laughing and talking, we started to walk faster as it got darker. The moon was not scheduled to come out early this night, but we hoped the forecast was wrong, or at the very least, that we would get out of the trees soon.

We were frightened by a rustling ahead. We began to whisper and slow down, just creeping forward. Farther along, we saw the tail of an opossum that was running along toward a big tree. A couple more of his kind hung from a limb, resting soundly.

We laughed with relief, until Lyle said, "I guess they'll be heading to our hen houses when we're asleep tonight." We lived very close to each other, so both of our chickens were in danger. Predators were always bothering them.

We continued our homeward journey, glad to have figured out the source of our fear.

There were a few birds still awake, some fluttering in the trees, and others singing unseen from the higher branches.

We knew that many of the other animals were getting ready to sleep. But the ones that worried us were the ones that only came out at dark.

We each took a deep breath. We had come through a small glade and were entering another batch of trees.

Out of nowhere, a loud scream pierced the night. We froze in place, listening. I said, "I wish we had waited and rode back on the hay wagon with the adults."

Watching for any movement in the dark, we began to slowly move again. The sound repeated, this time from a different direction. Our legs started to move more quickly, prompted by our racing hearts.

I whispered, "Do you think it's some of the older kids trying to scare us?"

"I don't know. They do like to see us scared," Lyle answered. "Do you think they would follow us after the picnic, knowing grown-ups will be coming right behind us?" Then I realized, "Most of our folks will be on the road, not out here in the woods."

Lyle stopped and I said, "Are there any animals that come out at night and holler like that?"

We moved on, the moonlight peeping through tiny openings in the cover of leaves. We were sure glad for the light, but it hadn't solved our problem.

"Oh!" I cried out, recalling something from our classes. "Remember yesterday in school?" I asked. "Our teacher said that hoot owls scream like that. And they only holler when they see a light."

Lyle let out a loud breath. "That's our mystery solved."

We laughed with relief again and started to run as we saw the edge of the woods where the field met the road.

When we reached our houses, we decided we would keep our scary adventure to ourselves. Our folks would only laugh and say, "You should have come with us. You're too young to walk home alone at night."

But we knew, the scariest thing about nighttime is the unknown. The more we learn, the less we have to be scared of.

We smiled as we said goodnight to each other. We now had one more thing that would never scare us again.

The Night Visitors
Bradley D. Watson

It seemed an ordinary night when the Robinsons headed to bed. The weather outside was typical for early autumn, the sky clear, the wind cool. Cliff gazed through the picture window at the sparkling tapestry of stars plastered on a velvet background. He felt them inviting him to other worlds somewhere far away. He stared a moment longer before closing the shades and turning off the lights.

Margie called from the bedroom, reminding her husband to make sure to lock up. Feeling his way to the front door, he opened it quietly and inhaled the autumn night. He loved the crisp air and the smell of winter coming. Reluctantly, he closed and locked the door, then headed off to bed.

For hours, a quiet rested in the almost complete darkness of the living room, broken only by the sound of the air conditioner kicking-off one last time for the night. The house slept, at peace.

After a few hours, however, a change began. In the center of the room, a blackness was gathering, almost invisible in the lightless space, formless like a cloud of ink. From its depths a small, round orb appeared. It hung motionless at the end of a pole whose other end disappeared into the splash of black. After a moment, the pole and orb were pulled back into the cloud of nothing.

It was then that three dark forms climbed from the undulating shadow. They could barely be made out in the room, for they were creatures of intense black, about four-foot tall. They did not seem to need any light in the room.

"Hurry," one whispered with a thin voice. "We have little time."

"I don't like this," the second quietly responded.

"The probe was right, wasn't it? It showed breathable air, livable conditions. We are still alive." The voices were kept low, trying not to be heard.

"I know, but I don't like stepping into a world that might be dangerous."

"You're just a coward," the third finally spoke. He was looking around the room, the lack of light no hindrance to his perceptions. "There is nothing for us to fear here. We are invincible. We can take what we want."

"Take what we *need*," the leader corrected in his thin voice. "We must have this planet to survive. And though the army is prepared to step into this world at our signal, it is our task to make the scouting trip, making sure the planet is ripe for our conquest."

"Why this one?" the doubter asked. "Why did they choose this world?"

"It was a long process," the first answered, trying to hold his temper. "For years our scientists have been searching the rifts we've created in space. All have been inhospitable to us. So many had destructive environments. And some had creatures that were unpleasant or inedible. We need nourishment."

"Why the hurry, though?" There was challenge in the voice.

"We have become desperate," he continued. "It has been kept from the common people, but perhaps you should know now. We are without food and need to find something quickly, or our species will die. The soldiers even now are barely held at bay. They must have rations or they will revolt and kill us all. And that cannot be allowed. We must survive.

"After searching through dimension after dimension, world after world, the council was close to despair. We had nothing . . . no hope. Only when this place, this one dimension, was discovered yesterday, did we finally have hope. It is the only one that fits our needs. We must move quickly. We have sent three probes into this world, and we can delay no longer. This one seems usable. It must be now."

"I don't like this one," the creature challenged.

"Twice in the last two days we have investigated this world. Our first probe showed conditions favorable to us, and a food supply most expansive, counting millions of life forms in a small area. Our second opening of a rift here was to pull one of the creatures through to see if it was edible. It was loud and fought back wildly, using a language I'm sure we could decipher, if it was worth our while. But we did find it to be enjoyable to consume. With so many of these on the planet, we can immediately be fed."

The figures continued their investigation, slipping silently through the room. One creature stooped down, examining a potted plant on the floor, testing its strength by pulling leaves from it. The leader was feeling the smooth top of a table as he considered its use. The final creature, still unhappy, had found the front window curtains. In curiosity, he pulled one back.

"Ahhh!" he said, much too loud, dropping the curtain back in place. As the others jumped to his side, he dropped to the floor, holding both hands over his face in pain. Wisps of black smoke were appearing by his hands, as if from a blown-out candle. He moaned.

"What happened?" the leader asked, trying to pry hands from the dark face.

Rocking back and forth, the creature would not let go. He managed to whisper disjointedly, "Through that . . . portal . . . it burns . . . pins . . . of pain!"

"Coward," one said under his breath, reaching for the curtain. The wounded one, hearing the movement, began scooting backward on the floor, away from the window, whimpering, "No, no, no!"

This creature, however, was more careful, barely parting the curtains, just a very tiny slit. With his own quiet exclamation of pain, he let them close again. "He's right," the creature hissed. "They have weapons up high. Millions of them, spraying light on the ground. We will need to warn the army. We must be prepared to protect ourselves from them. Not strong weapons, but many. They will burn."

"Come. We need to report," the leader said, "before the army begins its deployment. If we delay, it will be too late. If they come unprepared, all may be lost."

They reached to help their suffering companion from the floor, failing to see the human hand snaking around the wall, reaching for the light switch. There was a soft click, and white light swallowed the room.

The leader tried to scream, but the sound fell silent as his ability to speak dissipated. Like three dark pieces of wood in the center of a white hot sun, the deadly light vaporized all three creatures, leaving only the slightest hint of wispy darkness behind.

Cliff peeked around the corner, eyeing each part of the room carefully. "I don't see anything."

Margie appeared behind him, a bat held in both hands. "I'm sure I heard something."

Cliff looked through all the rooms carefully, making sure all was well.

"It must have been your imagination," he finally told his wife. "Let's get back to bed."

"Can we leave a nightlight on down here?" she asked.

"I don't see what good a little light would do, but if it makes you feel better." He flipped on the little hall light and put his arm around his wife as they walked back to the bedroom.

In the living room, now slightly lit by a dim light, the darkness found itself unwelcome.

One Damn Dime
Jay Harden

One of those rare moments when the world comes together for you—that's what it was, one moment around a safe campfire deep in the Missouri woods when something important becomes clear at last and destiny spawns meaning with no effort, as though the time arrived on schedule. Just a bunch of old warriors thinking out loud, without perfect words, without thinking too hard about the hardness of Vietnam more than four decades in the past, with words rolling forth that we alone could understand, words that would confuse eavesdroppers, self-evident words, requiring no explanation.

The weather was clear, too, and the stars were the same as they have always been, the same as they were shining then in that jungle. Our fire was crackling soft, and there was a peace lying over us along the Cuivre River that we never found in Southeast Asia, like an accidental gift. The beer helped and the harmonica called the memories along. We were all together again, only this time we had time to think and relax in the safe sounds and place we created. And we had acquired a luxury beyond listening, deep into knowing.

Curtis told his story offhanded and effortless, ready for birth in the familiar darkness. That night the general theme driving us all was the meaning of Vietnam now in our lives. What had we learned then and since then? Were we grateful for what happened—all of it—or were we full of selective regret?

When he got back, Curtis said, he returned to his old haunts in the projects of Pruitt-Igoe, a modern ghetto created by the best white intentions. He returned angry, like most of us, and he felt at home with the old anger around him still there: every emotion as it was when he left. No one else had changed in the meantime: same people and same behaviors, unaware, lost, without learning.

Not long after returning from combat, he said, he came upon a bunch of guys shooting dice in a corner of one of the buildings crumbling with grime and despair, kept unchanged like all the others by distracting alcohol and drugs. Broken bulbs and the evening shadows made it hard to see. The bet was a dime. A mindless argument erupted over the game. Someone felt cheated or someone had cheated, who knows? The man with the grievance just pulled out a pistol and shot him. Shot him six times. Emptied the revolver as easily and unconsciously as any man adjusting his junk. For a dime in 1969. One damn dime.

Curtis watched it unfold in slow motion, just like his combat in Vietnam, where the sequence and speed are surreal. The entire event lasted mere seconds, another memory seared forever and unwanted into his brain.

Curtis remembers this game often, but tonight he voiced that lesson he learned for the first time. He told us because it came forth from his soul without resistance and flowed out his mouth to help him understand the value of his time in Vietnam. He told us because the absence of judgment that we created around the fire spilled into him. And now, in the telling, he knows the meaning of that war personally, at least one meaning, at least for now.

Curtis said, because he was drafted and went to Vietnam, he had the choice when he returned to become one of those two guys shooting dice, or not. As he watched, he could see himself as either man easily: one as bad as the other. Curtis let us know in his inelegant, clean honesty that Army boot camp and combat showed him what he never knew he possessed. He found the liberation of self-discipline in his green jungle that still has not been discovered in the concrete combat jungle of the projects back home. Yes, he had killed many of the enemy. And in so doing, he learned to value life, precisely, his own life, and the lives of his brothers under fire, and the lives of brothers like him back in the world who did not. He had no feelings for the dead enemy at his feet, he said, but every dead G.I. he saw brought his heart to his throat. In a word, he learned to care. He discovered caring about someone else who cared about him and, in the process, to appreciate who he had been, what he had become, and where he wanted to go. For the first time, Curtis learned to care well for Curtis.

It took a prior lack of regard, a war, and then a dice game, to give Curtis a meaning to his war in Vietnam. Yeah, he said, he had some regrets. Yeah, he said, he would do it all again, too. Yeah, he said, all that life-taking saved his own and his friends.' He said it in his own words, uninterrupted, to the rest of us, listening with such a fierce focus and respect that the flames glistened at the bottom of our eyes. We knew what he said and, more than that, knew what he meant, and what an invitation his story was to us.

Good old Curtis. He opened the door, bless him. So we each, in turn, explained what that forsaken war meant personally, too, around a campfire, under a clear, starry sky in the woods by the Cuivre River, safe in our heartland, safe enough to release what we waited so long to say. Coming home is a process, we realized. That night, Curtis arrived. And, for a dime, we followed.

ANY ELEMENT GOES: Poetry

Midwest Heat in Summer
Claudia Mundell

Branches on the Osage Orange droop like arms of a giant,
Their withered leaves lusting for rainwater.
Blistered corn rattles stalks in bursts of breeze;
Ponds shrink to shallow and show the muddy banks
Where cattle stand seeking heat relief.

He heads for the house with face bandana red
As he wipes his sweaty brow and
Smacks brown dust from faded denim overalls,
Powdered earth that doesn't remember rain.

She looks at the counter of canning tomatoes,
Knows they can wait until the sun sinks.
She leads him upstairs, clicks on the fan.
They shed damp clothes, smell their own musk,
Then make their own heat before giving in to sleep—
An afternoon nap with dreams of thunder and rain.

An Army Wife's Residual Images
R.R.J. Sebacher

I sat at the picture window
Thinking and rocking / rocking and thinking
This might be the perfect solution
No more darkrooms with red and yellow lights
I could eliminate the necessity to feel
My work could stand on purely technical merit
Digital photography could let me continue
In my chosen profession

On weekend mornings he would enter my darkroom
Pretending he needed me to fix him breakfast
He would lift the lid on the fixer solution
Breathe in and paraphrase Robert Duvall's
Famous line from Apocalypse Now
"Ah nothing like the smell of fixer in the morning"
When he wasn't TDY
He never missed a weekend
Save the one his father died
That morning he just held me and cried
A luxury now denied to me
For the children's sake

When the Chaplain at my husband's funeral
Claimed we should be proud
The patrol had gone out in a blaze of glory
I finally understood the euphemism
Choke or go blind

How ironic / he had told me
His mission was to cleanup and save
That country in the Persian Gulf
While clearing a suspected sniper's house

His night patrol had triggered an IED
Homemade napalm or jellied gas
Made by mixing Tide detergent and gasoline

Darkness stops
A red yellow glow
Flashing to a screaming white
Faster than the mind can frame
Slower than the soul can shut

My hand reflexively snaps out
Trying to dodge the image of him
Developing in the silver salts
Of tears I cannot shed

I watched as a pure white moth
Immolated itself / drawn to the light
Then flipped the switch
Not needing its comfort to sleep
Like the moth my soul already seared
By the moon's cold red-gold illumination

The Gridlines
Bradley Bates

He gets happy at the roar and crunch of the teeth
eating oatmeal, granola, and the serenity
of sipping his green tea on this camping trip
through parts of the Grand Canyon.
They meet Manzanita, Bristlecone, and Ponderosa
on trails hiking until the sun begins
to deepen
his memory
like his Mom at the Harris House for treatment,
and his Dad at the hospital in the middle of Indiana
for a bleeding ulcer he couldn't get to
from the middle of Missouri in college.
Eruptions of mind noticing gridlines
disrupting forests in Northern Arizona
in comparison to the iron age in the center
of the US. Now, houses build themselves
up from the ground all along the street
he lived along during high school years,
and the deer have disappeared outside
the Greenway he rides his bike through
a paved trail on the banks of the Meramec
River. Twelve point bucks will almost
come up for a touch but back down.
They stomp, bark, and call the remaining herd
home eating again to continue, in safety,
but the elderly have their wisdom, no matter
the quirkiness that outlives them.

Frozen Phoenix
R.R.J. Sebacher

Spread eagled on a bloody cold stone slab
Veil of a lacy crystalized ice
Covers her majestic form and face
Father Frost attends cloaked in white
Fur she gives the animals in her season
Dead hollow bone that is their hair
Trims his collar, cuff, hood, and hem

Wailing over his lost love
Kissing his Hohner with frozen lips
Tonguing harmonic peal and repeal
In a soulful bluesy beat
Or is it the wind and wagging bells

No witches for they thought it governed by the moon
The bears, her mourning midwives, were there
They know she always dies at high noon
First spikes burst through the snow
Will be her funeral flowers
No one ever seems to remember
Winter dies birthing Spring

Lightkeeper

Nicki Jacobsmeyer

He
is a Lightkeeper,

lantern,   the eye of the sea   alarm,

beacon of hope,   L   I   G   H   T   disaster alert,

beam of brilliance,   shining without fail,   warning of danger,

refuge of night,   from dawn to dusk,   unknown strain,

guide   from dusk to dawn   radar

an unknown marine hero
stationed in the watchtower
following orders.

Keep replenishing the fuel

Keep winding the clockworks

Keep shining the brasswork

admiring in awe the   nature's

majestic beauty in   y o u r

own piece of secluded paradise

Keep working in damp dungeon

Keep climbing the spiral staircase

Keep tolerating the aching loneliness

enjoying   the peace of solitude and

the joy of   a simple fulfilling life

significant and s t a l k e d by the sailors

Keep hearing the shrills of the fog horn

Keep talking to the stranger in the mirror

Keep tormenting yourself with uncertainty

LIGHTKEEPER, THE EYE OF THE SEA, KEEP SANE.

ANY ELEMENT GOES: Prose

What We Wish For
Douglas N. Osgood

I read once about some German named Goethe. He said, "Beware what you wish for in youth, because you will get it in middle age." The truth is in those words. As a young man, I wished for little, but one thing I did wish for, I thought I got soon after. It didn't turn out that way, and I've wished for it since.

I rode into the town of Sowers yesterday. There was no one in the street to notice. Not much to this place, a few weather-beaten buildings assembled along a dusty stretch of the road connecting Dallas to Irving. There were a dozen businesses operating out of tents, including the saloon. I needed a drink, so I tied my roan to the rail in front and pushed through the partially open flap. Whiskey barrels supported a short plank that served as a bar. Behind the plank the barkeeper stood, back to the bar, humming some ditty while wiping out glasses. Otherwise, the tent was empty. I strode to the far end of the plank, my spurs jingling with each step. He must have heard them because he turned around. His glance was quick, but it found my face and then the tied down hog legs belted about my waist. He quickly averted his gaze.

"What's your pleasure?" he asked, looking at me again.

"Whiskey. Double."

"Don't I know you?"

"Never been here before." That was true, but I had been a lot of places, none for long. Towns ain't much on my kind stickin' around. I took my first good look at him. Medium height, white apron straining against his bulging belly, two days' growth. Nothing unusual, could have been any of a thousand men. Except for his hair. He had distinctive red hair like you might find on one man in ten thousand. I didn't know him. Did he know me?

I'd been hoping to stick around a while, maybe pick up some honest work. My pap had me workin' the farm from the time I was old enough to hold a hoe 'til I lit a shuck when I was fifteen. It wasn't the hard work that drove me off; I enjoyed that. It was the other stuff. After Ma died, Pa took to drinkin'. He was a mean drunk, and he was drunk a lot. I took the brunt of it, shielded Pru from him. After a couple a' years, I couldn't take any more. All I wanted was some peace. The preacher at Pa's funeral said there was peace in death. I should have found it in Pa's death.

The barkeeper stared at me for several seconds as he stroked the stubble on his chin. "Can't place ya, but you sure do look like someone I've met." He shook his head. "Maybe you're right. I must be mistaken." He sat my whiskey down in front of me.

"Easy to do." I downed it in one gulp and slammed the glass to the bar. *Whew.* I wasn't sure if I was relieved he didn't know me or refreshed from the drink. Maybe both. "Another."

He produced his bottle, refilled the glass and returned to his ditty and cleaning. I took my time with this one—finished it in two gulps. I tossed four bits on the bar. "Cover it?" I asked.

He glanced back. "More than. Let me get your change."

"Keep it," I said as I walked out.

My roan whinnied as I approached her; she always greeted me like that. I fed her a carrot from the stash I kept in my vest pocket for such occasions.

The livery, one of the three buildings in town, wasn't hard to find. Northeast corner of town next to the outhouses—gotta keep the stables and latrines downwind as much as possible. The stable boy said his name was *Jesús*. I made sure he knew to give my girl plenty of water and some oats. I gave him an extra bit to rub her down good. I grabbed my bags, but left the saddle over the rail of her stall.

I was halfway out the door when I turned back to the kid. "Any place a feller can rent a room in this town?"

A big, toothy grin crossed his face. "*Sí, señor.* My mama. She runs the cantina and has rooms upstairs." His finger pointed back up the street.

"*Muchas gracias.*" I remembered the place—right next to the saloon. It was the only place in town with a second story. Darkness had fallen while I was in the livery. There were no lanterns or torches burning outside, so the only light to see by was the hazy glow that filtered through the oiled canvas of the saloon walls and the flickering heat lightning.

As I passed the saloon, I heard the sounds of clinking glasses, falling poker chips, and men laughing. Familiar sounds. I was almost past the place when I heard the barkeep.

". . . in here this afternoon. I knew who it was soon's I saw him. Those tied down Peacemakers were a dead giveaway. Thought I might pee myself, I was so scared."

I froze. My heart lodged in my throat and beat a drum. And I waited for what was to follow. I've heard it a hundred times if I've heard it once. I just want some peace.

"I heard he killed thirty men in fair fights," said one man.

"I heard it was forty," chimed in another. Everyone started talkin' at once.

"No, it's twenty-three. I got it straight from . . ."

The real number would have disappointed them. Just ten, countin' Pa. Eleven, if you count Ma, but that wasn't my fault. Was it? Pa blamed me. Said it was my fault she got sick. Been carryin' it around fer more'n twenty years.

"I saw him in Missouri, ya know." That was the barkeeper again. I still couldn't place him.

"They say he's faster'n a frog eatin' a fly."

"I heard he beat John Wesley Hardin."

Where do they hear this stuff? I've never met Hardin. Besides, I heard he's in prison down here in Texas somewhere.

"Well, I ain't afeared of the likes of him. I been practicin' and everyone says I'm fast." The speaker sounded young.

There it was. Always that fool anxious to prove himself, prove how fast he was. They're never as fast as their friends think they are. Or as good. Lot different shootin' at a man. Cans wait 'til you're ready to draw. Cans don't shoot back. Why is it always a kid? How many of those ten were kids? Four? Five? Yah, five. *Ah, damn. Not again.*

What I wouldn't give for some peace. I came down to Texas to get away from my reputation. Figured since I spent most of my life wondering Missouri and Kansas, no one would know me here. What did the preacher say? There was peace in death.

". . . saw him kill a feller in Abilene town. Nerves of steel. Let the other feller draw before he reached. Took him right between the eyes."

Yeah, that one's right. Two years ago. He was a good man, but the railroad paid me handsomely to make sure he got dead. Felt bad about goading him into a fight, so I gave him a chance. I don't think he had ever fired a gun before. He still hadn't when he died. That was the last time I did it for money. Still have nightmares about it. Wife, two kids. *Damn.*

I shook my head trying to erase the memory. If I had any sense, I'd a' turned on my boot heel right there, collected my hoss, and headed out of town. Instead I pushed open the door to the cantina and walked in.

The *señora* gave me a room. She had a steaming pot of coffee and a plate full of *frijoles* and beef smothered in *mole*. I ate, but I didn't taste it. After, I went to bed.

Sometime in the middle of the night, I woke from a fitful sleep.

"Tucker. Gabriel Tucker. Come on out here. I ain't afeared a' you. I'm fast." The words were slurred. It was the kid from the saloon.

Damn, go home and sleep it off.

"We know you're in there, Tucker. What's the matter? Chicken? Yella-bellied?" There were more drunken hollers from the street. His friends. Great friends. Like to get him killed. I ignored them. I could pretend to be asleep as long as they didn't come knockin' on my door. Then I'd have to do something. I rolled over. Sleep didn't come for a long time.

I sat in the front corner of the cantina, back to the wall. Habit. Man in my profession wants to have his back to the wall, able to see anyone entering a room before they see him. I was nursing a bottle of whiskey from the saloon, a plate of beef and *frijoles* getting cold on the table in front of me. I was trying to forget. Forget Abilene. Forget the kid from last night. Forget the other kids in other places.

Forget Pa. Forget how much I miss Ma. All I've ever wanted was peace.

I was thinkin', too. Thinkin' about peace. Thinkin' about quiet. Thinkin' about life. Thinkin' about death. Nobody bothers you when you're dead. There's peace in death. I looked at the bottle, it was almost empty.

There was a commotion out on the street. It was the kid, again. Hadn't he slept it off?

"Gabriel Tucker. Come face me."

Shit. I just want to be left in peace. I guess not in this life.

"Come on, ya coward. Gabriel Tucker, big, bad gunfighter. He's yella."

I made up my mind. Maybe this'll turn out alright after all. Rising from my chair, I loosened the gun in its holster. Spurs jingled as I strode to the door and stepped out into the street.

A crowd had gathered along the street. The boy's friends, mostly, I imagine. At least they all look to be of an age with him. But there were a few others, too. I saw *Jesús* poke his head out'a the stable door and look this way. Then he ducked back inside. Smart kid.

"You lookin' for me, kid?"

"You ready to die, old man?"

"Kid, I'm gonna do you a favor. Go home. Forget about me."

"I ain't afeared a' you."

"Didn't say you was. How about if we agree that you're faster and leave it at that?"

"You're yella. I'm gonna be famous. Whole world'll know that Bill Haley beat Gabriel Tucker."

And come gunnin' for you, stupid kid. Gonna do your momma a favor.

"If that's the way you want it."

"Draw!" the kid shouted.

In a fight, I see everything as if it was happening real slow. I watched as the kid's right hand dropped to the butt of his gun. It seemed to take forever. I didn't move. His hand gripped the butt and the gun cleared leather. I didn't move. His left hand heeled the hammer back. I didn't move. He fired. I still didn't move.

White lightning tore at my gut. Everything blurred for a second. When my vision cleared, the ground was rushing up to meet me. He ain't fast, but he can shoot. God, my insides are burnin' up. I clutched my arms around my gut. It hurts bad.

I did my good deed. The kid'll go to prison where no one can shoot him huntin' a reputation. His momma can visit him. And I finally have some peace. I guess Goethe was right, it takes to middle-age to get what you wish for.

Little Light Above
Larry Duerbeck

Here we go, ladies. back here. Back to the start of a nasty, niggling, bit-by-bit bad day. We've all taken a run at a bad day now and then. Haven't we? Or felt a bad day take a run at us. Nothing terribly serious, no finding that lump in your breast but—.

Snaggy little things drib and drab along, grabbing at you one after another, and you wonder if anything will just slide easy.

Slide nice. Slide your way. The hope is there in the middle of all your troubles, in the middle of all your complaints, in the middle of everything you touch. The hope is for a happy ending to make it all turn out right, to make your day worth it. The hope is you'll be able to go over it again, check off a laundry list of dismaying entries. Right?

Sometimes life does go our way. Sometimes, our hopes are dashed. A whacking great last blast can cap off the whole crappy day.

So imagine, ladies. Imagine we're all here together, back at the beginning.

Friday morning, and you're happy. You're ready. You're set to go. But your garage door opener just says no. Just up and quits. Just as though it won some major appliance lottery and is telling you to drop dead, boss lady. It happens, right? Next, you try your luck with the wall switch. Nada. So you go to the red-handled, red-tagged, change-to-manual hangy-down cord. You reach up and pull. Click. Easy. It even sounds right. Click. Once more. Click. Encouraged, you now just have to lift the door.

Oophie. Stuck.

Stand back up. Consider. If tonight's date were here. Oh, yeah. He'd get this done. Tall, dark, handsome. And strong. Tall, dark, strong white knight. Ah, well.

Sister, it's all up to you. I get myself rebraced. Bend over. Grab the handle. Both hands. One hand over, one hand under. Interlock those fingers. A death grip. Squat. How becoming. Now.

Stuck.

Knees, thighs, lower back, shoulders—give it your all. Up through the glutes, the nape of my neck. Now!

"Mother—"

Zoom! Unstuck, I'm swept off my feet.

"Frumper!"

Too late, my death grip comes alive. Doubly unstuck, I drop. Plumped butt first on the garage floor.

As the door's rolling rattle dies away, I hear two-tone laughter.

Propped up on both forearms, I scan the sidewalk, search out the sounds. My lucky day. A mother and son. The kind they don't hardly make any more. A June-bug mother and her damned white-bread Beaver, both laughing at me. The mother's tittering is worse.

Worse, until after that brat's ha-ha-has, until the kid calls me back into playground sex play. "I saw London, I saw France—" No need to finish. We know the rest.

He sure did see. He hit a jackpot eyeful, accent on the jack, I'm sure. "Now, stop." Mother shook the little crumb's arm and regained her plucked-and-permed composure. "My dear! Are you all right?"

Bruised but unbroken, I call out to the world I am fine, thank you very much. June bug starts the two down the sidewalk. Tittering trails back and. "But Mom. I did!" He calls out the color, before being shushed. Time out to frown and count my small, blue blessing of combed cotton.

I lie back down and pretend I'm at the supermarket. Clean up, aisle five! No help, not even pretend. I get on my feet to add up the damages and nearly fall down again.

One heel snapped clean now, right thumbnail blown all to hell, pantyhose runs, cream shantung skirt smudged but good. And one bruised what that mother would have called her hip. Her right hip. Hip, my ass.

You hobble back inside and call the office. You explain.

I explained to the general manager. A man. One reason I have faith in the male sex. Another is my supervisor. A woman. Now there's a mother superior. She would have been peeved, pissy and full of cool reproof. More than usual, I mean.

Mr. Deltan laughed. I wanted to shower and shampoo in that warm laughter. "Honey, it sounds like you're in for a dry-dock day. But you're out and the seas are rough. Take care, and take your time."

Making repairs, I wonder if a wrecked manicure could serve as good ice-breaking material for early first-date flirting. A bruised hip may be a teensy premature, a little much. Perhaps, if all goes well, a nightcap. Or bottom.

Then, my car, my new car—well, secondhand—well, used—my just bought, merry little muscle-ette-mobile damn near decides not to start.

Doesn't want to. Come on, come on! Ah.

Ungrateful beast. Didn't I fill up the thirsty new steed tiptop full last thing yesterday? Yes, and now it's pinging like my oven timer as we roll at its own slow speeds. Never mind me and my right foot.

Some while later, I take another dip in Mr. Deltan's laughter. It feels chillier. "You interns! Next time you might want to try high test," he says. "Huh. I wouldn't own a car that didn't take to regular like a wino to Ripple."

And so the day drove me, ladies. Downhill. My date glowed before me, above and bright. Big as a sunset, a sunrise. But there also loomed the ETA. A shabby-to-tatters rain cloud, dark, persistent, and threatening all my radiant plans.

The ETA, I should confess, was my creation. My device. My responsibility. If I got to his place on time, then we'd hop into his beloved VW bug for a rock concert somewhere. The university grounds, I think. Who cares? My ETA.

6 p.m. was the latest. 6 p.m. was my deadline. 6 p.m. was all I cared about. He had his schedule. I had mine.

Naturally, the late start didn't further my interests. By the end of the day, my schedule had stretchmarks from all the meetings. Last of all was most of all, worst of all, longest of all.

Had to be. Of course. Re-upping our contract with a tenured professor whose trendy textbooks rose to be chart-toppers in their niches and far beyond. His latest title was a sure-fire bestseller. *Movies and Menace, the Male Malignancy.*

Mr. Deltan and the good professor got along as Scrooge and Marley must have. Much pleased to discuss, at congenial length, which sides of whose slices of what bread got the butter and jam.

So this last appointment, this late-on-a-Friday-afternoon appointment, ballooned into a cash-fueled big league bull session.

How is it money makes men so freaking chummy and long-winded?

Theory on male bonding is all fine and dandy. But sh. . . Sheesh! These two? Sparring partners. Money buddies. A pain in the butt.

Speaking of that. My bruise decides to make itself felt.

In my chair, I lean over and cross my legs and guess what? Ladies?

A damned strap of my newest, a special event poosh-em-upper from Aphrodite's Armoire, starts to dig in.

What, now?!

Yes, now. Time digs in. I shift and grit my teeth as the minutes limp, lame and all but halt. Still, I know how swiftly they race elsewhere.

Later, my poor poisoned little beastie croaks to life and pings me along at its I'm-doing-my-best ... umm, best. Yes.

There's a parking place! Nice and close. With time left on the meter. You dare to hope things may be looking up. Quick, now. A spray of perfume, a brush through long brown hair. Tilt the mirror. Hit the lipstick later. Maybe not an A plus, but damn, girl! A good solid A. At least for effort. Grab your purse and go.

I all but run to the apartment house and inside its vestibule, where a junior executive model, suited and male, and more junior than executive, stands before the bell board. He looks over.

"You new here?" I nod, somehow smiling back. "This palace, ha!, is wired so. You press the button. The bell rings. If the light above the buzzer button—there." He points. "One for each. See? If this lights up, then someone's pressed the answer button. Someone's home. Here, I'll show you. Hope she is."

He presses. Then. One Mizzsippi—Two Mizzsippi—Three. The light comes on. Not much to see. A dim dime-sized disk glows grubby toenail white. Not much, but enough for me. Him, too.

"Hallelujah. Well, I'm off. Say—!" He pipes me good.

"Nice. Looks like someone's set for some fine Friday night cuttin'. Cuttin' 'em." He snaps his fingers, showing off cuff and cufflink like a hip and cool old-timer. Bobby Darin, say. Snap!

"Dead. Looking good, lady, and good luck."

I say, "Thanks," to his trimly tailored back and, "I'll need it," to the rows of buttons.

In a few minutes, I'm kicking down the cobblestones. Well, stomping the concrete. Cursing my god damned day, my god damned luck, my god damned life. I'm like my supervisor on high test. Worse. Peeved, pissy and pouring over with reproof, lava hot. God damned sonofabitch. White light, white knight sonofabitch. Five minutes, by my Lady Accutron. Can't he wait five frumpin' minutes? For a lady looking good? His loss.

You, a-hole, are off my list.

So, we ladies live and learn. We do, don't we? We better. We live and learn to start up fresh and renewed. I lived and learned. Learned every day is my lucky day. God blesséd day, God blesséd luck, God blesséd life.

Since my luckiest day.

But not really every day since. Really every day since the day I first learned. The day I first learned, with the news, when the evening the rest of my God blesséd life dawned on me.

The day I first remembered. Really remembered.

So here we are ladies, back here. When I pressed the button and waited in vain for that little light above the name of my white knight. Ted Bundy.

Smitten
Stan Wilson

Cole Carson, a former Texas Ranger, rode slouched over in the saddle. A layer of trail dust covered his duster and black Stetson, turning them gray as the sky on a cold winter morning.

In a lone Sycamore tree at the edge of Scorpion, a hung man swung in the breeze, telegraphing the town's feelings: "Strangers not welcome."

Cole had trailed a thief who stole his prize stallion from Jackson Hole, Wyoming, to this hellhole in southeast Kansas.

He'd entered Scorpion, the belly of the beast, a pit where no one could be trusted.

***

The U.S. Marshal's office in Dodge City warned him. "Connie Hart, Scorpion's town marshal, is dangerous as any gunslinger you'll ever encounter. Cole, we've seen you both in action. You're fast, but she's faster and her aim's deadly. She's a crazy bitch whose favorite weapon's a sawed-off shotgun. Don't turn your back on her."

The search of the past months left him exhausted. He'd ridden over a thousand miles, across snow-capped mountains, windy plains and eroded bone-dry badlands.

He tied his horse to the hitching rail at Cherry's Blossom, the town's combination saloon and brothel, a hastily thrown together group of tents and wooden lean-tos. His spirits were boosted by the happy sounds from a honky-tonk piano playing in the background. Cole spoke with the saloon keeper, who told him, "The other day, Connie had a hassle with a drifter over who owned the black stallion. Watch yourself. She's as mean as any man and does damn well whatever she pleases."

Ignoring the warning, he hurried across the street to Connie's Livery Stable.

Connie Hart, the owner, dressed in tight buckskins and muddy boots with a shotgun slung over her shoulder, stared at him. Only her flaming red hair and hourglass figure indicated she was female.

Her pearl-handled revolvers and shiny marshal's badge glistened in the sun. She stood tall, radiating power—she was the Law in Scorpion.

"I'm Cole Carson from Jackson Hole, owner of the horse behind you!" Carson yelled as he hurried toward her.

"Prove it."

"That stallion's got my brand, a Double 'C' on his right hip. I'm here for him."

"Need better proof. Someone could've told you about the brand," she responded.

"Listen, lady, I raised him from a colt. He's mine." Carson had searched too long to back down without retrieving his favorite animal. Without a word, he snapped his fingers. The black rushed to him, gently nudged him like a playful kitten. When Cole raised his hand, the stallion reared and whinnied.

Carson continued, "When the bastard stole my horse, it wore a Mexican-style saddle with silver trim. The fenders of the saddle are marked with my Double 'C' brand."

***

Connie had mixed feeling about the bossy drifter who wore his guns tied low like a two-bit gunslinger. He wasn't about to tell her what to do.

Secretly, she burned with a desire to please the angry, domineering man with a windblown tan, in need of a shave and haircut, who'd looked like he'd not seen the likes of soap and water for months.

Carson's deep blue eyes pierced her like a Cherokee's arrow. She couldn't break the visual lock between them; his gaze petrified her.

She sensed his determination and suspected he wouldn't be denied that which he wanted. She'd seen that look from men at the brothel, when they selected their woman for pleasure. Deep inside, she couldn't hold back her thoughts of him and her in a haystack. The idea caused her skin to tingle. She couldn't resist the suggestive images flashing through her mind. He walked taller than any of the worthless, good-for-nothing cowpokes in that part of Kansas.

She asked herself, "Who the hell is this stranger, who paraded in here like he owned the place?"

"The saddle's in the barn. You owe two months for boarding the stallion."

He grinned as he paid the bill.

Carson didn't understand why, but Connie Hart stirred his emotions. The saloon girls standing in front of Blossom's were better looking.

Mysteriously, she'd ended up with his horse and saddle. Crooked lawmen, in his opinion, were the scum of the earth, even if one was a good looking woman.

Carson's mind, amidst chaos and confusion, knew she'd touched him deeply. He hadn't had any feelings since the murder of his wife five years ago. His soul knew, Connie's a dangerous woman, she'd became his challenge.

He strolled to the Chinese laundry and bathhouse. The crude sign propped against the tent stated a dollar for the bath and another for washing and ironing clothes. After being on the trail for months, a hot bath would heighten his sprits. They trimmed his salt and pepper hair and beard for a nickel. Looking in the mirror, a tall handsome man stared back wearing a Stetson and duster, once more black in color.

Cole returned to the saloon for the free lunch. The bartender asked, "Connie gonna let you have the horse? You know, she loves that animal. She's rode him every day the past months."

Carson didn't answer, his mind thinking about other chores. When in Dodge, he'd ordered a couple of new Winchester rifles and a case of cartridges to be shipped to Scorpion's Overland Stage office. They should be there by now.

The new lever action rifles were things of beauty. He'd requested the nickel plated receiver covers be engraved with the Double 'C' brand and hurried to his unfinished business at the stable.

He kicked every stone along the walk. His mind was in turmoil. What he'd heard hadn't dampened his burning itch for the woman. By God, now's a good a time as another to get it scratched.

With every step, he fought his crazy obsession—to seize her and make her his own.

A woman whom he'd been warned would beat him to the draw in a fair fight, and she didn't fight fair. He knew he had to be suffering hallucinations from too many meaningless, lone nights on the trail.

***

She heard him searching the stable for her.

"Lady, where are you!" he yelled.

"Out back. If you weren't so frigging blind, you would've found me by now."

She sat in the horse trough taking a bath—with her feminine charms covered in soapsuds. She didn't bother to hide herself. Like a couple of kids, they stared at each other without a whisper. The strange attraction linking them was as powerful as the springtime wind of a Kansas tornado.

He took a deep breath and pictured them snow-bound at his cabin in western Wyoming the upcoming winter.

"What are you doing here?" she asked.

He failed to notice her beautiful blue and white dress, the only one she owned, hanging on the clothesline. She'd planned to be wearing it when he returned.

"We have unfinished business."

Smiling, he moved slowly to the horse trough, stood with his hands on his hips as he looked her over like a judge at the local horse show. He hesitated for a moment, trying to make his mind up as to if she was worthy of the blue ribbon. His heart knew it had to be a gold one.

He leaned over, taking her head gently in his powerful hands, kissing first her eyes, then her neck, and finally her lips. A rush of pent-up passion exploded, uniting their hearts like a thunderbolt from heaven, as his fingers trailed lightly down her neck and across her delicate shoulders.

She rose slowly with soapsuds caressing her as they slide down the curves of her body. Her shaking left hand held the sawed-off shotgun with water dripping from the barrel.

He felt raging wildfires tempting to consume them.

Whispering, she cooed, "What took you so long? I've been in that damn trough all afternoon."

Pulling her to him—she eagerly returned his kisses.

She smiled, tossed the gun aside and locked her arms around him, determined never to let him go.

Carson prayed for a long Colorado winter.

Under A Crescent Moon
Tara Pedroley

When the sun went down on a Tuesday night in early March of last year, I knew in my heart that it was the perfect time to get Silas back. He was my one and only true love. We had spent many peaceful, romantic nights at his parents' house in Belltown, Missouri. Cuddled up under fresh lemon detergent scented comforters and blankets, we stayed up late watching outdated movies from the early fifties. Silas always wanted to watch *Rear Window*, teasing me that if he ended up in a wheelchair, just like the main character, that I would be the one taking over for him in case he got tired of "doing the driving." I told him that I'd always be there *for* him and *with* him, as long as we both saw faithfully fit. Unfortunately, later that year, he found himself being unfaithful, to me and to our summer romance.

The moon was of a crescent the night our relationship ended. The air had a certain bitter scent the night I snuck out to see Silas. I had to be sure to make it back home before my mother woke up at 5 a.m. to make a fresh pot of coffee for my father's return home from his overnight shift at the local lumber yard.

I realized that without hearing the sound of my sweet beau's voice, I couldn't make my shamrock-colored eyes close long enough to get rest, regardless of how exhausted the rest of my body was.

I climbed out of bed and smoothed out my long, straw-colored locks. I tucked a few strands behind my left ear, and secured it with a red bobby pin. I shoved my skinny legs into a dark wash pair of blue jeans and snuggled into a cotton-candy-pink hooded sweatshirt. After rooting around for a matching pair of shoes, I settled on a pair of navy blue flip-flops and closed my bedroom door behind me.

As I began to walk up the gravel road towards Silas's home, I shivered as the chilly air hit my face.

It was 2:37 a.m. when I reached the Buckman residence. The lights were off in the bedrooms, but the porch light was on.

I could hear muffled voices coming from the backyard, yet as I crept closer, the voices became whispers. I tiptoed past the bushes lining the sides of the house to see which nosey neighborhood kids may have trespassed on the Buckman's property.

As I approached the back porch, I could see a dull, circular glow on the ground, shining out from underneath the wooden deck. Of the four Buckman children, Silas was the only one who used the deck as his special hiding spot. He went under there whenever he needed a break from school, work, or everyday existence.

People in his life knew that he wanted to be alone when he went into hiding underneath the deck. It was his way of saying he wanted to be away from everyone.

Including me.

So when I got closer to the voices, I recognized Silas's low whisper. He was talking to someone. But who?

I turned my head to one side, leaning down closer to the voices, to try and tune in for any answer. Was it Ronnie, or Delva? Those were the only two siblings that I could think would be under there with him. Tommy Rickman from church? No, the other voice didn't sound like Tommy. Wait. I heard it again. It was the voice of another girl.

I heard a soft giggle, and then Silas began talking very low to her.

What were they saying? My hands started to tremble. My knees felt as though they would collapse any second if I stood there a moment longer. My throat grew very dry, and my stomach began to cramp.

Does Silas really have some other girl under the deck with him? I wondered.

Tears formed in the corners of my eyes, but I quickly blinked them back. I stared up at the dark sky above me, at the crescent moon, wondering what my next move should be.

I heard the quiet sounds of lips smacking together, and a shallow giggle escape her lips.

An angry wave of heat crept up the back of my neck when I realized that this female voice had been locking lips with *my* Silas!!

I swallowed the sudden taste of disgust that sat in my throat as I walked around to the other side of the deck and got on all fours.

That's when I saw them.

Silas had his arms around the shoulders of a thin-framed young woman. She was much like the size of me, only prettier, and with a bigger bust. She had thick, red, curly hair to the middle of her back, and blossom-blue eyes. The glow from the flashlight made her cheeks look pink and rosy, yet gave her a very soft peaches-and-cream look.

"What the hell do you think you're doing, Silas?!" I shouted, scaring the life out of both of them.

He scurried out from underneath the deck, desperately trying to button the first two silver buttons of his favorite maroon and navy striped flannel. "Caroline, I thought you were at home in bed…I…I…"

"Well, I was—But I thought I'd sneak out and see you. Yet I see that *you* have company!"

I stormed off, tears spilling down my cheeks.

"Caroline!" he called, running to catch up with me.

Picking up my pace, I shouted over my shoulder to him, "Good-bye, Silas."

"Caroline, wait. She doesn't mean anything to me, I swear."

I began to jog, the hood of my sweatshirt tapping my back as each foot hit the ground. My heart was racing. My stomach ached.

How could he do this to us?!

How? And who was that red-headed girl?

Thoughts of anger, sadness and confusion buzzed around my head like angry bees as I jogged the rest of the way home.

My mother was still in bed, the house was still dark and undisturbed when I reached my residence.

I slid my flip-flops off my feet, but didn't bother getting undressed. I was too distraught and emotional to even care. The sound of sad sobs shook my bed, until I finally gave in to exhaustion.

After that night, I avoided Silas.

Mr. Buckman said that I was still welcome to come over any time even though his son and I were no longer dating, but I never took him up on that.

For weeks, however, I would find reasons to ride my bike past the Buckman home, just because I missed Silas. I missed Mrs. Buckman's cherry pie with the flaky, vanilla bean piecrust. I missed sharing "Knock Knock" jokes with ten-year-old Delva Buckman. I missed hearing the sound of Mr. Buckman humming the tune of "Take Me Out to the Ball Game" while pruning the rose garden in the backyard. I missed watching *Rear Window*.

I missed everything.

Night after night, after I had gathered my school books together for school the next day, I would lie in bed with the lights off. I found myself tossing and turning. Some nights, I drank a half glass of warm milk and then climbed back into bed. I couldn't get comfortable. I thought about the night I found him and the red-headed hussy with perfect skin underneath the deck in the backyard.

I thought of the whispering and the kissing, and how he said she meant nothing to him.

I remember the days that I was actually *looking* for Silas, I didn't cross paths with him. But the days I wanted to *avoid* him, he showed up everywhere.

One evening, after solving one lengthy algebraic equation after another, I sat on our front porch sipping lemonade and watched the sunset. As I lifted the glass to my lips, I inhaled the scent of fresh lemons and closed my eyes, remembering the comforter that smelled of lemon-scented detergent that Silas and I cuddled up to when we watched *Rear Window*. It was at that moment that I knew it.

I knew how much I loved him, and that I missed everything we had shared together.

I knew one thing was for sure.

I needed to find Silas.

I needed to forgive him, so we could be together.

So when the sun went down on a Tuesday night in early March of last year, I knew in my heart that it was the perfect time to get Silas back. He was my one and only true love.

The moon was of a crescent the night our relationship ended, and it was as such when our new beginning awoke.

Darkness to Dawning
Susan Gore Zahra

In the dark of night, the outlines of poplars along the end of the lot reminded Adele of men's legs in black gabardine pants rising toward the sky. The garage behind her and the sycamore to her right seemed more like lady legs draped in dark worsted wool skirts. A few weeks ago, while she burned trash as Harry slept, the harvest moon rose above the poplars like a head bone connected to the hipbones. The Man in the Moon was as waxy yellow as Harry's face had been this afternoon while they waited for the undertaker to come take him from Oaknoll Nursing Home.

A gust of wind blew out the match before Adele could light the papers in the burn barrel. The moan of trees bending in the wind above her head chilled Adele more than the moonless, starless November night itself.

Adele threw the last of the pages detailing the type, dose, and site of each injection of insulin she had given Harry and each serving of food she prepared for him during the past thirty-some years, into the burn barrel. Dr. Marshall told her she could throw out all those records when they moved from the old house with too many stairs to the little bungalow closer to Jimmy and Will. He called her a miracle worker for keeping Harry from dying during the years before insulin was introduced to St. Louis in the 1930s. He told her Harry was damn lucky to have found someone young enough and strong enough to take care of him all those years. Adele felt a twinge of pride that Harry had outlived Dr. Marshall, followed by a regular charley horse of guilt for thinking such a thing. Harry and the doctor were the same age. Maybe if she had made fewer late-night phone calls, Dr. Marshall would have lived as long.

Adele offered some of her logs to the nurses at the home, but they assured her they would keep their own records. She both was worried that the nurses might miss something, and relieved because they might find she had made mistakes that caused the confusion and violent behavior leading up to taking him to the nursing home. What if she had done something to contribute to his death?

That was silly. Harry was 84 years old, much older than either of his parents had been when they died.

By the time the paper fire burned out, the apple pie in the oven was done. Adele put it on the rack beside the cherry pie she baked earlier, before the home called to tell her Harry had passed. Jimmy liked cherry pie, Will liked apple, so she baked one of each for Sunday dinner. Because their children loved cookies, yesterday was cookie-baking day. Their wives liked German chocolate cake—she would have ended the day whipping up a cake had she not been called to the home.

Probably she should bake a few more things in case people came by after the funeral. Maybe get another roast or a ham, definitely more potatoes. Jimmy told her she was going to give them all diabetes if she kept filling them full of desserts, but there was something soothing about finally being able to cook the way her stepmother taught her.

Stepmother? Adele pondered that word as she massaged her aching, gnarled fingers. Polly Jordan was the only mother she had ever known. She could remember calling her "Stepmother" instead of Mom only when one of her grandchildren made a family tree for a school assignment. That was so many years ago she couldn't remember which grandchild. Her father and older brothers made sure every new family member, from Harry to her sons' wives and several incoming cousins, heard how three-year-old Adele had clung to Polly's skirt and kicked up a huge fuss when her father and Polly were married. The preacher put a chair between them to let Adele stand beside her throughout the service.

Polly woke Adele every day, smelling of rose-water. Some days, Adele would pretend to sleep a minute longer while she breathed in a little more of Polly's sweetness. Polly had protected Adele from her father's drunken rages. She defended Adele's desire to stay in high school and took on some of Adele's chores to let her study. And, oh, how she had loved learning to speak French and reading poetry—Shakespeare's Sonnets, Dickinson, Longfellow.

A twinge of guilt rose from Adele's heart and tugged her fingers into tighter cramps. Had going out to gather eggs on cold mornings while Adele read "Evangeline" one more time contributed to Polly's frail heart? When Polly became ill for the final time, caring for two sons and Harry's needs already overwhelmed Adele. Her younger sisters took care of Polly. It seemed to Adele that instead of having a wicked stepmother, she had been a wicked stepdaughter.

Adele put on a pot of coffee while she made a list of groceries to prepare to feed neighbors and family making sympathy calls during the coming days. Jimmy could take her to the store after they made arrangements at the funeral home Monday morning. She didn't want to sleep yet. She didn't want to dream yet.

The 10 o'clock news was coming on, then the Late Show with an old movie featuring dashing young stars now long gray or long gone. Maybe after that, she could sleep without feeling penned in by long, tall legs and hearing that wailing way above her head. The wailing always woke her before she knew what it was. Adele told people she was in the habit of drinking coffee at night so she wouldn't sleep through Harry having a problem if his sugar dropped too low. She never mentioned the dream that had followed every crisis from her father's rages through Polly nearly dying in childbirth, on into her own birthing and raising children and battling Harry's diabetes.

Harry's armchair was in front of the TV, where he watched the Today Show in the morning and Walter Cronkite after supper. Beside the chair was a desk with a lamp, a dictionary, and *Reader's Digests* for Harry to read whenever he wasn't up taking a walk or gardening. Adele had never sat in that chair. Even during the weeks after putting him in the home, she felt like he would be coming in, wanting to sit in his spot. It was a good chair, sturdy, with arms she could use to boost herself up if her knees balked. She put her cup and saucer on the desk. The chair felt as comfortable as it looked.

Harry would have been in bed by now. Adele realized she could have sat in comfort while she listened for trouble all those years. But what if she had dozed too deeply? What if she had been unable to hear his thrashing and his teeth grinding?

Spencer Allen opened the news with pictures and the story of Eleanor Roosevelt's funeral. All those people, world leaders and past presidents withtheir wives, looked bereft, but no one shed a tear. Adele rubbed the back of her neck. Sadness welled up inside even stronger than it had at Harry's deathbed. Somehow it didn't seem right to shed tears for a stranger when she had remained dry-eyed and stoic beside her own husband. Her sisters had been inconsolable when their mother died, teary but more composed when their father died. Adele couldn't remember crying—not then, not ever.

The chair cradled Adele, softening the tension in her body. Stories about progress on the construction of the Gateway Arch and college football seemed jumbled together. Adele heard the roar of the MGM lion, but the image on the TV blurred and faded into darkness. She heard cellos and violins playing a vaguely mysterious theme that drifted into wailing and moaning high above her head. She could see those familiar, dark legs rising above her, feel the scratchy wool against her hands and cheek, hear first the high-pitched weeping, then something new that prickled her skin—a deep, male voice shouting.

Adele felt jerked up and up, shaken and jolted.

"See! See what you done to your mother!" Her father's voice roared in her ears. Damp, sour whiskey smell sickened her, then the dry mustiness of rotten potatoes. She felt herself fall toward a face as yellow and waxy as Harry's had been. A woman's face, bony, eyes closed, hands folded around a rosary.

"Mama! Mama!" Adele felt her screams scratch against her throat. She woke, sobbing and gasping.

Adele did not know how long the river of grief and guilt flowed from the deep well within her. As the darkness outside the window faded to gray, she smelled rose water. She breathed in the sweetness for just a little longer before she got up to peel potatoes and get the roast started in time to have dinner ready when Jimmy and Will brought their families over after church.

The End of Fifty-Two

George House

She always had a smile, a joy to see. My little girl died in the prime of her life at fifty-two.

By sheer luck, Bob Ross' painting show was on the Learning Channel. The television reconstituted his image. Sky colors were added to the canvas. Bob mixed burnt umber, ivory, black, and alizarin crimson, then daubed the paint to the landscape. He didn't like the additions and he began slapping oil over the still wet canvas, calling the obscured area a "happy little opportunity." The foreground was completed, dark color could be anything, a stream, a grassy mound, even time. Now for the mountains, a little phthalo blue added to the previously mixed paint, using a two-inch brush.

I pushed the "off" button on the television monitor and the phlogiston picture ceased to exist. Where did the image of the painter go? Did the DVD suck up the photons planting them on the surface, ready for viewing again? Maybe they were reflected into the infinity that is space, traveling skew to the light reflected into space during the original filming. Of course, the newly reconstituted stream of light would be fifty-two light days behind the original, because that was the timing and order of their creation.

Black seems to be the color of time, space, and the dead. Height, width, depth can be clearly seen in color, time moves the three-dimensional scene continuously straight ahead. Painting the passage of time is confounding, so Bob paints a time-space continuum. Two dimensions try to capture 3D rectilinear space where we live, and time is added as a third dimension, a motion picture. My girl can be seen at thirty paintings per second. Bob will find his paint separating into alizarin crimson and phthalo blue if time moves backward? It doesn't.

Bob Ross passed on in 1995. I imagine time going back to when our landscape was being painted in 1994 and, sure enough, Bob appears in my mind, brush in hand, frizzed lollipop of red hair.

What happens when he dies? His presence will no longer be in our time. Photographs would still show his image, but that is not him.

Where is my little girl?

The origin of my space-time universe would emanate from the dimensionless location of the big bang, radiating an infinite number of rays of time, not space. The rays are spreading out in all directions, never intersecting, meeting in an expanding spherical surface, the beginning of time. The painter cleaned his brush, slapping the bristles against the leg of his easel and dripping paint to the newspaper that covered the floor, it dried, it died.

Everything in our universe is on the This-life timeline. I imagine the instant of death would witness a change in the polar direction of time, the newly dead slipping from one timeline to another. Bob Ross might be there, painting the same landscape, applying cadmium yellow, adding warmth, not too much. Time progression yields new adjacent timelines—well, not really new, but newly seen, the divergence of rays makes room for observation. We are all still where we were when she died, on the This-life timeline. The first instant, she can see the old life, but divergence obscures vision as she goes over the black horizon on her New timeline. Her healthy body requiring neither sustenance nor maintenance, a big smile on her face.

I look for hopes, for dreams, for love, trying to imagine emotions following the one that died. I find no evidence that feelings persist in the after-death life. I have never been there, so what do I know? Living people enjoy memories of those passed, but the dead no longer need connections to their previous life. God is accepting, even demanding, all the love souls have to give.

My little girl is gone—just gone—needing nothing from me. I'm angry. I thought there would be more.

Others may find timelines containing Dante's Inferno, or St. Theresa's Crystal Mansion. There is a timeline for the place Jesus has "gone to prepare for us." I hope to move to this timeline when I die, and I hope to find my loved ones there with love to give.

Time ends when the sphere stops expanding. All that ever was, or is now, is on or within the sphere, all the universes, all the lives, all the things, all the time. The end of time begins with an incredible black hole at the point where the Big Bang occurred. It is sucking everything into itself, folding in, puckering, flushing down everything, even taking heaven, leaving nothing. Last in is the beginning of time. No more than a gum bubble popped and the air sucked out. Questions never answered, no life left to ask. Maybe waiting for the next Big Bang, but waiting is not possible since the black hole consumed all time.

Dog Tags

Sherry McMurphy

The elevator door opened on the fourth floor and Olivia
carefully stepped out. Walking toward Jack's hospital room, she
noticed dim lights reflecting from the nurse's station in an otherwise
dark hallway. She sat down beside his bed and gently placed his
hand in hers. Her heart broke, seeing him lie there so frail. Outside,
snow softly fell, blanketing the walkways and grass. Her thoughts
drifted back to another snowy night nearly sixty-three years ago.

Flashes of lightcoming from the hordes of cameras,
temporarily blinded Olivia when she stepped out of the limousine.
A cloud of pink chiffon and tulle floated around her legs as she took
her father's arm. Before them stood the Renaissance Hotel, aglow
with thousands of white lights against the backdrop of darkness and
softly falling snow. The red carpet held a dusting of white flakes that
glistened like diamonds. An elegant banner hung across the
entrance.

STARLIGHT WINTER BALL
NEW YEARS EVE, 1952

"Oh, Father. Isn't it just wonderful?" Olivia gushed.
"Everything is so grand and festive."

He smiled down at her and patted her hand, resting in the
crook of his arm. "Yes, darling. I'm sure it will be a beautiful night."

Crossing the threshold, they met the concierge, who collected
her wrap and his topcoat. Her father accepted a crystal flute of
champagne. The ballroom simply took Olivia's breath away.
Intimate dining tables, adorned with crisp linen tablecloths, fine
china, sparkling crystal glasses and shiny silverware, encircled the
marble dance floor, covered with couples romantically swaying to
the orchestra's music. Tall arrangements burst from the tables'
centers, bulging with colorful flowers and tea lights burning along
the base. Dazzling chandeliers hung from massive beams,

crisscrossing the tall ceiling. Men wore tuxedos while the women wore elaborate gowns with long white gloves, and were dripping in sapphires, rubies and emeralds. The entire venue was extraordinarily lavish and spoke of money and status.

"Olivia, our evening meal is planned for seven thirty. Please be prompt."

"I will, Father," she replied. She hugged him lovingly, then hurried off in search of her friends. Olivia wended her way through the guests until she noticed Ruth and Evelyn. She rushed over to them in excitement. They oohed and ahed over each other's formal gowns, hair styles and jewels, as women typically do when grouped together.

"I don't know about you two, but I think it's time to get acquainted with those gorgeous Army men," said Evelyn, eyes focused on the opposite side of the room. Ruth and Olivia turned casually—it wouldn't be sophisticated to whirl around. After all, they were now mature women, having turned eighteen years old. Huge smiles spread across their faces. Olivia pulled out her compact mirror for a quick peak and touched up her red lips.

"Ladies, I think Evelyn is absolutely correct. Shall we?" she said with a sassy wink. Placing her Coca-Cola down on a side table, she grabbed a flute of champagne from the tray of a passing waiter and sauntered toward the uniformed men.

Over the next hour, the ladies thoroughly enjoyed the night's festivities, laughing, talking and dancing with one bachelor after another. Olivia caught her father's watchful eye several times, but he never intervened. She arrived promptly for dinner, and then escaped just as soon as it was proper.

Walking back to her friends, Olivia's eyes fell upon a handsome man watching her intently from the opposite side of the room. Suddenly, he smiled. Her heart skipped a beat while her knees threatened to buckle. "Oh, my," she whispered as he approached her.

"You are an absolute vision of beauty," he smiled again, never taking his eyes off her. He brought Olivia's hand to his lips and kissed it softly. "Jack. Jack Hawkins," he said. "Would you care to dance?"

Stunned, Olivia simply returned his smile and nodded yes. *Well, isn't he quite the suave one.* They moved into each other's arms and remained oblivious to everything in the room until the crowd began the count down. "Four, three, two, one—Happy New Year!" they shouted. Jack and Olivia's lips came together in a kiss that caused an explosion of passion to rip through her body like nothing ever had before, with no idea if the sound of fireworks came from the knocking of her heart or from party horns and cheers. Two days later, Jack's platoon shipped overseas to fight in the Korean War. Jack and Olivia only had one evening together, but it's all it took to fall in love.

Jack stirred in the bed, bringing Olivia back to the present.

"Honey, how do you feel?" she asked.

He sent her a weak smile and then allowed his heavy eyelids to close again.

"It's okay, Jack. I'm right here. Go ahead and rest," whispered Olivia, rubbing his hand.

Jack knew he didn't have long in his earthly life. His days were numbered and he'd made his peace. Leaving Olivia behind gutted him, but he didn't have a choice. Burrowing deeper into his pillow, he thought back to the Korean War.

Tension along the 38th parallel was intense. Jack and his squad, which included his identical twin brother, Thad, didn't sleep more than four hours each night, running on simple exhaustion and fear. They'd had their boots on the ground for five weeks. The sound of gunfire and exploding bombs became a constant. Jack's sole comfort came from Olivia's letters.

Right or wrong—he occasionally shared some of Olivia's words with Thad as he wanted his brother to see what a wonderful person she was. Sometimes late at night, when they went out on patrol together, he would talk with Thad about his plans with Olivia after the war.

Three months into the platoon's tour, they took on enemy fire. Jack was struck down, but was rescued out of the trenches by his squadron and taken to a temporary field hospital. Thad paced the waiting area for hours while Jack underwent surgery to save his life. He pulled through the procedure but remained in a coma—too unstable to transport to an Army hospital. Distraught over his brother's condition, Thad was granted short-term leave in order to remain by Jack's side.

A few hours into the second day, Olivia's large bundle of letters came to Thad's mind. Retrieving the box Jack stored under his cot, he decided to read each letter to Jack in hopes that would wake him up. One by one, he read Olivia's words conveying her love for Jack. It was obvious she cared for the students in her kindergarten class. Thad knew Olivia would be a wonderful mother, something she dreamed of being when Jack returned. The stories she shared about showing her prize-winning flowers at the county fair, caring for her ill grandmother and volunteering at the USO made Thad feel proud of her.

As he continued to read, Jack remained unresponsive. But Thad realized he had unexpectedly changed through Olivia's expressive and loving words. By the time he finished the last letter, Thad was completely in love with Olivia.

Continuing his steadfast vigil over Jack into a third day, he noticed the dog tags hanging around Jack's neck. The raised letters read:

U.S. Army
Hawkins, Jack Edward
499-03-1234
O Positive
Lutheran

Running his fingers over the medal, he noticed his own dog tag was almost identical, except the given name, Thaddeus Arthur, and the social security number, off one digit, having been issued at the same time. Their blood type ran the same, a shared existence since conception. The thought of losing his brother was almost more than he could bear. He'd never been alone.

Jack's medical chart, attached to a clipboard, hung at the foot of the makeshift bed. Picking it up, he read through the damage done to his brother's body. If he'd been a second faster that day, he'd be the one lying in this bed and not Jack. *If Jack passes and I switch the tags . . . no, I can't even think that way. Can I? Would Olivia know the difference? We're identical twins, after all, and often confused for each other. I love her so much. If I lose Jack, I won't have to be alone. But, how could I do that to my own brother. Yet . . .*

Jack's hand moved. Thad's eyes flew to his face, bringing him out of his thoughts.

"Olivia," said Jack.

She turned toward him and took both of his hands in her own. "Yes, dear. What is it?"

"I love you, Olivia," he proclaimed, tears in his old weathered eyes.

"Oh, Jack, I love you, too," Olivia replied.

"You've been happy with me . . . haven't you, dear, all these years? We made a good life?" he questioned.

"Oh, yes. Please, Jack, you need to rest. Don't worry . . ."

"Livy . . . kids . . . I know how much you wanted them, and I'm so sorry I couldn't give them to you," he said, a tear running down his cheek. "I would've if . . ."

"It doesn't matter," she interrupted. Repositioning, she stretched out alongside him in the bed, wrapping her arm across his chest. He placed his hand on top of hers. "We settled that issue a long time ago. Why are you bringing this up?" she whimpered, struggling to hold back tears.

"My time is nearing, Olivia . . ."

"No, Jack. No. You'll get better and we can go back to our home," she promised.

"No, baby, not this time," he mumbled. Olivia began to cry, and Jack tightened his arms around her. "You know I've loved you from the moment I read your first letter, and every second since."

"My letter, what do you mean? You've always said you fell in love with me the minute you saw me in that pink gown at the New Year's Eve ball," she said.

Jack didn't reply, just held on to her tightly, "Jack, did you hear me?"

Closing his eyes, he kissed her forehead and whispered sadly, "Olivia . . . I have to tell you something."

Within seconds, a nurse walked into the room and unintentionally disturbed their conversation. She checked the blood pressure machine hooked up to Jacks arm. Olivia caught the look on her face and peered down at Jack. Crying softly, she leaned in and gave him one final kiss of goodbye.

A Day on the Farm
M.L. Stiehl

Grandma woke me in the morning.

"Get up. Grandpa is eating. He will leave soon to go get the hay in. Your Uncle Jay will be there at the barn already, with the team of mules and the wagon."

"Grandma, I'm going, too."

"No. You're too young."

"Please. I want to go. I'll ask Grandpa."

At breakfast, I asked Grandpa.

"It's too big of a job for such a little girl," he said.

"Grandma said that, too," I said. "But, please. I'll be good and do what you tell me to."

"Well," he replied, "you'd have to wear long sleeves and high-top shoes. And it will be hot."

"I don't care. Can I?"

"Go get dressed and we'll talk it over."

I ran to my box of winter clothes and got a long-sleeved shirt and overalls. Then, to the closet for my shoes.

"Grandma said, OK," Grandpa said. "But you need to eat plenty as you'll be gone until dinner."

I wasn't hungry, but I listened. I grabbed a biscuit with some honey and butter on it, and ran after Grandpa.

When we got to the barn, Uncle Jay had the mules harnessed to the wagon. He was surprised to see me, but he knew his mom and dad had approved or I wouldn't be there. He helped me onto the wagon and got the mules moving. These mules, Old Red and Old Blue, had been in our family for seven or eight years.

I asked Uncle Jay why I had to wear long sleeves. He said, "Hay scratches. And sometimes bugs are in the hay, too." I thought that was a good reason. I was going to ask why I had to wear shoes, but I forgot.

We went out the gate and up the one-lane dirt road to the field. The road was narrow, but we didn't meet many people on it. Riding on the wagon is fun, but I know riding back on the hay will be even more fun.

We crossed the ditch with a bump. When it rained, the ditch became a little stream that ran by the rock fence across the road from Grandpa's hayfield. That field was called the bottom field, and there were woods next to it. Above them was another field. There was also a road up through the woods to the top field. We had corn up there now, but would have dewberries later in the year.

We were now at the bottom field. It was full of hay, cut and ready to move. We went through the gate and started in the back of the field. The mules knew to stand still while we loaded the wagon. The reins hung loose, as just a touch to the bridle told the mules to move up.

Uncle Jay, Grandpa, and a man named Bill were in the field with their pitchforks, throwing hay on the wagon. Uncle Jay told me to stomp on it when it got high, to pack it down. I wasn't very heavy, but I guess it was enough to spread it all around. I did as I was told, and then knew why I needed high-topped shoes. Ha, ha. I also knew why Bill's boy can't do this. There was dusty stuff floating all around, and he sneezes and coughs until he gets sick from it. It doesn't bother the rest of us.

The hay was getting high. It was fun to stomp all around the wagon bed, and help, too.

I was jumping around when Uncle Jay suddenly yelled, "Stand still! Freeze!"

I knew not to ask why. I just did it. He came up on the wagon where I stood frozen. He took his pitchfork and quickly shoveled some of the hay off the wagon. I wondered what he was doing, but I never said a word, as he would tell me when the time came.

The next thing I heard was a gunshot, and Uncle Jay saying, "You got him." He turned and said to me, "We just threw a copperhead off. He's dead, now. "

I laughed, kind of quietly and low, and said, "Oh, boy."

He said, "Thank you for minding me when I called."

I felt so proud. When Grandpa or Uncle Jay complimented me, I got excited, as they didn't do that very often.

Grandpa asked if I wanted to come down. I told him, no, I wasn't afraid.

When the hay was high enough, they said it was time to go. They still had to get to the barn.

At the barn, they told me I'd better not tell Grandma about the snake if I wanted to go back to the field after lunch. If she knew, she might not let me go back. We don't keep secrets, but we do plan the best time to tell. My best time would be after we were through for the day.

Grandma had made dinner for us, of course, and Aunt Jenny helped her that day, since we had to work steadily in the field to finish on time.

Aunt Jenny is a black lady. She was my mammy when I was younger. Grandma needs her for busy days, like spring cleaning, thrashing days when lots of men are here for dinner, and wash days when she used the washboard to clean quilts, bed clothes, and the overalls and coveralls that Grandpa and Uncle Jay wore in the fields.

After dinner, we went to the barn and got the mules from their stalls where they had eaten, and took them to the pond to drink. They'd had a drink when we came in, but Grandpa said they needed to drink again after eating because it was so hot today.

The harness was put back on the mules and they were hooked to a rope that went into the barn to pull the hayfork up and into the building. Bill pulled another rope that opened the hayfork to release the hay into the loft. Later, Grandpa would fix the rope to a hayfork that releases the hay automatically, but for now it was broken, so the mules and Bill had to help. It seemed that if something was broken, Uncle Jay or Grandpa could fix a "Plan B" way to do things. The hay had to be brought in fast, in case it rained.

They said we would get to do hay in bales soon, but we don't have a hay baler, yet. It's still new. No farmers around here have one yet.

It took a while to get the hay off the wagon and go back to the field to get another load. Grandpa was telling us he had to check his bees before it got too dark to see how they were doing, and make sure that the hives were not too full of honey.

We brought the last load to the barn. I was getting tired, and our two dogs were already lying down around the yard.

Grandpa checked his bees. I couldn't get too close. He could go right up to the hives and pull out some rows with only his screened-hat on. He never got stung. He said you should never be afraid. They know if you are, and then they worry. I laughed.

Aunt Jenny helped with supper and headed home. She had to walk about half a mile through the woods to her house, way behind our house. There was a dirt road, but she didn't have a car. We all walked a lot. She'd come back tomorrow to help Grandma again. Grandpa said she needed the money. Her husband was kind of sick. He worked on the next farm over, doing timber work.

Having finished the last load now, I run to the house. I gather the eggs, and they're everywhere. Some in the hen house, some in machines sitting in the barnyard, and some in the barn. They lay them all over. I usually get around 15 eggs. Less, if the hens decide to sit on them. I never bother a sitting hen.

I also fill a little trough outside on our back porch, where the chickens, cats, and dogs drink. I pump the handle on the back porch and let the water run out and fill pans for them.

It's getting late, now. Grandma calls us to supper. We wash up and go to eat. We talk about our day. There's always something to talk about. Grandpa is still on his bees and how he needs to get the honey out. Uncle Jay says he has to sharpen a saw for some work he's doing. And someone is coming to get a haircut from him tomorrow evening. Grandma talks about how she needs someone to bring in some wood for the kitchen stove, which Uncle Jay agrees to do. I'm hot, so I talk about going to the creek to play.

It's very hot here in the kitchen. Grandma has to heat water for washing dishes, so we have to keep the fire in the stove going for that. When we finish eating, we leave and go to the front room, leaving Grandma to wash and dry the dishes and clean the table off alone. Grandpa smokes his pipe, while Uncle Jay makes some cigarettes on his cigarette-rolling machine. He taught me how, so I made some for him, too. He smokes one.

They go all day without smoking, as you are not allowed to smoke in the barn or the hayfields—they are full of hay and it's really not safe. Grandpa says no matches are carried in barns, because, even though we have cats, there are still mice in barns, and they can start fires with a wooden match just by biting the end of it. Sometimes Uncle Jay carries matches in the rim of his straw hat, but not if Grandpa catches him. Ha, ha.

Grandpa also had another rule for the barn. We can't lock horses or cattle in at night, especially when it's raining. Lightning could start a fire. Grandpa is afraid the barn might catch on fire and they couldn't get out. Every man who works for Grandpa knows his rules. Ha, ha.

He has other rules for the barn, too. We have to shovel manure out of the stalls frequently, and all harnesses, saddles, bridles, and halters are to be put in their places when we are through with them. Feeding troughs have to be kept clean. Safety and cleanliness are as important in barns as anywhere. He checks, too.

When Grandma cleans house, she says she wishes he was as particular with ashes and his pipe as he is with his barn. Ha, ha.

We sit on the front porch for a while, swatting flies and waiting for Grandma. We watch lightning bugs, which I catch and put in jars. I still seem to hear the katydids and the frogs at the creek. Uncle Jay says he needs to get some gigging done. The frogs are getting big.

Then, we head for bed. It's hot, even with the windows all open. We try to sleep in the breeze from the windows on the opposite side of the room. But we are so tired, it doesn't take long for everyone to go to sleep. And the feather beds feel so good, though hot. When you're so tired, it's okay, and a little breeze comes through late at night.

I'm so tickled, and learned so much today. I talk to the Lord and tell him of my dreams, and how happy I was to go to the hayfield. I thank him for the beautiful moon outside my window.

"Goodnight, for today," I pray. "Oh, yes. Thank you, God, for the snake not hurting any of us. Amen."

The Peddler
From Judge Lu's Ming Dynasty Case Files
P.A. De Voe

The cheerful tinkling of small bells contrasted starkly with the muted, bloodied body at Judge Lu's feet. He glanced over his shoulder and toward the bells' source. A tall man with a sprig of mugwort projecting out above his ear and a soft, dark hat tied with a red ribbon hugging his head, stood in a small crowd of curious on-lookers. Two candy-colored chest-high containers rested on the ground near him; one formed a base for a blue and green umbrella. Bells and good-luck talismans swung in the moist breeze as they clung to its blue edges. Each container sported scenes from stories past, designed to draw the eyes of passersby and entice them to buy a trinket. Now the carefully constructed cheerfulness went unnoticed.

Lu turned back to the corpse and his job. He began describing his findings to Fu-hao, the court secretary, who sat at a table in the impromptu investigative area. The notes would be included in the court's official death report.

"The victim is lying in the dirt, as if he was hit from behind and fell in place," Lu worked to keep his voice neutral. He reached out and nudged loose the navy blue band encircling the victim's dark cotton hat. The hat fell away. Stealing himself, he pushed his fingers through thick, matted hair. "The back of the victim's skull is crushed in. The area is linear, about finger length."

He stood up and Zhang, his guard, turned the body over and removed the man's shirt. No marks. Zhang rolled the body over again, exposing the now bare back. No marks.

"There are no other signs of trauma. Someone hit the victim from behind with one strong blow, killing him."

Nearby, two baskets of breakfast dumplings remained attached to a bamboo carrying pole, but sat at odd angles. The dumplings had tumbled indiscriminately onto the ground. Lu systematically circled the body, picking up a few items which appeared out of place: bird feathers, a short stem with mugwort leaves, a dirty piece of cloth, and a straight, flexible wire about three hands in length. With his back to the crowd, he tucked each one unobtrusively into the wide sleeves of his ankle-length, gray outer robe.

Along with the collection of random citizens, the growing crowd included several more peddlers with their various wares. Two of the peddlers drew his attention. One short, portly fellow had drums, clappers, cymbals, and other percussion instruments hanging off a strap running around his neck. The multicolored strip tying his cloth hat in place sported a toy double drum. The back of his right hand pressed against his forehead, allowing the wooden clappers he held to shadow his eyes. He clutched several long, thin metal mallets in his left hand.

An elderly man with an over-flowing cart stood next to him. Slim bands of paper fluttered from the cart's protective red and blue cloth roof. Small birdcages clung to the sides of the cart. As with the other peddlers, he wore a short coat over leggings and a muted, crumpled hat held in place by a strip of red cloth. A spray of yellow blossoms tucked behind his ear bobbed gently as he caressed a snowy white dove nestled in his hand.

Frowning, Lu observed the peddlers as he considered the objects tucked away in his sleeve. Had he found clues to the murderer or simply items lost over time?

He moved to the impromptu investigative area set up for him and sat in a folding chair near Fu-hao. Today's investigation wouldn't have the formal and imposing trappings of the official court—neither the setting nor his own official robes—but he wanted to get as much information as possible while details were still fresh in people's minds.

"Bring those three merchants," he ordered Zhang, pointing out the peddlers.

The three men blanched. Good. That was the reaction he wanted. Anxiety. Fear. Fear of the government and its courts.

The men promptly approached and fell to their knees. Lu silently scrutinized their bent forms.

"Tell me what you know of this man," Lu ordered.

The tall trinket merchant spoke up. "I sell every day from a location at the front of the path, just near the park's entrance. He's new, a stranger."

The elder bird peddler said, "He's a peddler, that's for sure, but I've never seen him before, either."

"And what do you say?" Lu asked the rotund drum peddler.

"I don't know. I can't be sure. I have my own business and no time for being nosy," he said, seeming to shrink.

"But you recognize him, don't you?"

The man ducked his head.

"Don't hide the truth. Tell the court," Lu said, his voice booming.

Exhaling the drum peddler said, "Yes. He's been around the past couple of days. He sold dumplings from his baskets. He seemed to want to find a permanent spot. Even though times are hard and we have fewer customers, still, many people come to the park."

The tall man's face twisted in a silent grimace.

"Did he find a spot?" Lu asked.

The drum peddler shrugged, turned his head away from the body, and murmured, "I don't think so."

Lu leaned forward. "Why not? All he needed was a patch of ground." He waved a hand out toward the park's grounds. "There's plenty of space for another peddler."

"Nonsense," the tall merchant interjected forcefully. "He was never here before today"

The drum peddler glared, "Are you questioning my honesty? Why would I lie?"

"How would I know? Maybe you killed him, crushing his head with one of your mallets and you're trying to throw the blame on someone else."

The drum peddler started to rise, but Zhang laid a massive hand on his shoulder, holding him down.

Drumming his fingers on his chair's arm, Lu struggled to hide his annoyance. The men were getting out of hand. Here in the park, outside the formal court's ambience, they seemed to forget the import of their behavior. He shot a quick glance at Fu-hao, whose brush flew across the rice paper documenting everything in the proceedings.

"Tell the court about your seeing this man," Lu said to the drum peddler.

"I didn't talk to him. As I said, he'd been selling his dumplings in the park. He carried them in baskets on his pole and remained mostly in one spot. I'd guess he was looking to set up a regular location."

"Where are you set up?"

"On the other side of the bamboo." He pointed to a small clump of bamboo slightly down and to the left of the dirt path in front of them.

"How could you see him from your stand?" Lu asked.

The peddler rubbed his right leg, "I have trouble standing all day and frequently sit on a stool. From such a low position I can see down the lane pretty well."

At that, the elderly bird peddler chimed in, "Yesterday, a screaming child scared my favorite bird and it flew over there," he gestured toward a stand of low, green bushes nearby. "I had to come over and coax her out. I'm sure, if this fellow had been along the path, I would have noticed him."

Lu nodded and turned to the tall peddler. "You also deny seeing this man. According to your friend here," Judge Lu pointed to the drum peddler, "he'd have been close to you and your makeshift stand."

"I don't know what that fool is talking about. He must have seen someone else. There are lots of peddlers in the park and the ones carrying baskets all look pretty much the same from a distance. My spot is up front and no one else was there, I can tell you that," he ended belligerently.

Judge Lu stroked his chin and gazed at the three. They all sold their wares in the same area. Why would one claim to have seen the dead man and the others not? He remained silently contemplating the men a moment longer, then leaned back into his chair.

"Tell me about your local guild," he said to the drum peddler.

Lu thought an almost imperceptible frown flashed across his face.

"It's true a peddlers' guild is being organized. Not everyone belongs to it yet. There are many questions to be considered."

"Who is the leader?"

The drum peddler cast a quick glance to his left. The elder spoke up, "I am the leader. We must form an association to set rules and regulate our members so we're not working against each other. If we don't, how can any of us succeed in these difficult times? As a group we can protect our own."

Lu turned toward the tall man. "And you also belong to this guild?"

"He does," the elder peddler answered for him. "My nephew here has been essential in helping to convince the others to join us."

"So, if the dumpling seller wanted to remain, he would be a member?"

"The organization would decide if he could join or not," the elder asserted.

"Why do you think this drum peddler insists he saw the dumpling peddler for the past couple of days?" Lu asked, tapping his chin.

The elder shook his head. "I can only assume he's lying. He killed the man himself and he's trying to confuse the court."

"That's not so!" the drum peddler jumped up before Zhang could stop him. However, before he could say more, Zhang's foot connected with his back, shoving him down.

"I didn't do it. He did." Quivering, he jabbed a finger toward the tall merchant.

The man scoffed. "No. You did and you'll pay for it."

The drum peddler banged his head on the floor before the judge. "Please, Your Honor, I can prove I'm not guilty."

"Then do so immediately."

Trembling, he said, "Look in the container with the umbrella. You'll find the murder weapon there."

"Zhang, open the box," Lu ordered.

The tall peddler's face contorted in anger as he watched the guard approach his candy colored containers.

Zhang pulled the door open, extracted a sturdy rod, and handed it to Lu. Traces of a dark, sticky substance were visible.

Blood. Lu held it up as the tall man shot a look of hatred at the drum peddler. The elder dropped his head in a low groan.

***

Later, back at the yamen, as Fu-hao finished the official report, he asked his brother what made him suspect the two were colluding against the drum peddler, instead of the other way around. And, why did he ask about a guild?

"It's to be expected that the peddlers would want to organize and, as is common, association members are often related in one way or another."

"But then, why did they turn on the drum peddler? As a guild, they should protect him and he should protect them," Fu-hao shook his head in confusion.

"Remember, the drum peddler said not everyone belonged to the guild yet. I noticed that both the tall and elder merchant wore red bands around their hats, indicating membership in a group. The drum peddler wore a multicolored band. He wasn't a member."

"But why would the guild kill the dumpling seller?"

"The drum peddler sold in the park for years; he had a right to be there. In time, the guild would persuade him to become a member. But the dumpling seller was different. By setting up his business in the park, he broke the new guild's unspoken rules. He aggressively went after the few coins people had to spend and was, therefore, considered a threat to the other peddlers' livelihoods and survival. It's a classic example of *fēn dào yáng biāo*—of people going their separate ways, without regard for others."

Fu-hao shook his head as he gathered the finished report's papers together. This evening the report would be sent to Judge Lu's superiors for review and confirmation of Lu's verdict of guilt.

PRESIDENT'S CONTESTS

For 2015, Saturday Writers' president, Tom Klein,
challenged contestants to write a story or poem inspired
by the following photo.

Photograph by Ryan Jacobsmeyer
© Ryan Jacobsmeyer

Saturday Writers 2015

PRESIDENT'S CONTEST: Poetry

Keep Faith with the Land
R.R.J. Sebacher

Metaphor for all of us – the small farmer's fate
Flattered by the banker's interest
Not realizing it was just on loan until too late
That bankers are just salesmen like all the rest
Rubes traded their heritage for shiny toys
Bargained away the land on which they stood
Ancestral homes were lost for fleeting joys
Bankers preyed on what the farmers forgot

The same substance of its creation – dust to dust
Now their homes rot and all goes back to woods
Tools auctioned off and land sold by the lot
Those who fed a nation now get the crust
Payback delayed until there's nothing in the pot
Then revolution or plague and only nature is just

Changes Must Be Made
Audrey Clare

A mile into Limbo's waiting lane—year after year
still standing—a tragic old house with doors unhinged—
mournful sad holds on.
Sightless eyes—expressions lost—from paneless windows—
a kinder city lives within
its walls & cries out its song.
"Changes must be made—or take me as I am."

Empty Gray Shell
R.R.J. Sebacher

The best of us left in the wreck
Of the family farmhouse
Trees now growing through eaves
Like thousands of others across the land

No time for boredom – plenty for laughter
Everyone setting down to dinner
Learning the three R's at the kitchen table
Parlor for funerals and weddings

Strong gentle shield for both kith and kin
Abandoned to whims of war – sickness – greed
Hidden weakness within foundation of rock
Was the mortar that held them apart

Understand – Oaks poking through the roof
Become the floors on which our youth will stand

Lesson in Black and White
(renga on a photograph of derelict farmhouse)
R.R.J. Sebacher

Man self-aware cries
About his abandoned past
No bird shed a tear
Over its abandoned nest
Which more important castle

Ghostly remembrance
Lesson of Ozymandias
Our mortality
American farmer's pride
Snapshot of humility

On granite bedrock
Faith in dreams and all our craft
Earth and time still laugh
Nature tells us it is time
Leave home now go to the stars

The Hidden Friendship
Tara Pedroley

The more I get to know you, the more I realize
That our friendship has always been there
 Even if we didn't notice.
  It was there, silent but obvious, just not to us
   It was floating, above our heads, we just never saw it
    As it was invisible to us.
     Others may have seen it, because they knew it was there
      They just never said much about it.
       Maybe it was because they knew
        That eventually, in our own way,
         In our own time,
          That we would find it.
           And once we did, we would hold it close...
            Close to our hearts
             Forever...

PRESIDENT'S CHALLENGE: Flash

The Good Buy
Bradley D. Watson

ENJOY!
Brad Watson

Sharon looked with unbelief at the house.

"Can't you see it?" her husband, Edwin, asked.

She swallowed. When they went house-shopping, she never dreamed they'd end up here.

"Ed," she said, a little more loudly than she was planning to, "this isn't even a whole house!"

Ed put his arm around his young wife's shoulder. "You're just not seeing the big picture."

Sharon's eyes were wide. "Oh, I see the big picture. It's a big mess! How can you even consider that . . . that . . . thing? It's barely standing. The only thing holding it together is the little bit of paint left on the outside!"

"Hon . . . hon . . . ," Edwin smiled as he squeezed her closer. "We wanted a fixer-upper, remember?"

Sharon wanted to scream in frustration. She couldn't pull her eyes from the disaster in front of her. "What about the others?" she asked, losing hope.

"Well," Ed began, "the one on Roosevelt, you remember, was in great shape. There wasn't much we could do to that. We could add a bedroom to the basement, but because of the neighborhood, it probably wouldn't add much value.

"And speaking of neighborhoods, the house on Wilson is a lost cause. No matter the work we put in it, we would still have a house in a neighborhood that no one would want to live in."

Her mouth open, Sharon tried to find something to say, but she was so in shock, she couldn't come up with words. "But..."

"Oh, honey," he said. "Can't you imagine it? This one is on acreage. Nothing to downplay the value that could be there."

"But, there's no house!"

"Sure there is. See? Two stories of home to work with."

"There are no windows. And the roof is just in pieces. There isn't even a door anywhere."

"It's right over there," he said, pointing to the piece of wood lying on the ground beside the remnants of the old house. "We just have to paint it, slap it back on."

"You're kidding," she said, turning to face this man who now seemed a stranger.

"Not at all," he said, his smile even larger. "Here's our chance."

"What can you possibly see in that mess?"

Ed turned her to face the standing pieces of wood on the old lot. "Don't you see?" he asked. "It's perfect. It was such a good buy. And it sets us up to win. Think about it. No matter what we do to it, it can only be improved."

Sharon had to admit he was right. She resigned herself with a sigh. "You're right. Even if it falls down while we work on it, that would still be an improvement."

Ed laughed as he took a last look at his new purchase. Sharon just drooped her head as she headed back to the car.

Why Me?

Bradley D. Watson

"Oh, man! Why is it always me?" Gary slammed the thin box to the ground in frustration. It disappeared into the darkness at his feet. The night sounds filled his ears as he reached into his pocket.

The light of his cell phone lit the name and number on the small slip of paper he held. Keying in the digits, it took a moment for the network to connect. He listened carefully to the expected voice.

"I'm sorry, but you have reached a number that is no longer in service. If you feel…"

He hung up and tossed the hand-held device through the open window into the beat-up '81 Honda Civic, cursing mildly under his breath.

He had known that the phone number sounded strange when it was given to him. Most phone numbers in the area start with one of three different exchanges. But what with local number portability, and cell phones keeping their numbers as their owners move around the country, any exchange or area code is possible nowadays. So, he had let them convince him that the number was okay.

He bent down to pick up the pizza, half out of its box, shoving it back in as much as possible. He couldn't avoid getting sauce on his hand, which he angrily wiped on his dirty jeans.

"Well," he said to no one in particular, "I'm not paying for this one."

With a jerk, he opened the car door, sliding the beaten pizza box across the bench seat.

"I told them this was a bad one," he said as he retrieved his cell phone from where it had fallen on the front floor mat, "but they wouldn't listen. 'You just don't wanna drive out there,' they said. Well, I'm gonna show 'em."

He turned back to the shadowy form looming above the overgrown gravel driveway.

"There's gotta be a better way to make a living."

He snapped a picture of the abandoned shell that used to be a home. The flash did little to light the edifice, but the picture was enough to make his point.

He crawled into the driver's seat and started the old jalopy.

Pausing, he made a decision. He rested the hand holding his cell phone against the wheel and began working with it. He attached the photo he had just taken to an email addressed to his boss. He added the text, "I QUIT!" He hit *Send.*

As he punched the accelerator with his foot, he laughed out loud.

He punctuated his decision with the pizza, which flew out his window, box and all, and disappeared again into the dark of the driveway.

The Refuge
Nicki Jacobsmeyer

Agonizing moans resonate around him.

William's cot is drench and reeks of rank sweat and fresh urine. The sound of hammering vibrates in his head. The fever is worse.

Bam-Bam-Bam

The soldier who brought him to this house insisted it was a refuge, a medical post. The reminder repeats in the back of his mind. William attempts to raise his head, but the throbbing pain and body tremors make it challenging. Across the room, a woman clutches her belly, swollen with life.

Bam-Bam-Bam

A frail arm covered in sores claws at William's chest, searching for salvation. The old man's eyes plead for the misery to end.

"Help me!" he moans.

His voice is familiar. It sounds like his neighbor James, but his face is unrecognizable from the infectious rash.

"Hold on, James, the doctors are coming." William scans the room for anyone vertical.

As they wait, William skims his body for signs of infection. Pockets full of pus cover his extremities that have become deep purple in color.

Bam-Bam-Bam

He rolls over in search of refuge and comes face-to-face with a petite elderly woman. Her eyes are closed, pain consumes her features. The rattle echoing from her chest is unmistakable.

A movement over his shoulder catches his eye. The soldier struts through the open doorwith a child cradled in his arms. He crosses the room and places her on an empty cot and tucks her in with a blanket.

Retching sounds bombard William from the other side of the room. The stench of vomit permeates the air, suffocating him. William reaches to cover his nose against the odor and feels a sticky substance. Blood is trailing from his nose into his mouth, tasting of iron.

"Help, officer, help!" William pleads.

The soldier turns in his direction from the child's bed. He stares into William's sunken eyes.

William sees a flash of understanding cross the soldier's face. Relief encompasses him.

The soldier pivots toward the doorway, his boots stomp across the decaying floor with precision.

Bam-Bam-Bam

The room becomes darker.

Bam-Bam-Bam

The sound rings in William's ears.

***

The soldier secures the doorway with wooden planks and hammers the final nail through the sign.

QUARANTINE: SMALLPOX

PRESIDENT'S CHALLENGE: Prose

A Place of Evil
Sherry McMurphy

Psychiatrist Dr. Ben Horton's tires crunched as he pulled up the gravel road in front of the house. In the seat beside him sat his patient, Killian, quietly staring out the window. Testing a new theory, he brought Killian back to the scene where an unspeakable event had occurred. In all these years, he'd never spoken a word or expressed any type of real emotion. Dr. Horton was hopeful that Killian would finally react if the memory were brought back to the forefront. He watched his patient intently and wondered what was going through his mind.

Killian was glad the house stood abandoned, empty and alone—just as he'd been for the past thirty years. The house, once pristine white in color and boasting a perfectly manicured lawn, was a home filled with love, laughter and companionship, a truly wonderful place that he'd called home. That is, until the night pure evil arrived.

Now, the color of the siding had grayed. The painted wood was chipped and peeling. Shutters, having lost brackets and screws, hung cockeyed. Most windows no longer held glass or screens and the back door lay in a pile of discarded junk. The roof sagged in sections with several rows of shingles missing. The weeds in the yard grew out of control. Rotted, leafless trees stood hauntingly around the yard. Nothing before him presented any sense of life.

Good, he thought. The house deserved it.

Killian would never accept the fate he'd been dealt, not really. They were all just kids looking to add some excitement to an otherwise boring weekend. They meant no harm, but with an unexpected sweep of fate, handed out by the house, everything changed, and he'd spent years locked in a cage, doped on medication and labeled a psychopath.

In the summer of 1982, after debating the issue for weeks, Killian and a group of friends decided they would hold a séance. Penelope and Tiffany were terrified of seeing a ghost. Nick, Conner and Colby were elated to have the supernatural experience. When Killian's parents announced they would be away for the weekend, they knew the time had come. The plan was to gather at Killian's house on Friday night and begin the event at straight up midnight.

Once everyone arrived at Killian's home, the furniture in the family room was pushed to the perimeters of the space. It was important to create a spirit-friendly atmosphere. Couch and chair cushions, placed in a circular design, adorned the hardwood floors in the center of the room. Tiffany placed a tablecloth, candlesticks and the Ouija board within the confines. Colby set up the video recorder and music. Penelope turned all the blinds and pulled the curtains closed.

"So, are we ready for this?" asked Killian, smiling excitedly.

"Hell yeah, Bro," said both Connor and Colby enthusiastically. Nick, nervous and unsure, squeaked out a faint, "Yes."

The girls didn't respond. Killian glanced at them. Their faces were almost green, as if they might puke.

"You girls aren't going to chicken out on us, are you?" *No way in hell I'm letting them off the hook. They signed up. They're sticking to it.*

The two girls exchanged a worried look. "No, but are you sure this is safe to do? I mean, it's not like any of us really know what we're doing," fretted Tiffany. She stepped closer to Penelope, clearly needing reassurance.

"Nothing's going to happen. We've been over this a hundred times. All were going to do is play with the Ouija board, and if we get to talk to someone, we do," Killian said. "Now, for the last time . . . you girls in or out? It's almost midnight and we have to start when the clock strikes twelve."

Killian's answer came when they all selected a cushion and sat down—Indian style. Using a lighter, Killian lit the first candle and then flipped the lights out. The room fell into darkness, shadows cast around the area from the lone flame. Several of them exchanged cautious looks. Connor and Colby giggled like two little girls, earning a disgusted glare from Nick.

"Tiffany, take my candle and light your own, then pass it around the circle until each of you has a flame," he explained. Centering the game board in front of him, he set the planchette among the alphabet letters and numbers. One by one, he focused his eyes on each of his friends and said their names. All confirmed they were ready, and then fixated on the clock. The grandfather clock began to dong. At the count of twelve, Killian placed a hunting knife in front of his crisscrossed legs. He wanted protection in case something went wrong.

The group of friends linked hands, closed their eyes and began the séance with a prayer.

"Spirits of the realm, we call to you in welcome and peace. We ask for protection from angry and evil spirits, and request only those with good intentions to join the circle. Let your presence be known. Your words be voiced. Your feelings be shared," Killian spoke. "The midnight hour reigns to weave and sync as one." They opened their eyes and glanced around the room. Everything looked the same.

Killian placed his hands on top of the planchette.

"Is someone there?" asked Connor. The flames from all six candles flickered rapidly. The girls gasped in fear and pulled back in an attempt to break the circle. Nick and Colby held their hands tightly and refused to allow them to break the connection.

"Do you have a message for us?" Killian asked. Almost immediately, his hands moved without will across the board. The point of the marker stopped first on the letter D then E and continued until the word D-E-A-T-H was spelled in full.

A muffled scream tore from Penelope's throat.

"Shhh!" the others said in unison.

The boys exchanged a wide-eyed glance. The two girls turned their heads to avoid the board.

"Death, hmm . . . Tell me . . . Are you talking about your death?" asked Killian, his hands rapidly sliding across the board to the number 5.

"Who are you? Can you tell us your name?" asked Colby. For more than fifteen minutes the group asked question after question, but the planchette did not move nor were there any other signs that a spirit had joined them.

Killian, growing impatient, snapped out, "Come on, asshole. Tell us more."

Two minutes passed. Nothing happened—five more minutes, again nothing.

With a deep sigh, Nick said, "Guess it's over. We gonna keep waiting or finish?"

Suddenly, a cold, brisk wind began blowing throughout the room. The friends turned loose of each other's hands, wrapping their arms around themselves to warm up. The candle flames wavered but never blew out.

"What the hell?" hollered Nick.

The wind grew stronger. The girls' hair whipped around their faces and obscured their vision. Nick's baseball hat flew off his head and sailed across the room. Connor and Colby tried to stand up but were held to the floor by an invisible force. Penelope screamed as the wind grew stronger and stronger.

The cushions they sat upon began to rotate in a rapid circular motion. The wind pressed against their bodies and twisted each one like a pretzel.

"I can't breathe!" cried out Nick.

"Help! Somebody help us!" screamed the others, over and over.

Chaos continued as their bodies wound tighter and tighter, until their shapes were grotesque and their eyes and tongues bulged from their faces.

And then, the wind abruptly stopped.

Complete darkness and utter silence engulfed the room. No one spoke. No one moved. No one breathed.

The police found the gruesome scene after neighbors reported people screaming. The group of friends sat on their cushions, still arranged in a circle, with one large stab wound in the center of each one's chest. Their arms were wrapped tightly around their necks like a rope, causing strangulation. Blood pooled around them and covered the floor within the circle. Written across the wall in blood were the letters that spelled, Y-O-U-R-D-E-A-T-H. Five people in the group were dead. Killian sat in a catatonic state, a bloody knife in his hand, smiling wickedly.

The police reviewed the video recorder and found no evidence to explain what had happened. They questioned Killian repeatedly but he never spoke a word.

Dr. Norton slipped the car into gear to pull away, when he noticed Killian's demeanor starting to change. His respirations had increased, sweat covered his upper lip and forehead, and he fidgeted in the seat. *Oh, my God! I've never seen him do this.*

"Killian, what do you feel? Are you uncomfortable being at this house?" he asked.

Killian did not respond but continued to stare intently out the window. When he began to wring his hands together and a look of fear swept across Killian's face, Dr. Horton pushed him further and asked, "What do you see? What has frightened you?"

To Dr. Horton's utter shock, Killian said, "The house is watching me and the walls are pulsating."

Fragility

Donna Mork Reed *God bless!, Donna Mork Reed*

Stepping across a pile of broken boards, Melinda hesitated so as not to shatter the frozen image before her. She stood in the open doorway, the door lying uselessly aside where past vandals had left it. Inside the house, silence reigned. Melinda took a bracing breath and stepped into the ramshackle house, pausing just inside to adjust to the darkness. Shafts of sunlight shone in from the back side of the house; dust motes floated in their own silent world.

Melinda walked cautiously across the creaking, wooden, dust-covered floor, avoiding the occasional broken floorboard. She paused several times, looking around, letting her mind open to receive whatever memories or thoughts came to her.

Melinda's fiancé, Martin, had proposed last week. As exciting as that was, she first had to deal with her past, or lack of past, as the case may be. She had shut out the memories of her childhood for so long, she was no longer able to open that door even a small gap to peek at what was truth. Truth now mixed with fragments of thoughts and dreams until reality was off kilter. No, before saying yes to Martin, she needed to set her mind straight, let the past in, and move on to better and brighter things. Determined, she pressed onward.

At the foot of the stairs, Melinda stopped and grasped the railing, giving it a shake to test its soundness. Though loose, it seemed to hold. Melinda looked up into the darkness. The hair at the back of her neck stood up, but she shook it off. No, this was now. This was not the past. There was nothing to fear here but memories. And that's what she had come in search of in the first place. Another steadying breath and she slowly made her way up the stairs, avoiding steps that looked least likely to support her weight.

At the top, Melinda turned and regarded the long hallway. Ghostly images rose in her mind. A small child. An angry hand slapping. A belt. A lock. Her mind shut down as echoes of yelling and crying filled her, and then, just as quickly, subsided. She walked toward the end of the hallway lit by open glassless windows inside otherwise dark rooms. The floor groaned in protest of her progress.

You could sell tickets here as a haunted house.

At the end of the hallway, Melinda stood in front of a door. It was closed tightly, much as her memories of this house were. She caught herself rubbing the old scars on her wrist that echoed the scars on her soul. They always tingled when she felt stress. She wiped her hands on the front of her jeans, as if wiping the tension away. It was time to open Pandora's Box, caution be damned. Melinda grasped the old metal door handle and turned it. At first nothing happened. She twisted it again, and then a third time, and finally the mechanism responded. The door creaked open unwillingly, adding to the haunted house feel.

From inside the large coat closet, total darkness glared back at her. She fished her cell phone from her back jeans pocket, turned on the flashlight app, then stepped inside. Even with the door open, sudden dread filled her. "Get out! Get out now! Run!" it seemed to say, but Melinda persevered. She sank down, lighting the wall by the doorframe with the dim light, searching. There, near the bottom of the frame scratched into the wood by a broken pencil was a message written in a child's clumsy letters, "Stop hurting me." Melinda traced her fingers lightly over letters barely visible in the faint glow, reaching out to touch the hand of a small child with curly, messy hair and tear stained face who did not understand why she wasn't loveable or why her parents hated her so much. A little girl who was so bad she had to be punished again and again, no matter how good she tried to be. She remembered scratching that message into the wood, hoping some sort of magic would occur, and that her parents would listen to the spell if not to the pleas from their small child.

"You aren't bad, little girl," Melinda spoke softly to the empty closet. "You are going to make it. You will survive and life will be good. Better than you can imagine. You are loved and will be loved by many." She smiled thinking of Martin and his unconditional love for her. She swiped a tear from her cheek and refocused.

Sitting back onto the pile of abandoned magazines and empty whiskey bottles in the bottom of the closet, Melinda stared at the message that called to her from across the years. She let the memories, painful and dark, return to the mind that she had so carefully walled off. This was still a part of her, in spite of her wanting to remove it entirely from her past. Maybe she had needed to erase it for a time to survive, but she was better now. She was grown and capable. What she had lived through had made her stronger, more determined, more self-reliant than any other childhood could have. Time passed unnoticed.

Finally, satisfied that she had found everything she needed, Melinda touched the letters a final time and said a silent goodbye. She then got up, retraced her steps down the hall, and carefully descended the stairs to the front door. She turned and looked back one last time. The evil ones who had done this to her were gone and no one could hurt her now. A teenage Melinda had built up her courage and walked out late one night long ago, leaving behind the only family she had ever known. She had survived. Scarred and changed and vastly different from an idealistic childhood, she was still a person who mattered, who had dreams, and who set and strove for goals. Now that she had found the lost memories, and knew for sure they were memories and not some nightmarish dreams from years before, Melinda was ready. Ready to press on and to live fully a life filled with love and blessings.

Melinda turned with finality and walked away, not running away in darkness and fear. This time Melinda held her head high and walked out in broad daylight, leaving behind the broken down rubble that had once been a house. You would never have called it a home. It surprised her how a large, sturdy, wooden structure with metal nails, screws, and large crossbeam timbers could collapse into a useless heap. Meanwhile a living, breathing, kind-hearted creature made of soft tissue, skin, and muscle could endure horrible abuse and stand upright after all this time. The resiliency of humanity never ceased to amaze her.

A Vision of Truth

Sherry McMurphy

"Brayden! Brayden, come quick," she hollered to her husband of three years.

"What's wrong?" he asked, rushing into her office. Lailey sat at her computer viewing engagement pictures she'd shot earlier that day.

"What is that? What do you see?" she stated, pointing to her screen.

Studying the photo, Brayden squinted to focus his eyes. A young couple sat on wooden stairs attached to the porch of an old decaying home. On the top step, a shadowy figure hovered. "Can you enlarge it?"

Lailey expanded the section. Clearly, the black and white area was not a trick of the light, but a figure of an adult woman.

"Looks like someone is standing there . . ." he said.

"Exactly," she interrupted. "I think it's a woman. The face is very unclear, but the clothes look like something worn in the thirties. I swear, Brayden, I never saw her when I shot this photo." Using the mouse, she clicked on additional pictures. "Look, she's only visible on that one picture. Could I have captured a ghost?" She shuddered.

"Damn, maybe. Was this taken at that old abandoned house off Farm Road 185?" Brayden asked. A six-year veteran of the police department, he was very familiar with the area.

Pointing at the photo, she explained, "Yes. I took this couple out there today to shoot their photos."

"Kids have held parties out there from time to time. I've had to go bust 'em up," he said, shaking his head.

"I just bet you did, Mr. Badass Cop," she said, smiling. "I wonder who she is. You think this was her home?"

"You don't know—for a fact—it is a ghost, Lailey. Don't you think you might be letting your imagination run wild?" He laughed, leaning in for a kiss when she shot him an "I'll kick your ass" glare.

"Humor me."

"I've no idea. My grandpa told me when he was a cop, back in the thirties—they discovered, sitting in one of the rooms, an abandoned copper still used to make illegal liquor. Apparently, during prohibition bootleggers secretly holed up in the house."

"I wonder what it looks like inside? Let's go check it out," she said, pushing her chair back, grabbing tennis shoes off the floor.

"Now? Uh . . . not a good idea."

Smiling wickedly, she tied her shoes. "Why? Oh, come on. I'll get the flashlights." She stood abruptly. Starting to rush away, Brayden's arm swung out and grabbed her around the waist.

"Wait just a minute. It's called B&E . . . as in a felony charge. I have no desire to be locked up tonight." He grinned down at her.

"Oh, come on. We can sneak in, look around and be back home before anyone even knows we were there." She wrapped her arms around him, nuzzling his neck. "We used to do stuff like this. For me," she insisted, batting her eyelashes.

With a heavy sigh, he agreed. "Woman, you're killing me." He smiled and leaned down for another quick kiss. "In and out—got it?"

"In and out—scout's honor," she promised, signing him the first three fingers on her right hand.

Twenty minutes later, Brayden killed the lights on his truck as they drove up into the yard of the abandoned house. Darkness engulfed them. Switching on the flashlights, they ascended the porch stairs while Brayden's eyes scanned their surroundings. Lailey opened the front door, cringing at the squeaky noise. Brayden stepped in front of her, lightly pushing her behind him for protection.

Standing just inside the house, they surveyed the interior by the beams radiating from the flashlights. Broken furniture lay scattered throughout the room. Tattered curtains hung from windows, and cobwebs swung from floor to ceiling. Maneuvering through the house, they came upon the dining room—used plates and glasses adorned the table. Lailey whispered, "It looks like everyone just abandoned their meal." Brayden nodded his head in agreement.

Without warning, the front door slammed shut. The lock clicked. Brayden slid his .45 out of the back of his jeans—and again, pushed Lailey behind him. Slowly, he walked toward the door, his weapon drawn and on the ready. Twisting the knob, he realized it wouldn't budge. "Shit."

Abruptly, loud voices and music erupted from the back of the house. Swinging around, he glanced at Lailey. He listened intently, and then cocked his head to indicate she should follow him. Cautiously, they walked toward the noise—laughter rang out. At the end of the hallway, they turned a corner and faced a room ablaze with light. Brayden and Lailey took a step back.

"What the hell?" said Brayden. Shaken, Lailey grabbed the back of his shirt as he wrapped his arm around her to draw her in.

The scene before them looked like something right out of a James Cagney movie. Several dapperly dressed men wearing fedoras, double-breasted suits and two-toned shoes, mingled in the smoke-filled room, puffing cigars, Tommy guns lying within easy reach. A man sat in a wingback chair, giving his full attention to a smartly dressed female splayed across his lap—laughing and kissing each other. A few other guests danced to a jazzy tune while balancing cocktails in their hands. A calendar hanging on one wall displayed the month of June, the year read 1933.

Lailey and Brayden exchanged a confused look. No one noticed them in the doorway. Mesmerized, they couldn't remove their eyes from the scene unfolding in front of them.

Suddenly, the back door flew open. Two men sauntered inside and instantly found firearms pointed directly at their head. The man in the chair abruptly stood.

"Damn! Fast draw," said Brayden as he and Lailey noticed two women rush to the aide of the woman now sprawled on the floor.

"Clyde Jenkins," bellowed one of the intruders.

"Who's asking," a man challenged.

Raising his hands in the air, he boasted, "Oscar Peterson. Your brother Eddie sent us out here to get some liquor." He looked around, laughing awkwardly. "Boys, we're not looking for any trouble here. No need for those guns."

"Throwing that door open like that, sure as shit's a good way to get yourself killed," he replied, studying the man carefully. "How'd you know Eddie?"

"Worked at the quarry together," said Oscar.

Clyde stared at the two men, mulling things over. "You can never be too careful. I sure as hell don't want to sell my wares to an undercover agent and end up in a cage. I've heard Eddie talk of you before." He shifted his eyes to his men and gave a nod.

Heading to the back door, Oscar paused to ogle the women. "Well, aren't you all some fine looking ladies," he said, causing the women to giggle. "We got a place on Sixth Street . . . if you know . . ." Oscar eyed Clyde cautiously. "If you ever want to join us," Oscar suggestively grinned, before walking out the door.

Clyde rushed the door, "I'll kill that bastard."

The woman who previously sat on Clyde's lap sashayed seductively to him. Wrapping her arms around him from behind, she hugged tightly. "Now, Clyde, don't be getting all territorial. You know you're the only one for me."

Lailey and Brayden continued to watch, standing in hypnotic silence.

Wrenching away, Clyde turned and looked her dead in the eye. Holding a glass of whiskey, he pointed his finger in her face. "I better be the only one for you. I'm taking a hell of a risk letting you be here, Eliza. I'm a dead man if you're high and mighty too-good-for-the-likes-of-me father ever finds out about us."

"Clyde, you're drunk—and it doesn't become you," Eliza threw back, dismissing him with a wave of her hand.

He grabbed her arm and yanked her toward him, their faces inches apart. "Don't smart mouth me. It doesn't become you."

"Clyde, don't," cried the other women. "Please, just let her be. We'll just go and you can relax." Both shot a concerned look toward Eliza.

Eliza reached for her purse, than caught the look in Clyde's eyes as he pushed her down into a chair. He walked to the other women and kissed their cheeks. "The boys will take you home," he said. "Thanks for coming, ladies."

"So, you proud of yourself, Eliza Hamilton?" he asked, his face red with anger. "You think being Daddy's spoiled girl gives you the right to speak your mind?" he snarled.

"Clyde, what has come over you?" His hand struck her directly across the face. "Clyde!" Grabbing her cheek, tears sprang to her eyes. "You bastard!" she screamed, jumping to her feet. Eliza instantly tried to run, but a second blow—this time from his fist—hit her, knocking her off her feet.

Brayden lunged forward yelling, "Mother F . . ." and crashed into an invisible shield hard enough to knock him back. "Shit, we can't get in."

Pounding their hands against the force, they hollered, "Stop," and, "Get away from her," but the abusive man never heard them. As if in slow motion, Lailey and Brayden helplessly watched Eliza fall back, her head striking the corner of the end table—blood spurting in several directions—before she came to rest on the floor.

"Oh, my God, Brayden," cried Lailey, disbelieving the violence that had just played out.

Brayden pulled her into his arms tightly and shielded her eyes. "Jesus, I think he just killed her."

"No!" she said, twisting her head in order to see. They stood in shocked silence.

Clyde knelt down and gathered Eliza in his arms. Shaking her, he screamed her name repeatedly. Eliza remained lifeless and bloody—eyes blank, doomed to pointlessly stare for all eternity. Seeing what his actions caused, Clyde moved quickly to hide the crime. Rising, he pushed several pieces of furniture toward the wall, and then rolled her body in the braided rug.

"We need to get out of here," Brayden said. Grabbing her hand, he pulled Lailey along as they rushed out of the now open door.

"Brayden, that poor woman—we can't just leave," she disputed.

They climbed into the truck. "He killed her eighty years ago. There's nothing we can do." Turning the wheel, his headlights sliced across the backyard. Brayden slammed on the brakes.

Clyde appeared before them carrying the rolled up rug—Eliza inside—to the back of the property. Tossing it to the ground, he picked up a shovel and began aggressively digging.

"He's burying her body!" said Brayden.

"Brayden, when I was here today, I noticed a wooden shed sitting in that same spot." They exchanged a knowing glance. Clyde had built it over the spot where he buried Eliza to keep the grave secret.

Back at their home, Lailey and Brayden went into research mode. It didn't take long to get a hit on their subjects.

"Lailey, look here," he said, turning his computer so she could read the archived newspaper article.

SOCIALITE ELIZA HARRISON PRESUMED DEAD

Reading it out loud, Lailey said, "Miss Harrison left her family home on Carnegie Drive to meet close friends at the picture show on the evening of Friday, June 3, 1933. According to her friends, she never arrived to meet them. An extensive search was conducted over several weeks. She has never been found."

"Well, we know why she didn't show up. Anything on Clyde?" he asked.

"Holy Crap, that bastard's alive. Look at this."

LOCAL RESIDENT OF ELDERBERRY MANOR TURNS 100

The next morning, Lailey and Brayden arrived at the manor and were quickly directed toward the lounge. Several residents sat throughout the room. Along the west window, a solitary man in a wheelchair gazed out the window.

"Mr. Clyde Jenkins?" Lailey asked.

Turning slowly, puzzlement displayed across his face. "Yes. Do I know you?"

"No, but I'm here about Eliza Harrison. Do you remember her?"

"Oh, dear God," Clyde gasped, eyes widening with shock. "I never thought . . ." before slumping over lifeless in his chair.

The Hunger

Bradley D. Watson

"But, Officer," Tara said, "This is all wrong! This wasn't here!"

"Ma'am," Sergeant Philip Albrecht said, placing a hand on her shoulder.

"No!" she yelled, pulling away as if touched by a lit cigarette. "You don't understand. This isn't the house. I mean, it is—but it was different. It was—younger!"

The officer reached out again. "Please, ma'am," he said, taking the woman's arm. "Relax. I want to help."

Tara heard the words as if through a wall. She was trying to piece together what she was seeing. She felt her eyes dart everywhere, like a hunted animal, not understanding why she was in danger, but knowing she needed to run.

"Talk to me." The officer pulled her arm lightly but firmly. "Tell me what happened."

Tara's mind was hazy. The morning light, brightening the eastern sky, couldn't seem to enter it.

The flashing red and blue lights gave the peeling white paint on the old house a strange glow. Tara allowed herself to be guided, moving sideways, her eyes never leaving the old, dilapidated building.

What happened? Where is he? She couldn't focus. Her thoughts were confused. She felt like a ball of thread. One big pull, and everything would come undone.

She was pushed carefully into the backseat of the squad car, her legs hanging out the door.

"Now, ma'am," the officer said, squatting down. "You told us at the station that your boyfriend was missing. That he'd been kidnapped. What makes you think that?"

I'm so dizzy. Do I want to go over this again? What good will it do? Her hand reached for her stomach. She wanted to throw up. *He must think I'm crazy.*

She looked up to see him waiting. She took a deep breath.

"We were...," she started, pausing to find her thoughts. "We were out, just having some fun. Jimmy and I." *Why were we out here?* "We'd spent some time at a friend's house and were driving around, just for kicks, y'know?"

"Had either of you been drinking, ma'am?"

Why couldn't he leave it alone? Can't he see? It's got nothing to do with alcohol.

"No," she said quietly. She flicked hair out of her eyes. *He doesn't believe me. He can see right through me.* She pulled her hair forward again, to hide herself—to disappear.

"Okay. Yes, we had a little to drink. But we could still think straight. It wasn't too much." *Am I fooling him? Can he see how much I had? I'm good at handling my liquor. I'm not drunk. I'm still in control, aren't I? I'm clearly thinking straight. Or am I?*

"Go on," he prompted.

What was next? I can't remember. Wait. Oh, yes.

"We came down this road, Elk Road. That's right. We just picked a road. Any road would've done, but we picked this one." Her eyes went to the house. "We shouldn't have, but we did." She paused. "Maybe something drew us here—I don't know. But we hadn't been here before, and we thought it'd be fun to go somewhere and, you know, just be together."

Why won't my hands stop shaking? I have to keep talking. I have to tell him the rest. He won't believe me otherwise.

"We passed that old wagon at the corner. See? The one just back there? And we heard noise coming from that big white house. I mean, the one that *was* here. I mean..."

What do I mean? What was here? How did it change?

"Take a deep breath, ma'am. Just tell me what you think you saw."

I know what I saw.

"The house. There was a party. Lights in every window. Voices and music everywhere." She gazed back at the windows, now just empty frames in a deteriorating wooden wall. An old faded piece of curtain hung half out of one opening, blowing in the wind.

They were there. Glass. Windows. I know they were. Some open. Some closed. Windows. And the man. That's right—.

"A man was walking down the road—staggering—like he was drunk, y'know? He waved, so we rolled down our window."

Wait. Was he real? Did I imagine him? No. I saw him. He had to be real.

"He told us about the party. With lots of stuff. Y'know. Stuff to help you—have fun."

"Drugs?"

He's testing me. He thinks I imagined it all. He's going to say I'm high. He won't believe me. But I have to tell. I have to find Jimmy.

"I—I don't know. Maybe. Probably. I don't know…"

"So what did you do?"

She glanced from the officer to the deteriorated building.

The house. Is it laughing? I feel it. What does it want from me?

"We parked over there," her arm swung to a place across the road with waist-high weeds. "We went inside and… and…" Her eyes widened as she yelled at the house. "What happened! Where is he?"

Why am I screaming? I have to stop. He won't believe me. He has to believe me. She glanced back at the house. *Those empty windows. Like soulless eyes. Watching me.*

"Ma'am," the officer said again, his voice sounding like it was coming from a long tunnel.

Has he been calling me all this time?

"Ma'am," he shook her arm. "Just tell me what you saw. That's all I'm asking."

"We went in. I remember, I was holding his hand. We went in. You know, just for some fun."

"Yes, ma'am."

It's so cold. Why am I so cold?

"There were a bunch of people there. All kinds of people. They had—they had—some stuff on the table. People were—smoking. They asked Jim to try something new."

It's getting darker? The sky is getting darker! Or is it? Could it be my eyes? Is there something wrong with my eyes?

"So," Officer Albrecht prompted, "he was asked to try something. Did he do it?"

"I tried to stop him. I said, 'Jimmy, you don't know these people. What if it's something bad?' But he wouldn't listen. He wouldn't. He pulled his hand away…'" She looked down at her palm.

I can still feel it. I can feel his hand there. Why can't I hold on? She rubbed the palm of her left hand with her right thumb, her right fist still closed tight. *His hand is still there. I know it. If I could just hold on.*

"He pulled his hand away?"

"Yes. I yelled at him. He wouldn't stop. They took him to a door in the back wall. I watched. He was laughing—they were all laughing—laughing as he went in. I watched him as the dark swallowed him up. Yes, that's the word. Swallowed. The others kept laughing. I screamed, but he was gone.

"A woman came over—still laughing, laughing—and grabbed my arm. She said it'd be all right, but I knew it wouldn't. She wouldn't let go. I pushed her, and I fell. I tried not to fall. I grabbed the curtain, but it caught on a nail and tore."

The laughing. Can't he hear it? It's still there. Stop it! Stop! I can't shut it out! Why can't I shut it out?

"It's okay," the officer consoled, pulling Tara's hands from her ears. "What happened then?"

"I jumped up." *Why didn't I leave? Would things have been different? Would the house still be the same if I hadn't stayed?*

"And?"

"I ran to the door. That hungry door—the one I didn't want him to go in—and—"

He's waiting. He wants to hear the rest. But it's all I've got left. All I have left of Jimmy. If I tell it, it's gone? I'll have nothing left.

But, maybe if I tell him—maybe if the words are gone, things'll go back the way they were.

"I opened the door—to tell him I was leaving. I shouldn't have thought about leaving him. But I did. I was going to threaten him, make him do what I wanted. I was going to say he had to leave or I was going alone."

Her eyes were back on the house. *That darkness. That emptiness. It's too much. The house is filled with it. Did it do this? Does it want me, too?*

"Focus, ma'am," the officer said. "What did he do when you said that?"

"Nothing." *How can I tell him?* "Nothing." *He's going to think I'm crazy.* "I couldn't." *Maybe I am crazy. But, I can't keep it in.*

"He wasn't there!" she exploded. "Don't you see? It was a little closet. It wasn't even a room. No one was there! I banged on the sides and kicked at the floor. They were all solid. Just a small empty closet. No one in it. Nothing in it. Nothing!"

"But, ma'am—"

"You don't believe me!" *Why should he. It doesn't make sense?* "You still don't see!" she cried. "I came out of the closet, and—and there was no one in the big room! It was empty!"

"They left?"

"No! Why aren't you listening? There was nothing! No tables, no drugs, no drinks. Nothing. No people, no chairs. Emptiness. It was like nothing had ever been there." *What am I doing? What's happening to me?* She could not help but look again at the empty eyes in the walls of the old house.

It's the house. It's hungry. I can feel it. It wanted Jimmy. It probably wants me, too. Or was that enough for now?

The officer's movements seemed to be in slow motion. He took her arms and lifted her to stand.

He wants to take me away. He wants to leave here. I can't let it have Jimmy.

"He's here!" she shouted. "Somewhere! He's got to be. He can't have just disappeared." She looked up at the old relic. "It's you!" she screamed. "You took him! You!" She tried to pull away. "I want him back! Give him back, do you hear? Give him back. You can't have him." She collapsed against the officer, sobbing. "Give him back. It's alive," she said. "It's taking us. It needs us. Well, you can't have me!" she laughed through her tears. "You lose! You can't have me! I won't go!" She began laughing and crying, her mind finally giving in to the fog that had been closing over it.

Officer Albrecht stared at the young girl. He wasn't sure what had happened.

"What's that?" he asked. She didn't answer. "In your hand," he said, pointing to her left hand. He wasn't even sure she could hear him anymore. He pried her clenched fist open and removed a small piece of material. "Wait here," he told her, pushing her gently back into the squad car.

Walking over to what was left of the old house, he held the swatch next to the old curtain blowing out through the paneless window. The torn edges matched perfectly.

When he returned to the car, he said, "I'm not sure what you saw, but we'll need a statement if you want to file a missing person's report." He watched as the girl stared over his shoulder. Her crying and giggling was disconcerting. She seemed unable to stop.

"Ma'am?" he tried asking again. She did not respond. Her eyes were vacant.

He looked down at the small piece of material in his hand. "Strange," he said to her, knowing she was no longer listening. "It's a piece of the curtain, just like you said." He looked back at the old house one last time. "What I can't figure out is, why this piece looks brand new, clean as the day it was purchased, but the piece it was torn off of, the curtain hanging out the window, is old and faded."

He closed his car's doors, turned off his whirling lights, and turned the car back toward the city. His passenger laughed lightly, talking to herself as he pulled away. She stared at the empty doorway in the dark.

The old house did not respond.

<u>CONTRIBUTORS</u>

Saturday Writers 2015

OUR WRITERS

Sarah Angleton

Sarah Angleton earned her MA in Literature through the Creative Writing Program at the University of Missouri. Her first novel has been accepted for publication by High Hill Press and her short and flash fiction has appeared in several anthologies and in the literary journal *Goldman Review*, as well as the online magazine *100 Word Story*. Sarah lives in St. Charles County where she writes historical fiction and blogs as the Practical Historian at www.Sarah-Angleton.com.

Bradley Bates

"I went to school at the University of Missouri-Columbia (BA English, Emphasis Creative Writing, 2004), Northern Arizona University (MA English, Emphasis Creative Writing, With Distinction, 2001), and Pacific University (MFA in Writing, 2007). I have the following books published: *Buddha Copper*, *One to One*, *Two Eyes: To Wander Like a River*, and *My Own Voyage*."

Phyllis L. Borgardt

"Writing is my passion since joining Saturday Writers. Before that I was an Occupational Therapist with a degree from Washington University and a Master's Degree from California School of Psychology. A widow with three children and four grandchildren, my family has always been supportive of my writing, painting, and educational pursuits.

I've completed two books: *Moments from My Wild Childhood* and *The Doctor and the Pole Dancer*. I'm presently writing a sequel to the latter."

Robert E. Browne

Robert E. Browne is a retired chief petty officer of the United States Navy. He and his wife, Adelita, live in Winfield, Missouri, where their three children grew up and now have families of their own. Their son, Daniel, is a petty officer in the U. S. Navy. Bob believes that for a work to be successful, it must stir the emotions within. Bob has won numerous literary awards for his poems, stories, and essays.

Patricia Bubash

Patricia Bubash received her Master's Degree in Education with an emphasis in Counseling from the University of Missouri, St. Louis. For more than 30 years she worked as a counselor, and facilitated classes at the local community college. Her work with families was the catalyst for authoring her book. *Successful Second Marriages*. She contributes articles promoting positive relationships: www.hopeafterdivorce, www.fizzniche, www.onelegacy.com. She is a Licensed Professional Counselor, and a Stephen Minister.

Cathleen Callahan

"A mathematician who discovered a poet within when a numinous dream awakened inner realms long ago, ...the thread [I] follow...[that] goes among things that change (William Stafford) is the poetry within. A high school drop-out (ah, a story) with several college degrees and careers in teaching, counseling, and poetry therapy, I'm now a retired visual arts teacher who has never let go of the thread or joy for life through all its wonders and tragedies."

Rose Callahan

Since a young age, Rose has enjoyed writing short stories and is pleased to say that she is looking to expand her portfolio to include a variety of story formats. When she is not writing, she enjoys reading, participating in cultural activities, and spending time with her family.

Sherry Cerrano

Writing has been an integral part of Sherry's life, never off her mind or far from her responsibilities. For 37 years she taught high school English in the Quincy Public Schools, making a living that incorporated her lifelong love of literature and writing.

Now retired, she is finally experimenting with her own creative writing. Sherry's goal is to finish a novel that is fun to read, a work which is still in progress.

Audrey Clare

Audrey Clare grew up in St. Louis, Missouri, during the time before anyone visited the moon or built the Gateway to the West (the Arch.) She moved around a lot because she was interested in many different cultures. After spending many years traveling, she moved back to St. Louis to be near her daughters. She continues with her artwork, painting abstract/expressionism, when she is not writing poems or fiction.

Kathryn Cureton

Kathryn Cureton writes from the basement lair of her hillbilly mansion, eight-tenths of a mile up a gravel road in southeast Missouri. She makes her living teaching physics and biology to high school students, who are not impressed with her status as a former high school valedictorian. Her spare time is spent collecting new clichés, chronicling the schemes of her hillbilly husband in a totally anonymous blog, and using prepositions to end sentences with.

P.A. De Voe

P.A. De Voe is a cultural anthropologist, which accounts for her being an incorrigible magpie for collecting seemingly irrelevant information. She writes contemporary and historical mysteries—the latter taking place in 14th and 15th Century China. *The Judge Lu Ming Dynasty Case Files* is a set of short stories modeled after crime stories traditionally written by Chinese magistrates themselves.

Larry Duerbeck

"I have been involved with show dogs since circa 1975. There are other aspects to my life, but not many and they are of limited interest. Even, I must say, to me."

Sue Fritz

"I am a retired elementary school teacher. I taught for 23 years. Upon retiring, I chose to follow my second passion in life, writing. I have taken several online writing courses. I have also attended several conferences in order to hone my writing skills. I am a member of Saturday Writers, as well as the Society of Children's Books Writers and Illustrators. I have been married for 24 years and have two children, both boys."

Marcia Gaye

Marcia Gaye enjoys writing poetry and most types of fiction and non-fiction. Her work has won awards in various categories and includes four dozen published pieces. A Christian, wife, and mother, she has lived in fourteen states, finding inspiration everywhere, mostly from her interesting family. She likes cats (real ones) and collects giraffes (not real ones). Marcia is active in the Missouri Writers Guild and three chapters, and is ambassador for Ozark Creative Writers.

Jay Harden

"I grew up in the deep South envying the eagles and hawks. Later, I survived air combat in Vietnam. Besides writing of love, war, and childhood, I enjoy photography, travel, music, and unconditional love of family. In the past year, I was featured on Channel Nine's 'Living St. Louis' and 'Stay Tuned' television programs. I also photographed the book covers for *Proud to Be: Writing by American Warriors*, Volumes 3 and 4."

Heather N. Hartmann

Heather Hartmann resides in St. Peters, Missouri, with her husband, two rambunctious dogs and two unique cats. She is working on self-control in the area of multiple manuscript writing while editing her current work in progress. Heather has been published in the *St. Charles Suburban Journal*. Seeing her work in print fulfilled one part of a lifelong dream. She is determined to fulfill part two of her dream, a published novel.

Jennifer A. Hasheider

Jennifer A. Hasheider has been an officer of Saturday Writers since 2012. She has published several articles on writing, edited many full manuscripts that have gone on to publication, and her short stories appear in local anthologies.

Stephen Hayes

Stephen Hayes is an award-winning Northwest writer and creator of "The Chubby Chatterbox," a blog focused on writing, culture and travel. Hayes is an artist and world-class traveler, and his work is an unabashedly sentimental exploration of growing up in the fifties, sixties and beyond. Aside from his blog, Hayes' work can be found in *Chicken Soup for the Soul* and *Not Your Mother's Books*.

Debbie Hedges

"I always wanted to write in my younger years and would make a brief attempt, but alas writing took a back burner to my teaching career and my family. Now I enjoy reading and writing in the genre of young adult. I believe I will always be a kid at heart."

George House

George House has written eleven technical papers, numerous training manuals and instruction books. Retirement afforded time to write his first fiction novel, *Grate Clinkers*, which will be out in March 2016. The short story, "The End of Fifty-Two," offers a different view of time and the event, death.

Diane How

Diane How writes poetry, short stories and has a romance novel in progress. She published *Peaks and Valleys* in 2011; has selections in the 2014 *Saturday Writers Anthology #8: Under the Surface*, and poetry in three other anthologies. Diane serves as president of the Pen to Paper Writing Club and is a member of the Saturday Writing Club. When not writing, Diane volunteers to record the life stories of hospice patients.

Nicki Jacobsmeyer

"I started entertaining my imagination by writing stories down in elementary school. A few years ago, I realized writing was my true passion and haven't stopped since. I write historical fiction and non-fiction, children stories, short stories and poetry. My work has been published in anthologies, and currently I'm writing a book for Arcadia Publishing, *Images of America: Chesterfield*. I live in O'Fallon, Missouri, with my husband and two boys."

Thomas Klein

A native of St. Louis, Tom served as the 2015 president of Saturday Writers while continuing his writing, refining his craft, and entertaining his readers with his imaginative stories.

Cathi LaMarche

Cathi LaMarche is a novelist, essayist, poet, and writing coach. Her work has appeared in over two dozen anthologies. She resides in Missouri with her husband, two children, and three dogs. When not immersed in the written word, Cathi enjoys cooking, gardening, and hiking in the mountains.

Sherry Long

"Born, to my surprise, in Iowa, I moved as quickly as possible to Missouri, via Omaha. Mom was a teacher, my father a bureaucrat. Reading was important in my family, so, naturally, I turned to writing. Most of what I wrote involved the internal drama of many school-age girls. It was practice. Now I write to communicate, to illuminate, to lead the reader to an idea and watch what happens."

Jennifer McCullough

Jennifer McCullough is a marketing and public relations consultant who has spent much of her career working in Branson, Missouri. She has written numerous travel articles for magazines, a personal blog about motherhood, and the occasional short story. Jennifer received the Missouri Writer's Guild Walt Whitman Major Work award for co-authoring *The Insiders' Guide to Branson and the Ozark Mountains, 3rd Edition*. She lives in St. Peters, Missouri, with her husband and their son.

Sherry McMurphy

"My passion for reading began as a very small child. Over time that love of reading developed into a need to write my own stories. I've been published nine times as an Opinion Shaper in the *St. Charles Journal* and have written a historical romance novel that I am currently editing. I enjoy attending author events and meeting with my two very close friends to edit together. I also enjoy spending time with my family."

Carol Mingo-Revill

Carol Mingo-Revill is a two-time cancer survivor who grew up on a farm in New England. She holds a Master of Arts in Holistic Thinking and presently runs a Writing and Healing cancer survivor group at the hospital. Carol has two married sons and one grandson, Benny. Married to artist Bill Revill, who also produces an Americana radio show, her world is rich with music, art, writing, and family. They reside in Meriden, Connecticutt.

Claudia Mundell

Claudia Mundell has a border war in her writing. With roots in Oklahoma, she grew up in Kansas, but her work life has been in Missouri. She has many memories from each state that work their way into her fiction and poetry. After raising a family and teaching, she now writes for pleasure. Her work has appeared in *MidRivers Review*, *Yellow Medicine Review*, *Rosebud*, *TEA*, *Good Old Days*, *Romantic Homes*, *Cactus Country*, and several anthologies.

Douglas N. Osgood

Doug Osgood's grandfather was raised on a reservation, was taught to shoot by a wild west show's trick shot artist, and eschewed that world to marry the love of his life. He taught his passion for westerns, especially Zane Gray, to his grandson, who now translates that same ardor into fiction he hopes his grandfather would have enjoyed reading. Osgood, a longtime resident of Missouri, has traveled the country seeking stories to write.

Tara Pedroley

Born and raised in St. Louis, Tara Pedroley has been writing since grade school. An award-winning poet, she recently took third place at the 2015 All Write Now conference. Tara loves children, holding a degree in Early Childhood Education. She writes several blogs, including one with advice on dating and relationships. Most of her time is spent writing, but she also enjoys dance, art, photography, and creating fun projects for friends and family.

Donna Mork Reed

Donna Mork Reed grew up in the Ozarks. With a B.S. in biology and an M.L.S., she is now a librarian. She resides in St. Charles with husband, Dave, and dogs China and Buster. She started writing in third grade and hasn't stopped. She is a member of the Saturday Writers. Her work will be in December 2015 *Joy of Christmas*, a Guidepost publication. Recently, her photography won awards at the Douglas County Fair.

Lester Schneider

Lester Schneider is an aspiring writer with no (other) published works to date. He is currently working on a mystery fiction piece with a locale in Olde Town St. Charles, Missouri. He does dabble with poetry occasionally because it appeals to his mathematical background.

R.R.J. Sebacher

R.R.J. Sebacher is an evil old bear/poet/midwife to the world's collective unconscious. His short term goal is to write poetry layered like an onion, which makes his reader weep in joy or grief. His ultimate desire is to focus the light of poetry so fiercely that it burns through the paper and sets the mind on fire. He would also like to remember where he left his car keys and his last girlfriend.

Gordon Smith

"I am a retired science teacher, living in Hot Springs, AR. I write short stories, essays, and poetry for the sheer fun of it! My wife, Carol, is a retired English and journalism teacher."

William A. Spradley

Born and raised in southeastern Nebraska, William A. Spradley spent thirty years in the aerospace industry, living and working all over the globe. He took up writing as another hobby to go along with framing, model railroads, gold and sailing. His writing style is a cross of many different authors, including Hemingway, O'Henry, and John Irving. He lives with his thoughts and enjoys long lunches and wine tasting.

M.L. Stiehl

M.L. Stiehl did most of her growing up in the country on a large farm. Her school years were spent in a one-room school house, where she had plenty of study time. To fill it, she began writing stories about her time on the farm, and about the things she imagined. In those days, her stories only entertained her fellow students and teachers. Now she hopes to entertain a much larger audience with her tales.

Doyle Suit

Doyle Suit and his wife of more than a half century live in St. Charles, Missouri, near children and grandchildren. They dance, play golf, travel, and enjoy bluegrass music. His first novel, *Baker Mountain*, is available at Amazon and selected bookstores. A second novel is in process of publication. A third is looking for a publisher. His short stories appear in *Cactus Country*, *Thin Threads*, *Good Old Days*, *Big Foot Confidential*, and numerous magazines and anthologies.

Carole Tipton

"For more than 30 years, I taught English at various levels: middle school, high school, university. I retired at the end of 2013 and have been working to find my voice—and courage—as a writer. Over the years, I've won a couple of writing contests, and have been published in *The NCTE Journal*: that article was subsequently run also in *Education Digest*. I live in Cottleville, Missouri, with my husband of 52 years."

Pat Wahler

Pat Wahler is a grant writer by day and award winning writer of fiction and essays by night. Her work appears in many local and national publications including *Chicken Soup for the Soul*, *Sasee Magazine*, *Cup of Comfort*, and *Not Your Mother's Book*. Pat, a life-long animal lover, ponders critters, writing, and life's little mysteries at www.critteralley.blogspot.com.

Bradley D. Watson

Bradley D. Watson started writing in fourth grade, and hopes to keep writing into his second childhood (which is fast approaching). 2015 V.P. for Saturday Writers, he has had several stories published in the club's anthologies over the last four years.

Stan Wilson

Stan Wilson enjoys creating imaginary stories based on science, crime, adventure and humor. Educated as an Engineer, he designs gadgets for "Internet of Things" applications. He grew up in Southern Indiana with hardwood forests, springs, rivers, caves and folks who talk with a southern twang. He's still married to the same woman after 56 years and has two grown sons and a calico cat who's in charge of anything important.

Lori Younker

Lori Younker has enjoyed the world of words with her international friends for over 30 years. Whether she is learning a new language or teaching her own, she appreciates the power of words to encourage and inspire. Lori and her husband raised three kids in warm and woodsy Missouri. Currently, she is president of the COMO Writers' Guild and donates her energies to recent immigrants and, of course, to her writing.

Susan Gore Zahra

Susan Gore Zahra has written stories since childhood. Several personal essays and theological reflections have been published. Since retiring from hospice chaplaincy, she has had time to study the craft of writing and to develop greater skill in writing fiction and poetry.

OUR PHOTOGRAPHER

Ryan Jacobsmeyer

Ryan Jacobsmeyer has always enjoyed photography and made an effort to see beyond the obvious. He enjoys catching little moments in life others may bypass. He has always used the tools at his disposal but only in 2014, with the guiding hand of his better-half Nicki, did he realize that photography was a true passion. He continues to hone his craft at any time possible and looks forward to sharing his passion with the world.